By the same author:

Me, You and Tiramisu
Crazy Little Thing Called Love
A Beautiful Day for a Wedding
The Family Fix
The Second Chance
The Sister Switch

Praise for Charlotte Butterfield

'Wonderfully original'

Katie Fforde, *Sunday Times* bestselling author of *Island in the Sun*

'A delight'

Sophie Cousens, *New York Times* bestselling author of *This Time Next Year*

'Gloriously life-affirming'

Heidi Swain, *Sunday Times* bestselling author of *The Book-Lovers' Retreat*

'The funniest writer I've ever come across'

Debbie Johnson, million-copy bestselling author of *The Moment I Met You*

'A heartwarming triumph'

Holly Miller, author of Richard & Judy Book Club pick *The Sight of You*

'You know it's good when you are snorting with laughter one minute and ugly crying the next!'

Amanda Prowse, author of *Very Very Lucky*

'Moving, page-turning and snort-laugh funny'

Becky Hunter, author of *One Moment*

'Hilarious, life-affirming and such a clever concept'

Jessica Ryn, author of *The Extraordinary Hope of Dawn Brightside*

'A pocket of joy'

Emma Cooper, author of *The Songs of Us*

A former magazine editor, Charlotte Butterfield was born in Bristol and studied English at Royal Holloway. She moved to Dubai by herself on a one-way ticket with one suitcase in 2005 and left twelve years later with a husband, three children and a 40ft shipping container. She now lives in the Cotswolds, where she is a freelance writer and novelist.

Charlotte Butterfield

ONE MORE Yesterday

avon.

Published by AVON
A division of HarperCollins*Publishers* Ltd
1 London Bridge Street
London SE1 9GF

www.harpercollins.co.uk

HarperCollins*Publishers*
Macken House, 39/40 Mayor Street Upper
Dublin 1, D01 C9W8, Ireland

This paperback edition 2026
1
First published in Great Britain by Hodder & Stoughton 2022
An Hachette UK company

Copyright © Charlotte Butterfield 2022

Charlotte Butterfield asserts the moral right to
be identified as the author of this work.

A catalogue copy of this book is available from the British Library.

ISBN: 978-0-00-876976-5

This novel is entirely a work of fiction. The names, characters and incidents portrayed in it are the work of the author's imagination. Any resemblance to actual persons, living or dead, events or localities is entirely coincidental.

Printed and bound in the UK using 100%
Renewable Electricity at CPI Group (UK) Ltd

Without limiting the exclusive rights of any author, contributor or the publisher of this publication, any unauthorised use of this publication to train generative artificial intelligence (AI) technologies is expressly prohibited. HarperCollins also exercise their rights under Article 4(3) of the Digital Single Market Directive 2019/790 and expressly reserve this publication from the text and data mining exception.

This book is produced from independently certified FSC paper to ensure
responsible forest management.

For more information visit: www.harpercollins.co.uk/green

To Team P, je t'aime, ti amo

I

When your family is an eighties pine dresser

My therapist's consulting room is also her utility room. It has a tumble dryer stacked on top of a washing machine; a cat litter tray; a shelf of breakfast cereals (including the supermarket-brand chocolate ones that I'd never buy my own kids – nine teaspoons of sugar in every bowl!); a big canvas with a cascading waterfall on it and a somewhat sexist box of 'man-size' tissues on a side table. The two latter additions turn it – hey presto! – from a functional family laundry room into a serene space for divulging your deepest secrets. It isn't entirely professional, but it's two minutes' walk from work and, most importantly, it's cheap – which is, after all, what most people look for in a therapist, isn't it?

Jackie has just asked me to describe how I feel about my family. She asked me the question in the soft, soothing therapist's voice she puts on in the morning along with her lip balm and elasticated skirt.

'They are – ' Which word shall I choose? I know I have to pick one that doesn't deviate from the script of what I am supposed to say, being a loving mother and everything. I'm about to finish my sentence with an insipid but positive word like 'lovely' when I look at Jackie, and she suddenly looks so smug, so together, so sorted – which is a bit rich as she's currently sat on a fold-up garden chair wedged beside a welly boot rack, underneath a wall calendar that has 'Kids at Dave's' written on every other weekend. She's also just had to raise her voice a little to be heard over the spin cycle.

Embarrassingly, I had never noticed any of these things before Fergus pointed them out after the one time he came with me. One time. Fifty-five minutes of therapy and he was cured. Didn't need to come again. For just under a pound a minute, his brain had been reset, his memories erased, his emotions realigned, and he was a new person. His side of the couples counselling successfully completed. Well done, Fergus.

Over thirty sessions and fifteen hundred pounds later, I still feel exactly the same.

'I bought an old pine dresser from a car boot sale a few years ago,' I start.

'Jess, stop avoiding the question,' Jackie says. It makes me feel bad for a moment. It's like she is actually invested in my happiness, not just counting the minutes until I leave and a far more open and honest client arrives to put their feet up on the beige IKEA footstool and spill out their secrets, necessitating a man-size tissue.

I hold my hand up to stop her interrupting. 'I saw it, this pine dresser, it was only twenty pounds, a real bargain. Don't get me wrong,' I continue, 'it's horrible – yellow, with ugly brown knots in it. But I knew that with a bit of elbow grease I could make it really fantastic. I bought a very expensive – and surprisingly small considering that it cost more than Liam's new trainers – tin of chalk furniture paint, and I ordered ten hand-painted china knobs off eBay. This dresser was going to be amazing. Everyone who came into my house would admire it, and it would make me so happy. But do you know what? What with work and life just getting in the way, I've never done it. Not even sanded it down or primed it. So it just sits there taunting me with its imperfections and potential. And I hate it every time I see it. Which is quite a lot, because it's in my bloody kitchen.'

Jackie's face is blank. If she knows where I'm going with this, she's not giving it away.

'That dresser is my family.'

'That's the most honest thing you've said to me in the last two years, Jess.'

I smile back at her. 'You're welcome.'

'It's not too late to paint it you know. To give it a sand down and a nice coat of paint.'

'Oh, I think it is,' I reply with a shrug that's designed to show quite how accepting I am of that fact.

'You seem very tense today, Jess. Let's end the session with a little relaxation. Close your eyes and think about a time you felt really calm and centered.'

'It's OK,' I say, putting my hands on the arms of the chair, ready to get up, 'we can finish early, I've got lots to do anyway.'

'Absolutely not, we've got fifteen minutes left, and I think you need it. Now close your eyes and breathe in for one, and two, and out, for one, two. And in, one, two, and out, one two.'

We need more surgical gloves.

'What are you thinking of, Jessica?'

'The ocean,' I answer automatically.

'Lovely. So, as you sit there on the beach, watching the waves gently roll in, I'm going to count back from five, and with every number you will feel yourself getting more and more relaxed, five – '

Does the dry cleaner's close early on a Wednesday? I'm sure it shuts early on a Wednesday.

'Four – '

Liam needs to wear his blazer tomorrow for the meeting that decides whether he's suspended or not. We're one of the few families who bought the thing, he's going to bloody well wear it.

'Three – '

When was my last smear test? I'm sure I need one soon.

'Two – '

Why does Molly hate me so much? I know she's sixteen, and sixteen year olds hate everybody, but she doesn't need to be so mean.

'One – '

What if Mum gets chopped up into tiny bits and fed to a pet anaconda by someone she's met Internet dating?

'You should be totally relaxed now, your mind completely free of all thoughts, as you listen to the slow and steady ebb and flow of the crystal-clear water, gently lapping on the sand. Are you totally relaxed now, Jessica?'

'Mmmmm.'

'Wonderful. What can you smell? What's that scent on the breeze?'

Someone else's perfume. 'The salty air.'

'Lovely. And what can you hear?'

The car engine turning off outside after that woman from work gives Fergus a lift home and it taking twelve minutes for him to put his key in the front door. 'The seagulls.'

'Fabulous. And are you there with anyone?'

Last time I took the kids to the cinema they made me sit in a different row. 'My family.'

'Fantastic. Just take a minute to breathe in and out. With every breath in, you're filling your body with positivity, and every breath out, you're getting rid of any negative energy in your body.'

Have I drunk enough water today? I don't think I have.

'And remember, you can tap into this fabulous feeling of being completely relaxed and stress free any time you want.'

I bet when the lab results come back Mr McDonald has high potassium levels.

'OK. And I'm going to bring you back now. As I count backwards from five, you're going to wake up and feel refreshed and carefree. 'Five – '

I wonder if someone's cleared that dead pigeon up from the street outside?

'Four – '

Did I leave the mince on the side to defrost or put it in the fridge?

'Three – '

If it's not in the fridge it'll be riddled with bacteria by now.

'Two – '

I need to drop off that nebuliser to Mrs Hendricks after work for her baby.

'One – '

We'll have to have something on toast. We can't risk the mince. Have we even got bread?

'And you're back. You should feel so much lighter and happier now, Jess.'

'Oh yes,' I say, 'that was marvellous. So much lighter. And happier. Thank you so much, there's your fifty pounds.' I stand up and stretch, shaking out my shoulders and cricking my neck from side to side to really hammer the point home that my body has been sat on a beach for the last quarter of an hour. 'Oh yes, so much more relaxed. You really are a miracle worker, Jackie.'

'Maybe next time we should talk about Anna.'

I shake my head, and smile brightly. 'Oh no, I don't think there's any need for that. Bye bye now.'

I'm ten minutes late running into work, sweat patches forming on my silk blouse. I smile when I see my favourite chicken salad sandwich on my desk with a note from Robert – one of my favourite partners in the practice – telling me to 'make sure you eat lunch!' I stow my bag under my desk and quickly wriggle into the white coat hanging on the back of my door, which has my name stitched onto its pocket, and take a deep, steadying breath. I can do this.

As usual, I can hear the waiting room way before I can see it. A baby's high-pitched shriek, a chorus of coughing and spluttering; an incubator filled with a hundred different germs and compromised immune systems. Pam on reception's loud voice booms that the next appointment is eight days away and although I can't hear it, it's easy to imagine the fruity words of outrage from the handset. *Eight days? That's ridiculous!* And they're right, it is.

Fourteen pairs of eyes look up expectantly from their phones as I walk in, clipboard in hand, and announce a name. Thirteen mouths sigh as an elderly man heaves himself up from his chair. It doesn't occur to anyone to help.

Now we're nine minutes into the allotted ten-minute consultation timeframe and the list of the pensioner's ailments is still growing.

'It's probably nothing,' he says, 'but I've been doing some research and . . .'

There are twelve patients after him, I still have to sign off all the prescriptions from the morning surgery and make four phone calls giving test results. I surreptitiously sneak a peek at my watch. If I call Fergus now, he may be able to pick the blazer up from the dry cleaner's – although it probably doesn't matter what Liam wears to the hearing tomorrow, the school are still going to suspend him. They're being far too harsh on him this time, though. After all, we're in the clutches of a heatwave. Not a 'let's head down to the supermarket, pick up some kebabs for the barbecue and fill up the paddling pool' type of heatwave, either. More a third-degree-burns, melting-pavement scenario, and all Liam did was start a sideline in selling ice lollies at break time. If anything, it was an act of kindness to his fellow pupils. He should be celebrated, not vilified. With a bit of common sense and gentle persuasion, I'm sure I'll be able to make the Head see Liam's act for what it was: a mature example of community spirit.

'. . . and I think I may have picked up a parasite when I was in the Congo.'

I tune back in to my patient. 'I'm sorry, what?'

'I'm pretty sure I have African Trypanosomiasis.'

'And when did you last visit the Congo, Mr King?'

'1958.'

I spend the journey home after work fantasising about a parallel life where I walk into the house and am met by enticing dinner smells wafting out from the kitchen. The newly picked-up dry cleaning is hanging over the bannister, the kids are showered and fresh faced, a glass of wine and a full bath is waiting for me. And someone, anyone, asks me about my day.

Back in reality, the front door is on the latch, the hall lights are on and the only reason I know I'm not about to confront burglars is that there are two pairs of scuffed school shoes and two school rucksacks left at the bottom of the stairs, but no one replies when I shout hello. I didn't really expect them to. Iris the spaniel thumps her tail in a vague sort of way, but even she can't be bothered to actually get up out of her basket to greet me. And there's no sign of Fergus at all.

I had four inches chopped off my hair and a head full of blond highlights put through just over a week ago. Robert even wolf-whistled when I came into work – which I know should have made me feel sexually objectified, but I'd be lying if I said I wasn't just a little bit pleased someone had noticed. Plus, he's not into women in that way. It was lucky that I hadn't been abducted that week because the description my family would have given to the police would not have matched me at all and I'd have never been found. Which actually doesn't sound too bad. Probably best not to tell Jackie that in our next session.

Hours later, the front door bangs and after a few seconds' pause, Fergus pokes his head round the living-room door. 'Wotcha,' he says in his soft Irish lilt.

'Hey,' I reply.

'Have you eaten?'

I nod. 'With the kids.' Which makes it sound a lot more convivial than the reality of sharing a table with two teenagers and three screens actually was.

'Anything left for me?'

'The lasagne we had on Monday is in the fridge, give it a sniff before you nuke it, see if it's still OK.'

'Nothing from tonight left?'

I can't fault his optimism. 'There was, but then Liam wanted thirds.'

'Oh, OK. I'll just have something on toast then.'

'We're out of bread.'

'Just some cereal then.'

'And milk.'

'Jesus, Jessica. Shops shut today, were they?'

'I don't know, Fergus, were they?'

I pointedly return my gaze to the TV and he slopes off to the kitchen. My phone, balancing on the arm of the sofa, pings with a new message from the Year 11 WhatsApp parent chat, which commandeers more of my time than a full-time job, husband, two children and a dog. It seems a boy has sent a picture of his genitals to the whole year. It is unclear if it is an act of deluded self-promotion or a mortifying mistake, but the sharpened talons of The Housewives of North London are out and motive isn't important.

Fergus comes into the living room holding his hot plate of lasagne with a white tea towel, the edge of which has orange ragu seeping into it.

'Someone's been sending penis pics to the Year 11 Group,' I say.

'Not guilty.'

I can't help laughing; he is still quite funny. Sense of humour. That's what every single person is looking for, it says so on every dating ad I've ever seen. GSOH. Make me laugh and I'll take my clothes off, that's what that means. So why don't I?

'You saw Jackie today, didn't you?'

'Yes, I saw her in my lunch break.'

'Ah.'

This is as far as his questioning ever goes, just an enquiry that I've been. That I am one step closer to being fixed. Mended. Happy. All issues talked through with a qualified professional. A little spot of mental management between a leg wax and a scrape and polish at the dentist.

I'd initially bought ten sessions of marriage counselling on a whim two years ago as a birthday present to myself after I'd read an article in a magazine about how it had revolutionised these women's relationships. The feature even had beaming photos of the couples, arms wrapped around each other, faces snuggling smugly into necks, to prove their new marital happiness. Fergus went to the first session and promptly declared it 'a waste of time', but for some reason I've kept it up, going by myself once, sometimes twice a month. It can't hurt.

We sit there in silence, the television flickering in the corner, giving us a legitimate reason not to talk to one another.

'So, tomorrow,' I say finally.

'Tomorrow,' he echoes.

'The meeting with the school is at nine, so we can drop Molly off first, then go to it.'

Fergus shovels another massive forkful of pasta into his mouth, waiting until his mouth is completely full before he starts talking, so that I can see the half-masticated food in all its glory. 'And how are we playing it? Totally his fault, totally our fault, totally the school's fault?'

I can't look at him any more, it makes me feel sick, so I turn back to the TV to reply. 'I think a mixture of all three, but we need to stay calm. We need him to stay at this school, so ultimately, a lot of grovelling, he needs to apologise, we need to say that we're dealing with it—'

'But we're not,' he says. 'We're pretending it hasn't happened.'

'We've taken his phone and he's grounded, so we are dealing with it.'

'Are we? Where is he now?'

'He's upstairs playing on the computer.'

'No he's not, I poked my head in.'

'Is he in Molly's room with her?'

'No, because that hasn't happened in about five years. He's not here, Jess – I thought you knew.'

I rise up from my seat. 'I'll call him and get him back.'

'We've got his phone.'

'Oh, for Christ's sake.'

2

Slice of lime with that?

'You are so lucky.'

'What, that I get to go back to that shithole in a week? Yes, Dad, I am so lucky.'

'Language!' I whisper-shout, peering around the thankfully empty school gates to check if anyone overheard. If it were an hour earlier there would still be clusters of whispering parents dotted about. I needn't have worried, everyone has already dispersed to their jobs, exercise classes, ironing piles or morning television.

'You made us look like absolute idiots in there, Liam,' I say as we stomp towards the car.

'What? What did I do?'

'You, with your, "I only wanted to keep my peers hydrated" nonsense. You knew that line would fire me up, and then I looked like a complete eejit.'

I feel such a fool – I even helped him load his cool boxes into the boot each morning. In between me firing off juvenile dehydration statistics and Fergus doing his, 'Oh, we were all young once, what's an ice lolly between friends?' routine, the stony-faced panel took great delight in saying, 'Mr and Mrs Bay, I don't think your son has been entirely truthful about why we're suspending him.'

'Are you calling our son a liar?' Fergus had asked, eyes flashing angrily. 'Because he has told us, and quite frankly we are appalled at the school's harsh stance on a child innocently trying to combat climate change.'

Even I had thought that was a bit much, but neither of us was ready for the head's retort of, 'We are suspending Liam for choosing to, ahem, innocently combat climate change through selling ice lollies made from gin and tonic and vodka cranberry.'

'Oh,' we'd both muttered in chastened unison. That told us.

I stand impatiently by my car, arms folded across my chest. 'So, what now?' I say to Fergus. 'Can Liam go to work with you today?'

'Me? No, of course he can't. What's he going to do, sort paper clips into size order?'

'You have interns, can't he be one of them?' I know for a fact that Fergus's company has a steady stream of eager young things happy to work for the cost of a Pret a Manger smoked salmon panini, because he is often tagged in their boozy photos on Instagram: #teambuilding, #allworknoplay, #bestbossever.

'He's thirteen,' Fergus says. As if I didn't know.

'I'm aware of that.'

'Are you also aware that he's standing right here?' Liam injects.

'I just mean, I can't take a thirteen year old into work with me.'

'He's not just *a* thirteen year old, he's *your* thirteen year old,' I say.

'Still here,' Liam chimes in.

'And he's *your* thirteen year old, too. Can't he go in with you?'

'To a doctor's surgery? What is he going to do? Take blood samples?'

'I don't know . . . get him to arrange the patients' notes in the filing cabinet?'

'The filing cabinet? We're not in the 1950s, we don't have a filing cabinet.'

I'm already late for the morning's surgery – my mind suddenly floods with images of newborn babies, pregnant mothers, frail pensioners, a thousand different germs and weakened immune systems all together in one place. I have a desperate urge for a double shot coffee to feel the welcome surge of caffeine flood my brain and I want to be as far as humanly possible away from Fergus. So, as I run into the crowded surgery fifteen minutes later, Liam is trailing sulkily behind me. I return the appraising smile Robert gives me as I sail past him, knowing full well that my pencil skirt accentuates the curve of my behind and allow myself to imagine him slowly unzipping it.

'Yuck, are you flirting with him?' Liam says, making vomit noises.

'Wind your neck in. He's gay.'

In between an infected leg abscess and a severe case of Strep throat, the school rings. I've got no idea how Liam could be in trouble when he's currently doing a stock take of sterile bandages, and impatiently say so, before the deputy head says that it is Molly he is calling about today. I'm sure that I detect a hint of pomposity in his tone, an audible eye-roll at having to disrupt his day with yet another incident involving a Bay child.

'Molly?' I reply. Aside from checking out of real life and existing purely in the world of pouting selfies and hashtags, she never gives us cause for concern the way Liam does.

'She missed her GCSE French oral this morning. I don't think that I need to tell you that this is very serious.'

'But she can't have! I dropped her off myself this morning, just before our meeting with you. I watched her go into her classroom.'

'Well evidently, she then went out of her classroom, Mrs Bay.'

'Doctor. Doctor Bay.'

'I'm sorry, what?'

'You said Mrs Bay, but I am a doctor.'

It was petty, and trivial, and totally unnecessary, but all control is slipping through my fingers like water and I feel a desperate need to impress him, to tell him that he's got it wrong, I'm not one of those mums they make documentaries about who let their kids run wild. Molly was thirteen before I even let her get her ears pierced, for goodness' sake. I put the phone down after promising I'll deal with it, and give the patient in front of me a smile. 'Right, let's take the swabs from your throat and send them off to the lab.'

As soon as I'm alone again, I pick up my mobile.

'Hello, Fergus's phone?' comes a chirpy female voice.

'Is Fergus there? It's his *wife*.' I put an unnecessary stress on the last word just in case there is any ambiguity about his marital status in the office. His wedding ring hasn't left the pot next to his electric toothbrush charger in months – apparently it doesn't fit any more. I don't want to ask if he means literally or metaphorically.

'He's just in a meeting at the moment. Can I get him to call you back?'

'Yes, it's very urgent. If you could interrupt the meeting—'

'Oh no, I couldn't do that.'

'Well, it would be great if you could, but if you can't, then the second he steps out, please tell him to call me.'

My phone rings about three minutes later.

'That was a quick meeting, or did the girl pull you out of it?'

'I was having a shit. But I could hardly tell her that.'

'You just said it to me.'

'We've been married for a hundred years. That's different.'

'I think I would still prefer to think of you in a meeting.'

Fergus clicks his tongue impatiently. 'Faye said that it was urgent.'

'Molly's gone AWOL. Missed her exam today, the school have no idea where she is.'

He gives a loud sigh. 'Oh, Jesus. How did we get it so wrong?'

'I think the most important thing is to track her down. Her phone's off, but can you use that app thing on your phone to see where it is?'

'Yes, hang on while I look.'

I drum my fingers on the table while I wait, seething. How could she be so stupid to mess up her future like this?

'OK. It's showing that she's in Tan & Glam tanning salon,' Fergus says.

'Are you kidding me? She's missing her French GCSE to get a fake tan?'

'*Mais oui.*'

Mum sits nursing a cup of tea at my kitchen table after she invited herself over. I'd like to think this impromptu visit was to support her only child in her time of need, but she admitted as soon as she'd made sure that we were alone that she had a date last week that didn't end at the restaurant and that she was a bit itchy, 'you know, down there', and needs the name of some cream. Like this week couldn't get any worse.

'So what did Molly say then? When you found her?' Mum says when I finish filling her in on Molly's Great Escape.

'She wouldn't talk to me at all. As usual. I knew she'd been crying because she had mascara all down her face, but she denied it of course, shrugged her shoulders and sailed past me. I'd still be none the wiser about what happened if one of her friend's mums hadn't called to tell me that just before the exam Molly had gone to the loo, and come back to the exam room with her skirt tucked in her knickers. Apparently she ran away in embarrassment when she realised and hid in the nearest place she could be by herself, which was one of those awful tanning cubicles of all places.' At least she'd had the sense not to actually use the sunbed – melanomas aside, those things must be riddled with bacteria.

'Poor thing.'

I look at my mother, baffled at her attitude. What part of this wasn't she getting? 'It was a real exam, Mum, not a mock or a little test – a proper exam that counts towards her future.'

'She keeps everything in, does that one. Wonder where she gets that from.'

I keep folding the laundry, making four piles, one for each of us, not meeting her eye. Molly's resembles the Leaning Tower of Pisa due to her hobby of changing her clothes every seventeen seconds.

'So, what are you going to do about it all?' Mum asks. 'I can't imagine my son-in-law is being particularly proactive about coming up with a plan to steer the kids back on the straight and narrow.'

When I'd first introduced Fergus to my parents, they'd liked him. But he was a different Fergus back then: a fellow medical student, a future doctor, with plans of specialising in the heady (and immensely fruitful) world of cosmetic surgery. What was not to like? Then he failed his third year exams, which wasn't surprising considering what was going on at the time, got asked to leave university, and took a junior role in a PR firm, which, ironically, represents many of the celebrities he might have operated on had he stayed at university.

'That's sort of the same, isn't it?' Fergus had said at the time, trying to make the best of it.

'No, not really, Fergus. It's not the same at all,' Mum had replied, disappointed that her new son-in-law would never be getting her discounts on the facelift she'd already decided to have thirty years into the future.

'We're just keeping our heads down for a bit,' I say in response to Mum's question, 'Fergus has gone into work this morning—'

'Leaving you here to hold the fort. Nice.' Mum sniffs.

' – to speak to his boss about some leave, actually.'

'So you're both off work for a bit, Liam's suspended, Molly's bunking off her GCSEs, and you're all just going to sit in the house feeling sorry for yourselves?'

'It's not like that at all, Mum! We're just taking stock of things. Molly hasn't got another exam until Friday, so it just made sense to be at home together.' When I'd called Robert to say that I'd be off for the rest of the week, he made a clucking sound that despite not containing any words was far more sympathetic than anyone else was being. 'Take as much time as you need,' he'd said, 'but make sure you look after yourself, too. Remember what they say: put your own oxygen mask on first before helping others.'

'Absolutely,' I'd replied, as if I were just off to have a hot stone massage that very minute.

Mum put her cup down and folded her arms across her chest. 'To be honest, Jessica, I think you need to consider stepping off this ridiculous hamster wheel of responsibilities for a bit, get the kids back on track, and sort out your marriage. Are you still seeing that psychiatrist?'

'Therapist.'

'Tomayto tomato.'

God, she's annoying. 'A psychiatrist is a doctor who can prescribe medication, a therapist listens to you talk.'

'And do you talk to her?'

'Of course I talk. We don't sit there in silence for an hour a week.'

'I mean *really* talk?'

'As opposed to what?' I say irritably. 'Tap dancing?'

'As opposed to smiling and chatting about everything except the reason you need therapy. I bet you squirt bleach down the lavatory before the cleaner comes, too.'

'I don't have a cleaner.' Which she knows all too well as she mutters about the state of my house every time she comes round. I speed up folding the laundry. I'm not bothering to even turn the inside-out socks the right way any more. They can do that themselves, surely.

'Jessica?'

'I don't want to talk about it.' I carelessly put Fergus's boxers on Molly's pile and it teeters ominously before falling over and scattering newly folded clothes across the kitchen floor like dominoes.

Fergus

Fergus's boss is away in his timeshare apartment in Majorca. He has been for the same two weeks each year for the last eleven years and will go back every year until he dies of a burst stomach ulcer in twelve years' time. He approved Fergus's request for a week's leave by email, telling him to 'take as much time as you need'. Fergus reads it, closes his laptop, and leaves for the office anyway, shouting down the hallway a swift, 'Bye, can't keep the boss waiting.'

Faye sits opposite him in the coffee shop next to work, twirling her long blond hair through her fingers and pouting. Both actions unsettle Fergus, because for a split second he sees Molly, not the woman he's been grafting for the best part of six months. He would, however, be horrified if he heard someone describe what he's been doing as 'grafting'; it is such a horrible word, so predatory. He'd have quickly shut it down, saying something like, 'It comes to something when a man can't be friendly with a female colleague! Honestly, this political correctness nonsense really has made the world a crazy place.'

Faye is younger than Jess, but she isn't young, not Molly young. She is actually slap bang in the middle between his wife and daughter. That isn't too young. For a friend to be. Everyone needs friends.

Faye has just finished telling him about this 'incredible speakeasy bar that he absolutely must visit, he'd love it'. He agrees that yes, he absolutely would.

'So you're going to be away for a week? Maybe more?' Faye pouts, sticking her bottom lip out. It's so shiny. 'Work is going to be so dull without you.'

Fergus nods. 'But I'll be on my email, and you can message me any time. In fact, please do – I'll be going out of my mind with boredom, so make me laugh.'

Faye has introduced Fergus to the world of humorous memes. Most of their WhatsApp chat is filled with pictures of animals or kids pulling funny faces, things that Jess would think were childish and a waste of time. Admittedly, Fergus is wasting a considerable amount of time looking for them.

'And you're not going away? You're just all going to be at home together?'

'I need to be there to support the family.'

'You really are such a great husband. I hope your wife knows how lucky she is.'

Under his shirt Fergus involuntarily flexes his chest.

3

Six hundred and thirty-two days and counting

Fergus's phone is screen-side down on the kitchen counter. I know what that means, I've read about it in one of the magazines at the surgery. I'm not stupid.

He's having an affair.

If I wanted to, I could turn it over and scan through the messages while he is in the shower – I'd be able to hear him coming down the stairs in time to put it down – but the sad thing is, I don't want to know for sure. I don't want to see what gushing words she's saying to him, or what lovely things he's written back. He even tried it on last night, coming out of the shower with a tiny towel wrapped around his waist like he was an Egyptian Adonis wearing a loincloth in size XS. He did look incredible, to be fair; maybe some of the times he said he was at the gym he was actually there. But I couldn't do it. I couldn't go from us not even sitting on the same sofa to entwining limbs and body parts, not when I'm pretty sure he's doing that during the week to someone that's not me. Someone who is younger, prettier and more supple because they have time to do after-work spin classes.

I hold out a plate of jam toast to Molly as she enters the kitchen in her school uniform. Molly shakes her head. 'I don't eat breakfast.'

'Since when?'

She shrugs and squeezes a lemon into a mug of hot water.

'That's not going to see you through the day.'

Molly turns to face me. 'You're a doctor. How much should I weigh?'

Teenage eating disorder statistics run through my brain as I carefully answer, 'Whatever is within the healthy range for your height and body type.'

'No, give me a number. How many kilos?'

'You're perfect as you are.'

'Give. Me. A. Number.'

'No, Molly, you're perfect,' I repeat.

'If I'm perfect,' Molly spits back, 'then how do you explain this?'

Molly plunges her phone in front of my face. The screen is dominated by a naked obese person being winched out of a first-floor window by a crane, with my beautiful Molly's head photo-shopped onto it.

My blood starts bubbling in my veins. 'Who sent you that?'

Molly averts her gaze and scowls. 'No one, doesn't matter.'

Liam chooses this moment to amble into the kitchen still in his pyjamas, making the most of his suspension, and picks up Molly's cold toast. He looks at the screen. 'I know who sent it,' he says, spraying crumbs everywhere.

'Shut up, Liam,' Molly hisses.

'His name's Kenzo. I saw him looking at fat people on his phone.'

'Kenzo?' The name sounds familiar. Then I remember. I'd found a screwed-up piece of paper in Molly's trouser pockets a few weeks ago, where she'd calculated the amount that Kenzo Preston loved Molly Bay. I seem to remember that it was a rather positive 86%.

'Isn't he a friend of yours, Molly?'

'I hate him.'

I open my mouth to parrot my mother, and say something like 'hate's a strong word', then realise that I hate the little bugger too.

Fergus

It's clear Faye likes him, thinks Fergus. Women don't flick their hair about that much unless either they fancy you, or there's something living in it. Even Jess in the early days had done more than her fair share of hair flicking to lure him in. *Jess. Don't think about Jess.* She rejected him again last night. He even came out of the shower wearing nothing but a tiny towel, his skin glistening after using her Jo Malone body cream, and Jess didn't look at him twice.

'Do you know that we haven't had sex in six hundred and thirty-two days?' Fergus told her, expecting her to be as aghast as him.

'How on earth do you know that?' Jess said.

'I keep a tally in my head.'

'So you still don't know that Wednesday is the day that the plastic needs to go out in the recycling bin, but you know that we haven't had sex for six hundred and thirty days?'

'Thirty-*two*,' he corrected her.

Jess ignored him and pulled her tartan pyjamas on. God he hates those pyjamas. It's like ten men-hating women sat around a table and purposely designed the most unflattering garments they could possibly come up with.

'I think this shows that you're using your brain power for the wrong things,' she said.

How were they ever meant to get back on track if she doesn't even fancy him any more? He doesn't think he's changed that much, a little thicker of waist and greyer of hair, but he thinks he's ageing quite well apart from that. Not as well as her, but then again, they can't all be perfect.

'So, um, Faye,' Fergus says, banishing thoughts of his wife from his mind and rubbing his toe along the fraying carpet next to the water dispenser. 'I was thinking of trying that bar you mentioned, the speakeasy one?'

'Yeah, you definitely should! You'd love it!'

'I mean, if you fancy a drink. Christ, I mean, I think we all deserve one after that meeting!' Fergus runs his hand through his hair, subconsciously saying, *Yes, I may be older than you, but look at how thick and luscious my hair still is.*

'Yeah, it was a bit of a shocker, wasn't it?'

'Yeah.'

'Do you know what,' Faye says suddenly, 'I could murder a vodka Red Bull. If you're buying?'

'Great! Brilliant! OK, let me just get my bag. Great!'

They have to walk slower along the pavement than he'd normally walk with Jess (*Jess, Jess*) due to Faye's height of heel and slimness of skirt but that just allows him to bask in the envious looks he's getting from every man they pass. Jess would be walking really fast. A to B. B to C. C to D. 'Quicker,' she'd snap, 'hurry up, stop dawdling, no the cloud doesn't look like Mickey Mouse, what a ridiculous thing to say. Come on, Fergus, mind the dog shit, God, you're slower than the kids.'

Fergus knows that it's far too soon to try to hold Faye's hand, although he does grab her elbow when one of her stiletto heels almost gets caught in a drain, so there is some touching, and it is electrifying, like a literal bolt pulsing through his body, waking every inch of him up. He's sure she felt it too.

'One vodka Red Bull and a bag of crisps,' Fergus announces, dropping the crisps out of his mouth as he reaches their table.

'I'm on the keto diet, so no carbs.'

'Oh, OK. Me too. I'll take these home for the kids.' *The kids, the kids.*

'You had a sandwich at lunch.'

'Yeah, I'm only carb free in the afternoon.'

Fergus takes a sip of his pint of bitter, instantly wishing he'd ordered something less middle-aged. A Porn Star martini maybe, or a Negroni. Something strong and sexy. Even the achingly hip barman had mumbled under his twirly moustache that no one had ordered an ale in months, they were actually thinking of getting rid of it. Fergus opens his mouth to ask Faye if she'd watched *Newsnight* the night before – he and Jess (*Jess, Jess*) had howled at the new candidate for Southwark's impression of the Prime Minister – but Faye gets there first.

'Do you watch *GoggleBox*?'

'That's the one where you watch people watching TV, isn't it?'

'Yeah.'

At the exact moment Fergus says, 'That's ridiculous,' Faye says, 'It's brilliant,' making them both take their next sip of their drinks in silent contemplation. A shadow falls over their table.

'Christian!' Faye shrieks. She jumps up, giving the six-foot-three shadow, who has stubble, a man bun, and an unnervingly large tattoo of a camouflaged shark on his arm, a passionate kiss – with her tongue. Fergus knows it is with her tongue because he can see it, darting in and out, pressing against the inside of the shadow's mouth like a trapped goldfish.

She breaks away and gestures at Fergus. 'Christian, this is Fergus, who I've told you about. He's like my Work Dad.'

'Pleased to meet you, sir.' Christian holds out his hand.

Work Dad?

Sir?

Shit.

4

An unusual aphrodisiac . . .

Robert insists on accompanying me on my lunchtime house calls, despite one being an infected bedsore and the other a leaky colostomy bag, so what he has to say must be really important. We stop off at the local park on our way back to the surgery to eat our sandwiches under a tree. He shifts his weight from one toned buttock to the other making his trousers appear tighter across his crotch. I pretend not to notice.

He gives a nervous cough. 'I wanted to talk to you because life is short, Jess, and I think your family take you for granted, and you really should be with someone who adores you. Someone who would even be happy watching you empty a colostomy bag if it meant being in the same room as you.'

For a moment, I don't understand and just smile bemusedly at him. Then it hits me and I freeze, the sandwich poised halfway to my mouth. Even if someone opened up the top of my head and poured plaster of Paris inside my body cavity, I don't think that I could sit any stiller than I am right now. Before I can think of what to say, his lips suddenly lock onto mine with such force that I completely lose my balance and fall back onto the grass. He takes this as an invitation to straddle me, pressing his stagnantly still lips onto mine even harder. There is no movement, no tongue action, thank the Lord – and what's more, absolutely no chemistry or thunderbolt of any kind. I am just a mute mannequin joined at the lips to an evidently straight man with a perfectly groomed, but incredibly itchy, beard.

I wriggle free and spring up, knowing full well that I've just flashed my M&S five-pairs-for-seven-quid pants to not only him, but all the suited sandwich-eaters in the park. I quickly brush all the grass off my clothes and hair. 'Um, Robert, that was unexpected.'

'So, when are you going to tell Fergus?' Robert says as we walk through the park back to the surgery. He's threaded his arm through mine, as though we're both teenage girls off on a shopping trip to River Island.

'Um, I think the thing is, Robert – the thing is . . .'

The thing is, Robert, I thought you were my homosexual friend-slash-boss until about three and a half minutes ago and now I'm reliving every horrifically embarrassing time I flirted with you because I thought I could, and while you're really lovely, and will make someone a delightful, if slightly over-attentive husband one day, I actually quite like the family I've got.

I like the family I've got.

I like the family I've got. That's a shock. Suddenly everything makes sense.

'The thing is, Robert, I'm married. Happily. Well, sort of. We're working on it. And I am very flattered, but I don't think of you in that way.'

He puts his hands into his pockets and nods slowly, avoiding my gaze. 'You thought I was gay, didn't you?'

'Um – well, I mean . . . I never, really, um – well, yes, sort of.'

He bangs the sides of his head with both his fists. 'Why does this keep happening?'

I'm pretty sure this is a rhetorical question and he doesn't actually want an answer, so I keep quiet and give him an embarrassed smile.

Robert coughs. 'It's probably best that we never speak of this again.'

'Yes. Absolutely. Never.' I mime zipping up my mouth and

then make a show of lobbing the imaginary key as far away as possible.

As I lie in bed later that night, the space next to me empty because Fergus wanted to stay up to watch a movie, I wonder if I was too quick to bat Robert away. Nothing's actually stopping me leaving Fergus. I could start again. Or I don't even have to leave him, I could just have a fling. Like he is. I could have a glorious, sexy fling where we meet in dimly lit cocktail bars; he'd have a bottle of champagne waiting in an ice bucket, and I would have had a bikini wax. And Robert is so thoughtful. A couple of years ago for my fortieth he bought me a beautifully illustrated edition of *Little Women* because I'd once mentioned in passing it's my favourite book; it was delicately wrapped in a square of protective silk. Fergus, in contrast, gave me a spa voucher. The gift you give when you don't know what else to give. I was so upset. I didn't show it of course, but I was really hoping he'd give me something that showed that he knew me better, something that proved that he still loved me. It didn't need to be expensive, just thoughtful. As the date of expiry loomed I started to wonder whether a weekend away with Fergus might actually be good for us, so I tried to rearrange my work shifts and organise Mum to stay over to surprise him, but a few days before the trip, the locum cancelled, and Iris stepped on a discarded syringe in the local park necessitating emergency surgery. So that put paid to that. This year on my birthday, Fergus bought me a hand-held vacuum cleaner because I'd mentioned that crumbs from the toaster always seemed to be on the kitchen counter. The kids' gift was saying 'happy birthday' to me. And even then, that was only after I'd said, 'It's my birthday today.' And Mum got me a bird feeder for the garden despite me never mentioning a liking for birds or indeed ever stepping into the garden for any reason other than to hang the washing on the line.

Every morning for the next week whenever I enter the doctor's pantry, Robert hurries out of it, so in some ways, work is now becoming very much like being at home. Friday, five days later, is different though. Robert is waiting for me in the reception, and ushers me through to his office before I even have a chance to say hello to Pam or hang up my coat.

'Is something wrong?' I ask as he points at a chair I should evidently sit in.

'Jessica,' he begins with a formality I don't recognise. 'I have been contacted by the local heath authority about a desperate need for a senior GP in another practice, and asked if I would consider loaning one of my doctors out. I immediately thought of you.'

'Me?'

'Yes. We're a little overstaffed here at the moment—'

'No we're not.'

'Sorry?'

'I said, no we're not. If anything, the opposite is true. You want to get rid of me.'

'Jessica, I—'

My blood pounds in my ears. 'Robert, this is ridiculous, I am not moving to another surgery when I've been at this one for fifteen years. My patients know me, I know them, it takes years to build up relationships like the ones I have. I'm not doing it just because you're a bit embarrassed about what happened.'

'You'd be running the practice.'

'What?'

'It's a small surgery, very small – only you, in fact, but you'd be in charge.'

'Of me?'

'What?'

'I'd be in charge, of me?'

'Well, you could put it like that, or you could look at it as the chance to get the experience of management.'

'By managing myself.'

'I don't think you're really approaching this with a growth mindset.'

I cross my arms across my chest. 'Where is it?' I ask sullenly.

'It's a little further than our normal secondment area.'

'I'm not going south of the river, Robert, the commute would be a nightmare.'

Robert picks up a paper clip to fiddle with. 'It's a little further than that. It's on the Isle of Forth in the English Channel. I've already put your name forward, so it's more or less decided. And your family would go with you.' His eyes soften. 'I know you think that I'm only doing this because of what happened, or didn't happen, between us, but I'm doing this as your friend. I think it's what you and your family need. The initial loan period is only six months, while they advertise for a full-time replacement for their doctor. So do that and then come back here. It's a second chance, Jessica. For all of you.'

I walk back to my consulting room in a daze, blood rushing in my ears. I must be able to turn this down. I'll contact my union. Yes, that's what I'll do. I have rights. He can't just try and kiss me then ship me off to a bloody island. I'll sue for unfair dismissal, even though I'm not technically being dismissed. Harassment. Yes, I definitely feel harassed. A tiny voice tries to tell me that I may, just possibly, have given him confusing signals, but I bat it away. Even if that were true, it wouldn't give him the right to banish me to the middle of the Channel to shut me up and save his blushes. How dare he!

I slump in my chair, not sure what to do first. Just out of interest, I lean forward and type 'Isle of Forth' into Google

– not because I'm considering going, I'm just vaguely curious. It's a tiny island halfway between England and France, just three miles by four, with seven hundred full-time inhabitants, more in summer. As I read, a strange feeling creeps over me, as though a virtual checklist I didn't even know I had is being filled in. It has an Ofsted Outstanding state school, so no more exorbitant fees – tick; it is car-free, so there would be no potential for joyriding in Liam's future – tick; plenty of pubs, but no mention of any private members clubs with perky hostesses – tick; the website also says there are plenty of pursuits for teenagers, like caving, orienteering and equestrian centres. That's what Molly needs to sort her out: a horse! Teenage girls love horses!

I suddenly remember what I'd told Jackie about my family being like an ugly eighties pine dresser. Well, maybe that's the London version of the Bays. The Isle of Forth version might be a beautiful duck egg blue with fancy knobs on it.

Fergus

'Don't say no,' Jess starts.

'No.'

'Fergus, I'm serious.'

'So am I. The very fact that you assumed I would say no, means that it's in all likelihood something that I don't want to do. So I'm saving you the energy of continuing a conversation, when we're both already in agreement that it's not going to happen,' he says, arms folded, shield up.

Her move. She stays silent.

'OK, fine, what is it?' he asks, unable to stop himself.

'I've been offered an incredible job, and I'd like to go for it.'

'I didn't know you were going for partner?'

'I'm not. It's not in my practice. It's – well, it's a bit further away.'

'How much further away?'

'The Isle of Forth.' Jess moves slightly back, as though she's anticipating the splutter of tea that is about to shower her . . .

'Where the hell is the Isle of Forth?' Fergus exclaims.

'It's in the English Channel. An hour from Guernsey. By boat.'

'An island? With how many people on it?'

'Seven hundred.'

'What would I do?'

'Well, I thought about that. If we rent out our house, that's the mortgage covered. There's an amazing school, and it's free. The new job comes with a house, so we wouldn't actually be spending that much, and so we could afford for you to start writing that book you've been talking about forever, and maybe you could do some freelance consulting. I know you'd miss your colleagues, but I'm sure you'd make some new friends.'

Work Dad.

'OK. Let's do it.'

'I knew you'd say that.' Jess slumps back in her chair. 'You're just so defeatist, and stuck in your ways, and you're going to be sat in your nursing home all alone, thinking of this exciting life you could have had, but didn't, because you're just too bloody boring.'

'OK, well first,' Fergus says, 'I wouldn't be alone, you'd be there.'

'No, I wouldn't. I'm now married to a man with a shiny beard and a sense of adventure.'

'You don't even like beards.'

Jess looks momentarily repulsed for some reason Fergus can't fathom. 'You're right,' she shudders, 'I don't. What's the second thing?'

'The second thing is, you didn't listen to me. I said, yes, let's do it.'

'Just like that?' Jess says, sitting upright in her chair. 'We'll just forget about the life we've got here, uproot the kids, leave our very stable jobs, and just bugger off to an island in the middle of the Channel to eat mussels every day?'

Fergus furrows his brow in confusion, 'I'm not sure I understand what's going on.'

'I didn't bring this up for you to decide that we were going to do it, I thought we'd spend the evening talking about it, going through different options.'

Fergus's head hurts. 'You said it was an incredible job. I said that I'm up for it. Why do we now need to spend hours gassing when we could just make the decision now, and then watch TV for the rest of the evening? I go back to my original point: you waste far too much time talking and dancing round every single thing you do. Just make a decision, stick to it, and move on. Done.'

'Just like that.'

'Just like that.'

That'll show Faye, he thought. *Work Dad my arse*.

5

'I am definitely not a Howard'

We wait for the kids in the living room. As soon as they clatter in through the front door amid a flurry of bag dropping and shoes being kicked off, Fergus tells them to come in and sit down on the sofa, which surprisingly, they both do without arguing about it. I wonder for a moment whether Fergus and I should stand or sit when we're telling them. Standing will give the announcement some gravitas, make it seem like a done deal. Sitting makes us seem more accessible, more open to negotiation, which we absolutely are not. I've taken inspiration from Jackie's consulting room and put a box of tissues on the coffee table, ready for the tsunami of teenage emotion that is about to engulf the room and everyone in it.

'Is it Grandma Joy?' Liam says. 'Has she—' He mimes slitting his own throat.

Horrified, I snap, 'No! Jesus, Liam, it's not that!'

Fergus steps in. 'Look, the last few months have been pretty rubbish for all of us. Your Mum – ' He adds 'and me' as an afterthought – 'have been working way too much, and we haven't been around as much as we should have been. Molly, you've had a few issues, and, Liam, you too. And we don't think that living here, in London, is perhaps the best thing for us at the moment.'

I search the kids' faces for clues as to how they are taking what Fergus is saying, but they are blank. I try peering into their earholes for hidden earphones and listen for the low buzz of pulsating music, which is the logical conclusion for their expressionless faces, but they are bizarrely clear.

'So, it's come at the right time, we think, but your Mum has been offered an opportunity to run her own practice in the country – a small village, on an island, where we won't have all these, er, distractions, of the city, and we can just enjoy being together.'

'A fresh start!' I interject, hoping my handclapping enthusiasm will be contagious, or at the very least evoke some sort of reaction from the two mute automatons currently sitting on the sofa. 'We can leave all the baggage behind and start a new life, as new people!'

'Can I bring my Xbox?'

I study my son. Are we not being clear enough? Does he think we mean this new life is going to just be for a weekend?'

'Um, yes, Liam, you can bring your Xbox. We'll take all our stuff. We're going to rent this house out, and then, later on, if we want to come back, we can.'

Molly has been completely, and uncharacteristically, silent. I squat down next to her, the way waiters do in American chain restaurants to make them seem friendlier. 'Molls?' I haven't called her that in years so I hold my breath waiting for the eye-roll that is about to happen.

I don't know what I'm going to do if they say no and refuse to go. This move is more to me than just geography. Over the last twenty-four hours, I've realised that it's everything we need. Everything I need.

'Can I get a new number?' Molly asks. 'So that no one here can find me?'

Since Knicker-gate she's flatly refused to go into school on non-exam days, and is already talking about moving schools for sixth form.

'Of course. The Internet's meant to be pretty bad there, anyway.'

'OK. How soon can we go?'

That's unexpected. Or maybe it isn't. Maybe I just don't know my own children as well as I think I do. Which is why we need to do this. This isn't my fault, or Fergus's, or the kids' – it's London's.

'I think I might start going by the name of Freddie when we move.'

I narrow my eyes at Fergus in the bathroom mirror. He is holding his toothbrush aloft, looking up into mid-air, hand on chin, as though he has just conquered a new land and claimed it at his own. All he is missing is a handlebar moustache.

'Um, what?'

'You said it yourself, it's a fresh start for all of us. We can literally be whoever we want to be, and Fergus has never suited me, so here's my chance to be something else. To be the Freddie I know I can be.'

'Why Freddie, though?'

'It's a bit posh, isn't it, and a bit rugby-playing—'

'Neither of which you are.'

'Because my name has been holding me back all this time! Imagine how different my life would have been if I'd have been christened Tarquin or Willoughby.'

'I've always thought that you look quite a lot like a Howard.'

'Howard!' Fergus spits out the word as though Howard is actually an animal in the same room as us who has just peed on the carpet.

'I am not a Howard!'

'Howard's not a bad name. I had a Howard in my class, he was a decent chap.'

'What would your name be, if you could change it?'

I rub my face cream into my skin in an upward circular motion, thinking for a moment. 'I've always quite liked the name Camilla.'

'Camilla would never be married to a Howard.'

'She would!'

'She would not. Camilla is married to a city banker called Tobias. Howard does the books for the local curtain shop. I can't believe you think I'm a Howard.'

'Fergus, give it up.'

'This, right here, is what's so wrong about our marriage. If you see me as a Howard, instead of a Rafferty or a Maximus, then there really is no hope for us. That's really annoyed me that has.' He throws his toothbrush into the holder and storms past me back into the bedroom.

'I don't know why,' I say, following him in and getting into bed. 'It's just funny banter.'

'You don't get it, do you? It's all about how we perceive each other, and it's quite clear that you don't see me as dashing and charming – you know, a bit mysterious.'

I shake my head in disbelief. 'We've been married for a million years, Fergus, of course you're not mysterious!'

'But I want you to think of me as this sexy beast, not as Howard the bookkeeper who can't grow a beard.'

'Well, stop telling me every time you have a bowel movement and showing me when you pull out a grey pubic hair, then!'

He looks confused. 'But you're a doctor. I thought bodies aren't meant to faze you?'

'They don't! But some things are best left private.' I can't stop myself adding, even though I know it will annoy him, 'Someone called Freddie would know that.'

I've been dreading breaking the news to Mum, but I needn't have worried. After a few seconds of yawning silence, all she says is, 'I'm going to have to get myself a proper GP now.'

I scratch my nose. 'I *am* a proper GP.'

'No, you know what I mean, one I have to make an appointment for.'

The removal van is booked and is due to arrive crammed full of our things a few days after we arrive on the island. The kids have said their goodbyes to their friends, which consisted of a flurry of sad-face emojis being pinged back and forth between their phones all week. Bizarrely, Fergus chooses not to have a big leaving party, even after I promise that I won't insist on coming to it.

'But you love a good party,' I say. 'I read about a new speakeasy bar that sounds right up your street. You could have it there.'

'I'm too old for all that nonsense,' he says, turning on the TV to watch the news.

Meanwhile, I've made the noises of 'we must stay in touch' with everyone at work and the school gates because that is what you are supposed to do, along with 'you must visit if you're ever in the area' (*the area* being the body of water that separates England and France), but I don't mean it. Every box that is packed makes me feel lighter, every 'goodbye' and 'good luck' card I receive gives me a little frisson of excitement that a better life is waiting for us.

6

New starts

There is a split second of perfection on the ferry. The four of us are standing in height order against the rail of the bow looking out to sea, totally unorchestrated, unlike so many of our #blessed family photos, which only come about through me persistently whining, 'Please, just try and look as though you like each other for one sodding second!'

The saline-scented wind whips our hair around our faces, which are all upturned to the cool afternoon air. It is one of those blink-and-you-miss-it moments of familial harmony that I concentrate on freeze-framing and storing in my memory bank forever. I know that if I whip out my phone to try to take a more reliable memento of the moment it will be gone, lost. Fergus will give me one of his disparaging looks, Liam will hit Molly, Molly will do the duck lips that she thinks constitutes a smile. But this moment, this is perfection.

Then Liam's new Nike cap blows off into the Channel, a seagull craps on Molly's arm and Fergus's phone rings. And my family are once again my family.

We draw up alongside the jetty and the ferry rudely crashes against the side of the dock, making me lose my balance. I instinctively grab onto Molly, who's the nearest to me. She shrugs my hand off her arm with a disgusted sneer before it contaminates her.

No cars are allowed on the island, so I've spent the last twenty minutes of the crossing thinking through the logistics of how the hell we're going to get the four of us, plus a dog, large dog bed, and seven suitcases – two without wheels and one with a broken handle – off the boat and through the streets to our new house, which is attached to the surgery. In the end, Fergus and I have to do two trips struggling down the gangplank onto the jetty, and back again to retrieve yet more of our belongings, which the rest of the passengers are busy tripping over and cursing – an excellent start to our brand-new life.

Suddenly, Iris starts barking as ferociously as a timid urban spaniel can.

'Iris, stop it!' I yank her lead, which is wrapped around my wrist, as I'm holding a suitcase in each hand. But Iris has found her voice and is now rising on her back legs against the taut lead, barking and snarling. I look up to see the cause of Iris's complete character overhaul, and come face to face with two massive black horses pulling a cart.

'You must be Dr Bay,' the man standing next to the horses says. He's a short, stout man in his sixties, shirtsleeves rolled up, his face tanned and weathered from a lifetime of enjoying sea air and cloudless skies. He puts out his hand. 'Keith Hodges. I'm your neighbour, and official welcoming party.'

I have to drop one case to the floor to shake his hand, then gesture at Fergus and the kids. 'This is my husband Fer—'

'Freddie. Nice to meet you.' Fergus pumps Keith's hand up and down enthusiastically.

The kids turn to me in confusion. I shake my head as if to say, 'Don't ask', and give Fergus a look that says, 'You're an absolute tool'. He smiles and gives me one back that says, 'Sorry, I can't hear you'.

There is absolutely no room for misinterpreting the look of glee on Liam's face as he clambers onto the back of the cart, after asking Keith how much he charges tourists for a horse-drawn tour around the island, while calculating in his head how he could buy a horse, cart, charge tourists less and still make a profit. The look of undisguised horror on Molly's face is just as easy to decipher, as she tries not to touch anything and lays out her jumper on the bench before sitting on it gingerly, her nose wrinkled. Thankfully Iris has calmed down, but only because Fergus is now carrying her.

'So you're from London,' Keith says as we clip-clop away from the port and towards the centre of the village. It's a statement, not a question, so demands no reply more complex than a 'Mmm'.

He follows that up with, 'Bit different here.'

Our eyes dart all around us, each of us taking in different things. I'm gratified to see a fairly large Co-op, nowhere near the size of the Tesco hypermarket at home, but surely large enough for what we'd need. A hairdresser's has yellowing sun-damaged posters in the window showcasing women with huge, pageant-style curls and once-neon eyelids. Fergus nods approvingly as the cart goes past two different pubs along the same small stretch of road, while Liam's eyes light up at the array of gift stores with garish inflatables strung along their canopies and carousels of fridge magnets, postcards and key rings. A collection of fishing nets stands in a pot next to one, along with buckets and spades and a sign outside declaring that inside there are 'six flavours of ice cream!' – a boast that apparently warrants an exclamation mark. I can tell by Molly's withering expression that she has yet to find anything on our journey vaguely pleasing. The artisan chocolate shop holds her interest for a millisecond more than the bookshop, cafe, art gallery or any one of the little cobbled side streets that I keep pointing out, exclaiming, 'It's so pretty.'

Molly doesn't think so. 'It's like the French town in *Beauty and the Beast* that Belle couldn't wait to leave.' She then starts humming 'There must be more than this provincial life'. To be fair, there doesn't seem to be a young person anywhere. And it's still the summer holidays, so it's not as if they're all crammed into the building we'd just passed that said that it was the school, yet looked more like a scout hut that you could hire out for birthday parties and bar mitzvahs.

'So how many people live here, again?' Fergus asks. I know that he knows, it had been the source of much mirth when I'd told him. 'Seven hundred,' he'd spat. 'I have more friends on Facebook than that!' I replied that that said more about his social neediness than anything else.

Keith thinks for a minute. 'Your family bring the total to a nice round six hundred and eighty.'

'I thought it was over seven hundred?' I say.

'It was a cold winter.'

'Oh.'

The cart abruptly stops outside a fishmonger's. 'Stay here a minute,' Keith orders, swinging his legs off the driver's bench and jumping down to the ground. 'I just need to pick up my dinner before Tom shuts for the day.'

I look at my watch. It's half-past two.

We sit in silence, our minds noisily processing everything we've just seen and I can hear every single thought from each of them.

'It's going to be OK,' I say out loud, to no one and everyone.

'You into skittles, Freddie?' Keith asks when he climbs back onto the cart. 'We have a pretty active league if you are. Always up for some new blood. Now more than ever.'

Fergus doesn't answer. I nudge him and nod towards Keith who is waiting for a reply from Fergus's posh alter-ego, who seemingly can't remember his own name.

'What, sorry?'

'Skittles. Do you like them?'

'The sweets?' Fergus answers, confused. 'They're all right.'

'A joker, I see. You'll get on well here – if there's something the islanders have, it's a sense of humour.'

Fergus and I look at each other, sharing the same thought about the need for one.

We pass a row of little fisherman's cottages, one of which has a National Lottery board outside it on the pavement. 'That's the luckiest newsagent you'll ever find,' Keith says. 'We've had four lottery winners on the island, and I'm not talking fifty quid either. The big ones. Six numbers each. You don't get that in London. Even your predecessor, Doctor Lewes – well, his wife.'

Liam sits forward in his chair, his instinct for success and money on high alert. 'Four people have won the lottery on this island?'

'Yep. Now we all buy a ticket twice a week. I'd do the same if I were you.'

'Not you,' I say, swivelling round in my seat to glare at my son.

'That's incredible,' Fergus says finally, after his brain has done the calculations. 'If you take away the under-sixteens who aren't eligible, that's one in every hundred people that has won the lottery.'

'It's a lucky place,' Keith says, pulling gently on the reins to stop the horses. 'Here we are. Home sweet home.'

It wouldn't have surprised me to find a corrugated iron roof balanced on mortar-less bricks and an outside toilet, but incredibly the house is worthy of being on one of the postcards sold in the harbour stores. Double-fronted, two-storey, sash windows, a front path flanked by sprawling lavender bushes ... It's perfect. So perfect that it even elicits a 'nice' from Liam, and not a single word of distaste from Molly, which is sort of the same thing as praise.

But then she sees the number of bees hovering around the lavender.

'Great, so we basically have to do a bush-tucker trial every time we leave the house,' she mutters, pushing me aside to be the first one in the house to bag the best bedroom. Meanwhile, Liam is holding his phone above his head and waving it around like a bubble stick, trying to get reception.

Keith helps Fergus unload all the cases from the back of the cart. 'Anything you need, just shout. And, Dr Bay, I'll need to come and see you this week about some more blood pressure tablets.'

Fergus puts his hand in his pocket and for one dreadful moment I think he intends to tip Keith like he is a brass-buttoned bellboy in a top hotel, but he is just retrieving his phone. 'You'd better give me your number then, Keith.'

'I don't have one. If you want anything, literally shout – that's my house just there with the green door.' He motions at a row of three houses directly opposite, each with a different coloured gate and door. I make a mental note to keep my and Molly's bedroom curtains closed most of the time: Keith says his blood pressure is already high, and the dwindling island can't afford to dip below the six hundred and eighty mark.

Three hours later, bedrooms have been assigned, the Xbox has been set up, suitcases are more or less emptied, a grocery shop is completed, and we've already had seventeen visitors.

Seventeen variations of, 'Yes, it seems very different to London', 'Yes, lovely fresh air', 'I know, four lottery winners, amazing', 'I haven't got my prescription pad with me right now, but if you call the surgery to make an appointment tomorrow, that would be best'.

'You did say that you hated the anonymity of London,' Fergus reminds me after I've shut the door on the last visitor and am standing with my back against it, eyes closed, breathing slowly in and out.

'Did I? Well, what did I know?'

'I think it's nice to be part of such a close-knit community.'

I raise one eyebrow. 'Doreen knew we were having pasta for dinner because Ruth who works in the shop had told Doreen's daughter the contents of our basket. She said "enjoy your lasagne" as she left.'

Fergus smiles mischievously. 'We could have some fun with this. We should do all our shopping on Guernsey, then pick up some weird stuff from the local shop each day. Something like a whole chicken, chocolate spread and some lubricant. Give them something to talk about.'

'I have no doubt we'll do that completely by accident, anyway.' I laugh, walking into the kitchen and taking a bottle of wine out of the fridge. 'Drink?'

'Absolutely, I'll get the glasses.'

Fergus

In twenty years of marriage, Fergus can count on one hand the number of times this has happened. The two of them politely bustling around the kitchen, one gathering the wine glasses, the other getting the corkscrew and opening a bottle for them to share together. 'Oops sorry, after you.' 'No honestly, you go.'

They have never even been on holiday together. Fergus told someone that once and they couldn't believe it. 'What, never?' they'd gasped, and he'd shaken his head. 'No, we never took our annual leave at the same time, so that we could cover the school holidays.' He'd punctuated this with an eye-roll and a muttered statement about 'the things you have to do, eh?' but in all honesty the thought of spending two weeks holed up in a French gite in the Loire countryside with Jess shooting daggers of disappointment at him over his morning croissants and lunchtime Brie baguette made him feel nothing but relief.

Every February he goes skiing with his friends, and every other year he visits his brother in Australia. One year he managed to squeeze in a trip to Oktoberfest in Munich, another year the Abu Dhabi Grand Prix. He used to make noises about her coming too, but she'd always said no – 'the surgery', 'the kids', 'the money', 'the time' – so he stopped asking. For her fortieth a couple of years ago he had given her a voucher for a romantic spa weekend for two after a female colleague suggested that's what he should do as it was a special birthday. She deserved a break, a bit of pampering, for a change. He'd phoned ahead and made sure that she could have the full works: facial, massage, mani pedi, even something called a Total Holistic Stress Buster, which sounded just the job. They even had a couple's hot tub in every room, wink wink. He'd held his breath while she held it in her hands, turning it over to read the T&Cs, seeing if she could cash it in for something more appropriate. She couldn't. It had stayed tacked up on their fridge, taunting him with a parallel life he could be living where his wife would squeal with excitement and immediately throw some barely there underwear into an overnight bag and book a babysitter. Almost a year later, one month before the voucher expired, Jess put it in as the main prize in a raffle draw at the surgery. This year he didn't want to risk spending loads of money on something she didn't want, so he bought her one of those handheld dust busters because she'd mentioned needing one so often, and it does get used every day, so it must have been a good gift.

Jess and Fergus both seem to be hit by awkwardness at being in the same room at the same time and Jess picks up her wine glass, 'I might just take this upstairs and call Mum, tell her we've arrived.'

Fergus picks up his glass too. 'Yes, good plan. I'll, um, stay here. Feed Iris.'

'Good.' She tips her glass towards him as she reaches the door to the kitchen. 'Cheers,' she says, turning briefly back around.

'Yes, absolutely. Cheers.'

7

Hypochondriacs and hilltops

It becomes quickly apparent on my first day of work that patient confidentiality doesn't appear to exist in the Forth Island Surgery. They've never heard of it, don't like the idea of it, and think nothing of announcing their reasons for visiting to every person in the small, wood-clad waiting room that more resembles a sauna in an Alpine lodge than a doctor's surgery.

'I'm seeing the doc,' they say to anyone who will listen, 'because I've got piles again.'

'Oh, you poor thing. That's the third time this year, isn't it?'

I've also realised that the only reason this island needs a doctor is for my prescription pad; my actual physical presence isn't necessary at all. Every patient I see in my first week has already diagnosed themselves by describing their ailment to someone else and getting a prognosis. Dr Google has nothing on the residents of this island.

'Penny said that I've got shingles.'

'Mike's neighbour had a wart on his finger just like this one, and then he needed his whole hand amputated. Good job it's my left one.'

'Don's wife had the same last year, it's definitely rabies.'

Then there are the patients who just want to have a look at the new doctor, booking an appointment merely to introduce themselves, have a chat, recount a chapter from their life story and to find out enough about us, the mysterious new arrivals, to pass on to whoever will listen down the high street.

The sixth person who replies, 'Oh no, nothing wrong with me today, Doc,' makes me march into the waiting room and ask the seven or eight people waiting there if anyone has any actual symptoms they are concerned about that need immediate medical attention.

Two people nod while the others sit with their cling-filmed plates of baked goods on their laps, gamely shaking their heads and smiling back at me.

I sigh. 'I tell you what,' I say, 'how about we leave the surgery just for people who feel unwell, and my husband and I will meet everyone else in the pub at six tonight for a drink?'

As six rolls around, Fergus has commandeered the length of the bar, a semicircle of men and women clustered around him. His audience are rapt and completely under his spell, as though he is a street magician about to bring a dead mouse back to life. He slaps male backs, kisses female cheeks. 'Hi, I'm Freddie.' 'Freddie, hi.' 'Nice to meet you, Freddie.' He accepts drinks; he buys drinks; he laughs at jokes and makes lots of his own, cementing his status as a 'bloody good bloke'.

Meanwhile, Molly and Liam sit slumped in the corner next to the fruit machine, sipping their Cokes and looking at the scene unfold in front of them with a mix of incredulity and embarrassment. I feel a prickle of frustration. Why can't they at least pretend they're having a good time? Meanwhile, I'm pinned up against a wall by two older women, one of whom is lifting her dress up to expose her bare, veiny thigh, pointing at a bulging blue knot above the knee.

'Can we go now?' Liam soon whines at me over the old woman's shoulder. Since his attempt to dislodge coins from the fruit machine with his elbow has not worked and his ration of one Coke and one bag of crisps has been devoured, the evening now holds no further interest.

'OK,' I reply. 'Can you take Iris for a quick walk before it gets dark? Apparently there's a fantastic view of the sunset from the public footpath on the cliff.'

The teenagers start walking towards the door.

'Stay together, though!' I shout. 'And don't let her off the lead near the edge. And don't you go too near the edge either, Liam. And stay together!'

It's fine. More than fine. It is completely safe. Forth is not London. And 'Violent Crime Isle of Forth' had yielded absolutely no Google hits. Nor had the more specific searches of 'Kidnapping Isle of Forth'; 'Rape Isle of Forth' or 'Murder Isle of Forth'. I haven't yet searched out any statistics for gun crime or stabbings, but my hunch is that across the board, the Forthians are an honest bunch. Complete hypochondriac gossips, but not a hardened criminal amongst them. It is fine.

A couple of hours later I leave Fergus in the pub and return home, ostensibly to sort out some things for the surgery, but also to check the kids aren't currently drifting towards the Normandy beaches. Just as I reach the front door, I see them turn the corner at the end of the street and feel a rush of relief.

'I saw this really rude woman up on the cliff,' Molly says as she hangs up the dog lead on the back of the boot-room door.

'Who?'

'An old lady with a nose ring. She was just sat on a bench up there looking out to sea. I tried to sit down next to her because it's the only seat up there and I was knackered, and the sun was setting, but she refused to move her bag, so I couldn't. Rude cow.'

'Molly! I'm sure she had her reasons. Maybe she was meditating.'

Molly narrows her eyes at me and gives a slow shake of her head before flouncing out of the room, officially dismissing me from the conversation due to having too few brain cells.

It's after midnight when I wake up to the bed shaking. 'Fergus, is that you?' I mutter into the dark.

A whisper comes back, 'I'm not Fergus, Fergus is dead. I killed him.'

If the voice saying this were not my husband's, I might feel more concerned by this proclamation. And while it is clearly my husband, his words are very far from clear.

'How much have you had, Fergus? You're absolutely plastered.'

'I told you,' he slurs, and even in the pitch dark I can see him swaying, 'Fergus is no more. I am Freddie. I am Funny Freddie. Thass what they're calling me. Funny Freddie. I've been reborn!'

'Stop shouting, you flaming idiot, and get into bed before you wake the kids up.'

'Would you like some of Funny Freddie? You know, inside you?'

'I can think of nothing I'd like less right now.'

'Thass mean. You're mean. Why are you so mean to me all the time?'

I feel a twinge of guilt, but push it aside. 'Get some sleep. Some of us have work tomorrow.'

'I love you, Jessica Rabbit.'

'Goodnight, Fergus.'

'Freddie.'

'Fergus.'

The next day I make two phone calls. My side of both of them is almost identical: I list the array of amenities on offer on the island (as I first say the word 'array' out loud I do feel a little disingenuous, but that doesn't stop me repeating it again in the next call). Then I run through the different people I've met, the setup in the surgery, the kids still feeling a bit isolated, Fergus's transformation into an alcoholic joker with a different name . . .

The first person I call, Jackie my therapist, tells me in her lovely, buoyant voice (which I know she's paid to have, but even so it's like a warm welcoming hug) that it all sounds 'very encouraging, and differences are to be expected'. The second one, to Mum, elicits the response, 'That sounds ghastly, when are you coming home?' I wish that I'd anticipated this and reversed the order of the calls, so that I'd be left with a nice inspirational glow to carry with me through the day, but you live and learn.

Word has obviously spread that my surgery is not an extension of the social club, because there are only two appointments in the book for Monday morning. The first is my neighbour Keith for his blood pressure tablets, the other one is a woman who I stood next to in the butcher's yesterday. I did think about introducing myself at the time, but the Londoner in me kicked in and wouldn't let my mouth open to say anything apart from, 'Four chicken breasts and half a kilo of lean mince, please.'

The woman extends her hand to shake mine as she walks in. 'I'm Maggie.'

'Jessica. Bay. Doctor. Jessica Bay. You can call me Jess.' I blush at my obviousness. *Be my friend, be my friend, be my friend.*

It isn't just that Maggie is beautiful. There is no disputing that she is certainly incredibly attractive – like, woman-in-a-shampoo-advert-running-through-a-meadow attractive – but more than that, I can just instantly tell from her smile that reaches her eyes that she's a good person, and God knows I need more of those in my life. She must be five or so years older than me; I'd put her at late forties, possibly older as she could be one of those women who age so much slower than everyone around them.

'Welcome to the island.' Maggie smiles, slipping her handbag off her shoulder and hanging it on the back of the chair, but not before I clock the subtle Prada lettering on the front of it and the glare of the sun bouncing off her teeth as she speaks. 'How are you finding it?'

'Fantastic. I mean, different, obviously, but great, yes, absolutely. It'll take some time I guess, but it's good. A complete contrast to what we had before, but it's fine, will be fine. I'm sure it'll all be OK soon.'

Maggie listens to my bumbling with a smile on her face, and when I finish speaking she puts her head on one side. 'So which is it? Fantastic, or pretty shit, but with hope for improvement?'

I laugh. 'Was I that transparent?'

'It's only to be expected. I grew up here, but my husband's from London and hates coming here at weekends. He's always on at me to move, but I love it here. I'm sure you will soon.'

I open my mouth to admit that actually I am finding it all a bit challenging, when Maggie says, 'Anyway, I'm sure you're busy, so I won't stop too long,' which shakes me back into my white doctor's coat. 'I haven't been feeling too well recently,' she says. 'I'm not sleeping, I feel hot then cold, and I've put on some weight.'

It's difficult to see where this extra weight may have attached itself on Maggie's lean body, but nonetheless I nod sympathetically and professionally. The symptoms Maggie is describing are classic menopause indicators, which is always a tough topic to broach: nature's harsh reminder to women that they were nearer death than youth. I enquire about Maggie's periods and ask her about her libido. You know, the obvious topics of conversation you bring up when you're trying to conceive a friendship.

'Oh my God,' Maggie says, hand flying to her chest. 'You think I'm menopausal!'

'It's certainly one thing to test for. I can run a simple blood test to check for FSH and oestrogen. But honestly, if it is that, you really don't need to worry, there are lots of things we can do to minimise the discomfort, it's something we all have to go through, and it's only to be expected at your—'

I glance down at her notes. What?

'Thirty-five. I'm thirty-five. This cannot be happening now.'

Thirty-five? Far from looking good for her age, as I'd previously thought, Maggie has evidently had an uphill paper round.

Ten tearful minutes and one intimate examination later, Maggie stands up, now sporting a small round plaster on the crook of her arm, and turns to leave.

Stop, talk to me more! Ask me anything. Tell me anything. Just stay and talk to me. The fact we've just discussed vaginal dryness doesn't mean that a beautiful friendship can't still happen. Surely?

'Well I must be off – I've taken up too much of your time, anyway.'

'You haven't.'

'Bye, then.'

'Yes, absolutely,' I reply, shuffling some random papers on my desk. 'Must be getting on. Busy, busy, busy.'

Liar.

Fergus

Fergus looks around at the kitchen. He should probably do something about the mess. Jess hadn't said it explicitly, but since he wasn't the one to actually leave the house to go to work, 'it might be nice' if he cleaned it up a bit. 'Might be nice' wasn't the same as 'do it'. 'Might be nice' essentially gave him a green card to have a lie-in and watch morning television.

It is one fifteen. Quarter past one. Fifteen minutes into his usual lunch break where he'd be queuing up in one of the busy Borough Market cafes he used to buy his lunch from. It's Thursday, so he might have had sushi today. Or Lebanese. He could murder some moutabel. Faye likes moutabel. So does Jess. Faye also likes tattoos and man buns while Jess is still choosing to stay married to him. And it is a choice, in this day and age, staying married. She could have left him many times over the last few years, but she didn't. If it were Jess who had been texting male colleagues at all hours, buying them endless low-fat mochas and going to wanky, overpriced, kitsch bars with them, he'd have ... what would he have done? Would he have left? He thinks of Molly and Liam, and the versions of him and Jess before it all started to go wrong. He actually hasn't got a clue what he would have done if everything had been the other way around, so it's lucky it wasn't.

Fergus decides he's going to make Jess some moutabel. She'd like that.

8

How do fools fall in love?

'So while you were out, I've been busy.'

The teetering pile of breakfast bowls with congealing milk pooling in the bottom of them are piled up next to the sink, Weetabix hardened and stuck to their sides; a tub of melted margarine with its lid off lies next to an uncovered slab of Cheddar and a chutney-smeared plate and knife; scattered dog biscuits are crunchy underfoot and the lounge curtains still unopened, despite it being five o'clock in the afternoon. It all seems to contradict Fergus's proclamation.

'Oh?' I say, trying hard not to let notes of scepticism seep into my voice.

'I've made you some moutabel.' Fergus spreads his arms wide as though he is a circus master, welcoming me to his show. 'I got the recipe off the Internet! Can you believe that the grocer's sells aubergines? That's a sign the island's on the up, isn't it?'

'Why?'

'Why what?'

'Why did you make it? It seems a bit random,' I say, picking up the margarine tub and putting it back in the fridge.

'Because you like it.'

'Oh. OK.' He is looking at me with such puppy-dog eyes, begging me to pat him on the head and tell him he's a good boy.

Jackie gave me a book once with the subheading 'The way that you felt about yourself when you first fell in love is the way you can feel all the time'. The problem is, it isn't the way I felt about myself that I'd like to regain, it's the way I felt about him. I am perfectly happy not being the sappy, ever-grateful twenty-one year old who can't believe her luck that Fergus Bay had asked her out. Me! Who would have thought it! He'd had a string of beautiful girlfriends since the start of university, he'd even received a written warning from the warden of our halls for having sex in the communal shower with a girl called Heidi from a Media Studies course. I, meanwhile, still had 'Lose Virginity' on a To Do list written in my neat handwriting at the back of my five-year diary. So no, I am very happy not to be that girl any more.

'Maybe after we eat it we can take Iris for a walk,' he says.

'Together?' I ask, with probably a bit too much surprise in my voice.

'Then we could pick up some fish and chips on the way home—'

'It's Monday, it's shut. And there's fifty grams of saturated fat in one portion, and the recommended daily allowance is twenty.' Sometimes I just can't help myself.

'OK,' Fergus says, looking a little flustered. 'That's fine, we have bread, we have beans. So what do you say?'

I decide to throw him a bone. 'I think that a walk sounds lovely.'

It's not lovely. It is freezing up on the cliff. The bright afternoon has given way to a blustery, windy dusk that is turning our romantic stroll into an exercise in endurance, with both of us keen for it to be over as quickly as possible. We huddle into our hooded tops, looking more like gang members planning a heist than a husband and wife taking the first steps to repairing our marriage.

'Looks like we're not the only nutters risking imminent death,' Fergus says, nodding towards a break in the trees on the cliff edge where two people sit on a bench, their heads bowed together deep in conversation. Iris's tail starts wagging, and she bounds towards the strangers before Fergus can clip her lead back on and curtail her fun.

'Oh, I know one of them,' I say. 'I met her this morning in the surgery, her name's Maggie.'

'Go and say hello.'

'I don't know . . . their conversation looks a bit intense.'

'Go on, I'm sure they'd love a new friend.'

I bite my bottom lip. It's been so long since I made a new friend, I've totally forgotten how to do it.

'Go on.' Fergus nudges me so hard that I stumble forward. 'Here, take the lead and get Iris, it'll be a nice opener.'

'What will I say?'

Fergus puts his head on the side, and adopts the voice of a parent talking to a nervous child standing on the edge of a busy playground. 'Do you want me to come and introduce you? I could say, "This is Jess, she likes saving lives, green vegetables and giving bees sugared water, who are you and what do you like?"'

I smile at his teasing. 'Stop it.'

'Go. They're not going to bite.'

He's right, they don't bite. But they don't exactly welcome me with warmth and love either. There's totally room on the bench for me to sit down too, if they would each shuffle up a bit, but neither of them do. If anything, they not so subtly stretch out their limbs, covering the space between them a little more.

'It looks like it'll be a lovely sunset tonight, despite the wind,' I say cheerily, sounding every bit as middle-aged as I feel, but I'm determined not to run back to Fergus with a 'they didn't want to be my friend' whine.

The two women nod, looking everywhere except the horizon. I guess that when you live somewhere with incredible sunsets every day, you become immune to its beauty.

'Do you come up here often?' God, I'm boring myself now.

'Sometimes,' the woman with the nose ring says. Maggie shrugs noncommittally, and I get the message: she might do, might not – what business is it of mine?

'It's a world away from London,' I say, determined to engage them somehow. 'Our dog can't believe her luck having all this space.'

'You better be getting back before it gets dark, though, dogs get lost up here all the time,' nose-ring lady says.

'Oh. Yes. Absolutely. OK. Well, nice to see you both. Come on, Iris.' I lean down and clip the lead onto the spaniel's collar. 'Bye, then.'

I know everyone has off days – God, in the last few years, I've had more than my share – but it's more than that, the looks these two women are giving me. It's like I'm an intruder, an annoyance they can't wait to get rid of, when all I'm trying to do is just be friendly. As I stomp back over to Fergus, I curse my own stupidity at ever thinking I'd be able to break into this community. These are going to be the longest six months ever.

'See, I told you it would be fine, what did they say? Are you meeting them again soon?' Fergus says, as soon as I walk back to him.

'Yes, they were lovely, definitely new friend potential,' I lie as breezily as I can. Nothing is to be gained in telling him the truth; I'm the one that uprooted everyone, I've got absolutely no right to find fault with our new lives now. I've got to be the perky one, the glass-half-full one, the 'everything's so much better here, isn't it?' one. Because if I'm not, what on earth did we do this for?

We pass a man walking two Dalmatians, who nods at us, saying, 'Freddie,' as he doffs an imaginary flat cap.

We say hello back, and I wait one, two, three seconds before turning to my husband and saying, 'While we're at it, can we talk about this Freddie/Fergus thing? Because it's starting to piss me off.'

'As is your continual reference to a man that doesn't exist any more. Fergus was a weak, annoying city boy; Freddie is a family man, a comedian, someone to buy a drink for, someone who values what he has. I am Freddie. You said that we could reinvent ourselves here, be the better version of ourselves, and that's who Freddie is.'

'So you want me to call you that too? When we're at home?'

'Yes. Then you won't slip up when we're out. And I like it better, it makes me feel all warm and manly.'

I bite back a snigger – warm and manly? – but he is so earnest, I can't laugh at him.

And he is the only friend I've got.

'OK, fine. I'll try. Hello, Freddie, I'm Jess.' I stick out my hand for him to shake, resolved to try and make this work.

His face bursts into a grin as he takes my outstretched hand and shakes it. 'Nice to meet you, Jess. Come here often?'

9

Stray cats and spider plants

Eileen Duggan comes with the doctor's surgery in the same way that an elderly tabby might be left behind when people move house, and the new owners gradually become less and less surprised when it keeps coming back until finally they relent and start feeding it.

In none of my interviews, or subsequent 'settling in' chats once I'd agreed to the move, did the subject of Mrs Duggan come up. The opposite was in fact true – I was led to believe that a receptionist was an unnecessary cost. Apparently, the Forthians are patient patients, all too happy to wait their turn at the walk-in clinic, where no appointment-making or crowd-control is necessary. And for every other type of enquiry, the interview board said, with what I did think was a slightly misplaced sense of pride considering the decade we're living in, they've got an answerphone.

Before we arrived on the island, I found it difficult to imagine how the surgery could possibly function without a receptionist, but even during my first week where I saw more apple pies than ailments, it was ... well, extremely orderly, in a way my old workplace had never been. So it is something of a surprise when, on my third week, I find the door to the surgery not only unlocked but propped open with a Yellow Pages, and the smell of extremely strong coffee and the dulcet tones of Elvis's 'Jail House Rock' puncturing the air.

'Hello?' I say gingerly, peering round the doorway, as if it is me that isn't supposed to be there, rather than the person I am yet to meet.

'Jessica Bay? Doctor? Eileen Duggan. Mrs.'

I can't remember exactly which Mr Man it is that jumbles up their words into an unintelligible order, but whichever character it is, they're currently scurrying about my surgery watering the spider plants that hang from crocheted pots suspended by ceiling hooks that to be honest I hadn't even noticed until this moment.

The old lady runs her finger along a bookshelf and tuts at the thin layer of dust blanketing it. 'Four weeks I've been away, and look, rack and ruin.'

'Um, Mrs Duggan?'

She stops wiping the table with the hem of her elasticated skirt and looks up. 'Dr Bay?'

'Do you work here?'

'Work here? I run the place!'

This is beyond confusing. 'But I didn't think we had the funds for any staff apart from me?'

Mrs Duggan laughs, her eyes disappearing into the quicksand of her wrinkles. 'Oh, I don't get paid, you silly sausage. I do it for free. To keep me out of trouble. I don't need the money. You better hurry up, surgery opens in three minutes and you've still got your coat on. Coffee? Cup of?' She doesn't wait for an answer and starts pouring thick, syrupy black liquid from the percolator into a mug and hands it to me.

It soon becomes apparent that a major perk to Mrs Duggan's terms of non-employment is unfettered access to a medical professional for the entire day. She sticks her head around the door between patients to say variations of 'Can I just show you?', 'What do you make of this?' and 'Is this normal?'. By the time I hang up my white coat on the back of the door I've seen more of Mrs Duggan's naked body than I've seen of my husband's in the last couple of years.

The only silver lining to the interruptions is the knowledge that a human body does not have an infinite number of things that can go wrong with it. Therefore at some point in the near future, the list will be complete, and Eileen Duggan (Mrs) will have to remain seated behind her desk every time the door to my consulting room opens and a patient comes out rather than jumping up, slipping in, and stripping off, before the next in line can heave themselves out of their seat.

I check my watch. It's just gone half past two, the surgery is meant to shut at two, but Mrs Duggan's daughter has just sent a photo of her son's mosquito bite and I have to confirm that it isn't measles ('Yes, there is a lot of it about'). I lean back in my chair so that the front legs lift off the floor. I feel momentarily rebellious at doing something I must have told Molly and Liam a thousand times not to do.

'I hope I'm not interrupting, Mrs Duggan said to come right in.'

I'm so startled I almost fall backwards, which, while mortifying, would at least prove my point about swinging on your chair being 'extremely dangerous'. I grab onto the desk to steady myself.

'My name's Nora, I met you last night up on the cliff?'

Without her nose ring, I've no idea at first who the older woman standing in front of me is. It's funny how a tiny piece of gold can define you as a person. Like a wedding ring.

'Sorry, my surgery hours have finished for the day.' I don't mean to sound so curt, but the way she and Maggie sharply dismissed me from their company last night is still fresh in my mind, bringing to the fore all those times at school the cool girls with their loosely knotted ties and undone top blouse buttons rolled their eyes at my strict adherence to the uniform code, however difficult it was to breathe. I never understood it; it takes far more energy to break a rule than follow it, or to be deliberately mean to someone rather than just pleasant.

'I know, sorry. I'm not here to see you as a patient, I just wanted to apologise about last night. I think we got off on the wrong foot, and I'm sorry. My friend Maggie and I were deep in conversation – she'd just had some bad news you see – and you caught us off guard. But I'd like to make it up to you and buy you a coffee, if you'd like?'

The effects of the coffee Mrs Duggan made me earlier are still lingering and the thought of another one sends me into heart palpitation territory, but my mouth pipes up before my adrenal glands can stop it. If we're going to last the full six months on this island, we're going to have to make an effort. 'I've just finished for the day, so that would be lovely,' I say.

As we walk to the only coffee shop on the island still open (working half days seems to be the norm here), I wonder if it was my chat with Maggie about her early menopause that was the 'bad news' she and Nora had been discussing. That would explain why, when I'd popped up with my breezy, over-eager 'Hello there!', they'd both looked at me like Molly usually did: as though I'd morphed into some sort of dung beetle.

There's no coffee machine in the cafe, only a kettle, and next to it a jar of Gold Blend and a box of PG Tips. 'Coffee or tea?' the smiling man behind the counter asks as we come in.

'Two coffees please, Dave. Karen's mum feeling better?'

'Grand now thanks, Nora, back on her feet. Take a seat and I'll bring them over, Doc.'

'How does he know who I am?' I whisper.

'Everyone knows who you are.'

As the conversation goes on, I can't help thinking that I've been to job interviews that had fewer questions asked. I half expect Nora to take an anglepoise desk lamp out of her handbag and shine it straight in my face. Maybe this is this what happens when people don't come into contact with new people very much. Or perhaps the rules of starting a friendship have changed so much since the last time I did it.

'How did you hear about the job?'

'My boss in London put me forward for it.'

'Did you ever meet our old doctor?'

'No, he'd died before I even heard about the island's existence.'

'So you knew nothing about us before?'

'No, nothing, everything is very new.'

New. And very unsettling. Even Jackie knows less about me, and she is currently in possession of quite a lot of my money, earned purely by getting me to talk about myself.

'So you've got two children?'

I nod.

'Siblings?'

I shake my head.

'Parents?'

'My mother, Joy. She's coming over next week to visit, actually.'

'Nice.'

'It would be lovely for you two to meet. She's going to be by herself a lot while I'm working, and I promised my husband Fer – um, I mean Freddie, that I'd find things for her to do so she wasn't hanging around him all day.'

Nora gives a little apologetic smile. 'I'm afraid that I'm not great with old people.'

'Oh, she's not *old* old, just seventy-one.' I stop myself from saying, 'Nearer your age than mine', because that would be very rude, but the unsaid phrase hangs in the air above us.

'Talking about age, I wanted to ask you something.' Nora picks up a sachet of sugar out of the pot and starts fiddling with it. 'I know the answer to this anyway, but with you being a doctor and everything, I thought I'd ask. I have googled it, but society being as consumerist as it is, all I can find is fancy skincare brands peddling expensive creams that I'd bet my house on not working. Regenerist this and rejuvenating that.'

There is a lot to dissect in that sentence. What exactly is Nora asking?

After a long pause, she says, 'So, is there anything else I can try?'

'For . . .?'

Nora looks exasperated. 'Ageing.'

'Ageing?'

'Yes. How can I stop it?'

'How can you stop getting older?' I ask slowly, my forehead crinkling in confusion.

'Yes. How can I stop ageing?'

'Um. Die?'

For a long agonising moment Nora surveys my face. I do the same back. We're like animals in the wild, sizing each other up.

Then Nora flings her head back and guffaws. 'Die! Hahahaha, that's hilarious! You're so funny! Die! You crack me up. I can see we're going to get on brilliantly.'

Just as I'm giving myself a mental high-five, her face rearranges itself in a split second. 'But seriously, is there anything I can use or take to stop looking so old?'

'How old are you, if you don't mind me saying?'

'Forty-one.'

Jesus! I work hard to conceal my surprise, but I can tell she knows what I'm thinking. What is it with the women in this town? The people who tout sea-air and sunshine as restorative miracle-workers may need to check their sources. I make a mental note to up my daily intake of water and buy a better sunblock.

10

Bench-gate

I'm pretty certain that Fergus hasn't as much as picked up a felt-tip pen since he was asked by his geography teacher three decades ago to outline the coastlines of the world's countries in blue. Freddie, on the other hand, is delighted with the new set of watercolours he's just had delivered by Amazon, via the Guernsey ferry.

He spends the early part of the afternoon on Tuesday painting the family fruit bowl, even adding a little bit of mould to one of the peaches for good measure. Who knew fruit could be so fascinating?

The stormy afternoon reluctantly gives way to clear, cloudless skies, and vibrant brushstrokes of pink, orange and purple fill the canvas he carries back down from the cliffs later in the evening, proudly showing it to me when he gets back. He is slightly less proud of the grass stains that cover the entire seat of his trousers.

'How did that happen?' I ask, pointing at his bum.

'I had to sit on the bloody grass, that's why. For the whole walk up there I'd pictured sitting on that one bench on the edge of the cliff between the trees. It would have been the perfect place to sit and paint the sunset.'

'So why didn't you?'

'Someone was already there. I recognised her from the other night. The one with the long hair and even longer legs.'

Maggie.

'I tried to sit next to her – I even said, "Hi, mind if I join you?" – but she waved me away with a flick of her wrist, as though I was an annoying fly at a picnic. Then she said, "I'd like to be on my own, if you don't mind." Well I did bloody mind. I minded a lot. It was rude, and totally unnecessary.'

'Then what happened?'

'She said that the other half of the bench had been painted so it was wet. I said, "They painted half the bench?" And she just shrugged and said, "Yes."'

'I saw her up there last night as well,' pipes up Liam. 'I took Iris up there, and when she saw me she picked up her handbag from the floor and put it on the bench so I couldn't sit down either.'

'What's her problem?' I say. I get that she's annoyed with me, but that's no reason to take it out on my family. I'm vaguely aware of sounding like a mafia don. *Family. Family. Don't mess with my family.*

'Do you think that maybe the bench is important to them? You know how when people die they dedicate a bench to them? Maybe they don't like other people sitting on it?' Molly shrugs. It's the first thing she's said out loud in days, so it takes us all by surprise.

But she might have a point. I make up my mind to walk the dog up there tomorrow and have a look. Surely they can't be sat there every evening? Don't these people have homes to go to?

The next evening, a Wednesday, Maggie and Nora aren't even looking at the sunset, they are reading their books. There are three other benches on the cliff, none of them facing the bay, though, which is inconvenient if you are there to admire the view. But it doesn't matter a jot if you are there to READING A BOOK.

Nora is knitting on the bench on Thursday evening. Evidently, her attempts at denying the ageing process are not going well. Her embroidered carpet bag, sitting alongside her on the bench, is huge and takes up the rest of it.

The two local pubs compete for the end of the week trade by simultaneously holding happy hours that run 5-7pm on Friday night where every drink is 50p. The town is deserted. Empty. Apart from these two public houses, which are crammed with islanders desperate to get absolutely sloshed for three pounds. Oh. And the bench on the cliff where three people sit. Three. Because Eileen Duggan (Mrs) has joined the sodding party.

Am I her boss if technically no money is changing hands? It's a grey area, made even greyer by Eileen Duggan's terse reply to my cheery 'Hello there!' as I approach her sitting on the bench alone on Saturday night, crossword in hand, chewing thoughtfully on the end of her pencil.

'Oh, you made me jump!'

Here's my chance. 'Mind if I sit down, Mrs Duggan?'

'Oh, no, you can't, sorry, Doctor. Something spilled on it, it's terribly sticky.'

I reach for the zip on my handbag, 'Don't worry, I've got wet wipes.'

'Oh no, it's horrible, you'll never get the smell out of your clothes, even after wiping it. See you on Monday? I've got a new mole that I'd like you to see, but it can wait until Monday. Bright and early?'

It's somewhat fitting that the Sabbath is the day of rest, because as the bench comes into view on Sunday evening, I can see the lean silhouette of Maggie curled up on it asleep, with her raincoat draped over her like a homeless person in a park. Except Maggie has the biggest house on the island and heating that comes on when you clap twice and say 'heating on', according to the man who delivered our oil for the boiler, so she certainly doesn't need to be sleeping on public benches. Instead of a litre of cheap gin wrapped in a brown paper bag, she has a Burberry-branded thermos flask lying on the ground beside her.

'Is everything OK?' I ask, peering at Maggie's sleeping body, watching for the steady rise and fall of her ribcage, just in case.

Maggie's eyes spring open, but she makes no attempt to sit up, or shuffle along, or do any of the things a normal, non-homeless person caught lying down on a communal bench might do. She just glares at me.

'Sorry, I didn't mean to intrude,' I say, backing away. 'Sleep well.'

I haven't been as obsessed about anything, ever, as I am now becoming about The Bench. I've even afforded the words capital letters in my mind to highlight quite how important this bolted-together pile of planks has become. I am desperate to find it empty. To sit on its hard wood, luxuriate in its discomfort, and enjoy a view of the sunset that has thus far been denied me.

Fergus

'You need to get a hobby,' Fergus says as Jess storms back into the house, huffing and puffing, banging cupboards and almost breaking the stem of a wine glass as she slams it down on the counter.

'It's just so – what's the word?' Jess replies angrily. 'Territorial. They're basically marking their territory so that any newcomer can't enjoy the jewel of the island.'

'Jewel of the island?' Fergus laughs. 'What are you? A travel brochure?'

'Why aren't you more angry about this?' Jess says, swivelling around to face him.

'About what?' He shrugs. 'A group of old women sitting on a bench?'

'A public bench,' she corrects Fergus. 'It's not theirs. They don't have any more right to sit there enjoying the sunset than us. And they've been there every day this week!'

'You can see the sunset from our garden. Why do you need to sit on a bench to enjoy it more?'

Jess groans in exasperation. 'You just don't get it. It's not about the sunset, or the sodding bench. It's about the fact that they've closed ranks on us, basically saying, "Bugger off back to London with your city ways, you're not welcome here."'

Fergus knows he has to tread carefully to make sure Jess's anger doesn't swerve off course and start aiming itself in his direction. 'And you don't think you're reading a little bit more into this than is actually there?' he asks tentatively.

'No. No I don't.'

'Would a Skype chat with Jackie help?' That was risky, he realises as soon as he says it. That marriage counselling session they'd done together a couple of years ago had made his whole body burn with discomfort. There was no way that he'd wanted to ever put himself through that again, so pretending he had no need for it was much easier than telling the truth. If he'd continued with it, sooner or later he knew they'd have had to talk about Anna and that wasn't somewhere he wanted to go. Kudos to Jess, though, for sticking with it. He's often wished he could be a fly on the wall during the sessions, except then he'd get sucked into that awful electronic blue light insect killing machine that sits on top of Jackie's tumble dryer. Between that and the hum of the washing machine it's a wonder any of Jackie's clients felt like opening up at all. He had hoped that as time went on, Jess would speak to him about her sessions, occasionally tell him what she and Jackie talk about. He asks, of course he does, trying to show her that he's interested, that he would listen if she ever wanted to talk about anything, but she never does.

'No,' Jess says. 'No, it wouldn't help, because she'll say what you're saying, and I'll feel stupid, when actually I know I'm right and you're both wrong.'

Fergus sighs. 'So tomorrow, go up there again and don't take no for an answer. If you honestly feel this way, then stop being so polite about it and tell them to budge up, move their bags. Sit on their laps if they won't move.'

Jess bites her lip, considering what he's saying.

'Do you think so?' she says.

'If it's that important to you, then yes, of course. Once you've done that, maybe take up yoga or T'ai Chi. You said you wouldn't be so stressed if we moved, so stop finding things to get stressed about. Do you want me to run you a bath?'

Jess gives Fergus a look so laced with suspicion and shock he wonders for a moment if he'd actually suggested running her a bath or by accident floated the idea of running nude around the island's mini golf course.

'A bath would be lovely,' she says finally, much to his relief and, from her expression, her surprise.

11

Can someone please tell me which side of the bed is the wrong one? Because it appears to be both . . .

I look at myself in the mirror while I brush my teeth.

I can do this.

I can show those stupid women that I'm here to stay, like it or not. Well, here to stay for as long as Robert makes me, and for as long as it's viable for the family's sanity.

'Cup of tea?' Fergus offers as I walk into the kitchen. Pre-move he never would have made me a cup of tea, and he brought me a wine while I was in the bath he ran for me last night. I smile at him gratefully. He's really trying.

Molly and Liam are sitting at the kitchen table. Molly is doing her homework while shovelling Cheerios into her mouth, drops of milk splattering the table and her textbook.

'I asked you last night if you had homework and you said no,' I say, accepting the outstretched mug from Fergus.

'It's only French revision.'

I roll my eyes sarcastically. 'Oh that's OK then.'

'Also, Mum, where's my PE kit?' chips in Liam. 'I don't know if I have it today.'

'I put it next to your school shoes last night so you'd remember it.'

'What about my shin pads?'

'In the bag too. You are thirteen though, Liam, you could start getting your own stuff ready.'

'Whatevs. Bye.'

'Bye.'

Mrs Duggan is true to her word and is waiting, mole exposed, when I turn up to the surgery half an hour later. 'Morning, Doc. I've just brewed a fresh pot of coffee. Look at this. My Clive says it's a freckle, but I've gone onto ratemymole.com and it said that it is in fact a mole.'

I suppress a sigh. 'I'm not a dermatologist, Mrs Duggan. If you're at all worried, you should make an appointment on the mainland with a specialist.'

'But can you have a quick look? And I've been feeling a little light-headed this morning – do you think that's related to the mole?'

'My first patient is already here.' I nod to an elderly man sitting quietly in the corner, oblivious to the newly watered spider plant drip, drip dripping onto his lapel. I reach up and unhook the plant from the ceiling, resting it down on the side table.

'Oh, that's just Patrick. He won't mind waiting a bit longer, he's got nothing else to do.'

This makes my hackles rise. 'But *I* mind, Mrs Duggan. I mind quite a lot. If you are genuinely worried about any one of your seemingly endless medical emergencies, then please make an appointment in the book. Now excuse me, I'm running late.'

My hands are shaking as I unclip my doctor's bag inside my office. I didn't mean to sound so curt. The sight of the old lady's jaw dropping and cheeks reddening was, oddly, not as pleasing as I thought it would be, but the incessant interruptions and the sight of Mrs Duggan's grey perm peering round the door with an 'If you have a minute, Doc?', just gets on my last nerve. It has nothing to do with the fact that she is part of The Bench committee that has closed ranks on me.

That has no relevance at all.

Halfway through the morning's surgery, a perfectly balanced four patients seen, four to go, there's a frantic knocking on my door and it flings open to reveal two of the waiting patients breathless with drama. 'Doc, you need to come, it's Eileen!'

I spring out of my seat and hurry into the waiting room, where Eileen Duggan is lying facedown on the threadbare carpet, the hem of her skirt risen up to mid thigh, affording the onlookers a glimpse of the varicose veins I know so well.

'What happened?' I ask, kneeling on the floor beside her, pulling the beige hem of her skirt down and checking for her pulse. It is racing.

'She just stood up to make herself another coffee and dropped dead to the ground.'

'She's not dead, she just fainted. But if you could move back a bit and give her some room.'

Just then, Mrs Duggan's eyes spring open and, embarrassed, she quickly tries to sit up.

'Take it easy, Mrs Duggan, you just fainted, but you're OK. Can I call anyone to come and get you? You should rest and drink plenty of water.'

The old lady licks her dry lips, preparing to speak. I reach for a pen to write down whatever name or number is going to come out of her mouth, but Mrs Duggan's voice, when it comes, says accusingly, 'I told you I was dizzy.'

'So then what happened?' Fergus asks later that afternoon when I recount the horror of my morning to him.

'I told everyone to wait, and walked her home myself.' I throw myself into the armchair in the corner of the kitchen. 'I feel terrible. She told me she felt light-headed this morning and I completely ignored her. Actually no, I didn't – I shouted at the poor woman. I basically made her faint.'

'So you literally crawled inside her body and made her heart beat faster and lowered her blood pressure?'

'Well, no, of course not. But I made her stressed and that, coupled with the strength of the noxious liquid she calls coffee, made her pulse go haywire.'

Fergus perches on the arm of the chair I've slumped in. I can sense his hand hovering in the air, somewhere above my head. He's obviously thinking about stroking my hair in a comforting, supportive, 'I care' type of way, and then remembers that we don't do that to each other, so he pats the top of my head instead, like you would to the family Labrador.

I think back over our marriage. I wouldn't even need all the fingers on one hand to count the times I've needed consoling. Jackie has asked me before why I don't feel that I need consolation or reassurance. 'Everyone does,' she said.

'Not me,' I replied proudly.

'And why do you think that is?' she said.

'Why do *you* think that is?' I replied, determined to make her work for every one of the fifty pounds I was paying her that day. She regarded me then with an expression I was familiar with from everyone else around me: disappointment laced with irritation.

'I've made a chilli for later,' Fergus says, jolting me back to our island living room.

There wasn't a natural link between what I'd been saying and his proclamation, but it's a nice gesture. First moutabel, now chilli. He hadn't cooked anything in London for years. He used to, though, in the early days of our marriage, flicking through the rolodex of *Good Housekeeping* recipe cards he took from his mother's house in Ireland after his parents moved to Australia, to be nearer his brother, and left us with an attic full of their rubbish. He used to make seventies classics like liver and onions, and what I remember was a pretty good steak and kidney pie, in the days where internal organs were more regularly consumed. I can't imagine serving up Molly and Liam such things now and that being OK with them.

'Maybe we could walk up to the school to meet Molly and Liam as they come out,' I suggest.

Fergus frowns. 'Won't they hate that?'

'No, it'll show we care.'

'Are you sure? They think we're complete idiots.'

'That was in London. Not here. Here we're all different.' I bend down to scoop up some Cheerios off the floor. '*They're* different.'

'Really? Can't say that I've noticed any massive personality shifts.'

I crawl underneath the breakfast table following the trail of Cheerios. 'Molly borrowed my hair straighteners this morning.'

'And that's good why?'

'Because we're sharing things, like sisters do. "Hi, hon, can I borrow your straighteners?" "'Course, hon, help yourself." "Cheers, darl, oh my new blue top would look great on you, borrow it any time." "Oh thanks, babe, I will."'

As I emerge out the other side of the table on all fours, Fergus studies me through narrowed eyes. 'None of that actually happened though, did it? I was there. She just waltzed in while you were in the shower and swiped them from your dressing table. She didn't borrow them, she waited for the opportune moment and stole them. And she didn't even bring them back. Hon.'

I stand up, brushing myself down, bits of yesterday's toast and crumbs from last night's baguette falling off me. 'You don't understand. It's a girl thing.'

Fergus nods. 'Sure. OK. And Liam? How's he metamorphosed into a more palatable human being?'

I rack my brains for a moment. 'He said "Bye" to me this morning.'

Molly is chatting with some other girls as she walks across the concrete playground over the painted hopscotch squares. When I see her, relief floods through me and I let my bunched-up shoulders drop. Molly has not been completely alone, she has already made some friends. Thank God.

Molly's eyes widen in horror when she sees us waiting by the gate. I don't understand why. We're not doing an improvised greetings dance dressed as unicorns, or holding a glittery 'welcome home' sign like you see in airport arrivals; we are literally just standing there, smiling, minding our own business, waiting for our daughter to regale us with tales of her second week at a new school.

'I am so mortified,' Molly hisses through her teeth as she sails past in a cloud of disgruntled teenage angst.

'Molly, wait!'

'Mrs Bay?'

I turn my gaze away from my daughter's rapidly shrinking back to the lady standing in front of me, who is holding hands with a boy who looks about Liam's age. Why won't Liam hold my hand any more? That should be the benchmark of a successful mother-son relationship, not whether he shouts 'Bye' or not as he leaves the house.

It's awful, but I can't even remember the last time I held either of my children's hands. It certainly isn't one of the moments I've made an effort to pin in my memory, but then you rarely know last moments are going to be last moments, do you? Otherwise you'd make more of an effort to lock them in. The last time I read them a story, the last time they asked me to lie with them at bedtime, the last time they asked me for a hug and not money . . .

The boy is wearing a short-sleeved shirt and sporting purple lips.

'Aren't you cold?' I say instinctively to him.

'That's what I've come to talk to you about,' says the woman, twitching nervously. 'Apparently your son won my son's jacket and cap in a game with very complex rules that no one apart from your son could understand.'

'I'm so sorry,' I say, mortified but unsurprised. 'I'm sure there's some misunderstanding. Look, here's Liam now.' I glare at Liam as he saunters over, wearing a fur-lined hooded jacket and cap that definitely aren't his.

My eyes are glowering while my mouth smiles. It's a complicated facial expression that I've spent many years practising in order to perfect it. 'Liam, this lady – sorry, I don't know your name?'

'Betsy. Mrs Betsy Jones.' She motions at her son who is busy staring at his feet. 'This is Zebedee.'

I instinctively reach down at my side for my husband's hand and squeeze it, warning him not to react, telling him, with every fibre of my being that yes, I know it's a *Magic Roundabout* character, and no, there is absolutely no need to say it out loud.

'Betsy, and . . . Zebedee. Hello, I'm Jess and my husband Fer-ddie.'

'Furdy? That's a strange name.'

I tighten my grip on Fergus's hand. *Don't, don't, don't.*

'Liam, do you have Zebedee's – ' When I say his name it comes out as a croak – 'coat and cap?'

It's a pointless question, when my son is quite obviously wearing them.

Liam shrugs. 'I won them.'

'Give them back,' Fergus says, nodding towards Zebedee. 'They're his, not yours.'

'But I won them.'

'This isn't the high-rollers' room at the Bellagio, Liam. You shouldn't be playing games where people have to give you things.'

'But I won them—'

'It's OK,' Betsy interrupts, backing away and holding her hands up as though my whole family are armed and dangerous. 'I don't want to cause any trouble. He can keep them.'

'No, Betsy, absolutely not. Here – ' I start tugging at the sleeve of the jacket, while Liam attempts to wriggle away. Fergus takes the cap off Liam's head and puts it on Zebedee's, then pulls at the other sleeve so the coat comes free in our hands. 'Here you go. So sorry about that.'

Betsy and her son start scurrying away. 'I hope we can still be friends!' I shout after her, while Fergus cuffs the back of Liam's head.

'Stop being a prize idiot, you idiot.'

'What? I won them!'

The four of us walk home in frosty silence, with Molly striding out in front. Due to the car-less roads and no busy zebra crossings to navigate, it is impossible for her to lose us – but boy is she trying. Behind her is a stony-faced Fergus, his arms petulantly crossed after I refuse to hold his hand. 'I'm not eight,' I said, embarrassed at the show of public affection that I'm not ready to make. He hasn't held my hand in years; why on earth would he want to start now? This is about the kids, sorting them out, not us. Not yet. He probably heard it on a phone-in on one of those morning TV shows I know he watches when I'm not there: 'How to regain your intimacy in three easy steps'. I'm walking behind him, deliberately slowing my pace to encourage a sulky, foot-scuffing Liam to catch up. There is zero chance of him holding my hand. Now or ever.

It isn't the happy and convivial family walk home from school I'd imagined. The now-warm Zebedee is bound to be regaling his mother with a minute-by-minute recap of his day – hopefully not spending too much time on the illegal hustling racket Liam had devised. Instead he'll be saying things like, 'Then we had science and it was so funny, Mum, you should have seen the magnesium burn, it was brilliant. Then it was English, aren't fronted adverbials a great way to start a sentence? Then we had lunch, it was yummy, thank you for cutting the crusts off my sandwiches, you're the best.'

I look around at the downcast heads of my own family. Why are they so sodding difficult? And for the millionth time, I push the thought out of my head that Anna would have made everything better.

With such a dramatic day behind me, I almost forget the promise I'd made to myself: to make tonight the night I'm going to seize control of The Bench. I look out of the kitchen window, at the almost-setting sun. If I'm quick I'll make it up to the cliff by the time it ducks beneath the horizon, but I'll have to be fast.

Does it matter though? Really? It is just a bench.

'I'll be back in half an hour,' I call out to anyone. No one. 'Come on, Iris.'

I don't believe it.

The Bench is completely empty.

No woman, no handbag, no knitting bag, no wet paint, no invisible patch of offensive-smelling nothingness. Just an empty bench begging me to sit on it.

So I do.

It is just as hard and uncomfortable as I've imagined, but the view is incredible. Perched right on the top of the hill, this bench has unfettered views across the whole bay. Colourful boats with tall masts bob in the harbour, gulls greedily circle the unloading fishing trawlers, the white tips of waves roll lazily beyond the harbour wall, and the sun dances on the skyline, delicately dipping inch by inch into the sea. This is what I need, this me-time, completely to myself, away from Liam's latest antics, Molly's mood swings, Fergus pushing me to move quicker than I'm ready to, Mrs Duggan's histrionics, and my inability to see the wood for the trees. Everything seems so much calmer up here. You can't blame the other women for wanting to keep something so magical to themselves. Maybe, just maybe, it has nothing to do with me, after all.

12

'I'm not being weird, you are.'

The next morning I look at myself in the mirror while I brush my teeth.

I've done it. I've actually done it.

I have shown those stupid women that I am here to stay, like it or not. Well, sort of. Sitting on the bench felt like an act of defiance. A two-fingered salute to their rudeness. Even if they weren't there to see it, I know.

'Cup of tea?' Fergus says as I walk in the kitchen. Two days in a row – I could get used to this. Molly and Liam are sitting at the kitchen table, Molly is doing her homework while shovelling Cheerios into her mouth, drops of milk splattering the table and her textbook.

'I asked you last night if you had homework and you said no,' I say, accepting the outstretched mug from Fergus.

'It's only French.'

'Again?'

'Mum, where's my PE kit? I don't know if I have it today.'

'Surely you don't need it again? I haven't had a chance to wash it yet?'

'I do. And what about my shin pads?'

'In the bag too. Where they were yesterday.'

'Whatevs. Bye.'

'Bye.'

Mrs Duggan is staying in bed for the day, under doctor's orders (mine), so I'm understandably on high alert when I see the surgery door propped open. Does the island even have a police station?

'Morning, Doc.' Mrs Duggan smiles as she sees me, my angry tirade at her yesterday obviously forgotten. 'I've just brewed a fresh pot of coffee.' She pulls the neck down of her jumper to expose her shoulder. 'Look at this. My Dave says it's a freckle, but I've gone onto ratemymole.com and it said that it is in fact a mole.'

Oh my God, it is worse than I thought; Mrs Duggan must have banged her head when she fell. I should have checked. Concussion and memory loss can be extremely serious.

'What are you doing out of bed?' I say softly, guiding Mrs Duggan to a seat in the waiting room. 'You shouldn't be up and about, and you certainly shouldn't be drinking that.' I take the full cup of thick, syrupy caffeine out of the older woman's hand and put it on a side table. 'From now on, it's purely fruit teas in this surgery.'

She peers at me, baffled. 'I'm fine! What am I going to do in bed all day? But can you have a quick look? And I've been feeling a little light-headed this morning – do you think that's related to the mole?'

Across the room my first patient of the day sits patiently waiting, oblivious to the newly watered spider plant drip, drip dripping onto his lapel. I narrow my eyes at it. I moved that yesterday – it's a ridiculous place for a plant. Mrs Duggan must have hung it back up this morning.

Mrs Duggan follows my gaze. 'Oh, that's just Patrick. He won't mind waiting a bit longer, he's got nothing else to do.'

I open my mouth to say that regardless of Patrick's apparent easygoingness, *I* minded, when a strange sense of déjà vu niggles at me. And Mrs Duggan really shouldn't be here, she should be watching *Cash in the Attic* under a duvet. 'Right, Mrs Duggan, I'm taking you home. You need to rest.'

'But I need to work! I can't just be pottering about at home all day.'

'I don't want you to potter about, I want you to put your feet up and stay hydrated.'

She wavers. 'I do feel a bit out of sorts, now you mention it.'

'There we are, then. I'm going to call my husband to come and fetch you and walk you home, and I'll pop by and check on you later.'

As soon as Mrs Duggan is safely dispatched into the crook of Fergus's outstretched arm, I turn to my first patient of the day.

'Sorry about that, Mr Linley. What brings you here again? Come on in.' I hold open the door of my office to usher the old man in before helping him painfully shuffle out of his wax barber jacket.

'It's my arthritis in my hands. Now the weather's turned, it's getting worse.'

'I thought I told you that it'll take more than a day for the medicine to work? The tablets should help you sleep straight away, but it's going to take a few weeks until you notice a difference in the pain and your mood. Have you come about something else?'

'But I don't have any tablets?'

'Didn't you pick up your prescription?'

'What prescription?'

I tamp down a flash of frustration. 'The one I gave you yesterday?'

'Yesterday was Sunday, and this is the first time I've ever met you.'

I narrow my eyes at him in concern. 'What year is it, Mr Linley?'

He looks back at me, mirroring my look of confusion. '2022?'

'And who is our Prime Minister?'

'I don't know, it changes so often.'

Fair point. 'What is your birthdate?'

'Seventh of November 1938.'

I open his file on the computer. He's correct, and he certainly seems lucid enough. I scroll down to the last entry where the prescription should be that I typed out yesterday. It isn't there. My brow furrows as I refresh the page. 'Sorry, this won't take a minute.'

There is no record of his appointment yesterday at all and I distinctly remember writing up the notes from his visit, particularly because even after all these years practising medicine, I still can't spell 'rheumatoid' on the first go. So where has everything disappeared to?

'So just to clarify, Mr Linley, you never went to the chemist to pick up your prescription?'

'I don't know what you're not understanding, Doctor, but you have never given me one.'

I shake my head. This is bizarre. 'I'll just print another one off for you now, then. But only one of them is valid, so if you do find the other one then just destroy it. I'll call the pharmacist to tell them there are two in circulation.'

'Don't you want to even examine me?'

'I don't need to. The synovial membrane of the joint capsule on your left hand is inflamed, which has affected the surrounding cartilage, leading to stiffness and swelling. Your right hand is displaying early signs of the same, but is significantly less severe.'

'And you can tell all that without even looking at it? They said you were good, but that's amazing.'

The next patient has come for their biannual smear test. Like she did yesterday. Why on earth would someone voluntarily want a speculum pushed against their cervix twice in two days? But once again, there are no notes on the system that the appointment ever took place, and the woman introduces herself when she walks in as if we are meeting for the very first time. By the third patient – a local beekeeper who has an infected cut that I definitely treated yesterday – I'm feeling very uneasy. Have I just imagined the whole day without actually living it? Perhaps I saw the patient list and visualised the whole thing, creating imaginary diagnoses and prescriptions and everything. I often dream about the patients I've recently seen, so maybe this is the next natural step: dreaming about the patients I haven't even met yet.

Gary Harris's cut has certainly never been properly cleaned the way I did it yesterday, and just like yesterday, when I go to the box of disposable gloves, I pull out the last pair. I go back to my computer screen where I remember sticking a yellow Post-it note reminding me to ask Mrs Duggan to order some more. But no note is there.

I'm either going mad, or I've developed a ridiculously accurate sixth sense.

Fergus

Jess comes crashing into the house just after lunchtime, which is unusual; normally Fergus can indulge his new pastime of watching an entire episode of *Loose Women* with his lunch before running around the house like a madman tidying away the morning's detritus before she gets home. She's already caught him out once today, returning barely twenty minutes after she'd left for work to ask him to take her batty receptionist home, the reason unclear to both him and the batty receptionist, who'd kept repeating that there was absolutely nothing wrong with her. He'd snuck back into bed after she'd left the first time, a treat that had now become a habit, and was just drifting off when he'd heard the front door slam, lifting him from horizontal to vertical in two seconds flat. He'd quickly stripped off and got in the shower, standing underneath the freezing jets and willing them to quickly warm up in the time it took for Jess to climb the stairs. She was none the wiser. He was the willing hero, able to step in, drop everything, and take time out of his busy day to help his wife. And he'd managed to throw together a chilli for dinner. Winning.

Fergus hastily turns off the TV and saunters into the kitchen, which Jess is pacing like a caged animal. 'What's happened?' he asks warily, not used to seeing her like this.

She swivels on her heel to face him. 'Something really strange is happening today.'

'Like what?'

Jess walks towards the armchair in the corner of the kitchen and folds herself into it as though her body is slowly deflating. 'Honestly, I've never had it before. It was as though I knew what was about to happen at any time. I knew who the patients were, I knew what they were there for. The phone even rang at midday and I knew that it was going to be Mum telling me off for not answering my mobile, even though she knew I was working.'

'You've been doing this job for fifteen years. I think maybe you've just seen it all and heard it all, so it's all very familiar, that's all.'

'You've made chilli for dinner.'

Fergus snaps his head up. 'How did you know that?'

'I told you, I know everything that's going to happen today.'

'You must be able to smell it.'

'Nope. I just know.'

Fergus perches on the arm of the chair Jess has slumped in. She seems so stressed, so tightly coiled. In London Fergus would have just left her to it, gone to the gym or for a run, given her the space to sort herself out, but it's different here. They're all living on top of each other, one person's mood is everyone's. Fergus instinctively lifts his hand to stroke her hair, but then he stops, his hand hovering a couple of inches above Jess's head. Would she like it, or would she bat his hand away and make him feel stupid? It feels natural, but on the other hand, totally unnatural and odd. Before he can change his mind, Jess reaches up, as though she's felt his hand interrupting the air's vibrations. She takes it and lays it on her head, moving it back and forth softly, showing him that it's OK, it's fine. She likes it. They sit like that for a minute, maybe less, though it feels more.

Fergus looks up at the clock and breaks the strangely companionable silence, saying, 'They'll be finishing school soon,' which makes something flash across Jess's face. She grabs her phone out of her bag and starts furiously tapping on the keypad. Fergus looks over her shoulder.

'I know what game you played today. It's not big or clever. Give Zebedee back his coat and cap NOW or I'm burning your Xbox.'

'What the hell does that mean?' Fergus says, bewildered. 'And who the hell is Zebedee? That's not a proper name, that's the spring with the moustache from the *Magic Roundabout*.'

'I knew you'd say that,' Jess says, with the note of exasperation in her voice that Fergus knows so well. The moment of intimacy just before is now completely lost.

'Let's walk up to the school to meet Molly and Liam as they come out,' Jess says, picking up her bag and putting an arm into her coat.

'Won't they hate that?'

'No, it'll show we care.'

'Are you sure? They think we're complete idiots.'

'I know they do. But that can't be helped.' Jess steps on a Cheerio pounding it into powder. 'Dammit.'

Molly's chatting with some other girls as they walk across the concrete playground, over the painted hopscotch squares. Jess pulls Fergus back behind the wall so that Molly doesn't see them as she sails past, laughing.

'Mrs Bay?'

Jess turns her gaze away from her daughter's rapidly shrinking back to the lady standing in front of her. She is holding hands with a boy in a fur-lined hooded jacket and cap.

'You look cosy and warm,' Jess says, smiling.

'I just wanted to introduce myself. I'm Betsy. Betsy Jones.' She motions at her son, who is busy staring at his feet. 'This is Zebedee.'

Jess grabs Fergus's hand and squeezes it tightly. Fergus doesn't really know why. 'Betsy, and Zebedee. Hello, I'm Jess and my husband Fer-ddie.'

'Furdy? That's a strange name.'

She tightens her grip on Fergus's hand to the point he starts wincing with the pain. What is she doing?

'I feel bad that you've been here nearly two weeks and I haven't popped over to say hello or anything,' Betsy says. 'You must be feeling a bit shell-shocked still? It's such a massive change for you all.'

'Aw, thank you,' Jess replies. 'It is very different, but we're getting there.'

'We must have a coffee, or even better a glass of wine one evening, properly get to know each other?'

'That would be lovely,' Jess says warmly.

Jess needs a friend, thinks Fergus. Betsy seems really nice – completely loopy when it comes to naming a child, of course, but really nice nonetheless. Jess has never really had any friends, or any need for them – unlike him, who feels the need to always have someone to message, to exchange banter with at the gym, at the pub, at the shop. You tell me yours, and I'll tell you mine. Jess isn't like that at all. 'Why would you tell me yours, and I'm certainly not going to tell you mine,' that's what she'd say. That's why it's so good she's still talking to Jackie on video calls. There is money changing hands, so it's not a conventional friendship, but at least it's someone for Jess to confide in. That's if she is. He hopes so.

On the walk home, Molly is a distant figure out in front. Liam strolls, hands in pockets, between Fergus and Jess. He isn't exactly regaling them with stories of his day like Fergus imagines Zebedee currently is, but he is speaking in multiple syllables, which is certainly on the right track.

After dinner, Fergus clears the plates away and stacks them in the sink. Jess brought that up in their one couple's session with Jackie, as though the root of all their marital problems lay in his inability to stack the dishwasher. Fergus is pretty sure that Jess realised as soon as she'd said it that it sounded petty and trivial. 'But it's not the plates,' Jess argued, 'or the pants next to the laundry basket. Never in it. Next to it. It's the underlying expectation that I would do it. That it was my role.'

'Do you think Fergus thinks it through that much?' Jackie responded, receiving a grateful smile from Fergus as she did. And then she'd followed it up with, 'Have you ever told him that it annoys you?'

Fergus can feel Jess's eyes boring into his back. Silently, he opens the dishwasher and starts putting the plates slowly in, one by one. Task complete, he turns around from the sink to see Jess smiling at him.

'Thank you,' she says.

'What for?'

'For putting them in the dishwasher.'

He shrugs, feeling a foot taller. 'It's not your job, is it?' He wipes his hands on a tea towel before throwing it on the counter, then thinking better of it, picks it up and hangs it on the hook. 'It's nearly sunset – are you not indulging in your new hobby?'

'What hobby?'

'Bench-spotting.'

She looks away from him. 'No. Been there, done that.'

Fergus's forehead creases questioningly. What can she mean? But he doesn't say anything.

Later that night as they lie in bed, he updates his fantasy football line-up on his phone and she reads a novel. It's only after half an hour that he realises she hasn't turned a page since she opened it. He considers asking her what's wrong, but decides against it. If she wants to tell him, she will.

13

A thousand types of mother

Seven days have gone by without another strange premonition or hint of déjà vu. Tiredness is the only explanation I have come up with for those hallucinations I had a week ago. More than tiredness – bone-numbing exhaustion. And stress. Even the most acclaimed neuroscientists in the world admit the brain works in ways they can't fathom yet. But it seems to have been a blip, thank goodness. I'm getting more sleep and life seems to have settled down a bit. Fergus is making a monumental effort in the house, the kids seem happier, so I'm more relaxed. That must be it.

I hear a buzzing noise, and look around the kitchen for a bee before considering that it might be electronic. My phone's upstairs, and then I spot Molly's on the counter. She plugged it in while she was having her breakfast before going back upstairs to brush her teeth. It's normally super-glued to her hand. When she isn't filming herself or her thumbs aren't moving rapidly across the screen, it's just there, being carried around like a pink, glittery tumour on her palm. It buzzes again.

I'm not going to look at the illuminated screen. I'm not that type of mother. I'm a thousand other types of mother, most of whom I'm not proud of, but I'm not the snooping kind.

Trust. That's what is important in a mother-daughter relationship. If you don't have trust, then there is nothing. When I was Molly's age, I had a five-year diary with a lock on it.

Even if I hadn't lost the keys within five minutes of receiving it, I wouldn't have locked it because I knew that Mum would never have looked in it. I used to keep it under my mattress for the sole reason that that's what teenage girls did in films, not because it was an added obstacle to my mother reading it. If she had, she'd have caught up on the goings-on in *Neighbours* and *Home and Away* and what I'd eaten for lunch and dinner – but the point is, I had trusted her not to look.

Which is why, nearly thirty years later, she felt able to query how to get rid of chlamydia.

That is the type of mother-daughter relationship that comes from trust. And even though Mum and I aren't into all that hug-it-out, sharing-is-caring business, I do want Molly to feel that she can tell me anything. Of course, I'd prefer it wasn't that she had contracted a sexually transmitted infection.

It buzzes again.

Stop it. Stop testing me. I am a good mother.

And again. Buzz. Buzz. Buzz. Buzz. Buzz. Buzz.

Before I can stop myself I grab it. *You dirty bitch!* one message reads. *Slut!* says another. I gasp, horrified. I scroll through the whole thread, the messages keep coming. I can't stop.

Have some respect!

They're lopsided. Freak.

Gross.

Hahahaha

Lucky Adam, they're huge!

You're such a whore!

Have you even reached puberty yet?

Molly, I don't know if you know, but Adam's sent pictures of your tits to the whole year. Sorry to be the one to tell you this. By the way, is the science homework due in tomorrow or Thursday? Xx

If I had a paper bag to hand, I would happily breathe into it, the way I've advised hundreds of my patients over the years to do to try and restore a semblance of control. I lean against the kitchen work surface, battling the nausea that takes me back sixteen years to when Molly was growing inside me, before breasts became something you photographed even if you weren't a glamour model, and were only used for babies to drink from.

Who the hell is Adam? And more to the point, where the hell can I find him?

I scroll up the chat to see the photo of Molly that has caused so much drama. Thankfully it was just a cleavage shot, an 'arms pressed into the body to make your boobs look bigger' shot, no nipple action, nothing that you don't see on every high street every Saturday morning in summer. I squint closer at the photo, at the background. The tiles look very much like the ones in our upstairs bathroom. Has she literally just taken the picture as she was getting ready for school? Sent it off, then wandered downstairs and had breakfast?

'Is that my phone?'

I swing around to see Molly standing in the doorway, nostrils flared like a bull waiting to charge. 'Are you looking through my phone?'

'No, I – Molly, I wasn't, I promise. It just kept buzzing and I picked it up and all these messages were on your home screen, and so I—'

'I can't believe you'd do that! Give it here.' She reaches out to grab it, but I tighten my grip and hold it up high out of her reach. At five ten I'm still taller than her, but probably not for too much longer.

'Molly, I read something that's going to upset you, and I want you to know that I'm going to help you work it all out.'

I'm vaguely aware of the home phone ringing while I'm talking, in that I consciously have to raise my voice over the sound of it, but I make no attempt to pick it up. Molly needs me more.

'I don't need your help, just give me my phone!'

It buzzes again in my hand.

'Mum!' Liam shouts from the living room. 'Grandma Joy's on the phone. Her ferry came in early and she's waiting at the port.'

'Say I'll be there soon,' I shout back, going on tiptoe so Molly can't reach my stretched hand.

'Go. I don't need you,' Molly spits.

I know that Molly means that I'm not needed in that particular minute, before she knows what she is about to deal with, but even so, her words sting. How many times has Molly yelled out, 'Mum, I need you,' throughout her childhood? 'Mum, I need you to wipe my bum.' 'Mum, I need you to help me open this.' 'Mum, I need you to get me a snack.' 'Mum, I need you to help me work out what x is equal to.' And how many times have I yelled back variations of, 'in a minute' or 'ask your dad', or 'I'm a bit busy at the moment', confident that there'd be another 'Mum, I need you' in a few more minutes.

Except now, she's saying she doesn't need me. I've missed my chance to be helpful.

Molly keeps jumping up, trying to seize the phone from my hand. When I speak, all my words tumble out as if they are joined together.

'Molly, someone called Adam has sent a picture of you to some other people, and now everyone is messaging you about it.'

Molly stops jumping.

'What?'

My voice is more measured when I reply, 'There's a photo, apparently of you – well, some of you – and somehow or other, this boy called Adam has got hold of it, and – well, shared it.'

She blushes a furious red. 'You're lying.'

'Molly, why on earth would I make this up?'

'Give me my phone.'

'I will, absolutely, but before I do, just know that we can sort it all out, it's all going to be OK.'

Molly doesn't say anything, she just stands there, one hand on her hip, the other held out, with her palm turned upwards.

'Fine. Here.' I reluctantly hand it back. 'But please talk through what you're going to do with me first.'

Molly snatches the phone out of my hand, gives me one last contemptuous glance, and turns on her heel, throwing over her shoulder a withering, 'Hurry up, you're going to be late.'

'Take no notice!' I call after her. 'It'll all blow over.'

'And that's exactly why I don't ask you for help, because that's bollocks,' snaps Molly, twenty seconds before the front door slams behind her.

Liam picks up his school bag from the floor and walks out, toast in hand, shouting over his shoulder as he follows his sister, 'She's right, Mum. That was shit advice.'

Of all the mornings for this to happen, it has to be when Mum's arriving.

Or arrived. Early.

Why today? Any other day I could have gone to work, put this out of my mind until lunchtime, come home and talked to Fergus about it. But instead, I need to run down to the port, pretend that everything is absolutely rosy and feel the weight of the lie when I reply, 'Yes, everything is brilliant, really good,' when Mum asks me how I am.

To give credit where it's due, by the time lunchtime rolls around, Mum hasn't made any disparaging comments about the island, although I can see it is killing her not to. Instead, she's spent her day plucking inoffensive words out of the air to fling about, like 'pleasant', 'agreeable', 'nostalgic', 'quaint'.

Words that say, 'I think you need your head examined', while not actually saying that.

After 'enjoying' two instant coffees in the cafe ('I haven't had a Nescafé in ages!') she buys two battered paperbacks from the second-hand book rail in the newsagent's ('It's a very economical way to read, but I am glad I've got some hand sanitiser in my bag!'). We then wait patiently for the grocery store to open after lunch – an hour after advertised on the little paper clock on the door because Ruth, the lady who runs it, 'had pasta for lunch and fancied a nap'. I steady myself in anticipation of the criticism that is about to pour forth from Mum's mouth, but instead she simply says, 'What refreshing honesty. I love a nice after-lunch nap myself.'

After school Liam and Molly make a valiant attempt at looking pleased to see their grandmother, perhaps due to the fact they both know she would not have arrived empty handed. Regardless of what their motives are, I'm thankful they don't stamp all over Mum's enthusiasm for being reunited with her only grandchildren. Liam even lets her hug him, and I can't help feeling a twinge of jealousy.

Molly has barricaded herself into her room since getting back from school, greeting every knock from either me or Fergus with a 'Go away', saving the 'Fuck off' for her brother.

'Molly, I just want to know how your day went,' I say through the door. 'Was everything OK, with the – you know, the messages?'

'Go. Away.'

'It's all going to be forgotten about soon you know, tomorrow there'll be something else to talk about.'

'Go. A. Way!'

'Dad's getting fish and chips for dinner. Do you want cod?'

'Nothing.'

'You have to have something. I'll tell your dad to get cod then.'

Silence.

Then a small voice from inside the room says, 'Battered sausage.'

It's Fergus who suggests that I take Mum up to enjoy the sunset from the cliffs and to pick up the supper on the way back, possibly just to give him an hour's breathing space, but whatever his reason, it's a good idea. I've spent the day lugging her round to all of Forth's top sights, which took just over an hour, and I've only got this sunset up my sleeve, and then I'm done. Spent.

'Oh, it's beautiful.' Mum sighs, glimpsing for the first time the view across the whole bay from between the break in the trees as we approach the top of the hill.

My heart sinks as I see Nora's familiar long, grey hair cascading down the back of the bench.

'Is she a friend of yours?' Mum asks as we near the peak.

'Of sorts,' I reply, which is kind of true. We've had coffee once and now we avoid each other. Isn't that what friends do?

'Hello. You must be Jess's mother. I'm Nora,' she says, rising slightly from the middle of the bench and holding out her hand for Mum to shake.

'What a fabulous view!' Mum gushes, looking out to sea. I'm so glad she likes it as much as I do.

'You know, the cliff is even more beautiful in the morning.' Nora smiles. 'You should come up here then.'

We look up at the vivid streaks of purple, pink and magenta painting the sky. I fail to see how an ordinary morning sky would rival that. That was like going to the African plains to watch the annual migration and just staying long enough to watch the animals limbering up and doing their stretches, then going back to the hotel before it all starts.

I open my mouth to move Mum along – it's not worth getting into an argument about it – when Mum says, 'What utter tosh, look at the sky, it's glorious. Budge up.' And wiggles her bottom in front of Nora's face until she has no choice but to shuffle along the bench and make room for us. The three of us sit in stony silence, or at least Nora and I do; Mum seems completely oblivious to any ill-feeling and is just enjoying the view.

At the point that the base of the sun is just about to start touching the sea, Nora leaps up, standing just in front of us, her back to the sunset, completely obscuring our view.

'What are you doing? We're going to miss it!' Mum shrieks, waving her hand back and forth trying to bat Nora out of the way.

'I thought I saw a wolf, over there,' Nora says breathlessly, pointing behind the bench so we both swivel round in our seats to look at the empty expanse of green. 'It was huge, with really big teeth!'

The woman is clearly completely nuts. I turn back around just in time to catch the sun extinguishing its fire in the water. It is just as beautiful as the first time I saw it. I breathe in, feeling the stress of the day wash away. Molly will be fine, it'll all blow over.

Meanwhile, Mum is still looking over her shoulder for the invisible predator and misses the whole thing.

14

A thousand (and one) types of mother

'Cheers for making me a tea, but I wanted a coffee.'

'It's not for you, it's for Mum,' I reply as I fish the teabag out of the cup, then feel bad for not even considering making Fergus one too, especially when he's made it his morning routine to make one for me.

'Won't it be cold when she gets here?'

'I'm taking it up to her.'

'She's here? I thought her ferry didn't get in until nine a.m.? It's only seven.'

I study my husband carefully. Has he been drinking?

'Of course she's here, she arrived yesterday. I took the day off, we all had fish and chips for dinner.'

'Yesterday was Monday, the chippie was closed. Today is Tuesday, the day your mum arrives. We said we'd have fish and chips tonight for her first night.' He says all this slowly, as though I'm an invalid, gabbling nonsense.

I shake my head. 'You're wrong. It's Wednesday.' My heart starts to pound faster as I take the stairs two at a time, fling open the guest-room door and find the empty bed, pristine with newly ironed linen on it, and a stack of white towels stacked on the end of it.

It's happening again.

I've imagined the whole thing.

I sink wearily down onto the bed. Fergus sits beside me and puts his arm around my shoulders. 'It's OK, Jess, you've been so tired recently, and working so hard. It's just your mind playing tricks on you.'

He must be right. It must be the stress of yesterday, with Molly and everything. But then that didn't happen.

Just then, across the corridor, the door to Molly's bedroom opens and I see her step out, a bath towel in one hand and her glittery phone in the other.

The bathroom door has barely even shut before I'm hammering on it. 'Molly, you have to let me in. Just let me in a second.'

Molly opens the door a crack. 'What?'

Fergus stands behind me, one hand on my arm. 'What are you doing?'

'Just let me in a second, Molly,' I plead. 'I want to talk to you.'

'You're being really weird,' Molly says, but she does open the door enough to let me in.

I shut the door behind me and speak in a hushed tone. 'Look, I have no idea how I know this, but I think you are planning to send a photo of yourself to a boy called Adam. That's fine – I'd prefer it if it was of your face, but that's your choice.'

Molly's face flames beetroot red and my heart leaps; my hunch is right.

'But please, please, think about whether you can trust him, OK? I'm not saying all, but some sixteen-year-old boys keep their brains in their pants, and he might think it's funny to send the picture on to his friends. In fact, I know he will. You're new here, we all are, and we're just trying to find our way, find the right friends, and we don't yet know who we can rely on. While you're still figuring that out, please don't do anything that might backfire. OK?'

I stop talking and wait for the explosive retort of, 'You can't tell me what to do!', but it doesn't come. Molly looks thoughtful, her eyes looking to the left as she contemplates what I've said. She shrugs. 'OK.'

'OK?'

'OK.'

'OK then.' I turn to leave.

'Mum?'

I swivel back to face Molly, who is still clutching her towel to her chest. 'Yes?'

'Thanks.'

My heart soars. It was just one word, but it's the nicest thing she's said to me in ages. Fergus is still waiting in the corridor outside the bathroom when I come out. 'What was that about?'

'I have no idea,' I answer honestly. 'It's like I get these flashes of the future, and it's as though I've done it all before.'

'Like déjà vu? I get that all the time. Like, I walk into a room and then think, I've done that before, but then that's because it's the lounge, and so I have.'

'No, not like that. Like much more than that. Like I've actually had whole conversations and it's literally as though I've already lived the day.'

Fergus guides me back to our bedroom, and for once I let him.

'Look, why don't you go back to bed for a bit. Your Mum's not going to be here from Guernsey for another hour and a half.'

'Her ferry's going to be early.'

'What? Did she call from her hotel?'

'No, I know it is.'

'I think you need to call Jackie. See if she can do a Skype consultation. I think you're just really tired and it's all got too much for you. I'll go and pick up your mother, you stay here and get some rest.'

Maybe he's right. Our lives have been turned upside down in the last month, nothing is normal any more. A lavender-oil-infused bath, a kava root capsule and some lemon balm tea, that's what I need.

Or failing that, seven days of my mother staying. Oh good God.

'Darling, Fergus has filled me in on the walk back, you poor thing. You do this all the time, you take too much on, always have, you say yes to everything, go at it a hundred miles an hour, and then completely burn out like one of those small birds that fly across deserts and then collapse with exhaustion.'

Even though I've got my eyes shut, I can tell by the way I'm having to tighten my abdominal muscles to stop me rolling off the mattress that Mum is perched on the edge of the bed.

'I watched a documentary about it,' Mum continues inexorably. 'There's this breed of birds – I can't remember what they're called, it adds nothing to the story anyway – but they migrate from Italy to Australia – or Austria, doesn't matter, either or – and they tag team taking the lead so they don't get tired, first one goes in front, then the other one. Now, I'd never say this to Fergus, or if I did, I'd have to choose my words carefully, men's egos are fragile things, but that's the problem in your marriage, darling: you don't take turns at being in charge, and then you end up incapacitated in bed, absolutely burnt out.'

I try to sit up but Mum pushes me back down. 'Absolutely not. You're staying there.'

'Mum, I'm not ill. I'm just a bit stressed out, that's all.'

'Well it would mean shuffling things about, and quite a lot of reorganisation . . . I do have two dates and a funeral. But I can stay as long as you need me to.'

'Whose funeral?'

Mum shakes her head dismissively. 'No one important. Well, not any more.' She giggles, then obviously immediately feels bad about such a flagrant disregard for human life and covers her mouth with her hands. 'But seriously, I didn't really know him. I'm sure I'd be more upset if I did.'

'So why are you going to his funeral?'

'The wake's at the golf club and they've just had a renovation and I haven't seen it yet. Linda said the carpet's just horrible.'

I close my eyes; it's going to be a long week.

'That's it. You rest now. Looks like I arrived in just the nick of time.'

I can't sleep. The kids are at school and Fergus has taken Mum out for a few hours so it's not because the house is too noisy, it's because my thoughts are. I have my laptop balanced on my knees over the duvet, and my fingers are flying over the keyboard typing *neurological disorders, hallucinations, precognitive dreaming*. One report I read even attributes the feeling of déjà vu to a mini seizure that is reassuringly 'nothing to worry about'. Another website shrugs and lays the blame at the feet of one of my past lives, while another labels it the 'tuning fork phenomenon', where a person's brain momentarily matches the frequency of someone in the afterlife. At that I slam the laptop shut and huff the way only someone with twenty years' experience of reading medical journals can.

The thing that I can't shake is the clarity of the dreams. Every conversation I had in them was lucid, each mouthful of food was flavoursome – the few chips I stole off Fergus's plate last night were perhaps a little too salty, and once I stopped picturing my arteries literally furring up with every bite they were actually delicious – but the point is, nothing was blurred around the edges the way it normally is in dreams. It is as though everything had actually happened. Except now I know it didn't. It can't have.

Maybe I'm having a nervous breakdown. Do I feel overwhelmed? Yes. Am I socially isolated? Absolutely, this bloody island is filled with bloody witches. Extreme mood swings? Not that I've noticed, but Fergus would be the best one to answer that. Changes in sleeping habits? No, I enjoyed a full nine hours last night after that lovely walk on the cliff. *The one that never happened.*

I shake my head as though I'm trying to dislodge water in my ears. It's so confusing working out what's real and what's imagined. Perhaps it's worse than a nervous breakdown. Maybe I'm having a psychotic episode? Could I feasibly be a schizophrenic whose signs and symptoms have lain dormant like Vesuvius, lulling everyone who lives around me into a false sense of security until one day burning lava buries everyone alive?

Fergus

Fergus thought it best to leave Jess to sleep, she looked absolutely exhausted. The toll of organising the whole move and the demands of a job like hers was bound to catch up with her at some point; she's only human, however much she pretends not to be. He also thought it prudent to take Joy out of the house before she rearranged any more of the kitchen cupboards, and Jess heard her tutting and muttering things like 'have you no plates that match each other?' and 'pasta next to the cereals?'.

The day wasn't actually as bad as he thought it would be. Normally he would have tried anything and everything to not be trapped with his mother-in-law, and he knew the feeling was entirely mutual. She'd say things like, 'Oh sorry, Jessica, I didn't realise you had company,' whenever she'd popped round to their house in London and saw him sitting there, as though he was a distant relation or acquaintance who popped in at deeply inconvenient moments, not the person who paid half the mortgage. But today, it was as if a silent truce had been made.

'I made you a mint tea,' Fergus says, gently placing it down on the bedside table next to where Jess lies on her back with her eyes focused on the ceiling. 'Are you feeling any better?'

She shrugs. 'I don't know.'

'Did you sleep?'

'I'm not sure. Maybe. How's Mum been?'

'You know what? She's been all right. She even said that she hadn't had a Nescafé in ages, and she bought herself two second-hand paperbacks from the rack outside the newsagent's. She used up half a bottle of hand sanitiser afterwards, but still! We had to wait for a bit for the shop to open, Ruth was delayed for some reason.'

'She was having a nap,' Jess said matter-of-factly.

'I doubt it, not when she has a business to run. Anyway, I was thinking: why don't you take your mum for a stroll in a bit, get some fresh air? It's going to be a lovely sunset.'

Jess shakes her head vehemently, 'No, I'd rather stay here.'

'But the fresh air,' Fergus says weakly, unsure of what other argument to pull out the bag.

'If you're so worried about the freshness of my air, I'll open a window.'

He shifts his weight from one foot to the other, frowning as his mouth refuses to form the words inside his brain. 'I'll give you this advice for free,' Joy had said to him earlier, as though it's standard practice to charge relatives for unsolicited opinions, but this particular time she'd do him a favour and give him a discount.

'What's Mum been saying?' Jess says, guessing the reason for his unease.

'Just that I should be more assertive with you.'

Jess raises one eyebrow. 'Is that right?'

'She just said that part of the reason you're not yourself lately is that you're doing too much, and I should chip in more, take some of the burden off you.'

'You made chilli the other day. And it was delicious.'

He puffs out his chest a little. If she thought that was good, wait until she tries the rainbow trout enchilada recipe he's been working on. He doesn't know why he left all the cooking to Jess in London; her job was just as demanding as his, perhaps even more so because people could actually cark it if she had an off day, whereas if he did, the worst that could happen would be a press release wouldn't get sent out. His bosses would think it a life and death situation, but it really wasn't.

'So what other gems did my mother come up with?' Jess asks.

'She also said that you told her that we hadn't slept together in two years.'

Jess groaned and put a cushion over her face.

'She then spent ages telling me about tantric bloody sex and how hours of sensual massage can bring couples back together. And she wrote down the name of some erectile dysfunction tablet one of her recent lovers used which, and I quote, "made him last for hours". So, you owe me.'

'Fine,' Jess says through gritted teeth. 'But only if you come too. The bag will be really heavy from the chippie, so you can carry it. Molly will want a battered sausage.'

Half an hour later, the three of them have almost reached the peak of the hill, where the row of trees lining the clifftop gives way to the clearing with the best vista over the bay.

'Oh, it's beautiful,' Joy gushes.

Fergus notices that Jess barely looks at it. She's turned pale – maybe it was too soon for her to come out. He takes her elbow. 'I see we have company,' he says, gesturing towards Nora. Jess doesn't seem surprised to see her, and makes no attempt to walk closer or greet her.

'Let's go,' Jess says, pulling Fergus away. 'Come on, Mum, it's not worth it.'

'Don't be silly, I didn't climb that hill for nothing!' Joy cries shrilly.

Hearing voices, Nora turns around, 'Hello. You must be Jess's mother. I'm Nora,' she says, rising slightly from the middle of the bench and holding out her hand for Joy to shake.

'What a fabulous view!' Joy gushes, looking out to sea.

'You know, the cliff is even more beautiful in the morning.' Nora smiles. 'You should come up here then.'

'What a strange thing to say,' says Fergus, gesturing at the vibrant strokes of purple, pink and magenta in the sky. 'Look at it, it's magnificent. Come on, Joy, Jess, there's room for all of us.'

'Budge up then, Nora.' Joy wiggles her bottom in front of Nora's face until she has no choice but to shuffle along the bench and make room for them. Jess's head pounds with the familiarity of it all. Any minute now Nora is about to leap up, hands waving about – three, two one . . .

'What are you doing? We're going to miss it!' Joy shrieks, flapping her hands wildly in front of her, trying to shoo Nora out of the way of the setting sun.

'I thought I saw a wolf, over there,' Nora pants, pointing behind the bench so Joy and Fergus swivel round in their seats to look at the empty expanse of green. 'It was huge, with really big teeth!'

Jess doesn't turn, or move, or even blink as every aspect from the day wooshes up and over her. Molly's phone, Joy's visit, the fish and chips, the cliff, the wolf.

And right in front of her the sun tumbles into the sea.

15

A thousand (and two) types of mother

Spending the day in bed has not been relaxing. If anything it has made me more fidgety and restless, so I'm not surprised when I wake up half an hour before my alarm, before the slice of sunlight that normally dissects the floorboards appears around six thirty.

'Go back to sleep,' Fergus murmurs next to me, half his face hiding in the pillow.

'I can't, I'm going to go into work early to take the messages off the machine, check there's been no emergencies.'

'But it's your day off.'

'No it's not.' I swing my legs out of bed. 'I'm back at work today, I only took the one day.'

'But I thought you wanted to get your mum from the ferry this morning and then spend the day showing her around the island?'

I stop completely still in the pitch-black bedroom. Not again. This is not happening again. 'What day is it?' I ask quietly, already knowing the answer.

I hear the rustle of sheets that suggests Fergus is also sitting up in bed. 'It's Tuesday. Are you OK? Jess?'

'Fine. I'm fine. Absolutely.'

The bedroom is suddenly flooded with light as he switches on his lamp. 'Jess? What's going on?'

There is no point going through it all again, we did that yesterday – or in the imagined yesterday – and all it did was make him think I'd lost my mind. Which quite clearly I have, but I don't need his pity, or another enforced day in bed, which it turns out never even bloody happened.

'Having a senior moment, that's all,' I say, climbing back into bed.

'You're forty-five.'

'Yes. But haven't you seen how living on the island is prematurely ageing all the women on it?' I say, with a jolliness I'm definitely not feeling. 'Molly's going to need a hip replacement by the time she's twenty-one if we stay here too long.'

Saying Molly's name out loud makes me remember the next stage in the day. It's too early for Molly to be up yet, so while Fergus dozes next to me I impatiently wiggle my toes under the duvet until I hear her pad across the landing. The bathroom door has barely even shut before I'm hammering on it. 'Molly, you have to let me in, just let me in a second.'

Molly opens the door a crack. 'What?'

'I need to talk to you,' I plead.

'You're being really weird,' she says, opening the door just enough to let me in.

I shut the door behind me and speak in a hushed tone, trying to remember what worked well when I last did this. I mean, when I last imagined doing this. Whatever. 'Look, you're going to send a photo of your breasts to a boy called Adam. Don't.'

'I don't know what you're talking about,' Molly stammers, her face beetroot red. 'Get out. Get out of the bathroom. Leave me alone.'

I feel a dart of panic. This isn't what happened before. I wildly search my consciousness for the right words I'd used in the dress rehearsal, the words that worked. The ones that made her look at me with gratitude, not hatred.

'Look, it's none of my business, but please, please, think about whether you can trust him, OK? I'm not saying they all are, but some sixteen-year-old boys are complete idiots, and he might think it's funny to send the picture on to his friends. In fact, I know he will. We're all new here and we don't yet know who we can rely on, and until you know for sure, please don't do anything stupid.'

'Because *I'm* stupid, is that it?'

'That's not what I said, I said don't *do* anything stupid.' Did I use the word stupid in my hallucination? I can't have done because Molly even thanked me yesterday, rather than looking as though she wanted to pick up the loo brush and poke me out of the bathroom with it, as she is now. 'Look, Molly, I'm sorry if I've made you upset. I've been having some really strange dreams recently, and in one of them this Adam boy sent a picture of you to all his mates and it made you really upset. So on the off chance this dream is going to come true, I just wanted to warn you. That's all.'

'Fine. You've done that.' Molly clutches the towel tighter to her chest. 'Now can you leave?'

'What was all that about?' Fergus asks when I walk wearily back to our bedroom and sink onto our bed.

'I honestly don't know. It's like I'm trapped in a really bad dream. I could be dreaming now. I'll probably wake up tomorrow morning, and you'll tell me to get my Mum from the ferry again. The poor woman's been on that bloody ferry for three days now. She could be halfway to the Caribbean in the time it's taken her to get here from Guernsey.'

'What are you talking about? You're worrying me now.'

I rub my face. 'It's fine. I'm fine.'

'Why don't you stay in bed for a while, get some rest, I'll go and get your mum.'

The words are barely out of his mouth before I yell, 'No!' She cannot be left alone with Fergus to impart her newly acquired sexual wisdom to him, and I cannot bear another few hours lying in bed, wondering how long it's going to be before my brain implodes for good.

I start pulling my clothes out of the chest of drawers. 'Let me just get dressed and I'll go and get her, whizz her round the island, have a coffee—'

'She'll moan about it being instant.'

'No, she won't. Then we'll go to the newsagent's, she can pick up a bit of holiday reading and—'

'She'll never buy a second-hand one, she'll say they're covered in germs.'

'Do you know what?' I reply, slicking on some lip balm. 'I think she'll surprise you.'

I run down to the ferry before it's even docked, and Mum seems genuinely delighted I'm there to greet her off the boat. I should have done this the first time. Then I remind myself that this is the first time. Gaargh!

The rest of the day is uneventful. I make sure we buy the supplies we need from the grocery store before it shuts for lunch, just in case, and as it gets towards dusk I deftly bat away Fergus's suggestion of a sunset stroll. I can't face another altercation with Nora, fictional or real.

'No, we've done too much today, I'll take Mum another day. Can you be a love and go down to the chippie? Four cod and chips and one battered sausage? Not too much salt on the chips, please.'

'Who's the sausage for?'

'Molly.'

'Did she say she wants that?'

I scrunch my face up, suddenly doubting myself. Did Molly say that? In real life? Everything is blending into everything else, getting mixed up and it's getting impossible to know what has actually happened.

'I'll just run up and double check,' I say.

'Molly?' I ask Molly's closed bedroom door. 'Cod or sausage?'

'Sausage,' Molly shouts back. Followed by a surprising, yet very welcome, 'Please.'

Just as I turn to go, the door opens. 'Mum?'

'Yes?'

'You know what you said this morning, about the photo? It wasn't going to be of my whole . . . chest.'

'OK.'

'I mean, I don't want you thinking I'm sending pictures of my tits to boys.'

'OK.'

'And I didn't anyway.'

'Good.'

'I mean, even if you hadn't said what you said, I probably wouldn't have done it.'

'Good.' I nod, smiling. 'That's good. Try to remember that people should like you for your personality, not your cleavage.'

'Whatevs.' Then the door shuts again, Molly on one side and me on the other, but as I stand there in the corridor, I can't help smiling at the mini breakthrough. Just like the other version of today when we were in the bathroom together.

I really hope today is a real day.

16

TFI Wednesday

Please let it be Wednesday. Please let it be Wednesday. Please let it be Wednesday. If I repeat it enough, with enough feeling, maybe I can make it happen. I can't bring myself to open my eyes just in case it hasn't worked, so I just lie in bed, in the half-light, with whichever morning it is seeping in through the crack in the curtains.

'Aren't you getting up? You're going to be late for work,' Fergus says from the doorway to our en suite, his skin still glistening from the shower.

'Work? I have work? It's not my day off?' I jump out of bed with an enthusiasm and vigour for work unrivalled in history. 'Yes! This is brilliant! Whoop whoop!'

'You're a complete nutcase,' Fergus murmurs after me with a laugh.

'Heard that!' I shout back.

I even beat Eileen to work, such is my zest for the surgery this morning. When Eileen does arrive, she's sporting a rosette like the ones horses win at pony club gymkhanas, pinned proudly to her cardigan. A giant '80' adorns the middle of it.

'Mrs Duggan! Is it your birthday?' I ask, a little unnecessarily.

'It is! Eighty today.'

'That's amazing, congratulations, happy birthday. I can manage here if you want to take the day off to be with your family.'

'Oh no, they're all coming round later. I'd just be twiddling my thumbs at home.'

'You must tell me what you'd like me to get you for your birthday. Do you drink? I could get you a nice bottle of sherry or something?'

'Oh no, Dr Bay, I haven't touched the stuff in years.'

'Chocolates? I'll nip out at lunchtime and pick you up a big box to have with your grandchildren later.'

'With my diabetes? Not likely.'

That's the first I've heard of Mrs Duggan's diabetes, and I do know my receptionist's medical history quite well. 'OK then . . . oh, I know. How about I buy you a little china frog to add to your collection?'

Mrs Duggan smiles. 'How do you know I collect frogs? Who's been gossiping?'

'No one,' I reply unthinkingly. 'I saw them in your glass cabinet when I took you home last week.'

Mrs Duggan's smile starts to fade, a look of confusion replacing it. 'You've never taken me home.'

'You know, after you fainted. I saw it in the corner of your living room. You had a few big ones; one had a fishing rod, the other had a shopping bag. Then lots of little smaller ones. You showed them to me. One had a kilt on and was holding tiny bagpipes.'

The older lady stares at me, peering into my eyes as if she can see beyond them, the way I've done hundreds of times when the children were little, scrutinising their faces for signs of a lie.

'You've done it, haven't you?'

'Done what? Mrs Duggan, I don't know what you're talking about.'

'Don't lie to me,' she says, waving an arthritic finger in my face. 'You've done it. I know you have.'

'You're not making any sense. Done what?'

Mrs Duggan runs round the other side of her desk and picks up the surgery phone. 'I need to call the others,' she mutters to herself.

'What others? Mrs Duggan, are you feeling ill again? Why don't you sit down?'

'I knew this would happen. I knew it,' she says, dialling a number and waiting, tapping her fingers on the table. 'The minute Ted Lewes died and we knew we'd get a new doctor, I knew it would happen. I told them, they didn't believe me. I said, just watch, the wife will come in here – that's when we thought the doctor would be a man. I said, the wife will waltz in and find out. I knew it.'

I stand there mutely, not sure what I'm meant to have done.

'Nora, it's Eileen. She knows. She says she doesn't, but she does ... The doctor ... I have no idea. Clueless. But she does ... You better tell Maggie ... No, I've said nothing. I can if you like? Oh, OK then, I'll wait ... Yep ... OK. Yes, I promise I'll wait ... See you soon.'

Through the whole impassioned phone call I still just stand there, gamely waiting, trying not to gaze around the room for hidden television cameras. Mrs Duggan replaces the handset and smiles brightly at me. 'Shall I pop the kettle on?' she asks, as though nothing unusual has just happened at all. 'The first patients will be here soon. I'll bring it through to you while you get yourself sorted. Come along then.'

I let myself be bustled out of the waiting room and along the small corridor to my office, feeling suddenly homesick. London had many faults, but it had never made me feel as though I were living in a reality TV show. The whole island is completely mad.

Twenty minutes pass, and no patient shows up. I'm about to go and ask Mrs Duggan to call them when the door bursts open and the three figures of Nora, Maggie and Mrs Duggan cast ominous shadows across the floor. It feels like there should be some sort of orchestral music accompanying their arrival, such is the heightened level of drama in the room. I stifle a nervous giggle. They seem so serious, standing in the doorway, as though they have to wait for the cymbals to start before they can take a step forward.

'Ladies,' I say, standing up. 'To what do I owe this pleasure?'

Maggie and Nora come in, while Mrs Duggan hangs back furtively by the door, glancing through it as she closes it, double-checking we're all alone. Oh, the drama. Molly would love this. So would Mum. I just find it faintly ridiculous.

'How do you know Eileen collects frogs?' Maggie starts.

The question throws me. All this hype, and they want to know about novelty frogs? 'Um, because I saw them?' I offer hesitantly. 'I didn't break in, if that's what you're thinking?' I don't know why I said that. Nerves I guess. It's pretty unsettling, having the three of them stare at me, firing bizarre questions at me.

'When did you go to her house?' Nora asks. 'Which day?'

I think for a moment. When was it? With all the days repeating themselves, I've got no idea about the real passing of time any more. 'Last week?' I offer tentatively. 'Tuesday? No hang on, let me look in the diary, it was the day I saw Mr Linley.' I flick through last week's appointments on the calendar on my computer. 'Monday,' I say triumphantly. 'Last Monday. The nineteenth of September.'

'That was the day you sent me home,' Mrs Duggan says slowly. 'Your husband took me. You didn't come to my house.'

Of course I didn't. That was right. I'd called Fergus, and he'd come to fetch her. I was going to check up on her later but I called her instead. I went to her house on the day that didn't happen, the one that I imagined. So how on earth do I know that she collects frogs and could literally draw a floor plan of her house, right here, right now? I must look as confused as I feel because Nora suddenly reaches across the table and puts her hand on top of mine, which only increases my feeling of baffled panic.

'You poor thing,' she says. 'You have no idea, do you?'

Maggie turns to Nora. 'None of us did, though, did we?'

'I started taking tranquillisers when it happened the first few times,' Nora says. 'I miss them, actually – you feel really floaty.'

'Will one of you please tell me what's going on?' I say loudly. 'I have no idea why you're here, and nothing you're saying is making any sense.'

The three women exchange looks and nudge each other, eyes widening. They're acting the way the kids do when something's broken and no one wants to be the first to own up – *you do it, no you do it, no you do it.*

Nora takes a deep, noisy breath in. 'Have you ever sat on the bench at the top of the cliff?'

I stare at her. The speed at which these random unrelated questions are coming is making my head hurt. 'You know I have – you were there, too. When you pretended you saw a wolf.'

Nora gave a slight, almost imperceptible shake of her head, as if to say to the others, 'That never happened.'

'The thing is, Jess – can I call you Jess?' Maggie checks, and I nod. 'The thing is, Jess, we think you might have inadvertently, perhaps, stumbled upon something that you shouldn't have done.'

'Something that we've all tried very hard to stop anyone from stumbling upon,' Nora adds.

'Something that you really have to forget that you ever knew about,' Maggie continues.

'Do we make ourselves clear?' Nora says, and I detect a note of . . . is that menace, in her voice? How unnecessary.

'Not really,' I say.

'The thing is,' Mrs Duggan starts. 'The thing is—'

'The thing is,' Maggie interrupts, 'that you really shouldn't go up to the cliff again, at all. It's extremely dangerous, and as your friends – ' She pauses, just as aware as I am that we are no such thing – 'we feel it's our duty to warn you that really bad things can happen up there. So from now on, please walk your dog on the beach, or the field behind the school, or literally anywhere else.'

'Why?' The lunacy of this conversation is making me brave. 'Why should I do what you say? There's obviously something important up there that you don't want me seeing.' I rack my brains for a plausible explanation. 'Oh! Are you all witches and that's where you meet and you draw a magic circle out of salt and chant and cast Wiccan spells?'

Maggie rolls her eyes. 'No.'

'Do you sacrifice things? Is that why you didn't want me taking Iris up there?'

'No. Don't be ridiculous,' Maggie snaps.

'Yeah, that's crazy,' says Nora, who the more I look at her, could totally be a Wicca High Priestess. Her long grey hair cascading in waves around her face, the nose ring, the kaftans – it all makes perfect sense.

'Oh my God, that's it, isn't it? Every time I've seen you up there, you're about to have a meeting!'

'The bench makes you go back in time,' Mrs Duggan blurts out.

Maggie's eyes widen. 'Jesus, Eileen!'

'For God's sake, Eileen!' Nora adds, shaking her head in disbelief.

'What?' Eileen says defensively. 'I don't want her going around thinking that I'm a witch.'

The four of us stare at each other. Or rather I stare at

them, Nora and Maggie scowl at Eileen and she scowls right back at them.

Maggie's the first one to break the silence. 'Look, Jess, I don't quite know when or how you've managed it, but you've obviously sat on the bench when we haven't been there – which is impossible because we're always there – but you have, and you've obviously gone back in time. I just hope not too much damage has been done.'

'Look at her,' Nora says, nodding at me. 'She's completely shell-shocked.'

'How many times have you gone back to some time in the past?' Maggie asks, an urgent edge to her voice. 'Once? Twice?'

I shake my head disbelievingly. This isn't happening. This isn't real. I'm a forty-five-year-old married mother of two with a stressful job who is quite clearly having a mental breakdown. This very conversation might not even be happening. Those tranquillisers Nora spoke so highly of before would be very welcome any time around now.

'Should we slap her?' Eileen says. 'I mean, I don't think I can, she's basically my boss. But one of you two could.'

'Shut up, Eileen. She's just processing it all.'

'Jess? Can you hear me?' Nora says loudly, leaning across the table to peer into my face. She smells of eucalyptus oil. She turns back to face the other two. 'I think she's passed out.'

'Three times.'

'What?' Maggie says, looking at me.

'I think it's happened three times,' I repeat slowly. 'The first time was last Monday, when Eileen fainted here in the surgery—'

'I never did! I've never fainted in my life!' Eileen says indignantly, as though she's the absolute poster girl for medical perfection.

'But if she went back a day, to before it had happened, you wouldn't remember that you had, would you? If she stopped it happening,' Maggie reminds Eileen.

'That was the day I took you home,' I say, 'so I saw your house, and your frog collection then.'

Nora exhales. 'Monday was Eileen's night on the rota! So that's why she wasn't on the cliff that night, leaving the bench empty for you to sit down on it!'

'You have a rota?'

Maggie nods, 'Of course we do, that way it's never unattended. Apart from last Monday, apparently.'

'Sorry,' Eileen says sheepishly.

Suddenly the menopause symptoms, the need for anti-ageing products all make sense, these women have effectively been reliving the same days over and over, getting older much more quickly than everyone around them.

'Who else knows about this?' I ask. Is everyone on the island just going around hopping between days?

'Just the four of us in this room. We think. We actually have no idea if anyone else knows about it, but since we put the rota in place no one has tried to sit on the bench at sunset, so we're assuming it's just us.'

Eileen smiles. 'If you tell anyone, we'll have to kill you.'

My eyes must have widened at that before the three of them burst into laughter. 'We're not really going to kill you,' Nora says, 'but it really is best for you not to tell anyone. And don't do it again, it really is very dangerous.'

I have no idea what's fact or fiction, whether I'm awake or asleep. But I can feel the breeze from the open window, hear it rustling my papers, smell Nora's overwhelming essential oils. Every sense is heightened, and yet none of it can possibly be happening.

I think back to how I managed to intervene in Molly's cleavage debacle, and Liam's run-in with Zebedee, and

Fergus touching my hair, and Mum and I enjoying a day together, and I have no idea what's real and what's imagined.

'Do you understand what we're saying?' Maggie asks slowly, enunciating every word. 'That bench is dangerous. Travelling back in time is dangerous.'

'So why do you do it?' I ask, deciding to lean into the lunacy. It's my dream, I can behave any way I want.

'We don't,' Maggie replies, shaking her head. 'Not any more.'

I think for a second. 'If what you're saying is true, you could even win the lottery!'

The three women start shuffling their feet, shifting their weight, looking away. No one whistles, but it wouldn't have been out of place. And then it clicks. 'Oh my God, you're the lottery winners! You memorised the numbers, went back a day and won the lottery! That's why you've got a Prada bag and a Burberry flask, Maggie! And Mrs Duggan, that's why you turn up to work here every day for free – because you're minted! I'm not quite sure where you're hiding your money, Nora, but Jesus Christ, this is insane. What else have you done? Have you solved crimes? Do you tip off MI5 the day before someone bombs something? Do you tell presidents of countries the day before a wildfire so they can start cloud-seeding to make it rain? Vaccines! We could go back to when people died of diseases we've now cured! Franklin D. Roosevelt had polio – we could stop that, he'd never need to be in a wheelchair! Think of how different that scene in *Annie* would be if he could walk? Have you ever been back to Pudding Lane and told the baker to always have a bucket of water next to his bread oven? George Orwell and Jane Austen – they supposedly died of tuberculosis, we could go back, slip them a few antibiotics and goodness knows how many more novels would be around now for A-Level students to study.

We could be like Superman, but we're women and there are four of us!'

To give them their due, they let me manically ramble on about all the different ways we could change the world for quite a few minutes more before Maggie holds up her hand to stem the flow.

'Right, well, clearly, you're a little excitable, which is understandable. But there are a few things we need to make clear about this. You can only go back to change something in your own life. Something that you have done, or not done. You can't change anything in anyone else's.'

And then I think of Anna.

I feel a painful stab of guilt that she wasn't the first thing I thought of. I thought about Jane Austen before I thought about her. I don't know why that surprises me, though. I've spent the last twenty-three years doing my damnedest not to think about her, so when I finally manage it, when she doesn't pop into my head without warning, why does that make me feel so bad?

'What if I caused someone's death?' I ask. 'Could I stop that happening?'

Don't cry, don't cry. You've kept a lid on this since 15 December 1999, don't go there now.

Maggie eyes me uneasily, 'It doesn't seem that you can change things like that.'

'I once ran over our cat,' says Eileen mournfully. 'Lovely ginger thing she was, so we went through the whole charade of burying it, my boys recited a poem, my husband wore a suit, but I went up to the bench that night, went back a day, woke up – Garfield was still alive. Then at four o'clock, the exact time I ran him over the day before ... I didn't even get in my car, too afraid to, but the damn thing only went and ate the rat poison my husband had put in the garage. Dead within the hour. Another funeral. Then I went back again that night, after getting rid of the rat poison. Sat on the bench. Again, the next day, my car stayed in the drive, poison in the bin, then five o'clock rolls around, it has a seizure. Another funeral. I saw the vet afterwards, asked if there was anything that could have prevented it, he said no, it was always going to happen.'

'What you have to understand, Jess,' says Nora gently, 'is that your day is made up of millions of seconds, and if you change one of them, it has a knock-on effect on the rest. We've all felt what you feel now, thrilled at all the possibilities, but please don't dabble in it – just leave what's in the past there, and live for now. Look at me and Maggie. We look much older than we are because we kept trying out different ways of living, different ways to be happy. Get it right the first time so you never need to go back.'

They stay for another half hour or so, saying in a hundred different ways what Nora just did. I smile. I nod. I say that I absolutely one hundred per cent will never look at the sunset again. I even agree to go on their rota to guard the bench from anyone else.

I'm so convincing that I even believe myself, for a moment.

17

Gardening is a dangerous business

'What's wrong with Mum?' Liam asks Fergus as he passes the bowl of carrots right in front of my face.

'I can hear you, you know,' I say. 'And nothing's wrong.'

'Did you have a bad day, love?' Mum asks me. 'Did you lose a patient?'

I snort. 'I'm the island GP, Mum, not an ER doctor in inner city New York.'

'You can get sepsis from a splinter nowadays,' Mum adds helpfully. 'I read it in the paper. You never used to die from splinters.'

Molly's eyes widen. 'I had a splinter yesterday. Mum,' she whines, 'am I going to die?'

'Unlikely.'

'There was a story in the paper about a woman – pretty as well, she was, such a shame, it's always the pretty ones – and she was gardening one day, got a rose thorn in her finger, dead by the end of the week.' Mum looks around triumphantly, her point proven. 'Gardening never used to be considered a dangerous hobby, but now, thanks to sepsis, it is. That's why I'm glad I only have a patio.'

I can feel Fergus's eyes willing mine to meet his over the steamed broccoli. *Come on, Jess,* he's urging me, *this is comedy gold.* I look up and for a couple of seconds we share a look of silent laughter.

'Sepsis is not a new thing,' I say finally, 'we're just more aware of it now. People have always got infections.' I pass the gravy to Liam. 'Why are we talking about sepsis over dinner, anyway?'

'So why was your day so bad, then?' Fergus asks. Typical, I think: more than twenty years I've waited for someone to notice me, and now they do, all I want to do is to slink back into oblivion.

'It wasn't bad,' I reply, hoping to shut this line of questioning down. 'It was a fine, normal, day. How was yours?'

I left Fergus and Mum alone together all day today, much like I did the day before yesterday. The only difference being I was now the only one that remembered that day, because for everyone else involved in it, it had never happened. And buoyed up by the fact it went so well then (minus the sex advice), I thought they could do it again. Except when I mentioned it last night it was immediately clear that given the choice between in-law bonding time or a bout of sepsis brought on by gardening, both would have opted for the latter. 'I'd be happy just sat in the waiting room at the surgery,' Mum proclaimed. Clearly the prospect of reading five-year-old magazines and being surrounded by all the island's bacteria in one go was so much more preferable than spending time alone with my husband.

'I've got a, thing,' Fergus said, when I suggested it last night as we got ready for bed.

'A thing?' I replied.

Fergus ran his hand through his hair. 'Yes, a thing. For, um, work.'

I really don't want to beg, but it would be wonderful to have a husband and mother who actually liked each other. 'Please, Freddie. It would mean a lot to me. I can't take her to the surgery, and she's come all this way to see us.'

'I doubt she's come all this way to see me.'

'Please?'

He sighed. 'Fine. But if one of us doesn't survive the day, it's not my fault.'

But I'm guessing by the fact that they're both currently sitting around the kitchen table and neither of them is in a body bag, it went better than expected. Mum flashes me a smile. 'It was good! Fergus and I had lunch at the pub – The Swan, not The Fox, we'll do that tomorrow, won't we, Fergus?'

There was so much in that sentence that seemed incredibly unlikely. Mum and Fergus had both gone out of their way never to be in the same room in London; surely geography couldn't change a habit of a lifetime?

'I had chicken tikka masala. You wouldn't have thought it, would you?' Mum says.

'You like Indian food,' I reply.

'No, I mean, you wouldn't have thought that they'd have it at all. On the island.'

'We do have food here, Mum.'

'I know that, but it's funny, isn't it?'

Of all the funny things I've found out today, the fact that The Swan serves curry is not one of them.

I still have so many unanswered questions, and yet when Maggie asked me outright, 'Do you have any questions?' before the three of them left, I just shook my head mutely. They must have thought I was a right idiot. They tell me I've travelled in time, and then I have nothing to ask them about it. Then the second I was alone in my office my mind was flooded with things I needed answered.

If I can only change things that have directly affected me, what would I want to alter? If I hadn't promised not to, of course. So this is all completely theoretical. Just for fun. A lark. An innocent game of what-ifs that will absolutely not result in me traipsing up the cliff to the bench.

Molly had a particularly awful bout of chickenpox when she was young, which has left her with a deep gouge in the left side of her forehead. Should I go back and stop her having that play date with her little friend Laura, who came out in spots a few days after? But then, it was because of her chickenpox that I got the job in the GP practice that I then stayed in for the next fifteen years. When I took Molly there, I overheard the partners talking about needing a new family GP.

I could go back to that time a few weeks before we moved, when I'd found Molly curled up in the tanning salon the day of her French oral exam when those bastard boys laughed at her getting her skirt stuck in her knickers . . . I could get her to wear trousers instead of a skirt that day, I could say that it was in the wash. Molly wouldn't have failed then. And she wouldn't have been so humiliated. As for Liam, he's had so many incidents over the years that I would happily change. It would be great to delete a few of his suspensions off his school record to make it easier for him to get into university. But how can I go back further than just one day? Is that even possible?

Could I change anything about Dad's death? My chest hurts as I contemplate the possibility. Maggie and the others made it clear that I couldn't bring him back, but I could still change so many things about it. I feel a familiar stab of guilt that I always feel when I think about it. It was such a busy day at the surgery, which I know is no defence, but it's true. I was in the middle of lancing a boil, telling the patient not to share towels, wash it with antibacterial soap, showing them how to dress it with gauze, and then Mum phoned three times in a row, and I declined it every time, muttering something like, 'for God's sake' under my breath. As I showed the patient out, the receptionist called me from her desk. 'Your mum called, she said to call her back as soon as possible. I think it's important.'

'It's always important. Next patient please.'

By the time I'd dealt with the immunisation of three-year-old twins and a suspected case of type 2 diabetes, the receptionist called me again and said that this time Fergus was on the line and it was very urgent. My blood froze in my veins; he never called me at work.

When I got there, having squeezed through every amber traffic light and ignored every speed restriction on the journey, Dad was lying on the floor of his bedroom, propped up against the bed, his legs at strange angles to each other as though his whole body had folded and crumpled like a sheet of used paper. His face was white, one side drooping tellingly, his hands clammy, and there was a wet patch spreading on the groin of his trousers. I grabbed the bedspread off the bed and covered him from the waist down; he wouldn't have wanted anyone to see him like that.

I crouched down next to him and said, 'Dad, can you hear me? It's OK. Are you in pain anywhere?'

His breathing was ragged and weak. 'My arm is numb,' he panted.

'Get an aspirin from the cupboard and pound it up,' I yelled to Mum, who was in the doorway, her hands cupping her face. 'Now.' I turned back to Dad. 'It's OK, we need to get you to a hospital. How long have you been feeling poorly?'

'This morning,' he slurred. 'My arm is heavy and everything's a bit blurry in one eye.'

The missed calls. The messages.

Mum rushed back in with the powdered aspirin. 'Dad, you have to open your mouth and take this. Mum, you need to call an ambulance. Tell them the patient is having a suspected stroke.'

The whole time we sped towards the hospital, Fergus and Mum following the ambulance, I didn't let go of Dad's hand once. Why didn't I answer the calls? The emergency team was waiting by the open doors to Casualty, and he had a CT scan within half an hour of arriving. The first five hours were the most critical, and he needed clot-thinners as soon as possible. I shouted this at the doctors and they looked irritated and told me to wait outside. I paced the corridor outside the imaging unit, trying to forget all the stats and figures I knew. None of them mattered. He could be in the ten per cent who recovered completely.

Except he wasn't.

Would it make a difference if I went back and changed how it happened? If it was always going to happen, if he was definitely going to die that day and I really couldn't do anything to stop it, then I could at least make sure it was a good day. I would answer Mum's calls – hell I might not even go to work, for the first time ever. I'd take him out to lunch, somewhere no more than a hundred metres from the finest stroke unit in the country. I'd make him have a blood thinner with his meal. I'd crush it up and put it in his food. I'd do something differently. Anything.

'Shit! Mum's crying!'

'Jess! Do you need to go and lie down?' Fergus asks, getting up from the table and walking round to behind my chair. He hovers, unsure of what to do next.

This is mortifying. 'No, sorry, something in my eye. I might just go and swill it out. You carry on without me, I've finished anyway.'

Up in the bathroom, I grab the sink with both hands and look at myself in the mirror. I need to be more careful. I can't let my mind wander off into the past, and make the family suspicious that something's going on. We're all living in each other's pockets now, the separate lives we all used to lead are now completely entwined. I have to hold it together better. Ignore what I know. Forget that I have the chance to change things that are best left well alone.

Fergus

In the shocked silence Jess leaves behind, it occurs to Fergus that that's the very first time he's ever seen her cry. That's not normal. Not when they've been through what they have. But after Anna, it's as though everything shut down for Jess – for both of them, if he's being honest with himself. And instead of grief, and love, and emotion, came duty and responsibility and the need to fill every micro-second of every day with being busy.

Seconds seem to last twice as long for Jess as they do for everyone else. What other people can achieve in ten minutes, she can do in five. Fergus is usually only a third of the way through any plate of food as Jess is up from the table, stacking her empty plate in the dishwasher and boiling the kettle for a herbal tea to aid her digestion. She's always the first to shower, eat, change and leave the house in the time the rest of them are still stretching, yawning and having a morning scratch. But tonight at dinner Fergus watched her through narrowed eyes as she pushed the same piece of potato round her plate for minutes, staring at it as though it held the secret to eternal life.

Fergus thinks back to how Jess was slowly eating her way through the food on her plate in colour sequence – all the peas first, then meat, then potatoes. They hadn't had one recently but something like a stir-fry would blow her head clean off if this was now a new habit. *I'm a worse husband than I thought I was*, he thinks, *if this isn't a new thing but I've just never noticed it before. Did I used to pay so little attention to her?*

He should go upstairs and check she's all right. It was obvious that the old 'got something in my eye' line was just an excuse. She was properly upset about something.

He pushes back his chair to follow her but Joy lays a hand on his arm and gently shakes her head.

'Leave her be,' she says quietly.

'But—'

'She won't thank you for it.'

Fergus hesitates. Is it still true that Joy knows Jess better than he does? That letting Jess calm down alone is better than offering help? It doesn't feel right to just sit there and pretend his wife isn't sobbing upstairs while they all eat Cornettos from the freezer for dessert. Maybe if he tidies up the kitchen first and then takes her up one of her sorbets in a bit, when she's had a chance to compose herself, that would be better all round. As well as loading the dishwasher, tonight he also sweeps under the table.

18

Having a new toy and never playing with it

Jackie is leaning so far forward in her chair that her face is filling my laptop screen, and I can see it's been a while since she plucked her eyebrows. Not that women should conform to society's expectations of beauty – I told Molly that when she spent her pocket money on a tube of hair removal cream when she was thirteen and I'd refused to buy one for her. But still.

'I'm not sure what you're asking me, Jessica?'

To be honest, I'm not sure either. But I need to speak to someone about this, and she was the only person I could think of. 'Don't worry, I was just being silly,' I say, batting my question away as though a flick of my wrist could make it vanish.

'There's nothing silly about anything you say, Jess. Every thought you have is valid.'

'Not all of them,' I mutter.

'There must be a reason why you asked me that, Jessica. Do you feel like you want to rewind time?'

'I asked *you* that, Jackie. Would *you* rewind time if you had the chance?' There's a silence, in which I assume Jackie is thinking about how spending three years doing a psychotherapy degree brought her to the place where she's sat in front of a laptop on a fold-up garden chair in a laundry room speaking to someone who has spent a sizeable amount of money on trying to feel better, but who clearly can't be helped.

'Who's paying who, Jess?' she says finally. It's a valid point.

I just about stop myself from correcting her with 'whom'. 'I just mean, is the past best left alone?'

Jackie laughs. 'If everyone left their past alone, Jess, I'd have no job.'

'True, true.'

'People's past, like it or not, makes their present what it is. And unresolved situations from the past can affect our whole lives.'

'But if you had the chance to change the past, would you take it?'

'Wouldn't that be wonderful,' she says. 'To have the gift of hindsight and not make the mistakes we did.'

'So you would?' I press on. 'You would go back and change things?'

'Is this about Anna? Are you ready to talk about her?'

'Forget I asked,' I say, and gently close the laptop.

My mind is buzzing with the possibilities. Assuming all this is true of course, and I'm not trapped in some bizarre social experiment that will be aired on a satellite channel in early spring. Which moment is worthy of erasing and pretending it didn't happen? Molly left my hair straighteners on this morning and they burned a hole in the bedroom carpet, meaning that when we leave in five months, we'll have to replace it. But I'm not going to repeat the day for the sake of a couple of hundred quid. Yesterday I walked in on Fergus sitting on the toilet in the unlocked bathroom, his phone in one hand, his trousers round his ankles, a definite need for a quick squirt of air freshener in the room, but again, the need to alleviate our mutual embarrassment by erasing the day and starting over wasn't that extreme. I just said, 'Sorry, as you were,' shut the door, then ordered a bolt on Amazon.

I'm pretty sure that a couple of days ago, on Wednesday, we all had food poisoning from the chicken curry I made from the leftover Sunday roast, but sidestepping a few hours of stomach cramps and diarrhoea isn't worth reliving the whole day for, just to cook a different dinner in the evening.

I'd be lying if I said that the thought didn't cross my mind every time I squirted a good dollop of toilet bleach down the loo in between someone using it, or as I used my nail scissors to cut off the worst burnt bits of bedroom carpet, or as Fergus avoided my eyes as I handed him a glass of wine last night, that all it would take was a trip up the cliff then all this would be fixed, but a promise is a promise. And even though I knew in all likelihood I was going to break it, I felt I owed it to those I made it to, for the reason to be worth it.

That is until Friday morning arrives and the school phones Fergus, who bounds breathless into the surgery to find me. Liam has broken his arm playing rugby. It's too swollen to operate on today, so we're looking at surgery within a day or two followed by eight weeks of plaster. He's currently lying on the sofa, drugged up to the eyeballs on very strong pain-killers while Fergus researches ferry timetables to Guernsey to see the orthopaedic surgeon I've just spoken to on the phone.

I'm sure I'm not the only mother who would take her dog for a walk in the evening to think about her options, perhaps stopping along the way for a nice sit down on a bench she is timetabled on a rota to be on anyway, to truly contemplate the situation, maybe even allow herself a couple of minutes to watch the sunset and to recharge her batteries before going home and hiding her son's PE kit so the next day at school he has no choice but to stand on the side of the rugby pitch during his Friday PE lesson, watching his friends beat the crap out of each other.

And now thanks to the little reset, we're not spending our Saturday on our way to the orthopaedic day clinic on another island; instead, we're all off to watch a fully intact Liam and Fergus play their first game in the local five-a-side island football league. Molly was going to stay at home because 'we're all lame', but she changed her mind when she saw me empty the contents of the fridge into the cool box to take with us. So here we are, all walking down the hill to the school playing fields, together. This is a much better way to spend a weekend. Of course, I do feel a little guilty that I went back on my word, but this was absolutely not a frivolous reason. If you couldn't use the bench's power for something like healing the sick, what on earth was it there for?

When Monday rolls around, Molly is in a panic: it's the day of the French oral she ran out from last term at her old school. After a lot of paperwork and plea-bargaining for her to be given special consideration, the exam board has agreed for her to re-sit her oral at the new school, and her grade to be changed should she pass. Seeing as she got a D and needs at least a C to get into university in a couple of years' time, a lot hangs in the balance.

'OK, Molly,' I say over breakfast, 'pretend I'm a hotel receptionist, and ask me for a single room for four nights.'

'That role play never comes up any more, 'cos everyone just uses booking.com or Airbnb. Pretend you work at the train station.'

She has a point, but I still press on. 'Shouldn't you know the hotel one anyway?'

'If it's not going to come up then what's the point?' Fergus says.

'Yeah, Mum. What's the point?' Molly echoes in a nasally voice I'm absolutely certain I don't have. God, it's infuriating when they team up against me.

'Fine, OK then. *Bonjour, Mademoiselle, comment puis-je vous aider?*'

'What does that mean?' Molly asks blankly.

'Hello. Miss, how can I help you?' I reply.

'But that's not what they'd say!' Molly whines.

'What would they say then?' I ask.

'*Qu'est-ce que vous voulez?*'

'But that means "what do you want?" They wouldn't say that,' I argue. 'French people are mostly very polite.'

'God, you're so annoying!' She flounces off, slamming the door on her way out, and I shrug at Fergus as if to say, what did I do?

When she walks back in the door six hours later after school she ignores my cheery request for a rundown of her day, gives a grunt when I ask about the exam, and dissolves into floods of tears when I ask what she wants for dinner.

The hotel question came up.

If it wasn't an actual GCSE exam then I wouldn't even be considering it. Kids need to learn that if you don't revise properly for a test then you need to face the consequences. But this isn't an ordinary test. These aren't ordinary consequences. Molly failing this could mean the difference between university or not. Employment or unemployment benefits. A house or a cling-film-wrapped sleeping bag under a railway tunnel. In short, I really have no choice but to trek up the hill to the bench come dusk. Then to insist at breakfast the next morning that she needs to memorise the phrase '*je voudrais une chambre simple pour quatre nuits s'il vous plaît*'. And yes, she would like breakfast and a newspaper. *Merci*. But after this, I am absolutely never doing it again.

Then Wednesday happens. Against every ounce of common sense and local advice, I chance it with the local hairdresser, despite all their faded posters in the window warning me not to. Each sun-worn, permed woman with neon eyelids is literally screaming at me to turn away and not do it. Go shopping, horse-riding, fishing – anything but give money to Teresa the island hairdresser, who has magazines in the salon older than Molly. But I don't listen. *How bad could it be?* I think to myself as I merrily stroll inside.

The hair on my right side is now an inch shorter than that on my left and my once-blond highlights are the colour of the inside of a Cadbury's Crunchie. Now, when you place this latest catastrophe next to a broken limb and a failed exam potentially leading to lifelong unemployment, granted, it seems less calamitous. But that's only because you aren't here. I've never been the type to care too much about what I looked like on the outside – I've never smoked and I always drink two litres of water a day, so I'm pretty certain my organs are all operating as they should, and what my hair looks like is not important when you put it side by side with liver function – but honestly, it really is awful.

I am poised to absolutely deal with it myself with a pair of kitchen scissors and some out-of-date home dye I found in the grocery store, were it not for Fergus stomping around the house this afternoon livid with himself for forgetting to send off an invoice for some consulting work he's done, meaning that he's missed that month's deadline so it will roll over to the next month. My legs walk up to the cliff that evening on autopilot, telling Eileen who is sitting there doing her knitting that she can go home. Thankfully, when I wake up again on Wednesday morning I remind Fergus to deal with any outstanding admin, cancel the hair appointment, and the money that I save on getting my hair done I spend on chocolate, because thinking about Crunchies made me really want one.

Fergus did say that I needed a hobby. And now I have one. Everyone is winning. I am doing absolutely nothing wrong. I wouldn't have even found out about the bench if I wasn't meant to. Obviously someone, or something, wants me to do this; to make things better, easier. It's like anything: it's only a problem if I make it a problem. And that's absolutely not going to happen.

19

Pandora has nothing on me

It's now early October, the leaves are starting to take on a warm autumnal hue, and the evenings are edging earlier into the late afternoon. Mum has been staying with us for nearly three weeks, and while no specific return ferry crossing was booked when she arranged her journey out, the expectation was – and I don't think it's unreasonable for me to say this – that there would definitely be one. How I bring this up though, I have no idea.

'You have to!' Fergus whispered last night when we were lying in bed. 'She bought two new cushions "for her room" yesterday. House guests don't normally refurbish their rooms.'

'It's hardly refurbishing!' I hissed. 'She just likes cushions.'

'I like Sky Sports but I don't install it in every friend's house we stay in.'

He had a point. Dad used to say that house guests are like fish: they go off after five days. We were now on Day Nineteen. To say that we've reached our expiry date is an understatement. But that makes it sound like it's been trial after trial and surprisingly, perhaps, it really hasn't. On balance, it's been an unmitigated success. Before she arrived we were bumbling along, getting on as best we could with the weirdness of island life, our new living arrangements making us all feel a little unsettled with the proximity of each other, and then she arrived, and we all pulled together a bit more. First of all for appearance's sake – I'm sure all of us were keen to avoid an intense conversation with her about the difficulties of change – but then I'm not sure whether we just started to believe the lie, or whether it genuinely began to get better, but we seem to have turned a corner and part of me doesn't want her to go. I like the company. I like *her* company – which came as something of a shock when I realised it.

'I've joined a book club,' she says to me later in the afternoon as we sit on the sofa and have a cup of tea. I didn't have any patients today, so after I sent out emails reminding all my patients over sixty-five of the flu vaccine drive tomorrow and over-watered the spider plants, I came home early.

'I'm sorry, what?' I say.

'I've joined a book club.'

'That's what I thought you said. Is it an online one?' I ask hopefully.

'No, silly, it's every other Tuesday in the function room at The Swan. We're doing *Fifty Shades of Grey* for the first one. Doreen invited me to it this morning.'

Oh dear God. Come on, Jess, you have to say it.

'But I thought you had lots of things to go back to in London? Dates and funerals, those sorts of things?'

'I do. Well, I did. I missed the funeral, but as it turns out, that's OK. The family only went for the bronze package at the golf club, so just sandwiches and sausage rolls, no desserts or alcohol. It was over and done within an hour. I'm glad I didn't rush back for it.'

'So you're going to be staying for a bit longer, then?'

'I think so.' She takes a sip of her tea, and I notice that her hand is shaking a little. 'That OK?'

'Yes, of course!' I gush. 'Absolutely! We're loving having you here. Stay as long as you like!'

As well as the power of time travel, I seem to have developed the ability to see into a different room, because I can feel Fergus's eyes boring into my skull from behind the closed living-room door. 'Excuse me for a minute,' I say, backing out of the room, and Mum starts flicking through a copy of *Country Living*. I really hope she hasn't started a subscription to be sent here.

Fergus is exactly where I knew he'd be: standing in the hallway, hands on hips, steam coming out of both ears. I motion for us to go into the kitchen, and gently shut the door behind us.

'What?' I hiss.

'You know what,' he hisses back.

'What was I supposed to say? She's my mother.'

'Which is exactly why I'm not contacting the courts to get her forcibly removed from our property. It's been three weeks.'

'Exactly, it's only been three weeks. Which is not a lot.'

'Last year you wouldn't let my parents stay for more than a week, and they'd come all the way from Australia! You made them book into a Premier Inn for the next two weeks!'

'Which we paid for,' I mumble.

He gives me a piercing look, which I can't quite meet. 'It's got nothing to do with the money, it's the fact that you didn't want them staying with us.'

'Yes, but that was different.'

Fergus looks outraged. 'Because it was my parents? Your mum can move in without even consulting me, while my parents need to have their breakfast sitting next to a photo-copy machine salesman from Swindon every morning instead of their own grandchildren.'

'Sort of . . .' I say. I can't bring myself to say 'yes' even though that's exactly what I mean. 'I know they don't like me,' I add, 'and it makes me feel a bit uncomfortable in my own house.'

'And that's exactly the reason why your mum needs to go now, too. "Oh, Fergus, I bet you're enjoying being a kept man." "Oh, Fergus, you should start making jam, with all those fruit trees in your garden." "Oh, Fergus, you'll have to join the WI soon!"

I have to bite my lip to stop myself from laughing, 'She's just making conversation.'

'No, Jess, she's making a point about you being such a sodding high flyer and me being a complete waste of space. She's always done it. They didn't want me as a son-in-law, they wanted that bloke – your godmother's son, what's his name? Barry?'

'Harry. And no, they didn't.'

'I bet your mum had already written the wedding invitations. She told me a couple of days ago, actually, that he's now got his own cosmetic surgery practice in Dubai. Spends most of his time making fake knobs for Saudis at ten grand a pop. Lucky Barry. Just think, Jess, that could have been your life. But no, you ended up with me, a drop-out, a complete fuck-up who couldn't make it as a doctor.'

'But you chose to leave medicine, no one forced you to.'

'I failed the year, I'd have had to repeat it.'

'So? You could have done it.'

'We needed money, Jess, we were having a baby for Christ's sake.'

'You could have reapplied after she died, if it meant that much to you. You could have become a doctor. Anyway, I thought you liked your job?'

He rounds on me. 'I hated it! I hated the fact that you achieved our dream and I didn't. You stuck at it. I gave up. You're the success story. I'm the failure.'

'Fergus—'

'That's another thing: your mum keeps going around the island telling everyone my name isn't Freddie.'

'Well, it's not.'

'I thought you understood why it's important to me.'

'Yes, but you can't expect her to.'

'You did.'

'Yes,' I shrug, 'but I have a vested interest in making my life as easy as possible.'

'What's that supposed to mean?'

'Just that what makes you happy makes me happy.'

'Since when?'

'What?'

'Since when?'

'What do you mean since when? Since we got married!'

'What absolute bollocks. You've always done exactly what you want to do, it's no wonder this family was in such a mess.'

We've forgotten we are meant to be whispering. 'Whoa, hang on a second!' I shout. 'You're saying that everything that's happened with us – with Molly and Liam – was my fault?'

'I didn't say that, you said that.'

'But you think it?'

'It's no coincidence that now you've taken your foot off the pedal a bit, everyone has settled down.'

'And that has nothing at all to do with the fact that you're at home now too instead of chasing around after young girls half your age?'

This obviously hits a nerve with him, as his face starts colouring. I feel a surge of satisfaction.

'What the hell's that supposed to mean?'

'I'm not blind, Fergus, I have eyes! And a nose! I saw what was going on, all the messages, the nights out, the cheap perfume – I'm not stupid!'

'Well, if you were remotely interested in me I wouldn't need other women to laugh at my jokes or feel good about myself, would I?'

There it is. He might as well have poured petrol all over the argument, the speed at which it now goes up in flames.

'How many affairs have you actually had?' I cry. 'Come on, do you need one hand or two to count them? Shall I call one of the kids in to borrow their fingers too?'

He stares at me, aghast. 'Jesus, Jessica, do you think that little of me?'

I've gone too far down this road to haul myself back, although all the warning lights are flashing at me to do so.

'I don't know what I think of you any more, Fergus – Freddie – whoever the hell you are. It's not as though we know each other very well at all, is it?'

'What do you mean by that?'

I decide to just carry on, get it all out, say everything we should have said to each other years ago. After all, I can erase the day, pretend everything is fine tomorrow. He won't be any the wiser that anything's wrong and I'll have purged myself of all this anger that's been gnawing inside me for years.

'I mean, you felt sorry for me, didn't you? Me the mousey nerd, you the college heartbreaker. I had an all-right body, shame about the face, you gave me a pity shag, then another one, then another one, then oh shit, got me pregnant, that wasn't meant to happen. Forced to marry me, dropped out of uni, I lost the baby, but it was too late, you were trapped.' I can't stop the words tumbling out of my mouth, each one gathering speed, building up momentum towards the awful crescendo I know is going to happen, but I just can't stop it. 'Your parents can't stand me. They think it's totally my fault you left medical school – how could I have been so irresponsible as to get pregnant? For people like them it's always the woman's fault, for some reason. And how dare I not look like every ex-girlfriend you ever had. "It's strange, you're really not his usual type" – your mum actually said that to me when she met me, and I know what she meant. She meant types that had much better genes to pass down to her grandchildren, and what was going on with my anatomy that meant that it would make a child that would only live for four days? "We've never had anything like this happen on our side," she said when Anna died. I can never forgive her for that, and you never said anything, you just stood there in the hospital like a damn plastic mannequin letting her say those things.'

'OK, OK.' Fergus takes a step forward. 'If we're going to talk about what our toxic mothers have done over the years, that's fine. How about when your mother said that Anna's death was "probably for the best"? How about that?'

'She didn't mean it like that, she just meant because we were so young.'

'I wasn't so young that I didn't know what I wanted, and neither were you.'

'Yes we were! We were twenty-one years old without a sodding clue what to do so we thought, we might as well try and make a go of it. Nothing else to do. Two kids later, bills, jobs, life, and here we are. Completely bloody stuck.'

There's a silence as we both take in what I've just said.

If only I'd said all that in front of Jackie, she'd have been able to wind the angry threads into neat little balls of twine that made sense. That's what I've been paying her for. This. Not to hear some rubbish about pine dressers. But I didn't say it then. I shouted it across our rented kitchen, in the middle of the English Channel, twenty foot away from where my mother is sitting, cold cup of tea poised to her lips, the magazine on her lap open on a double-page spread on 'Ten Things to Do With Pumpkins'.

'Is that how you feel?' Fergus says finally. 'That you're trapped?'

'I think that's how *you* feel,' I say, sure that I'm right.

'Don't assume you know what I'm thinking, Jess, because you don't.'

'Do you think you know me?' I ask, hands on hips, knowing for absolute certainty that he hasn't got a clue.

'We've been together for more than twenty years – of course I know you.'

'Well, you're wrong,' I say, more quietly. 'I've been wearing a mask for so long now, even I have no idea who the real me is any more. So you've got no chance.'

Fergus runs his hands through his hair. 'So, what now? Shall I leave? Is that what you want? Because you clearly have no feelings for me left at all – and that's if you ever had any in the first place.'

'That is unfair, Fergus. I loved you very much.'

'Loved. Not love. Wow, OK – so at least I know where I stand.'

A flare of panic rises, as I realise that came out all wrong. 'I didn't mean that. I still love you, of course I do. You're the father of my children.'

'Ouch. OK. So as the father of your children, you still love me, but as your husband, not so much. Wow.' He sinks down into a kitchen chair and looks at his hands clasped on the table in front of him.

'You're putting words into my mouth,' I say. 'I think life has just got in the way of us enjoying each other's company. But that's changing, isn't it? The last few weeks have been better than the last ten years put together.' I sit down next to him. 'Haven't they? Don't you think we're getting on so much better now we're here?' I reach out my hand to lightly touch his arm but he flinches and pulls away.

'I did, yes. Until you said all that.'

'I didn't mean—'

'Yes you did. You meant all of it. You can't take it back.'

'But I didn't mean for it to come out like that.'

Fergus stands up. 'I'm going to take Iris out. Get some air. Think about all this.'

I glance up at the kitchen clock; it's quarter to six, there's only forty-five minutes until sunset. Only three-quarters of an hour to make this right. 'I'll take her.'

'No, you stay with your mum, she'll want to talk about everything she's just heard. Slag me off some more.'

That's another reason I need to get rid of this day and start again. I don't want Mum to have heard any of this. Screw 'communication is key'; functional relationships thrive on secrecy and unvoiced issues. Jackie should have that on a poster above the framed print reminding her clients to 'Just Breathe'.

'I think we both need to go out and calm down. You go down the beach and I'll go on the cliff,' I say, as though I'm being magnanimous, and not desperate.

'The tide's in. I want to go on the cliff,' he says petulantly.

'Fine. We'll both go on the cliff.'

Fergus slams his chair in under the table. 'You go on the fucking cliff, Jessica. You win, why is that not a surprise? I'll go down the pub.'

It's Maggie's turn on the bench tonight. I completely forgot that as I stamped my way up the hill after shaking my head warningly at Mum when she came out of the living room and started to talk to me. She looked pale and shellshocked at having no choice but to hear everything Fergus and I had flung at each other. The sooner I can restart this godawful day again the better.

Maggie's head swings around in surprise when I sit down alongside her.

'What are you doing here, Jess? It's my night. You don't need to be here.'

'I just fancied some air,' I say. 'You can go home, Maggie – no need for both of us to be here.'

'No, you're OK, I'm just thinking through some things. It's easier to do that out of the house.'

I know very little about Maggie's home life. I haven't even met her elusive husband, who works back in London but comes here at weekends. She doesn't have children, and I guess that the onset of the menopause has shut that door for good.

'I know what you mean,' I say, sitting down next to her.

'Tough day?' she asks.

I nod, looking out to sea. The sun is still low in the sky; we have a few minutes yet until it sets.

'Kids playing up?' she asks.

'Remarkably, no. Not this time.'

'You don't need to talk about it. I never do.'

I want her to confide in me, I do – I sense she's just as lonely as I am – but I need to look at the sunset, and I don't know how I can do that without her realising, or being rude. 'Why not?' I say, not taking my eyes off the horizon.

She shrugs. 'It's no one's business but mine, and no one needs to hear me rabbit on about my woes, do they? Not that they'd believe I could have woes, not when I live in the biggest house on the island.'

The sun is now touching the ocean, and I stare at it, unblinking. She'll understand.

'Jess, stop looking at it! You can't look at it.'

I ignore her.

'Jess, don't do it, it's really dangerous playing with it.'

'I know what I'm doing,' I say, my eyes fixed on the orange sun.

'Jess, please stop it. For God's sake, Jess, stop looking at it.'

I wonder what it is that's happened to Maggie, and Nora, and Eileen to make them all so anti . . . this. Maggie even tries to grab my chin, to move my face away from the horizon, but I wrench her hand away, staring at the sun all the while. What is her problem? Why is she so against us doing it? Surely this is not a burden, it's a gift.

The sun has completely disappeared. I sigh with relief, give Maggie a thin smile, whisper, 'Sorry, but it's important,' and walk slowly back down the hill.

Fergus

Jess is right about one thing: she clearly doesn't know him at all, Fergus thinks as he hands over another fiver in return for another pint of bitter. Surely all the grief, all the crap, all the years had to have meant something, otherwise what was actually the point of it all? They should have left each other years ago if all she said was true. And it absolutely wasn't. Of course it had been a shock to discover she was pregnant – they were twenty-one, for crying out loud – but if anything, that cut out the years of indecision and questions about when would be the right time to move in together, when would be the right time to get married, to start a family. Because God knows, it was her and only her he'd ever wanted to do that with. Jess was so headstrong, so ambitious, so *sensible*, it never would have been the right time for her. She'd have always felt there was something else they needed to put into place first – to be further on in their careers, more money saved up – so in so many ways he was thrilled some of the decisions had been taken out of their hands. But she, it turns out, wasn't. Stuck. That's what she said they are. He doesn't feel stuck. Either one of them could have left at any time; they weren't chained to each other, forced to spend eternity in a sexless marriage. Yes, he used to have mild flirtations, but surely everyone wants to feel they're still attractive and smart and funny from time to time. Maybe it did go a bit far with Faye, but he never would have actually done anything with her because he knows that, deep down, he loves Jess just as much now as when he first met her.

She keeps everything in, that's her problem, he thinks as he takes another swig of his drink. She doesn't let on to people when she needs help. Doesn't talk about what's bothering her. Not necessarily to him, but to anyone – Jackie, a friend, literally anyone. A problem shared, problem halved, that's what they say.

'Hello, Freddie, how are you doing? Fancy another one?'

Fergus looks up from staring at his pint. 'Oh hello, Keith.'

'Christ, you look like you've got the cares of the world on your shoulders, mate. Everything all right?'

Fergus gives Keith a wide grin, his belief in the importance of open and honest communication put back in its box and its lid sealed. 'I don't know what you're talking about, mate, you've caught me wondering who Tottenham are going to get in the cup draw.'

A small voice in his head whispers 'hypocrite', but he drowns it out with a large swig of his beer.

20

Toys sometimes break, though

I can barely breathe with all the alcohol fumes smothering the bedroom like a whisky-soaked blanket. The night before last, which was actually last night because I've gone back a day, we only had a glass of wine each, and were in bed by nine thirty, so it's really odd that the room reeks like this. Unless Fergus got up in the night and drank alone? But then it didn't smell like this yesterday morning, which is today. God, this is confusing.

He's still asleep next to me, snoring heavily and loudly, his mouth open. Yes, he is definitely the source of the stench. I look at my phone next to me: half six. I know I'm not going to have any patients today, and the emails and plant watering can wait a day, so I decide to stay at home. From what Fergus said in our argument yesterday/today, a day spent keeping Mum away from his air space might be in order. Especially if he smells like this.

But when I pad downstairs, to my surprise, Mum is already up, dressed and eating a slice of toast at the kitchen table, which is really odd as she wasn't yesterday.

'Morning, Mum. You're up early. Cup of tea?'

'I've booked myself on the first ferry off the island.'

I spin around from filling the kettle from the tap and look at her. 'What?'

'I think it's best if I go home.'

'But that's ridiculous. What about your book club?' I say before remembering that she doesn't know about the book club yet: Doreen will only ask her about it later on this morning.

'I've read it already.'

I don't have time for this to sink in before Molly and Liam come in, grab a banana each – hadn't we run out yesterday? – and shout their goodbyes.

'I won't see you for a while, kids,' Mum shouts down the hall. 'I'm leaving this morning.'

They both come back in the kitchen, looking confused. 'Why?' Liam asks.

'I thought you were staying for a while longer, Gran? You said you were going to come and see me in *Chicago*?' Molly has surprised and delighted all of us by not only auditioning for, but getting, the part of Roxy Hart in the school musical. I have my suspicions that Mum had a hand in it, but I'm not sure how.

'Sorry, darling, but I do need to go now. House guests are like fish; they go off after three weeks.'

'Is Mum making you go?' Molly glares at me with narrowed eyes.

'No, absolutely not, darling, but I can't stay here forever.'

Liam looks at Mum with his big, brown eyes, and for a second I think I glimpse them shining a little with tears. He blinks. I must be wrong.

'But you said you were really sad in London,' Molly says. She did?

'You said that you've been happier here than since Grampy died.'

Mum smiles brightly, but there is no mistaking her watery eyes. 'I have loved being here, it's true, but this is your home, not mine, and it's too small for all of us. I need to go back to my own friends and my own home.'

'But you hate it there. You said that it's where people go to die lonely, horrible deaths.'

I am stunned. When exactly has Mum been having all these chats with Molly? Molly, who only speaks if it's to ask when dinner will be ready and if I have any money.

'And you said that you don't have any friends, because the only friends you ever really had were Grampy and your brother, and that's why we need to look after each other, because family is the most important thing,' Liam adds.

I'm looking at Liam, then Molly, and Mum, all sat in a triangle, both of my children holding one of Mum's hands, begging her not to go, wondering if I've woken up in some parallel universe where all my nearest and dearest have had personality transplants. Since when do they have this bond? In London they barely looked up from their phones when Mum visited, and now they're having deep and meaningful conversations about life and death and loneliness.

'Elodie's mum rents out bedrooms in her house,' Molly says suddenly, 'I know she does! And she's really nice. She has a nose ring. You could stay there if you don't want to stay here.' Molly glares up at me again. 'Mum can ring her now and ask.' She turns back to Mum. 'Why don't you do that?'

Liam adds, 'Elodie's brother Nico has an Xbox and a PlayStation and a Wii.'

'Well I certainly wouldn't be bored, would I?' Mum laughs, dabbing at her eyes with a tissue. 'Look, you two push off to school, you don't want to be late. And I'll talk more to Mummy about it, OK?'

They leave amid a flurry of forced promises that Mum won't be getting the ferry after all. As soon as they're gone, silence descends on the house once again. Mum and I stare at each other. She's the first to speak. 'I never meant for Fergus to think that I dislike him, or don't approve of him.'

'He doesn't think that!'

She smiles sadly at me. 'Jessica, I heard everything yesterday.'

Yesterday. My heart sinks. This can't be happening, I did everything right, everything the same as I've done before. Why didn't it work?

'I'm really very sorry that I've caused so many problems coming here.'

'You haven't!'

'Not just by coming here now, but over the years, it seems. I think you and Fergus need to have a proper, calm, talk about everything that came up in your fight yesterday, and work out where you go from here. I think you've both got a lot of unresolved anger about things that's built up over the years and if you two stand any chance of making it work, you need to talk about it. And I need to give you some space to do that.'

I sink into a kitchen chair alongside her. 'But I don't want you to.' And I realise I really mean it. I don't want her to go. The last three weeks have brought us closer than we have been in years, the rift between us has almost healed and if I let her get on that ferry, then she'll be gone and I won't get her back.

Mum sighs and covers my hand with hers. 'I don't want to either, but Fergus, Molly and Liam are your family now, and you need to focus on what's best for them.'

I have a flashback of a few minutes ago, seeing my two troubled teens holding hands with Mum at the table, all their bravado and attitude stripped away, until they were just two grandchildren not wanting to let their grandma leave.

'I'm going to call Nora,' I say, my voice firm. 'Don't go anywhere.'

Fergus is still comatose when I get back from walking Mum, her two suitcases and her two new cushions the few hundred metres to Nora's, who was delighted with her new lodger. 'We're going to have so much fun!' she said, clapping her hands together. 'I make my own gin, you know!'

An hour later I sit at the end of our bed, debating whether to wake him up or not.

I still can't work out why now, of all the times, it didn't work. I did the same thing I had always done before: sat on the bench and looked at the sun as it dipped into the sea. I wasn't by myself – Maggie was talking at me – but then Nora had been shouting about wolves and wildly waving her arms about before and it still worked, so it wasn't that I needed to be alone. So why was this time different? And when I really needed it to work, as well. I wouldn't have minded being stuck with orange hair, not really, and we would even have managed Liam being in plaster for two months and Molly's life wouldn't have been ruined because she can't order a baguette in a boulangerie. I would happily swap all the other times for this one. This is going to be so much harder to mend.

'Are you sure you want to fix it?' Jackie said this morning. I messaged her as soon as the kids had gone to school, asking for an emergency video call.

'Of course I do,' I replied without thinking, keeping my voice low so that I didn't wake Fergus up.

'Just stop a second, Jessica, and think,' she said, her voice dripping with honey. 'There's a reason why this all flared up now. This argument was years in the making, and it's all out there now. You can't take it back.'

Clearly.

'So the question is now, do you both acknowledge what was said and find a way to reach a resolution? Or do you mutually decide it's too hard to address these issues?'

'I thought you were a marriage counsellor?' I said tersely. 'I want you to make our marriage better, not tell me it's too hard and to get a divorce.'

'Is that what you heard me say?'

I closed my eyes then, tilted my face to the woodchip-wallpapered ceiling and took a deep breath in. I didn't know what she'd said because I was only half listening, weighing up the two routes I could go down. Stay or go. Or a third – one that Jackie has no idea about. I could try and make it all go away again.

Fergus stirs under the covers.

'Hey. I got you some water and paracetamol,' I say.

'Thanks.' He tries to sit up, groans, and falls back down onto the pillow.

'What time did you get in?'

'Dunno. We had a lock-in. You were asleep. I tried sleeping on the sofa downstairs but it was too cold, so I came up here around four.'

'You didn't need to sleep on the sofa,' I say gently.

He grunts something unintelligible.

'Look, about yesterday—' I start.

'Not now.'

'But we need to talk about what we said to each other.'

'Not now, Jess. My head kills, you're late for work—'

Dammit. I've completely forgotten the surgery, because I'd assumed it was yesterday, when I had no patients. Oh God, today is the day all the pensioners are being vaccinated for flu. And as the average age of the island is one hundred and twelve, the queue will be round the block by now!

'I'd better go. Look, get some more sleep, have a shower, and let's go out for dinner later, yeah? We could go to the pub.'

Another groan from under the duvet, and I stifle a laugh.

'OK, maybe not the pub. I'll make a plan. Just sleep. And drink some water.' Telling him to stay hydrated means I care. He knows that. My mouth starts to form the words 'I love you' because it seems like the moment needs it, but I stop it coming out just in time. We've never been the couple for whom daily declarations of love roll off the tongue. I feel foreheads and top up water bottles, and iron the family's underpants. He keeps the ice-cube tray filled up, assigns family accounts on Netflix and always gives Iris her worming tablet. I'm slowly starting to realise that in our own way, we were actually saying we loved each other all the time, we just never really noticed. But if I say it now, he'll probably assume I'm only saying it because of the argument. Better to wait until later.

It's the tenth of October. It is drizzling. It's around ten degrees. And there are currently around thirty senior citizens huddled under their umbrellas, shivering into their Marks and Spencer anoraks, more in need of a flu shot than ever before.

'Sorry,' I gasp. 'I'm so sorry I'm late. Come on in, everyone, the heating's on, Mrs Duggan will make everyone a nice cup of tea, come on in.' But Eileen doesn't seem to be here – her hours are still a mystery to me – so I flick on the kettle and usher everyone inside until no one's left in the cold. The waiting room now resembles a commuter train at rush hour, just with fewer briefcases and more hip replacements.

'OK, who wants to get stabbed first?' I say brightly from the doorway of my consulting room, needle in hand.

Two hours later I sit back in my chair and close my eyes. I haven't had time to contemplate my marriage all morning, which is probably for the best. But now the rush is over, it's all I can think about. I have visions of Fergus emptying the wardrobe, stuffing his clothes into a holdall, deliberating over which family photos to take with him, if any. I have a sudden, overwhelming urge to go home.

He hasn't packed anything. He's eating a bowl of cornflakes at the kitchen table. I feel weak with relief.

'Hey,' I say, flinging my keys into the bowl on the counter and shrugging my coat off.

'Wotcha.'

An onlooker wouldn't know that less than twenty-four hours ago we'd hurled insults at each other like we were playing catch with a tennis ball.

'Where's your mum?' he says between mouthfuls.

'She's staying with Nora,' and in response to his blank expression I add, 'The nose ring lady. She rents out rooms.'

'Something I said?' he asks. He does this, using comedy, flippancy to address an issue. Though I still find it aggravating, Jackie's voice in my head reminds me that at least he's addressing it.

I take a seat at the table opposite him. Far enough away to not make him feel crowded. Near enough to show I still like him. Which I think, bearing in mind the content of yesterday's argument, I need to prove.

'About yesterday,' I begin.

He keeps chewing.

'I think we need to talk about what we said.'

He reaches for the box of cereal and pours another bowlful.

'Freddie?' I hope that by using his new name, I'll show him his feelings do matter.

He looks up at me. 'Yes?'

'I think we need to talk about yesterday.'

'OK. Go on then.'

I take a deep breath, and in that moment I'm glad my trip to the bench last night didn't work. In this moment I know that I have no choice but to try and mend my marriage this way. Not by digging a hole to put my head in, or by sticking my fingers in my ears and singing really loudly to drown it all out, or by sitting on a bench at sunset and making it all go away.

This.

'When you sat next to me that day in the lecture hall and said, "Hi, Jess," it was literally the best day in my life.' I pause, searching his face to see if he's hearing me. He's still chewing, but less noisily and slightly slower than before. 'I had no idea that you even knew my name, let alone would want to sit next to me. Then, when we both got the same train down to London from York and you suggested us sitting together, my heart beat so fast for the whole journey – and bear in mind, trains went a lot slower then. The first time we slept together I kept the condom wrapper as my bookmark for the whole of the term.'

He smiles, clearly delighted, and it changes his whole face. 'You didn't?'

'I did.' I grin. 'The librarian gave me the dirtiest look when I forgot to take it out from a book I borrowed when I returned it.' I feel my grin sliding off my face. 'Then, when I got pregnant, everything changed. You just left, for weeks—'

'It was one week.'

'It felt like weeks, Fergus. It felt like I told you I was pregnant and you just disappeared, leaving me to figure it all out by myself.'

'I was twenty-one.'

'So was I!'

'But I was a twenty-one-year-old boy, who knew nothing. I was a gormless child, who just got told the news that his life was going to change forever.'

There is no point reminding him that I was too. That I was just as terrified as he was. I sit there quietly, waiting for the penny to drop.

'I know I shouldn't have run away,' he says slowly. 'I should have stayed with you. But I couldn't. I panicked.'

'Neither of us wanted to get married, and we should have stood up to everyone, to my mum and dad, to your parents . . . we should have said that it wasn't what we wanted, but we didn't.'

'I wanted to marry you.'

'Don't rewrite history, Fergus – Freddie, sorry.'

He half smiles. 'You can call me Fergus. Fergus was the one that did all those things that made you feel like that.'

'We were bullied into marrying and we were bullied into keeping the baby,' I say, speaking the truth about it for the first time.

'If you had decided not to, I would have supported you.'

'But I couldn't make that decision myself. I was a mess, a complete mess. I had your Catholic mum fresh off the plane from Ireland shouting the odds, carrying a brand-new pushchair in one hand and your grandmother's engagement ring in the other. I had my parents blankly refusing to consider any other option. And I had you, shrugging your shoulders, telling me that it was up to me, as though I'd just said, "Shall we have pepperoni on our pizza tonight, or not?" And then, when we're still coming to terms with it, my wedding dress not even back from the dry cleaner's yet, she's born. Twelve weeks early. And we're told that it was due to my placenta not functioning properly and she probably wouldn't survive the week. And it was my fault.'

Fergus shakes his head and leans forward in his chair. 'It was not your fault.'

'I spent the first twenty weeks of her gestation thinking about getting a termination. I poisoned her with my thoughts. She was getting all her nutrients from me and I was barely eating, thinking dark, horrible thoughts all the time, and then she died. Of course it was my fault.'

I don't know when I started to cry, but the tears are flowing fast down my cheeks, landing with a drip, drip, onto the wooden table. In more than twenty years I've never cried about it. Never. Not once. I thought that if ever this happened, if there was ever a day where I'd let myself think about this, talk about it, then the walls would close in and the floor would fall away from under me. Fergus moves his chair closer to mine, and takes my hands in his.

'It was not your fault, Jess. None of this was your fault.'

'I wasn't even with her when she died,' I sob. 'You were. I wasn't. I couldn't bear to see her all hooked up to thousands of tubes, the machines beeping, her little naked body kept alive by all those pumps and pipes . . . I couldn't do it, and so she died, and I wasn't even there.'

'It was very peaceful. She wasn't in pain.' Fergus's voice cracks as he says this, and I look up to see a tear roll down his cheek too. It's the first time I've ever seen him cry, and it makes me catch my breath. Gone are the shields of bravado we've both built up over the years, and in their place are two people, a mum and a dad, utterly broken at the death of their child.

'But I wasn't there,' I gasp. 'I wasn't there, Fergus. I was her mummy and I wasn't strong enough to be there.'

'She knew you loved her.' His thumb moves rhythmically over mine, stroking, back and forth.

'Did she? How did she know? I spent months pretending she wasn't real, and by the time I realised I did love her, after all, it was too late. *I* was too late. She was gone.' I sniff and rub my eyes with my sleeve. 'And then, when I could have put it right, when I could have given her a beautiful name and a lovely funeral, I didn't. I said, "Call her whatever you like," and we let the hospital cremate her.'

'We were in shock, Jess. We just went along with what the doctors suggested, what our parents said would be best. We would do everything differently now, but back then we did what we were told to do. What we thought was right.'

'Do you ever think about her?' I ask.

'Of course I do. Do you?' he asks gently.

'It's a constant battle not to,' I admit for the first time. 'Because if I did let myself, I honestly think I'd fall apart.'

There's a few seconds of silence, and I realise that we've both been doing exactly the same thing. I've thought for all these years that we had both dealt with this in completely different ways, but the opposite is true.

'Why have we spent so many years pretending we're OK when we're not?' he asks.

I take a moment to think – really think – about his question. 'It started then, that week, when we lost her. Instead of dealing with it together, we struggled on alone and that paved the way for how we lived. Every time I was anxious or sad about something I kept it in because I didn't want you to think you'd been forced into marrying someone weak and pathetic.'

'But because you were so strong all the time I didn't want *you* to think that *I* was the weak one, so we created this life where there was no room for talking about anything that really mattered. We both made ourselves so busy, filling every minute with work and distractions, that even if we'd wanted to talk about her, what had happened, we couldn't. Not because we didn't want to, but because we didn't have time to.'

I rub his thumb with mine. He's always had really soft hands.

'And now things aren't so manic, we start to fall apart,' he adds.

'Or we finally start to put ourselves together,' I say, and then without meaning to, I let out a giggle. 'Oh my God, that sounded so corny.'

'Jackie would be so proud.'

'Finally I know where my money's gone.'

'Didn't you say she had a conservatory put on her house recently? Our dysfunction did that.'

'And she had a lovely half term in the Balearics.' I smile, enjoying this mini respite from arguing.

'See? We're basically providing a community service.'

'You're right. We've given her a lovely life.'

'Does she still have to shout over the noise of the spin cycle?'

I shake my head, smiling. 'No, she's got a new model, it's much quieter.'

'We paid for that too. The woman is living the dream.'

I cover my mouth with my hand to stop any more comments coming out. 'We shouldn't be mean about Jackie. She's really nice.'

'She is. And I'm glad you talk to her.'

I pause, knowing what I want to say next and not knowing if I'll be able to. 'I like the name you chose for her. Anna. It's really pretty.'

'You've never said that before.'

'I should have done.'

'We both should have done things differently.'

I can, I think. I can still go back and do it differently.

But I won't.

Fergus

As he lies in bed later, Fergus thinks back over the day. It could have gone either way, the argument. Fergus wouldn't have been surprised if Jess had chosen the other route, the one that would have seen him packing a pathetic sports bag filled with clothes and family photos to remember them all by. It all needed to be said, though. Possibly not flung at each other across the kitchen like live grenades, but definitely aired. Tonight after getting everything out in the open they even sat next to each other on the same sofa. On purpose and not just because there were no other seats available. He opened a bottle of wine, poured them both a large glass, and instead of making a beeline for the armchair on the other side of the room or taking his laptop into the kitchen like usual, he sat down next to her. He was a bit nervous, second-guessing her reaction, really hoping she didn't ask him what he was playing at. She must have been able to feel the nearness of his arm mere inches away from hers because he certainly could. The hairs on his arm were standing up and he could sense her tense up at first, and held his breath waiting for her to ask him to sit somewhere else, politely of course, or perhaps get up and move herself. But she just tucked her leg underneath her and reached out for her glass. He can't remember what they watched, but he can clearly recall the way it felt to sit next to his wife again.

21

Most toys come with instructions, but some don't need any

You normally only need to ring people's doorbells once and then leave. Anything more might be considered pushy. They're either there and want to answer the door, or they aren't there or don't want to answer; it's as simple as that. But I know for a fact that Maggie is in so I've rung it twelve times so far, and she's still not answering. The curtain upstairs twitched on the first ring, so it's futile her pretending that the house is empty.

'Maggie?' I call up. 'Are you in?'

The front door opens – not a lot, but enough for me to finally meet Maggie's husband. His large frame blocks the view inside and even in a navy towelling dressing gown I can tell he's a charismatic charmer. After all, I'm married to one. Or was. I seem to be married to a completely different man these days.

'Can I help you?' he smiles, standing in the foot-wide gap of the open doorway, his brown hair slicked back, wet from a shower.

'I'm so sorry,' I say, giving him what I hope is an ingratiating smile. 'I was after Maggie, but I didn't mean to disturb you.'

'I've just got back from London,' he says, putting one arm up on the door frame, allowing me a glimpse of an incredibly hairy chest. 'We were having a little afternoon reunion.'

Oh Jesus.

'I'm so sorry,' I gabble. 'I'll call her later. Or not. Tomorrow. I'll catch up with her then. Sorry again.'

'What did you say your name was? I don't think we've met before.'

'Oh Jess. Jess Bay. I'm the new doctor here. Well, for a while.'

'A doctor? Brains as well as beauty.'

What a creep. I back away uneasily down the white gravel driveway towards the two stately pillars flanking the entrance that are begging for a fancy electric gate to be attached to them, if the Isle of Forth was an electric-gate sort of place. Thinking about it, I'm not quite sure why they need such a big driveway on a car-less island.

Just before I step onto the road, I turn around once more and look up at her house, and as I do, I glimpse Maggie standing in the upstairs window. Something about the way she stands there, bath towel tucked around her, watching me, makes me feel a little uneasy. I feel bad that whatever message she's trying to give me, I'm not getting.

I walk from Maggie's to Nora's to pick Mum up for a coffee, saying hello to everyone who passes me. I'd been in supermarket queues sandwiched between my old patients in London and it hadn't occurred to either of us to acknowledge that fact, and yet here, it's like I'm suddenly visible – real.

Molly and a teenage boy I assume to be Nico, Nora's son, are sat eating ice creams on the low wall outside her house. I start to say that October is a strange time for ice cream, but then instead I just tell them to enjoy them. Nora opens the door and ushers me in.

'Is that your son?' I say, nodding at him.

'Yes. I may be mistaken, but I think he has a little crush on your daughter.'

'Good luck to him.'

'She's very polite. A credit to you and Freddie.'

Is she? I go to make a joke to that effect, but I stop myself. Maybe Freddie's not the only one trying to reinvent themselves. 'I met Maggie's husband just now,' I say. I don't want to be thought of as a village gossip, so this is a good, casual starter, it's conversational, not prying, although obviously that's my goal.

'Did you?' Nora says, motioning for me to sit down on the sofa alongside her. 'How is the bastard?'

Her choice of words completely throws me, which she obviously picks up on because she follows it with a laugh. 'Oh, excuse my language. He and I have never really seen eye to eye. He represented my husband in our divorce.'

'Oh. Sorry.'

'Don't be. My husband was a complete arsehole who had a whole other family in Guernsey that I never knew about.'

'Oh. Sorry,' I repeat, not really sure what one says to that.

She shrugs. 'What can you do, eh? But Oscar – that's Maggie's husband – well, he was fairly instrumental in me losing pretty much everything I had as he managed to make my ex-husband seem like the wronged man. So forgive me for my rather skewed view of him. Also, he's not very nice to Maggie. But that's none of our business. I'll just get your mum.'

'Um, Nora? Before you go,' I say, 'can I just ask a couple of questions about, you know – the um, bench?'

Nora darts her eyes left and right to check we're alone, then makes a point of going to the door that leads into the hallway and closing it quietly. 'What do you want to know?'

I smooth the tie-dye sheet that is covering the sofa with my hand. 'How does it work?'

'What do you mean? I thought you've done it? Maggie even told me that you did it last night. Which has pissed us all off, incidentally, because we thought you'd agreed not to.'

'It didn't work,' I say sheepishly.

'Oh. I see. Yes, now I think about it, I wouldn't know about you having done it if it had worked, would I?'

'No. And although I'm glad it didn't work now, at the time I really, really needed it to, and I want to know why it didn't, when it has before.'

She hesitates. 'I don't know whether I should tell you . . . I don't want you to think it's OK to do it all the time, when it's not.'

'I really won't do it again,' I say, meaning every word. 'I'm just interested in why it works sometimes and not others.'

'The thing is, when you sit on the bench, you have to—'

'Hello, darling, I thought I heard your voice!'

'Mum! Hello!' I say, far too loudly and too enthusiastically.

'Have I interrupted something?' Mum asks, looking first to me, then to Nora, then back to me again.

'No, nothing at all,' we chorus, far too suspiciously to throw Sniffer Dog Mum off the scent. But thankfully she lets it go.

'Well, then, ready when you are.'

Once our coffees arrive at the cafe, she wastes no time on small talk and jumps straight in with her characteristic frankness. 'So, are you and Fergus going to stay together?'

'Of course we are.' I say this without conferring with him, because the alternative, a future without him in it, is suddenly unbearable to think about.

'Have you talked today?'

'Yes, when I got back from morning surgery.'

'And?'

'And we sorted some things out.'

'Some or all?'

'Some.' I sip my coffee, relishing the buzz of the caffeine. 'It's going to take longer than a lunch break to put everything right.'

'But you think it can?' she asks earnestly. 'Be put right?'

I nod thoughtfully. 'I hope so.'

She sits back, clearly relieved. 'I think I've played a rather big part in all your problems.'

'Not really. A little part maybe, but not a starring role. Don't flatter yourself.' I smile, taking another sip of my Nescafé. I'm actually starting to prefer it.

'We were only doing what we thought was best, you know. For you both. I'd change it if I could. I wouldn't wish what you went through on anyone, especially not my own daughter.'

'It's fine. It's done. We can't change it now.' *Liar liar, pants on fire.*

'He's a nice man. Fergus. Funny.'

I smile. 'Yes.'

'No one's going to be good enough for Molly in your eyes, Jess.'

It takes me a second or two to join the dots between what we were talking about and what she just said. Then I realise. This was never about her not liking Fergus, it was about her loving me. And I get it. The smartest, kindest, most prolific donator to every charity fund going could want to marry Molly and I'd still assess him through narrowed eyes and give him the smallest Yorkshire pudding at Christmas.

Mum shakes her head. 'My mum was very disappointed when Prince Charles married Diana, because she was convinced I was a better match.'

'That would never have worked,' I say.

'Because of Camilla?'

'No,' I say, deadpan, 'because he's really into gardening, and you won't go outside now because you're terrified of getting sepsis.'

Mum lets out a loud giggle and swats my arm affectionately. I laugh too, and reach out for her hand, taking it in mine and squeezing it. She squeezes back and smiles. 'You're doing OK, Jess. You're doing OK.'

'And are you?'

She takes her hand back, pulls the shutters down. But this time I'm not going to let her.

'What do you mean?' she asks, not meeting my eye.

'Well, you haven't explained why you're not keen to go back home to London. You seem to have told the kids how unhappy you were, but not me.'

'You're busy.'

I shrug. 'Not especially. Not now. I'm really sorry if I've made you feel that I didn't have time for you, especially after Dad ... you know. I didn't mean to make you feel like you couldn't talk to me.'

'You don't want my woes as well as yours.'

'Yes, Mum, I do. I'd like to help. If I can?'

'You're lucky,' Mum says, giving me a sad smile, 'that you and Fergus have always been independent from each other, you've always led different lives. Me and your dad didn't. What he did, I did – we even worked in the same company for forty years, always taking our tea breaks, lunch breaks together. I can't quite explain how it feels when half of you just ... goes, like that – ' She snaps her fingers. 'Poof. Gone.'

I hadn't thought of it like that. My reflex after his death had been to sort out all the logistics of it for her: change the bills into her name; find her a smaller place to live that's less upkeep; sell his car, separating her life from his in practical ways. I thought that by doing those things I was acknowledging that I knew how tightly bound together their lives had been, how blurred the line had been between where she ended and Dad began, but Mum couldn't care less that I'd taken his name off the TV licence – in fact she might have preferred it stayed on there, I didn't ask. But as she finally tells me how she's really feeling, I realise that none of that really mattered and I should have been there for her emotionally. What matters is not that I buy her a new phone, but that I reply to her text the same day, or even message her without it being a response to one of hers.

'I thought that you'd moved on a bit, Mum,' I say weakly, knowing it's no excuse. 'You've been on lots of dates, met some nice people.'

'I've filled my time, Jessica, so I don't have to think about him, because if I did I might not get out of bed. I don't want to die alone, Jess. I want to feel butterflies again, feel the love that me and your dad had. But London is full of strange people, and all those dates I went on just made me feel worse, not better.'

I don't know what to say. 'That's what antibiotics are for,' I manage at last.

She gives me a sharp look. 'I mean emotionally, Jessica, for goodness' sake.'

'I know, I'm sorry. I'm just trying to lighten the mood.' I take a deep breath. 'OK. Look, Dad would want you to be happy, not lonely, and he'd be thrilled you're here, with us, and not in that godawful retirement village, so that's good. Now we just need to find you a lovely companion. This island is full of men your age.'

Mum crinkles her nose. 'But if it didn't work out I'd have to see them every day. That would be awful.'

'What about Guernsey? I'm sure there are lovely old seadogs living there. Why don't you join that website again and see if you can start chatting to one, and then you get the ferry over for lunch one day or something? That'd be something to look forward to?'

She is noncommittal, but I see her eyes starting to dance again with the possibilities and feel a wave of relief – and pride that I'd helped get some of her sparkle back.

Later in the evening, Mum heads back to Nora's and the kids retreat upstairs, sparks almost coming off their trainers with the speed at which they disappear after I say that I'll wash up. Fergus is sitting on the kitchen floor next to Iris's bed, stroking her velvet ears, when a knock comes on the back door.

'I'll get it,' I say, pulling my Marigolds off and throwing them onto the counter next to the sink.

I open the door and gasp out loud. Maggie is sheltering under an umbrella, the fur-lined hood of her coat pulled up over her head.

'Oh my goodness, Maggie, come in, you're drenched!' I stand aside for her to come in, but she doesn't move.

'Can we talk somewhere a bit more private?' she asks, obviously hearing the noise from inside my house.

'Of course!' I cast my mind about. 'I can grab the key to the surgery and we can go there?'

A few minutes later and we're sitting side by side on the sofa in the waiting room – I thought it was better than sitting opposite each other over my office table like I was about to diagnose her. I make us both a mint tea, and when I hand her a steaming mug she says, 'I'm really sorry about interrupting your evening. I just wanted to come and see you as soon as I could get away.'

It's an odd choice of words. Especially for someone who doesn't have a job, no children, and a husband who lives away most of the week.

'It's fine,' I say. 'I'm always free for a chat.'

'I spoke to Nora earlier on.'

'Oh?'

'She said that when I saw you on the cliff last night, it didn't work for you, and you wanted to know why.'

I can't help guilt showing on my face. I promised that I wouldn't do it at all, and now they all know that I completely went back on my word.

'I don't think you quite understand what you're doing.'

'I'm not doing it any more,' I blurt out. 'I've stopped.'

'Since when?'

Again, I know I must look sheepish when I admit that it has only been about ten days. It's hardly a milestone worthy of a badge.

Maggie smiles sadly. 'I was like you at the start, doing it all the time over tiny things that don't even matter. I once had a manicure and they shaped my nails round instead of square, and I repeated the day to get it right.'

I try to look surprised, as though the thought of using this power for something as trivial as nails (or hair!) would never cross my mind.

'I scraped the side of my bike along a wall once, and instead of just paying the garage the money to repaint the scratch, I redid the whole day. Break a favourite ornament: do the day again. Be a bit grumpy with someone in the shop, feel bad about it: do the day again. I was absolutely addicted to it. Addicted to getting it right. To making my day perfect.'

'I'm not addicted,' I say with a little laugh. Too late, I realise I sound smug and superior, and blush.

'Maybe not yet, but it can happen really easily. You'll start to question yourself over everything – could this be better the second time around? What could I say or do differently if I had another chance? And before you know it, you're thirty-five, desperate to have a family and your body's going into menopause.'

'But how could that even happen?' I ask, unable to put aside my cement-strong belief that I know how human bodies work.

She shrugs, 'Honestly, Jess, I have no idea. We think somehow whatever time you spend in the past gets added to your body when you come back to the present. It's the only explanation we've come up with.'

'But that means you must have done it thousands of times! Why on earth didn't you stop doing it, when you realised you were ageing faster?'

Maggie gives me a slow, sad smile. 'Why does a gambler think "just one more bet" or an alcoholic, "just one more glass"? I kept promising myself that each time would be the last, but it never was. The need to make things perfect was just too much, I couldn't stop. Nora was the same. She was so desperate to make her husband stay that she changed herself in every way she could think of, and when that didn't work, and he still left her, she tried to be someone else.' Her voice changes then, and takes on a new intensity. 'So be careful. I've ruined everything messing about with time.'

'I wouldn't say that.' Even as I say it I know it's a stupid thing to say. I hardly know anything about these women; the only thing bonding us is the thing that we're not allowed to do, so I am completely unqualified to disagree with her, but she looks so sad and broken, I feel the need to console her.

'What have you changed so far?' she asks.

I shrug, wanting to downplay my interest in it. 'Not much. Nothing important.'

'That's what you think, but every single decision you make affects the next one, and the next one. Every tiny aspect of your life has a consequence, and a reaction, and what you think is not important might not be on the face of it, but the thing that happens because of that just might affect everything. And if you go back to change one tiny thing, much more significant things may have been altered as a result. Do I make sense?'

I nod. I think I follow. 'Anyway, the last time I tried – when I saw you up there – it didn't work, so it seems a bit hit and miss. Is there a secret to it working all the time?'

'Like I'm going to tell you that,' she says, laughing. 'You'd only do it more.'

'I wouldn't,' I promise emptily.

She shakes her head. 'I'm not telling you, Jess. It's honestly not worth thinking about. Just forget you ever knew about it.'

That would be absolutely impossible for anyone to do. I press on, determined to get answers to at least some of my questions. 'Can you only go back a day at a time?' I ask. 'Or further back?'

'You can go back to whenever you like, but the only way to come back to the present is to sit on the bench again at sunset. Eileen once went back thirty years to see her dad again, before he'd passed, and she was stuck in the late eighties for a year or so because the bench wasn't there, so she couldn't come back. I told you, it's really dangerous.'

I take a deep breath before I ask my next question, because I have no idea if she's going to answer it or whether it might result in her clamming up and walking out.

'What happened to you, Maggie? Why are you so against it?'

She looks me squarely in the eyes. I know that she's assessing whether she can trust me or not, and the fact that she carries on talking obviously shows that she thinks she can, which makes me happy. 'One of the first things I did when I found out about the bench was win the lottery. Nora said that she did, too. I felt bad when we told you about it, and you were excited about giving people antibiotics and vaccines and stopping the Fire of London, and my first thought when I knew about the bench was a gun-metal-grey Range Rover with heated front massage seats – and the irony is I live on a sodding car-less island! But there we are. When I won the lottery, I was ecstatic. Fourteen point six million pounds. It was a rollover. It was brilliant. I knocked down my sad little bungalow, I even bought the bungalows either side of it for double what they were worth, bulldozed them all to the ground, and built the house of my dreams. I went to the

Maldives for Christmas – we had a slide going from our suite into the ocean, it was wonderful. Until it wasn't. Then it was really, really bad.'

'How?'

She stops for a minute, then she must decide she's got nothing left to lose so takes a deep steadying breath and starts talking. 'About five, maybe six years ago I was deeply in love with this wonderful man. He taught PE at the school. I was a teacher there, too. History. I loved it. Ironic really, considering that I've spent so much time changing my own.'

I had no idea that she used to be a teacher. Looking at her now, with her designer bag, manicured (square-tipped) nails and expensive tailoring, it's difficult to imagine her with chalk dust down her shirt, patrolling the playgrounds.

'We loved each other so much, but if the school found out we were dating we'd have lost our jobs. They were really strict on that rule. It's the only school on the island so it's not as though we could have got other jobs, so we had to keep it secret. I'd only just found out about the time travel, completely by accident by sitting there at sunset, like you did; that's why years later I came up with the idea of the rota, so it couldn't happen to anyone else. I thought being rich would make everything easier as it would mean that we didn't need to work, and we could just be together without any worries. But it made everything so much harder. Friends and family were tapping us for money the whole time, getting angry that we wouldn't clear their mortgages, or we wouldn't upgrade their cars – people on the island that I've grown up with, shaking their heads in disgust that we wouldn't put five hundred quid behind the bar whenever we walked into the pub. We became recluses. It was too much for him in the end and he moved away. He begged me to go with him, to leave everything behind, give all the money away and live a simple life, but I couldn't. I'd grown up with my parents struggling for money, working multiple jobs, and that's not what I wanted for us. So he left. A while later, I met Oscar in the first-class lounge at Heathrow. I was only there because of the lottery win, there's no way that our paths would ever have crossed when I was a secondary school teacher at the Isle of Forth school.'

She takes a steadying breath. 'Rich, entitled men are, would you believe it, pretty rich and entitled. And I hate him. I actually hate him. I hate what he's made me into, I hate that I was ever so shallow to think that winning the lottery would make my life complete. I hate the fact that I've wasted so much time with him, wasted so much time trying to make my life better, when it was actually pretty great before. I miss Tom, the kids at the school, the other teachers. I miss being normal, and liked for being me, not constantly wondering when people are nice to me, how long it's going to take until they ask me for money.'

'Give us a tenner.'

Her head slightly tilts as she assesses what I've just said, then realises it's a joke designed to defuse the seriousness of the moment and she laughs. She has a really pretty laugh. I realise that I've never heard it before. 'Sorry, I'm not used to people teasing me.'

'I'm sorry, I shouldn't joke about it. I appreciate you opening up to me about this, it's obviously been very difficult.'

'I'm not telling you any of this for you to feel pity for me.'

'I know you're not. But I do. I feel very sorry for what you've gone through, and the way that it's turned out.'

'What I've told you is just the tip of the iceberg. But I wanted to tell you enough to warn you, to tell you to enjoy the life you've got and stop pissing about trying to make it perfect, because you'll end up worse than you were before.' She looks at her slim, gold watch. 'I should go.'

As I watch her head back out into the stormy night, her distinctive Burberry umbrella blowing inside out, proving once and for all that money can't triumph over nature, I think back over the evening. I appreciate her coming – it was very brave of her to open up and share her experiences purely to save me going through the same thing – but all the same, it sounds like she was completely out of control. I'm a doctor for heaven's sake. I'm trained to be level-headed, sensible and open-minded.

I conveniently forget that I'm also meant to be honest and ethical.

22

Don't sweat the small stuff

Maggie's words stay with me all night and into the next day. I replay them over and over in my mind whenever I can. It seems to me that she did two things wrong, each at opposite ends of the spectrum. First, she made monumental, life-altering changes. She went from being a teacher to a multi-millionaire in a day. Of course that path was never going to be easy; marking essays on the democracy and dictatorship of pre-war Germany one minute then having your sunglasses polished for you next to an infinity pool in the Maldives the next – 'Fruit kebab? Lovely, don't mind if I do.'

Maggie got greedy, which was her downfall. She should have gone for five numbers and the bonus ball, not all six. No one needs that kind of money. A couple of nice holidays a year and maybe a sofa upgrade and an American double-door fridge, that's the sort of comfortable lifestyle you want, not a walk-in wardrobe with rails that rotate by a remote control. It's like people who say they want to be famous. They don't. They want the odd person to tell them they're brilliant, they don't want pictures of them buying loo roll and thrush cream splashed all over the Internet. Everything in moderation.

Secondly, she got hung up on perfecting the minutiae of a day. That's where she slipped up. I know that I once went back a day to sort my hair out, but I don't think that I can quite explain how bad it was. I really couldn't have fixed it myself. It was that or wear a hat for a month, so that's completely different to nails, which grow back so much quicker. And I only did that because it had happened on the same day that Fergus needed help; I wouldn't have been so shallow as to repeat the day for a hairstyle alone.

She did say something that I hadn't thought of, though, about Eileen. I've been so hung up on what I can change for the better, it hadn't even occurred to me that I can go back to relive a moment and not change anything at all. I could see Dad again. I could go back to a time when the kids sat on my lap, and I can breathe in their scent, I can read them a bedtime story, I can redo it and appreciate it so much more this time, because I know what they are going to change into. How quickly it is lost.

I could see Anna.

The next day I wait for Eileen to work her way through her morning patter, answering mechanically as I do most mornings: 'Yes, it is very wet', 'Yes, Evelyn is a bit late with the post today', 'Peppermint tea for me please', 'No, I didn't see Emmerdale'. And when there is a break in the conversation, as there always is at the point where she removes the teabags from the mugs because, bless her, she's not a multi-tasker, I jump in.

'Maggie came to see me yesterday.' I speak quietly because my first patient is due any minute.

'Oh? She all right?'

'She was telling me more about how bad the – you know, the bench, has been for her. She mentioned that you once went back and got stuck in the past. That must have been awful.'

She finished removing the second teabag before speaking. 'Oh God, it was! Don't get me wrong, I loved seeing my parents again, and my boys were younger. And I was slimmer – a size twelve I was, and I thought that was fat back then! I used to squeeze a tiny roll of skin above my jeans and wail to my husband, "Look at that. Look at all this fat." I didn't know what fat was back then! If I thought then that one day I'd be lugging this barge of a body around, I'd have been horrified! So it was nice to be slim again for a while.'

'So what happened?' I ask, trying to veer us away from middle-aged spread and back on track.

'Well, I went back to my dad's sixtieth birthday party. We surprised him, you see. It was at the village hall, here on the island. It was lovely, everyone came, we had bunting, and a DJ, it was smashing. I danced with him, laughed with everyone, we even had vol-au-vents with prawns in them. The salads had three dressings: thousand island, French, and honey and mustard.'

'Lovely,' I murmur.

'And then, obviously it was too late to go to the bench straight after the party because I'd missed the sunset, so I had already decided that I would stay the night back in 1987 – October it was, the fifteenth – and then come back to the present, the next evening. But I'd forgotten, you see, that after the party, my Dave and I had had an almighty row. We were both a bit tipsy, it wasn't a great time for us, arguing most of the time back then – the boys were teenagers, never saw them, so, truth be told, I couldn't wait to get to the bench the next night. But the weather was shocking and I couldn't even get up the cliff, let alone sit on the bench, so I had no choice but to go back home. I woke up the next morning to see Anne Diamond on breakfast TV, telling us all to stay in our homes because there'd been an almighty bloody storm in the night. Shanklin Pier on the Isle of Wight had even fallen into the sea, the same sea that we lived in the middle of! Well, it was three days before I could go up to the cliff again – if I'd gone before, I'd have been blown clean off – and when I did, you won't believe it, but the bench had gone! I thought it had been carried over the side of the hill onto the beach below, and taken out to sea. It was probably bobbing merrily about next to Shanklin Pier! I sat on the grass where it used to be and hoped for the best, but nothing happened. Anyway, I was distraught. I wrote to the council about replacing it, I even bought a bloody bench from the garden centre on Guernsey, and lugged it up there myself. Didn't work. I was stuck in nineteen eighty bloody seven and eight for nigh on eleven months. Mind you, Thatcher was a good prime minister. Better than the lot we've got now. But it was horrible. I had to bury my dad again. I didn't want to do that once, let alone twice. Awful time. And I was so scared of doing or saying something that would change the lovely life I have here so I was on tenterhooks the whole time, trying to do everything the same as what I did the first time round. Does that make sense?'

Her story is making my head and my heart hurt. 'So how did you come back?'

'One of my letters or phone calls must have worked – I did write a lot of them – because one day, September it was, the council reinstalled the bench – apparently it hadn't been washed out to sea, it had been in storage in the council's basement all that time after being found on the beach – and I came back to my normal life that night. But do you know, the oddest thing happened: when I came back, I had to squint to see the morning newspaper the next day, and it turned out I needed glasses! That's when I realised that messing about with time makes your body get old so much quicker – something I can't really afford at my age!'

I smile. 'Is this when you tell me you're really in your thirties?'

The door of the surgery suddenly clangs open and we both jump, so engrossed in Eileen's memories that we'd forgotten where we were.

'Morning, Doc, Eileen.'

I stand up and plaster my professional face back on. 'Mrs Garret? Come on in.'

It's a busy morning. It seems as though everyone on the island has a sore throat, and the chemist has run out of Strepsils. There should be another batch arriving on the ferry later today, but in the meantime Ruth is going to have a run on ginger and honey in the local shop. I definitely took the convenience aspect of my life in London for granted when we lived there; the idea of running out of Strepsils would have been absolutely ridiculous. There were a dozen local shops who with just one phone call would have brought some packets straight to the door, along with a pint of milk and some custard creams. I didn't miss much else about it, though.

There's no time to ask Eileen anything else, and even if there had been, her morning of reminiscing seems to have put her in a downcast mood. Normally I can hear her chatting away to the waiting patients whenever my door opens, and if it's not her voice I can hear, there is almost certainly some Elvis pumping out from the stereo in the corner, but the mood today is different.

'Is everything OK, Eileen? I hope I didn't upset you this morning?' I ask, when the last patient of the day has been dispatched to Ruth's shop to buy some salt to gargle with while he waits along with the rest of the island for the drugs to come in.

She shakes her head. 'I'm all right. It just took me back.' She sighs, giving her shoulders a heavy shrug. 'Which is the problem, isn't it? Going back. Your memory plays tricks on you, and you only remember the good things without the bad, or the bad things without the good.'

'I'm not sure I follow,' I say.

'I wanted to go back to Dad's birthday party, because I remembered it being a wonderful night. We danced, we laughed and there were three salad dressings, thousand—'

'Yes, you said.'

'Yes, so I did. But you see, over the years, I'd forgotten that the night ended with an argument, and the awful storm that followed it. So it wasn't all good. And then the times that you think, that was an awful period of my life – actually, often it wasn't entirely bad. People still sometimes said kind things, you still had moments when you were happy in amongst all the sadness.'

'Is that the last time you went back?'

Eileen nods. 'To be honest, I only did it a handful of times before that, more for fun than anything else, but getting stuck in the past scared me. It's not that I didn't want to risk getting stuck again, or looking older – Maggie thinks it is, but it's not. It's that I don't want to see or change anything else, I don't want to interfere with my memories any more. Your brain remembers what it wants to, and I don't want to bring to the front of my brain things that I'd buried at the back. They're at the back for a reason.'

But what if they're not meant to be stuck at the back? I wonder. What if you only put them there because you didn't know any better? 'How did you go back so many years?' I ask her, making sure that I phrase it nonchalantly and ask it with a tone of voice that's conversational, not curious. As though I'm not asking for myself, you understand – just to be polite.

'Same way as you did,' she replies.

'To be honest, it's been a bit hit and miss with me. Sometimes it's worked, sometimes it hasn't.'

'Are you sure you were thinking about the moment you wanted to go back to? You have to replay the thing in your head while you look at the sunset. You can't get distracted and let your mind wander off. You probably did, that's what must have happened. It's happened to me a couple of times too, believe it or not.'

It all makes sense now. My pulse starts racing. The first time it happened, I was thinking about all the things that had gone wrong that day – me snapping at Eileen, her fainting, Liam stealing Zebedee's coat, none of my family talking to each other. The same for the next time: my mind had been filled with thoughts about Molly's cleavage photo and Mum's arrival on the island. Without even realising how it worked I was doing it right, which is probably the only time in my life that I've got something right without sweating blood trying.

The only time it hadn't worked was when I was sitting on the bench with Maggie on the day of my and Fergus's argument. She was shouting at me to stop looking at the sun and I was trying to block her out, so I wasn't thinking of anything to do with earlier in the day, just how annoying she was being, that's why it hadn't worked.

Thank you, Eileen, and your wonderful ability not to filter your thoughts before you open your mouth.

23

Charming conman looking for love, laughter and all your money

The home phone rings just before five a.m. on the morning of Sunday, 2 November. Before either of us move to get it, Fergus and I swap a look that even in the pre-dawn fogginess says, 'This can't be good.'

It was a middle-of-the-night phone call that announced my grandma's heart attack, which killed her four days later. Another one – and I'm not sure this counts as it was dialled at lunchtime in Australia, so technically it might count as a daytime call – told us that Fergus's brother had been bitten by a venomous insect and needed his thumb amputated. So, understandably, neither of us are in a hurry to answer this one, but as I'm the only doctor who isn't separated by a body of water from everyone else on the island, I have no choice.

The voice on the other end of the phone is raspy but familiar. 'Jessica, it's me. I'm using the phone in the hotel. Can you come and get me? And can you bring your purse?'

'Mum? What's happened? Where are you?'

'I'm at the Redwood Lodge hotel in Guernsey,' she says, as though it's absolutely normal and natural to be at a hotel on a different island, rather than tucked up in bed in Nora's spare room two hundred metres down the road.

I rub my eyes. 'What on earth are you doing there?'

'I'll tell you everything when you get here. Can you hurry, though?'

'It's going to take a while, Mum, I'm not going to lie.' As it's a Sunday the first ferry doesn't leave until eleven, so I'm faced with five hours pacing back and forth over the floorboards in the house, wearing them down. Fergus makes a few phone calls and one of his new fishermen friends agrees to take me on his trawler. Fergus insists on coming too, and after I make all the noises I think he knew I would about being a strong, confident woman, and totally able to deal with whatever is happening, I'm grateful he persists. Both for the emotional support and also because quite a few times he manages to stop me falling over the back of the boat after it lurches into the waves.

Four hundred and eighty-three pounds. That's the amount that I've put on my credit card an hour later, after my wobbly sea legs somehow took me to the hotel. So before I've even brushed my teeth this morning, I've somehow spent our monthly food budget. And I have absolutely nothing to show for it apart from a very chastened mother who met a charming sixty-year-old grifter called Sidney on greyhairtwinkleintheeye.com. He invited her for a slap-up meal followed by an overnight stay at one of Guernsey's finest hostelries, champagne sent up to the room, the works – and then legged it with Mum's purse before sunrise, leaving her with the bill.

Had it not been for a weak bladder prompting a pre-dawn toilet break, Mum wouldn't have discovered the missing man, and missing purse, until after he'd tried, and probably succeeded, in using her cards in numerous shops up and down the length of St Peter Port. Thankfully I am able to cancel all the cards before the shops open. As we go through the revolving doors of the hotel out onto the street I try to make a joke about it being lucky Mum's conman was so old and doesn't know how to shop on the Internet, or it would have been a different story, but Mum doesn't find it funny, murmuring, 'Too soon, Jessica,' into the ground, which her eyes have been resolutely chained to since I picked her up.

'I feel such a fool.'

We're sitting in a cafe a few streets away from the hotel. Fergus has bought us all a big pot of tea and a scone each. Mum's remains untouched on her plate.

'Don't be silly, Joy, the world is filled with conmen,' Fergus says bracingly. 'You weren't to know.'

'He was so good looking, and a good ten years younger than me. I should have known that he wouldn't look twice at me without a good reason.'

'Mum, you're a really attractive woman,' I say, and it's not a platitude – she really is.

'I'm an old stupid woman, Jessica, that's what I am. An old woman who's lonely as hell and is desperately trying to remember what it's like to feel wanted and loved.'

I stare at her. That's the most honest she's ever been in front of Fergus. She doesn't cry (she's not the crying type, I get that from her) but she's as near to it as I've ever seen her. For all their bickering and eye-rolling, she and Dad were deeply in love for nearly fifty years, and until recently I've never stopped to imagine, really imagine, the gaping void he's left in her life, and the desperate need to fill it with something that helps her step out of her loneliness. I feel so guilty that I suggested this date in the first place. Well, not *this* date, no daughter would knowingly set their mother up with an unscrupulous thief, but I certainly convinced her to give dating a go again.

'We love you,' I offer simply. I know that's woefully inadequate, but there's nothing else I can really say. I don't know how she feels; I haven't had a marriage like hers, not until this last month anyway, and I'm not entirely convinced this new phase in mine and Fergus's relationship is permanent.

'I don't know why,' Mum says sadly. 'I cause far more problems than I intend to.'

'No you don't.'

'I've made awful decisions with you, ones that I really regret. And I obviously haven't learnt anything, because I'm still making a monumental mess of my life.'

'No you're not. You can't blame yourself for this, or any of it, for that matter. You did what you thought was best in the moment. That's all any of us can do.'

'I'm a burden to you, Jess. I've messed up your relationship. You've got enough on your plate with young Liam and Molly, you don't need me adding to it all.'

'But you don't add to it. I actually like having you around.'

'We all do,' Fergus adds. 'And I think I need to apologise about what you heard the other week. Tensions were running high and I said some things I shouldn't have, Joy. I hope you can forgive me and come back with us.'

I'm a little stunned that Fergus said that. I didn't ask him to apologise to Mum. I wouldn't either, because he was actually right about most of it, but the fact he has, off his own back, just shows that he's not the same man that I left London with in August.

Mum shakes her head. 'There's nothing to forgive, Fergus, I'm ashamed of how I behaved back then, but I'm not going to come back to the island, I've made my mind up. I'm going back to London tomorrow. You can send my things on to me.'

'No, please don't, I don't want you to. You're unhappy there.' I try to reach out for her hand across the cafe table but she moves hers away and picks up her empty handbag, placing it primly in her lap.

'I have to. If I didn't know it before today, I do now.'

'Joy, please, you've just had a really rubbish thing happen to you. I'm sorry you had to go through that, but come back to Forth with us.' Fergus reaches over, and places his big soft hand on top of Mum's paper-thin one. 'Please?'

A moment of silent tension hangs over our table while she considers what he's said.

'Thank you,' I mouth to him as she gives a small, reluctant nod and allows us to lead her out of the cafe and towards the ferry port.

Being November, sunset is mid-afternoon, so I only just make it to the bench in time as the ferry doesn't dock back on Forth until two thirty. Apparently Mum met Sidney online a fortnight ago, but only agreed to meet, aptly, on the night of Halloween. ('I remember it was then as Molly came to call for Nico in her costume, and I was about to telephone Sidney for the first time.') So when I'm sitting on the bench, breathless from the run up the hill, it's easy to go back to that day: I just picture me buying the pumpkin from Keith's allotment on the morning of 31 October and wondering why it was that I'd never bought one before. (After spending over an hour trying to carve it, breaking two knives and bending a pair of kitchen scissors in the process, the reason became clearer.)

When I wake up in the morning, the first thing I do is check my phone (yes, it's 31 October again!), head straight to Nora's and sit at her kitchen table while Mum has a shower upstairs. It's easy to log into Mum's laptop; her password is literally 'password', which makes me realise that enrolling her on the community course on cyber security for the over sixty-fives last year was a complete waste of time and money.

The most recent email in her inbox is from him. Sidney Callahan. If that's even his real name. They've been messaging for a few days. I scroll through the thread.

> *S.D. Callahan: I see from your profile you like musical theatre and vegetarian food? My favourite is Miss Saigon, you? And although I'm not strictly a vegetarian (don't shoot me, haha) I am partial to a nice roasted vegetable quiche.*
> *Joy Potter: I also like Miss Saigon, although Les Mis is still my favourite. Have you ever tried laying asparagus on the top of your quiche? It is delicious!*

Oh my days. This is awful and it's making me nauseous. Thank goodness Fergus and I are getting back on track and I never have to make flirty small talk with strange men on the Internet. I scroll through to the last message.

He is suggesting they meet up in a couple of days' time. He apparently lives on the south coast of England, but goes to Guernsey frequently:

> *Not to be presumptuous you understand, but I'd love to treat you to dinner and the Redwood Lodge has a magnificent sea view.*

I'm delighted to see that Mum hasn't replied to this message. I'm just in time.

> *Hello, Sidney, thank you for your lovely message. Sadly I won't be able to meet you after all. Please don't message me again, as I don't think we'd be very compatible. Have a nice life, Joy.*

I'm about to press send, I am, I promise. But then another thought pops into my head, and I delete what I've just typed and write instead,

Hi, Sidney, that sounds wonderful, I look forward to meeting you finally. See you at 7 p.m. on Saturday night. I'll be wearing green. Much love, Joy x

Once I'm sure it's sent, I delete all the emails from him from her machine and block his email address from ever being able to contact her again. I slam the laptop shut just as Mum swoops into the kitchen, a towel wrapped around her head. Clean of make-up and devoid of her normally backcombed hair, she looks every one of her seventy-plus years, but aside from that, her eyes are dancing with excitement and anticipation. I feel momentarily bad, before remembering why I'm doing this.

'Sorry for keeping you waiting, darling,' she smiles at me then her face freezes. 'You look guilty, what have you done?'

'I'm sorry, Mum, but you had an email when you were upstairs, from a man called Sidney. He seemed a bit forward, so I googled his name, and it turns out, he's already married.'

'He's not!' she gasps. 'The scoundrel!'

'I know, it's awful. So I took the liberty of blocking him so he won't be able to message you again.'

She sits down heavily onto a dining chair. 'Honestly, what is wrong with people? Oh what a shame. While I was in the shower I'd just made up my mind to meet him. I was looking forward to going to Guernsey this weekend.'

'I know, sorry, Mum. How about you and I go to hit the January sales after Christmas? We'll make a weekend of it.'

'Would you really do that? You'd spend the weekend with me?'

'Of course I would,' I say, a little sad that it is such a shock to her that I would even consider it. 'I would say that we'll ask

Molly as well, and have a three-generation girls' shopping trip, but I know she wouldn't come.'

'She'll come back to you eventually,' Mum says, with a certainty that's a little disconcerting. But I haven't got time to dwell on it; I need to think up an alibi of why I need to go away for the weekend and look up ferry times to Guernsey on a Saturday afternoon.

It's not unlike that scene from *Pretty Woman* where the lady is sitting at the bar of a luxury hotel, resplendent in a beautiful flowing gown, waiting for her date to show up with diamonds – except the man I'm meeting intends to steal my jewellery, not give me some. I'm also not remotely resplendent, but I am wearing lipstick, for the first time in ages. The bar is, however, surprisingly really nice, dripping with an old-school glamour that oozes sophistication, with its oak-panelling, heavy red drapes and opulent candelabra that casts long, seductive shadows over everything, including me.

'Joy?' comes a deep, gravelly voice from behind me.

I swivel around and can't help catching my breath. Mum had said that he was attractive, but what she didn't say was that Sidney Callahan stepped out of a Next catalogue and straight into the bar at the Redwood Lodge.

'Wow, you look so much younger in person,' he says lasciviously, not quite licking his lips, but I can tell he wants to. He really is very good looking. 'Normally it's the other way around and ladies publish a photo from two decades ago, but you've done the opposite. Sorry, how very ungentlemanly to talk about a woman's age. Forgive me.' He puts his hand on his chest to really hammer the point home that he's speaking from the heart.

'I have to be honest with you,' I say.

He raises an eyebrow, waiting for my confession.

I smile coyly, 'I've had some work done.'

'Haven't we all,' he simpers. 'Shall we? Great dress by the way, it really brings out the green in your eyes.'

I just about stop myself from rolling my eyes – which are brown, by the way.

'And your hair is a lot longer than in your photo.'

'I've got extensions. They say money can't buy happiness,' I laugh, 'but it can shave years off you.'

We have four courses – I insist on it. We're near France after all, we need cheese. And a nice bottle of red to go with it. Perhaps one from towards the end of the thick, leather-bound wine list, instead of one from the first page like everybody else does. 'It's only money, after all, isn't it?' I giggle. Is this what it's like to be Maggie, I wonder?

He leans in, mere inches away from my face and his aftershave is musky, expensive. 'How about a nightcap, up in my room?'

'Are you suggesting I spend the night with you?' I say from underneath my eyelashes. I'm glad I can't actually see the way I'm behaving because it is shameless and mortifying, but it is all for a good cause.

'I'm a gentleman.' He smiles. 'I wouldn't dream of being so forward. Just a drink, then the rest is up to you.'

'Well, I hope you have a suite.'

'I can upgrade?'

'Why don't you go and do that while I powder my nose, and I'll meet you back in the bar?'

I hardly recognise myself when I catch sight of myself in the mirror in the ladies. My cheeks are flushed, my eyes are alive – it's almost as though my mind hasn't told my body that it's all an act. He doesn't really want to sleep with me, I tell myself, although I'm sure I could glimpse a bulge in his trousers that wasn't there before as he trotted off to reception as quick as he could. A tiny part of me – minuscule, so small I don't even know why I'm mentioning it – muses that it is possible that I could actually be pulled into all sorts of rude positions by this debonair stranger on a hundred-count Egyptian hotel bedding, and then go back again and erase the day. He has however, slept with my mother. Sort of. But it's certainly an option.

In fact, why stop there? I have the ability to just delete days and rewind time whenever I feel like it, so why don't I spend the weekend doing all the things I've always wanted to but never had the nerve to before? I could snort cocaine, sleep with a woman, bungee jump off the Eiffel Tower! Actually, I've never wanted to do any of those things – I'm remarkably unremarkable when it comes to experimentation, I don't know why, I just don't have the gene for spontaneity – but if I wanted to I absolutely could. The possibilities are endless. I'm starting to think that this time travel thing is wasted on someone like me.

'Sorted?' I purr as I re-join Sidney in the bar.

He dangles the key seductively in front of me and I see that the room now has a name not a number, which means it must be expensive. 'Sorted. Shall we?'

'Do you mind if I nip up ahead of you, to put something a lot less comfortable on?'

His eyes pop out of his head on cartoon-like stalks. Yes, he definitely licked his lip then. 'Absolutely. I'll give you a fifteen-minute head start.'

'Why don't you order some champagne?' I suggest. 'Put it on the tab.'

As soon as I'm up in the room, I pull out a sheaf of monogrammed hotel writing paper from the leather folder on the desk and pick up the matching pen.

Sidney,
   Thank you for a truly wonderful evening, I'm sorry I've had to go suddenly, leaving you with the bill for dinner and this gorgeous

suite – it must have cost you a fortune! But if you're the gentleman you keep telling me you are, you wouldn't have let me pay my share anyway, so I know you won't mind.

I know my exit may seem very abrupt, but I suddenly remembered that thieving conmen aren't my type after all.

Much love, Joy xx

24

New friends and lock-ins

A few uneventful weeks later, I have a drink with Maggie. It isn't planned. Fergus has a skittles match and I surprise him by coming down to the pub and watching him play, which makes his eyes light up like a child spotting their busy parent standing on the sidelines of a school football game. We've been doing more of this type of thing lately: him bringing my lunch to me at the surgery; me suggesting we watch a film I know he'd like to watch, that in the past I'd have dismissed out of hand. We even held hands when we walked Iris the other night together on the beach. It felt unnaturally natural, if that makes any sense.

Maggie popped into the pub to buy herself a bottle of wine to drink alone at home, and I asked her if she fancied staying to have a drink with me. I'm a bit bored if I'm honest. Skittles isn't the most adrenaline-inducing game at the best of times, and with nine players on each team, Fergus has his turn every twenty-five minutes or so, and I didn't bring a book.

The words, 'I'll get this round,' are barely out of Maggie's mouth before I insist on getting the next one. I don't want her to assume that I'm like all the other people who just want free handouts, but apparently I don't mind her thinking that I'm either a complete desperado with no friends or an alcoholic lush.

'I'm glad you moved here,' she says a few minutes later, slipping onto the bench next to me and handing me a large glass of red wine.

'Really?'

'Really. You've brought some life back into the island. You and Freddie. Everyone says so.'

'Rather unexpectedly, the island's sort of done the same to us,' I say.

Maggie raises a thin designer eyebrow. 'Oh?'

I take a sip of my drink. 'We weren't very happy in London, to be honest. We barely saw each other, the kids were running riot, Fer-ddie was doing God knows what with God knows who—'

'Do you think he was having an affair?'

Well, I screamed as much to him a few weeks ago. But if I honestly stop to think about it? 'No.' I shake my head. 'I don't. But I think he might have done had we not changed our lives. And to be honest, I don't think I was far behind him.'

'Oscar's got a girlfriend in London. Her name's Shelby.' Maggie says this in a way that someone might say, 'I'm thinking of getting a trim tomorrow' or 'the soup of the day is minestrone', because if there was a hint of emotion or sadness in her voice then I certainly couldn't detect it.

'How do you know?'

'Oh, you know. The obvious: new aftershave, new monogrammed cufflinks, things no one buys themselves. His phone's off ninety per cent of the time when he's in London. Oh, and the small fact that she's called me and told me.'

'What?'

'Yes. A while ago now, she phoned me one afternoon and told me that he doesn't love me any more, and I must stop blackmailing him to stay.'

'And are you?'

'Am I what?'

'Blackmailing him?' I wonder as I say it if I've overstepped the mark, but when a friendship starts off the way that mine and Maggie's did, with one of you holding a speculum in one hand and a tube of lube in the other, no subject is really off limits.

'Am I heck. I want him to leave. I even packed his things for him that very day, but he begged me to have him back. If anything, it's the other way round. He said that if we ever split up he'd take everything and make sure by the time he was finished with me I'd be nothing.'

'What a charmer.'

She shrugs. 'He's not one of the UK's top divorce lawyers for nothing.'

'Would it be so bad though?' I ask, because from where I'm sitting, Maggie's got nothing to lose. Not really.

'What? Being nothing again?'

'It doesn't sound like you were nothing before, Maggie. It sounds like you were much happier, living a simpler life. Doing a job you love, with a man you love.'

'But that was before I knew any different, wasn't it?'

'Is it worth it, though? Is having it all really worth putting up with all the other crap that comes with it? Is it worth staying married to such a creep?'

Maggie takes a sip of her wine, considering my question. 'He's not a creep all the time. He's actually quite sweet sometimes. He bought me a beautiful orchid last week.'

'And it didn't cross your mind that he got two for the price of one, and Shelby's currently watering hers?'

She flinches as though I've slapped her. 'Oof, you don't mince your words, do you?'

'Not if I can help it.' I cover her hand with mine. 'Look, I know we don't know each other really well yet, but I'm glad that you feel that you can confide in me. I'm a good keeper of secrets.'

'You haven't got much choice to be anything else living on this island, do you?' She laughs. 'And you thought your life would be less difficult living here!'

'It's both simpler and far more complex than I could ever have imagined.' I take a sip of my wine. 'Can I ask you something, though?'

She nods.

'Why not change it? Why not wipe it all away and start again from before it all went wrong? You know how to. Why not use it?'

'You mean go back to being a teacher? The simple life?'

I shrug as if it's a no-brainer, which to me, as yet unburned by the bench, it is. 'Why not?'

'I have thought about it. But I looked him up – Tom, I mean – online, to see where he was, what he'd done with his life, and there was a photo of him on Google images . . . Hang on, I'll show you.'

She digs out her phone from her bag and her fingers fly across it. A photo fills the screen. An attractive man with an open, smiling face is carrying a baby girl and holding hands with another little girl, both pretty and blonde. The three of them have the same pointed chin and dimples.

'So as you can see,' Maggie says, her voice determinedly upbeat, 'he's obviously moved on. And I couldn't live with myself if I thought that me going back might wipe these two little girls out. We have no idea how this works, not really, and it was too big a risk. She smiles at me weakly, all bravado stripped away. 'So there we go. I made my bed with fine Italian linen, and now I have to lie in it.'

'But even if you don't go back that far, you can still go back and not meet Oscar? Take a different flight, use a different airport. It doesn't need to be Tom or Oscar, it could be neither. You could meet someone else.'

'I'm never changing anything again,' she says firmly. 'Not through the bench, anyway. I'll have to put up with him for a bit longer while I figure out what to do.'

'Here's to leading complicated lives,' I say, holding my glass out, and Maggie clinks hers against it.

As promised, I buy the next wine, and once I know that the glass Maggie had bought was double the price of the house wine I would have chosen had I gone first, I pledge to drink this round considerably slower. We're halfway through it when the door to the pub bangs open with unnecessary fanfare and six old, already fairly tipsy, women laugh their way inside, not unlike a Beryl Cook painting. I turn to Maggie to raise my eyebrows at her in a conspiratorial 'look at the state of them' type way, but as I do I glimpse Eileen Duggan in the middle of them – linking arms with my mother.

'Isn't that your mum?' Maggie says, smiling over at her.

'Looks like it,' I say from between my fingers. Mum gives me a wave as she congas to the bar.

'Why doesn't she join us?'

I search my own feelings for why I'm finding the thought of it so uncomfortable. 'We don't really have that kind of relationship,' I say at last.

'What kind would that be?'

'The mother-daughter going out drinking together relationship. She's my mum, not my friend.'

'You're not going out drinking with her. You're out with me, she's out with them, and you've both ended up in the same place. Her name's Joy, isn't it? Joy, Joy! Coo-ee.'

'No Maggie, don't—'

But it's too late. Mum squeezes next to us on the bench, her cheeks flushed, her eyes twinkling with the effects of two or three gin and tonics.

'Hello, daughter of mine. Fancy you being out in a pub!'

'I could say the same to you, mother of mine,' I say drily.

'Me and the girls from the book club thought we'd have a pre-Christmas night out.'

'It's December the first.'

'Exactly! It's Christmas!' Her Noddy Holder impression is outstanding. 'It's Maggie, isn't it?' Mum leans across me to shake Maggie's hand. 'It's so nice that Jessica's made a friend. And such a pretty one.'

I'm suddenly six years old again. In a park. Standing next to a girl with curly hair and a dress with a bow as a belt as Mum prods me closer to her – 'such a nice friend'.

'You should be getting back to your friends, Mum. They're probably wondering where you are.'

'Ooo, you're right. OK, help me up a second. Right, see you two later. Lovely to meet you, Maggie. See you in the week, Jess.'

We watch her wobble her way to the bar. Keith's joined the throng and hands Mum a Baileys, which she gratefully accepts. I definitely made the right decision going to Guernsey and thwarting Sidney's assault on both her belongings and her self-confidence.

'She seems fun,' Maggie offers.

'Doesn't she?'

'I sense some Mummy-issues.'

I laugh. 'No, she's great. We're closer now than we were. It's a work in progress.'

Maggie studies the group of women at the bar for a few seconds then says steadily, 'I lost my parents when I was a teenager. Life's short, Jess.'

Fergus

It makes a change for it to be Jess's turn to comically tiptoe up the stairs, shoes in hand to try to muffle the sound of her footsteps. Someone hasn't told the floorboards to play along, though, as every step she takes is accompanied by a loud, obnoxious creak. Fergus smiles as he hears her telling them to shush, but they don't appear to be listening.

'Did you have fun?' Fergus asks from the dark bed that Jess has just bumped into.

'Sorry, did I wake you?'

His skittles match ended around nine, and Jess and Maggie were having so much fun, laughing, properly laughing, that even though he was planning on joining them, he decided not to, so he feigned tiredness and left them to it. 'No, I was dozing, but I couldn't sleep properly until I knew you were back safely.' The house was far too quiet and empty without her in it this evening and he didn't like it at all, wandering through the rooms, starting a TV programme, turning it off, picking up a book, putting it down, he just couldn't settle. Even the kids asked a few times when she'd be back and didn't want to go to bed until she returned. 'It's been really odd you not being here tonight,' he says. 'I think that's the first time I've been in the house at night with the kids without you here.'

He half expects her to reply something along the lines of, 'Now you know what it feels like,' but she doesn't. Maybe that was then. This is now. Biting remonstrations and snippy asides was what the old them did. Not this one. Not island Jess and Freddie. Island Jess and Freddie are fun, yet calm. Loyal, dependable, a real family-oriented couple. The type of couple that spoon each other in the darkness, her fitting her slender body into the curve of his back and reaching for his hand to hold as she falls asleep.

He likes this version of them a lot.

25

Christmas comes but twice a year

I shouldn't have done it. What was I thinking? I clearly wasn't thinking. It's all going to go horribly wrong. I did it on a complete whim. I'd promised myself I wasn't going to ever go back more than a week or two, if at all. I didn't do all the checks beforehand, either, so now I have no idea whether I'll be able to get back or not.

It's Mum's fault. She put the idea into my head this morning as she was helping me space out the baubles on the Christmas tree, while Molly was out with her friends and Liam and Fergus were at football. I'd asked them before they all scattered to their different parts of the island whether we should all do it together later, but I received a resounding 'Nah'. If Mum hadn't reminded me how much I used to love helping her and Dad do it when I was young, and followed that up with a sigh saying, 'It's such a shame your own family have never been interested in doing this with you,' then I wouldn't have even thought about it.

'We *did* all used to do it together,' I insisted. 'We'd put Christmas music on in the background. Fergus was there too, I know he was, and we were all singing and laughing. Fergus lifted Molly up to put the star on the top of it . . . she must have been nine or ten.'

'This one?' Mum said, taking it out of the box. The gold was tarnished in places, allowing the metal underneath to shine through.

I took it, handling it as delicately as though it were made of priceless gold. 'Yes.'

'You should probably get a new tree soon, this one looks like it's on its last legs.'

Bringing the plastic tree we've had for years was a last-minute decision, born mostly out of necessity as the tenants for our house in London needed the loft space.

'Why haven't you ever had a real one?' Mum asks. 'They're so much nicer.'

'I don't know really ... Fergus always wanted one, but I always said no. Too much mess that I knew no one would help me clear up, I guess.'

'They give off a lovely smell. Especially when the fire's going as well. You should get one this year.'

'Do you know what? I think we will. Don't take any more of this one out, Mum, I'll chuck it out for the bin men on Friday, or maybe I'll put it up in the surgery. I'll ask around where to get a real one tomorrow.'

Her words came back to me when I sat on the bench later reading my book. It was my turn on the rota. I'd done such a good job of not even considering a journey back in time since my trip to Guernsey a month ago to sort out Mum's love life, yet tonight it was such a battle to keep my eyes on the page and not look up at the sunset. I honestly wasn't going to, that wasn't my plan at all, but suddenly I was gripped with an almost violent urge to prove her wrong. We did have lovely Christmases where we all decorated the tree together and had fun, I know we did. I looked up, thought about decorating the tree the year Molly was nine and Liam was six – he had sloth pyjamas then, which he looked so cute in – then I looked quickly down at my book again, my hands shaking.

I've got no idea if it will work or not. All the other times my gaze stayed fixed on the sun on its whole journey into the sea, but tonight I couldn't have looked at it for more than five seconds, if that. So I'm probably worrying over nothing. But even so, as soon as I get back from the cliff I bring my laptop upstairs to the bedroom and research as much as I can about early December 2015. My heart sinks as I read that it was the wettest month ever recorded, with 230mm of rain in the UK. But it was also the warmest December ever, too. No mention of any major disruptions to rail, or ferry crossings. Or freak storms down south – only Storm Desmond on the fourth, but that was up north. And I'm certain that we always used to put our tree up after that. If it does work and I wake up tomorrow back there, then somehow I'll need to find my way to Poole, get the ferry to Guernsey, then the ferry to Forth to get back to now. Can I print out the ferry timings? Is there some way to take some money with me? This is the first time I might wake up in a different bed, not on the island. I've got a different bank card now that wouldn't work then, so there's no point taking that, and even if I stuff some money in my pyjamas or down my pants, chances are I'm going to wake up wearing different ones.

'Stop moving,' Fergus groans next to me. 'You've been tossing and turning all night.'

Have I? I know I haven't slept but I did think that I'd done a good job of pretending I have. 'Sorry.'

'Why can't you sleep?'

'I don't know.' *I do.*

'Is something bothering you?'

I can hardly tell him the truth: that I am absolutely terrified of waking up tomorrow in the same bed in a different city, with the same man with a different name, all because I want to decorate the same tree with different people. So I say, 'I don't know whether to stick with turkey this year or do a goose.'

'We've never had goose.'

'No. I thought it might be good to try something new. We've got to put the order form back into the butcher's by the end of the week.'

'And this was keeping you awake?'

'Yes. It's a big decision.'

He turns his pillow over to the cool side. 'I know I made a promise not to belittle any of your worries, that every anxiety you have is valid, but Jesus Christ, Jess, just pick a bloody bird and go to sleep.'

A few minutes pass, and an electrifying thought occurs to me: if I don't go to sleep then the day can't change. I can't time travel. It's not like the bed will start spinning and twirl me off like Dorothy in *The Wizard of Oz*; I physically have to go to sleep in order for it to work. So I won't. I'll go downstairs and have a double espresso followed by an energy drink. If I stay awake, I'll stay in the present.

'Jess. Go to sleep,' comes a whisper to my side.

'How did you know I'm not?' I whisper back into the darkness.

'Because you're wiggling your feet from side to side at a hundred miles an hour. Would an orgasm help you sleep?'

He's said similar over the years, even through the two-year drought, and I've always heaved an annoyed sigh at his suggestion.

Tonight I am tempted to say yes, but I don't. When that does happen, and I know it will soon, I don't want to be distracted by something else. And also, he's right: historically they do make me sleepy, and I need to stay awake. But it's encouraging that the idea of it was actually very pleasant indeed.

★ ★ ★

I wake to the noise of a police siren screaming past our house, and my heart in my mouth. Well, that's that then. I'm back in London.

The alarm says that it's four a.m., and there's a space in the bed beside me where Fergus should be but isn't. It surprises me for a moment, because I've got used to him always being around, before I remember that this is seven years ago, and him not being here at 4 a.m. wasn't unusual then.

He eventually stumbles in after about half an hour, bumping into the chest of drawers, stinking the room out with the coat of alcohol fumes he's wearing. He seems to have lost his feet because taking his socks off is apparently impossible.

'Fergus?' I whisper into the dark.

'Who else did you think it would be?' he slurs before turning his lamp on and blinking at the sudden brightness that pierces the room. I forgot how much I hated that wallpaper.

'Where have you been?'

'Iss my Christmas party. I told you it was tonight.'

'I know, it's just really late.' Or early.

'What, miss me, did you?' He laughs, as though that's the funniest joke he's ever heard.

'I just wondered where you were, that's all. Have you had some water?'

'Oh yes, I must remember to have some water. Because I'm only five.'

I don't say anything else. There is no point.

I can't go back to sleep. For one thing, the fumes of tequila are far too strong, and for another, it's really unsettling to be back in the pattern of non-stop bickering, each of us taking immediate offence at what the other is saying. So at around five thirty I slip quietly out of bed and go downstairs. Iris doesn't run to greet me the way she always does, and then I remember that she hasn't even been born yet; we didn't get her until 2017. It makes my head spin. I instinctively run my hands through my hair and stop in shock. Most of my hair's gone. I have a utilitarian short back and sides that at the time I thought was practical. In reality, I think, catching myself in the hall mirror, it makes me look like Fergus's shorter, less attractive brother. What was I thinking?

I sit down at the kitchen table, the room illuminated by the single corner lamp I've turned on. I'm nursing a cup of hot water and lemon because I can't find any fruit teas in the cupboard, for the reason that I used to solely exist on caffeine and didn't start buying herbal teas until we arrived on the island. *The island*. I push the thought away.

I thought I was coming back to 2015, but instead, there's a 2016 calendar hanging on the wall in front of me, and I'm trying to work out where in the month I am. On Friday 9 December in Fergus's handwriting it says 'Work Do' so I guess that it's Saturday the tenth. Which means, according to the calendar in front of me, we've got someone called Peony's wedding at four. I rack my brains, then groan. Oh God, that was a rubbish wedding. Why have I come back to today? I wanted the day when we put our tree up together, not a day where I have to feel about sixty years old and the size of a baby elephant next to all the leggy young things Fergus works with.

A couple of hours and three cups of lemon water later, I hear footsteps on the stairs and my heart starts beating faster. I don't know who it's going to be, but I feel a lump rise in my throat. I had no idea I'd feel this emotional about seeing the children younger.

Liam walks in the kitchen, yawning. His two front teeth seem too big for his seven-year-old mouth and his hair is still messed up from sleeping. He's wearing the pyjamas that have a picture of a sloth holding the branch of a tree, the ones I remembered on the bench. I rise up out of my chair to hug him, but he takes a step back. 'Liam darling!'

'What are you doing?' he asks, making me recoil slightly.

'I'm giving you a hug.'

'Why?'

'Because you've just got up.'

'And?'

'And I wanted to say good morning.'

'Why?'

'Because . . . it's nice, I suppose.' I'm baffled. Why does he think that's unusual? 'What do you want for breakfast?'

Liam eyes me with suspicion. 'What, you're going to do it for me?'

'Of course I am. What do you want?'

'I don't have to have Weetabix?'

'Not if you don't want them? Cheerios?'

His face lights up. 'We have Cheerios?'

As he says this, I remember that this is my old kitchen, my old cupboards, my old shopping habits of getting the same contents from my online Ocado account delivered at the same time every week. It was quick, healthy, no stress, no deviation, no room for spontaneity. I open the cereal cupboard, saying a little prayer beforehand that a magical box of Cheerios would magically be in there, but no.

'Sorry,' I say. 'Weetabix?'

He groans and rolls his eyes. 'Fine. Why are you here? Don't you have work?'

I almost drop the cereal box. I'd completely forgotten that I used to have Saturday surgery. I glance up at the clock. Just after eight. I could call in sick. Yes, that's what I'll have to do. I'm not going to waste my only day back in the past going to work and then Peony's wedding.

'I'm not going in today. I'll call in sick.'

Liam stares at me. 'You've never called in sick. Even when *I* was sick.'

'I'm sure I have,' I say weakly, knowing full well that he is telling the truth.

'You dropped me round to Angela's, and I vommed on her sofa. You gave her a hundred pounds when you picked me up for it to be professionally cleaned.'

'I did?' It was vaguely familiar. But then I used to do that a lot, throwing money at situations to make them go away. I should have cleaned it myself, or at least offered, but that probably wouldn't have even occurred to me back then. I let Iris off the lead in the park once and she went straight to a family's picnic and snuffled her snout into their sandwiches. I literally threw a few five pound notes at them and carted her off – I'm not even sure I said sorry. Situation dealt with, tick, people financially compensated for the inconvenience, tick. Though that event hasn't even technically happened yet, I blush at the memory. Hopefully when it happens in a year or so I'll react differently.

I leave Liam to his cereal – the same cereal the poor boy has had every morning since he's been allowed solids – and go into the living room to phone work. A voice answers that I don't recognise. It's not Pam.

'Hello, this is Dr Jessica Bay, I'm afraid I can't do my surgery this morning, I'm, um, I'm not very well. What? No, there's no need for me to speak to Robert, if you could just pass the message on, I'm very sorry. No really, I'd rather not, if you could just – oh hello, Robert, I'm really sorry, but I'm not feeling very well this morning and I really don't want to pass it on.'

My pulse is pounding. I've never missed a day of work, and I know that I never did right up until we left for the island, so I've never needed to call in before, which is why it doesn't occur to me to try to sound ill. For any other boss this might be a precursor to an incident of rage, but Robert simply says, 'Oh you poor love, let me know if you need a bed bath and I'll be right over.'

How the hell did I ever think he was gay? I must have been in absolute denial that anyone would ever find me attractive; that, and the fact that I was in desperate need of a friend, any friend. I just couldn't see it at the time.

Molly is sitting opposite Liam when I walk back in the kitchen. Like me, she has much shorter hair than she does now and her body is also completely different, much more . . . rectangular. She looks like a different child, except that I know it's her from the way she doesn't look up from her phone. Did she really have one when she was just ten? I thought she was a bit older when we'd bought her first one . . .

'Mum's pulling a sickie,' Liam says in a sing-song voice.

Molly doesn't even pull her gaze away from the screen. 'Why?'

'I thought we could put up the Christmas decorations today.'

My children look at me in confusion, their matching, pale foreheads furrowed as though it's the middle of June and celebrating Christmas is the most ridiculous thing they've ever heard of.

'It's Christmas in less than three weeks,' I explain nervously. 'Wouldn't you like that?'

'No thanks,' Molly said, taking refuge from my apparently strange behaviour behind her phone again.

'Will you shout again?' Liam asks.

'What do you mean?'

'When I was five you shouted at me because I put too many on one branch and didn't space them out.'

'I'm sure I didn't—'

'Yeah, then you moved everything that we put on after we'd gone to bed, so when we came down in the morning it looked like a different tree,' Molly adds, her voice flat.

'Then you made us stand in front of it so you could put it on Facebook,' Liam says.

'Hashtag blessed. Hashtag bollocks.'

'Molly! Language!'

Molly scrapes her chair back. 'I'm going back to bed.'

'Well, I won't do any of that this time. Shall I get the decorations out, then?' I call cheerily to her retreating back.

'Whatevs,' she shouts back without turning round.

I sigh. This is not going the way I'd hoped. But I can't give up this quickly. I turn to Liam. 'Would you like to help me, Liam?'

'Not really.'

I pause and think hard. 'What happened last year? Who decorated the tree last year?'

'What?'

'You said that I shouted the year you were five. What happened last year?' Why do I not know? How can this not be a memory?

'You were at work so Dad did it with us. It was really fun, we had music on and wore Santa hats.'

I feel sick, realising now that of course, that was the memory I was telling Mum about, yesterday-in-the-future. I'd claimed it as my own memory, but it wasn't. I'd walked in the door late one evening, exhausted from work, to see Fergus holding Molly up to put the star on the top of the tree. I didn't even stay to admire it. It would have been so easy to tell them that it looked good, that they'd done a great job, but I didn't. Instead I'd poured myself a large drink and took it up to the bath. I'd even sighed loudly about having to run it myself after a long day at work. That's why I didn't go back to that time; I can't travel back to a day that never actually happened. I'd appropriated the memory of us all doing the tree together as my own, even though I wasn't even there. When I was on the bench last night, I'd thought about Liam in those sloth pyjamas, which took me back to now. Oh my God, this is so complicated to navigate.

But I'm here now. It might be too late to change last year's Christmas, but it's not too late to make this one different.

I have to wake Fergus up in order to get the decorations out of the loft as the ladder unfolds right in the middle of our bed.

'What are you doing?' he groans, somewhat unnecessarily I think, as I'm standing on the bed with a giant stick in my hand, prodding the hatch open with the end of it.

'Getting the decorations down. We're going to do the tree today.'

He rubs his eyes. 'Why?'

'Because it'll be fun!'

'No, it won't. It won't be fun at all. Your phone will go, you'll have to rush off, the kids will carry on with it and invariably get it wrong, you'll get cross, the kids will get upset, and it'll all be shit. So no, we're not putting the tree up.'

I breathe a deep, steadying breath. I'm not going to let this ruin the day. I didn't come back here to just mutely stand by and let this family who I barely recognise carry on the way they are.

'Come on, Fergus, get up, have a shower, and let's go and buy a tree from the garden centre.'

His eyes spring open. They're hopeful, but laced with suspicion. 'A real tree?'

'Why not?' I shrug, smiling broadly.

He narrows his eyes at me. 'Are you drunk?'

I laugh. 'No, I'm not drunk. Come on – get up, have a shower, and let's get some rope to tie it to the roof. I'll tell the kids to get dressed.'

Fergus literally bounds out of bed like he is seven years old on Christmas morning. I can hear the shower being turned on and him singing 'All I Want for Christmas is You' as I go to rouse Molly and get Liam dressed.

Liam runs around the outside area of the garden centre excitedly shrieking, 'This one, no this one, no, this one!'

Molly hasn't taken her phone out of her pocket once, and is strolling around the trees. She's not smiling, but not grimacing either. It's a win!

'How big can we go?' Fergus asks me.

'Well, our ceiling is about eight foot, so . . . seven foot?'

'Seven foot!' he shouts. 'That's brilliant!'

To continue this Hallmark movie-esque scene, I decide to treat us all to steaming cups of hot chocolate in the garden centre cafe while the tree is packaged up in netting and tied to the roof of our car for us to take home. My whole family looks at me with a mixture of open-mouthed shock and deep concern when I suggest it. Fergus looks so worried, it wouldn't surprise me if he reaches over to feel my temperature, except it's normally me who does that.

Before we leave, I stop at a carousel by the till which has white baubles with names written in candy-cane red on them. I pick out a Dad, Mum, Molly and Liam, and hand them to the cashier. I know they all think I'm mad, but I don't care.

'Are you OK?' Fergus asks after we've spent the afternoon decorating the tree to the sultry tones of Mr Michael Bublé, and we've gone upstairs to get ready for the wedding.

'Yes of course. Why?'

'You just seem . . . different.'

'Different how?'

'Well . . . Happy.'

26

Mending breakages

'I can't believe that you've been together for nearly twenty years! Do you have any tips for us on how to keep the spark alive for that long?' the bride asks. I have to keep calling her the bride because I've forgotten her name again. I know that it's a flower, but not Lily or Rose. It's one of those names that you can't help commenting on when you hear it, or if it comes up in the roll call of credits at the end of a film you'd turn to the person next to you and say, 'Imagine being called that!' I only saw it on the calendar this morning, so there is really no excuse for not remembering it. Particularly as I've now attended her wedding twice.

It's a question we've been asked before, many times, so we have our answers ready and waiting, shining matching, practised smiles at the happy couple, mere hours into their marriage. Bless them.

'When you find out, make sure you tell us!' Fergus says. Cue guffaws and a back slap from the groom.

'I think the key to staying married is, never get divorced.' I smile, putting my arm around Fergus's shoulders. He subtly shrugs it off so that my hand falls limply to my side.

'You two are so funny, you must just laugh all the time,' the bride gushes.

All the time.

'It's just fun fun fun in our house,' says Fergus.

'Come on, Peony – ' *Peony.* ' – we need to go around four more tables before they can serve the dessert. Enjoy the rest of the day, thank you so much for coming.'

'And for the gravy boat,' Peony adds. 'We've decided to make it a tradition to have a family roast with both sets of in-laws every other Sunday, so it'll get a lot of use.'

'That sounds really – lovely.' I keep my smile fixed in place until I'm sure the newly-weds are definitely out of earshot.

Fergus stands up, throwing his napkin on his chair. 'Make sure they leave me dessert – the chocolate one, nothing with fruit. Just going to the loo.'

As I sit alone I watch Peony throwing her head back with laughter at what someone as equally hilarious as me had just said on the next table. People often say that brides 'glow' but it is incredible the way this young woman just radiates happiness. The groom, Fergus's much younger colleague Simon (although to be fair most of Fergus's colleagues were much younger, PR certainly seems to be a young person's game), now has his hand on the small of Peony's back. He is barely touching her, just skimming her skin with his fingertips, just enough for her to know that he's there, just standing next to her, just being in love. While she is still talking to the guests on Table 4, not even pausing for breath, Peony reaches round her back and her fingers find her new husband's, brushing the very tips of his fingers with her own.

It's a secret signal. *'I love you so much.' 'I know you do. And I love you.' 'I think you'll find I love you more.'* I miss Fergus. Not the Fergus who has just gone to the bathroom, the one I left at home last night.

'That paté's gone right through me, and there's no bog roll. Have you got any wet wipes?'

'What?'

Fergus stands impatiently next to me with his hands on his hips. 'Have you got any tissues or wet wipes in your bag?'

I feel a surge of guilt: I should have remembered the paté was off and told him to have the ham and melon, like me. 'I might have some tissues ...' I rummage through my handbag, momentarily elated at finding my favourite lip balm I'd thought I'd lost in an inside pocket. No wipes though. 'Oh, hang on – ' I remember this now from before, giving him a used tissue from my sleeve. I pull it out – 'You can have this. It's a bit snotty, but fold it over.'

Fergus grabs the tissue out of my hand and waddles back to the bathroom.

The dessert plates are cleared away, the speeches have been laboured through – I forgot that the best man had used a PowerPoint. It was just as laborious second time around. I take my phone out of my bag and dial home. The babysitter, a cheery sixty-something Welsh neighbour called Angela, answers on the fourth ring.

'Everything OK there, Angela?'

'Fine. I haven't seen the kids at all. It's like being staff in a hotel, isn't it? I took their trays up to them in their room, they took it from me without a word, the door shut again, and now I've just gone up to find the trays with empty plates outside their door. Is this what it's always like?'

Was it?

'Also,' Angela says, 'you said in your text message that you'd like me to put your tree and decorations up for you while you were out, but I see you've already done it. It looks lovely.'

Who the hell outsources their family Christmas decorations to their babysitter?

That would have been me, I guess.

Fergus gives no argument at all when I suggest leaving the reception early. Five years ago, first time around, we stayed until we were so paralytic we had to stop the taxi twice on the way home for him to be sick, and I had my head out of the window like a drunk terrier. Tonight, we're home by eight. The kids are meant to be asleep, but I know they're not. They weren't even asleep the last time we came back from this wedding, and that was after one a.m.

'I'll just give the kids a kiss,' I say, kicking off my heels inside the door while Fergus pays Angela.

'Good one,' he says. 'Bye, Angela, thanks again.'

'Night, Angela.' I wait for the door to close behind her before I ask, 'What do you mean?'

'About what?'

'You said "good one" when I said I was going to kiss the kids.'

'Just that you don't normally do that. You say, time for bed, they go upstairs and play video games until I prise the controller out of their sweaty hands when they're asleep.'

Really? I'm sure I was more hands-on than that, I must have been. I know I wasn't going to be winning any awards for my parenting skills, but I wasn't that bad, surely? Not when they were this young? I head upstairs to prove him wrong.

'Knock knock, hey, Moll, can I come in?'

Molly's sitting cross-legged on her bed when I peer round the door, her phone propped up on a cushion facing her, her own reflection sullenly looking sideways at the rude intruder in the doorway.

'Whatcha doin'?' I say in what I hope is kid-speak.

'Nothing. What do you want?'

'Just wondered if you fancied a chat about anything? We haven't talked for ages, and I want to know what's going on in Molly Land.'

'Why?' she asks with narrowed eyes.

I tentatively sit down on the edge of the bed alongside her, and when she doesn't object, I continue, 'I have no idea who your friends are at the moment, what you like doing . . . Tell me anything.'

'Why?'

'Because I'm your mum, and I'm interested. In anything that interests you.'

She shrugs. This could go either way. Then she says, just as cautiously as I sat down, as though she too is testing the water, trying something new and strange, 'I've got netball try-outs next week. I'm the tallest girl in the year, so the coach wants me to try out for goal shooter.'

'That's brilliant!' I exclaim. 'Which day next week? I'll make sure I iron your PE kit for it.'

'Thursday.'

'If you like, we can go to the sports shop tomorrow and get a netball hoop to attach to the back wall, so you can practise shooting?'

Her eyes light up. 'Can we? I was going to use my Christmas money to buy myself one, but then I thought that you'd say that it would ruin the wall or something.'

Now that she's mentioned it, I remember her buying herself a netball hoop and I did refuse for it to be drilled into the wall, so I bought her a stand for it that wobbled really badly. 'Nonsense, of course we can get one,' I say. 'If you get in the team will you be playing other schools?'

'Yes, the fixtures start after half term next year so we'll have a couple of months practice first, but alternate Wednesdays and Saturdays we'll be playing other schools. Or the team will. I don't know if I'll be in it. Probably not. I'll probably be shit.'

I ignore the expletive and say encouragingly, 'Well, I think you'll be awesome. Like you said, you're tall, you're strong, and if you put your mind to it, you can do it. Whatever it is. And if you do get in the team, I'll make sure that I swap shifts at work so I can be there handing out orange segments at half-time.'

'Orange what?'

'Don't they still do that? No? OK then, I'll be there shouting as loud as I can. Give me a M, give me an O—'

'Stop it. I'm embarrassed for you.' But she's smiling.

'Fine. I'll be quietly cheering you in my head, accompanied by the occasional loud hand clap.'

She averts her gaze as she asks, 'Would you really come?'

'Of course I would.' It makes me feel really sad that it's even in question, but then why wouldn't it be? The first match I ever went to of hers was just a few weeks ago on the island. I lean in to kiss her cheek, but she puts her head down and my lips land on the top of her head. It's better than nothing.

I go into Liam's room next, and am met with the exact replica of emotions: curtness, then mild irritation, then apathy, then mild interest, followed by incredulity, suspicion and then gratefulness. All because I say that I'll ring the Intellectual Property Office on Monday morning and see if his new invention can be patented. Before I do anything else, I write on a Post-it note on my bedside table, so it's the first thing I see when I wake up. *Buy netball hoop for the wall TODAY and ring IPO office re. trademarking Liam's invention of a see-through toaster.* Which is, actually, a really clever idea, because if you could see your toast toasting, you'd be able to fish it out at the perfect level of brownness. He is going to change the world one day. Or at least make an awful lot of money from it. How am I only realising this now?

I head back downstairs and suggest we get a Chinese takeaway and watch one of Fergus's action films that he loves and I really don't.

'But you hate films like that. And you said that Chinese food has that bad sodium thing in it.'

'Monosodium glutamate. Yes, but it tastes really good.'

'Tell you what,' Fergus says, retrieving the takeaway menu from the kitchen drawer, 'you've gone out of your way today to make it brilliant for everyone so why don't you choose the movie? I draw the line at anything with Hugh Grant in it, though.'

As I hand him the DVD he looks back at me and something happens. It's a fleeting, blink-and-you-miss-it moment where we're suddenly connected, and neither one of us is wanting to be anywhere else.

A couple of hours later as we get into bed and I turn out the light, Fergus says, 'Today's been one of the best days for ages.' And I know that he genuinely means it. A real Christmas tree, a hot chocolate, a free bar, a takeaway we don't normally have and he's ecstatic. And twenty minutes of me sitting on the kids' beds listening to them talk about what is important to them sent them off to sleep happy too. If it was this easy why didn't I do it before? Then I remember, with a jolt, that nothing was easy back then. I was lonely, and exhausted, and was doing the absolute best I could. It was all well and good smug future-me waltzing back in here making judgements on all the things past-me had done wrong, like some kind of Supermum, but at the time there was no other way to do things. I was a taut wire stretched to breaking point either waiting for someone to notice and help me, or counting the seconds until I snapped in half completely. Rather than judging her, I now feel achingly sorry for past-me.

Once I'm sure Fergus is asleep, I sneak back downstairs and double-check on my old laptop that the ferry timetable hasn't changed in the last five years. Annoyingly, before I can do that, I'm locked out of my laptop twice because I didn't input the right password. How can I be expected to remember one from six years ago?

In order to reach Forth by sunset, which being December is around 3.30 p.m., I need to be on a train to Poole from Victoria Station by 8 a.m. It suddenly occurs to me that until I leave 2016 for good, they'll all wonder where I am tomorrow if I've left before they get up. I can't even use the excuse of work as it's a Sunday. Where could I be? What would they believe?

The sad thing is, I realise, as I sit in the dark kitchen alone, that until today, until we all did things differently, no one would probably have even noticed that I wasn't there anyway.

Fergus

Fergus isn't sure what actually happened today, if he's being completely honest. But it was bloody brilliant.

27

> Mansions are so overrated.
> And don't get me started on the
> Maldives. Ghastly place . . .

I can't say goodbye to Fergus or the kids, because I'll cry and completely blow my excuse for not being around all day. No mum or wife would give an emotional, tear-filled hug to her family – especially not the mother and wife I was – before leaving for a day of Christmas shopping at Westfield. Which is where my note on the fridge says I am. So instead I gently kiss their sleeping heads, breathing in the scent of Molly and Liam's childhood one last time, and close the front door before anyone wakes up.

I stand for a minute on my doorstep. The doorstep I'd raced down every morning for fifteen years, medical bag in one hand, car keys in the other, rushing, rushing, always rushing. I could stay forever. No one would know. The future hasn't happened yet for them, they wouldn't know any different. It's not as though there's another version of us that's going about their business on the island, oblivious to the fact I'm in London six years before, because 2022 hasn't yet dawned. I could stay here, now, and drink it all in, make it better every day, not just for one day. Last night, when I was on my old laptop planning my route home to the island, I went onto Ocado and amended the online shopping order to also include Cheerios, peppermint tea and four Cadbury's chocolate selection boxes to open on Christmas Day. After that I sat there in the semi-darkness thinking of what else I can do, how else I can change the 'us' of six years ago.

I have the same thoughts now, standing on the street in front of my old house, one magnet pulling me back inside, the other drawing me back to the island. If I stayed longer, made different choices, put the children, me, Fergus first, just think of how much I could improve everything. But then it's not just up to me, is it? I know it's not all my fault; Fergus was hardly blameless for the state we were in, but change has to start somewhere and I ache to get going with it now. I have to make my mind up soon because they'll all wake up any minute and take the decision away from me. Part of me hopes they do.

I'm suddenly woken from my daze by a familiar voice calling my name. 'Jess! You're up early!'

'Mum!'

Mum is half walking, half running down the pavement towards me, shaking a white envelope at me. 'I thought you'd all be asleep. I was just going to post this through your letter box.'

'What is it?'

'Your Christmas card. We're delivering them all by hand this year, do our bit for climate change.'

It's unclear what part of delivering post by hand after driving round London in a diesel car does, in Mum's eyes, influence climate change for the better, but I don't say anything. My blood suddenly runs cold.

'We?'

'Me and Dad. He's in the car, he couldn't be bothered to get out.'

I have to reach out to hold Mum's arm. I can't breathe. Coming back was about my children, recapturing their younger days. Proving a point. This wasn't about Dad, it never even crossed my mind that he would still be here, it seems he's been gone for so long, I've blurred my memories of when he was here and when he wasn't.

'Ian! Ian! I think she's fainting, don't just sit there, you silly man, come and do something!'

A car door slams and a minute later my dad's arms are under mine, holding me up. His cold, dead body warm against mine; his breath that shouldn't be there now as strong as my own. 'There we go, love, that's it, just sit on the step there, easy does it.'

'I'll ring the bell for Fergus to come,' Mum says.

'No, no don't. Don't disturb him,' I gasp, reaching out to grasp my dad's hand tightly, before he can disappear again. His hand is warm with blood pulsing through his veins.

He puts his other arm around my shoulders and draws me closer to him until I'm resting on him, my head on his chest, and great, heaving sobs wrack my body, torrents of tears lashing my face. I can't let him go again, I can't.

Mum kneels down next to him, stroking my hair as though I'm four again and have just fallen off my bike. A hug, a kiss, a few kind words and everything will be all right. 'Whatever's the matter, darling girl?' she murmurs.

'Just let her be, Joy,' Dad says gently. 'Just let it all out, Jess, sweetheart, let it all out.'

Five years, twenty years, forty-five years of being strong, keeping it together, not falling apart all comes gushing out.

I can't stop sobbing and, what's more, I don't even try.

I don't know how long we sit like that. Me, Mum and Dad. Together. The way I'm sure we used to when I was small. The way we should have done the night we lost Anna.

I can't go back now. How can I say goodbye to him again? But then how can I stay, knowing that I'll have to live through his death again?

But I don't want this to be the last time he sees me, puffy-faced and vulnerable. The last time I saw him before he had the stroke, he was adjudicating an argument between me and Mum about something completely unimportant, whether a carbonara sauce should have cream in it or something ridiculously trivial, one of our many heated discussions that neither of us would back down from, him helplessly trapped in the middle between the two women he loves the most. But not this time. I won't let that happen.

I want us to laugh, to have fun, and for our last time together to be something magical. Not many people get this second chance to rewrite scenes from their lives the way they should have been written. I do, and I'm not going to waste it.

'Shall we go into town and see the lights?' I say, snapping out of my misery as quickly as it snuck up on me. 'We could go to Harrods and Selfridges and have hot chocolate, and maybe a glass of champagne with lunch.'

Mum stares at me. 'Harrods? Champagne? Are you mad?'

'Why not? Come on, Mum, it'll be fun. When was the last time the three of us did anything like this together?'

'But we have seventeen more cards to deliver, and some of those are south of the river.'

'I'll buy you some stamps and we'll post them in town. Come on, let's go.'

'I've taken a joint of pork out of the freezer and it's defrosting now, it'll be wasted,' Dad says. 'You can't refreeze meat, you know.'

'You can get listeria,' Mum adds.

'No you can't, that's from dairy,' I say, determined not to let my idea be cast aside in favour of defrosted pork or postal deliveries.

'Salmonella!' Dad announces with pride.

'Eggs and chicken. Come on you two, it'll be fun. Get in the car, come on, let's go.'

'I haven't driven into the city for years, Jess, I wouldn't know how,' Dad says.

'OK, I'll drive.'

'You're not insured on our car.'

'Fine, we'll get the train.'

'I haven't got my senior citizen's pass with me.'

'I'll buy us tickets. Come on, Dad, Mum, let's go.'

'Darling, honestly, it's a nice thought, it is, but neither of us have our thermals on, and if we're going to be walking around town in this weather, we really should have wrapped up a bit warmer,' says Mum.

'And I need to take my tablets at lunchtime and I haven't got them with me,' Dad adds. 'We'll do it next year, but we'll plan it properly.'

'Please.' I can feel tears pricking at my eyes again. Please don't let it end like this. I won't be here next Christmas. *Neither will you.*

'Westfield!' I say, thinking of my fictional plan. 'That's all inside, full of Christmas spirit. Let's go there, do a bit of shopping, have some lunch ...' I tail off because they're both looking at me as though I've completely lost the plot.

'Westfield? Two weeks before Christmas? On a weekend? It's going to be mayhem,' says Mum.

'I've never been inside a shopping mall,' Dad says, with the same reverence and pride someone might announce that they've never smoked a joint.

'Well, today could be the day!'

'And I really never want to, Jess. Horrible, soulless places. We really appreciate the thought though, darling, but we have set aside today to do all the cards – the roads are quieter on a Sunday.'

'I could come with you?' I say weakly, because if spending a couple of hours looking at the back of my Dad's head is the best I can get, I will gladly take it.

'I've got all the dry cleaning on the back seat, darling. Our best winter coats got ruined on Remembrance Sunday with the downpour, so I've just had them cleaned.'

'Can I not put them in the boot?'

Mum looks horrified. 'It cost eighteen pounds each to clean, so we don't want them getting creased.'

Dad looks at his watch. 'Sorry, darling, but we must press on, good to see you looking brighter.'

'The cafe at the end of the road opens at nine,' I say weakly, 'it's only quarter to now, we can have breakfast together?'

Mum shakes her head. 'We had porridge this morning.'

Dad pats his belly. 'I'm absolutely stuffed, couldn't eat another thing.'

'A quick tea?'

'We'll be needing a wee before we've even gone over Hammersmith Bridge if we do that,' Mum says.

I feel like screaming in frustration at their refusal to deviate from their plans, to inject just a tiny bit of spontaneity into their day. To put me and the three of us before stupid Christmas cards that will be recycled in three weeks' time and posh woollen winter coats that wouldn't crease even you balled them up inside a bin liner, let alone laid them carefully flat in a hatchback's pristine boot. But then I remember that today doesn't matter for them; as far as they're concerned, they can spend tomorrow with me – or the next day, or the next, or the next . . .

Mum pulls me into a hug. 'Bye, darling, enjoy your shopping. We're just giving the kids money again, like you do, is that right?'

Money? We give a seven and ten year old money? 'Actually, it would be great if you could give them actual presents, if you don't mind, I'd like them to have things to put under the tree, and to open.'

Mum's shoulders slump. 'Well, when am I going to have time to get something now?'

I must be the only one who sees the irony in what she says, considering I've just spent the last ten minutes begging them to come shopping with me.

'At the garden centre yesterday in the toy department Liam saw a wooden Jenga set he liked, and Molly loved a door sign with her name on it. They'd love those. And you like the garden centre.'

'We could go on Tuesday,' says Dad to Mum. 'They have half-price cream teas for pensioners then.'

'We would ask you to come with us,' Mum says to me, 'but you'll be working, won't you?'

'Remind me on Tuesday morning, and I'll meet you there for lunch,' I say, sure that even when I'm back in the future, the past me will make sure I go.

My goodbye hug with Dad goes on for much longer than it normally would. I kiss his papery white cheek, breathing in his mix of shaving foam and his musky cologne for an extra few seconds as he pulls away. Because unlike six years ago, I know it's going to be the last time I can.

'You're going all soppy in your old age, Jess.' Dad laughs, playfully pushing me away. 'See you Tuesday then, love.'

'Yes. Tuesday.'

I have to turn away before they see my eyes filled with tears, so I pretend to be putting my key back in the house's lock until I can hear their car's engine start up. Then I let myself have one more look.

I raise my hand up as they sail past me, Dad keeping one hand on the wheel as he waves with the other.

Then he's gone.

★   ★   ★

Despite having to get a train from Victoria an hour after the one I'd planned to, I somehow manage to get on the boat back to Forth as the sky is darkening. *Come on, hurry up*, I silently will the passenger ferry. A few of us are braving the bracing wind standing on the bow, while the more sensible majority are huddling inside the cabin. I need to be outside, to feel the wind whip my face with its icy hands, breathing in the lung-numbing air with greedy gulps. A metre or so along the rail, there's a couple passionately kissing. Her long brown hair is blowing all around them like a blizzard and his arms are wrapped tightly around her back, pulling her further into his body.

I miss Fergus.

I go to look away, not wanting to be caught staring at them, but something about the back of the woman makes me take a second glance. I know her, I'm certain, but I'm not sure from where. It'll come to me.

I'm exhausted. 'Bone tired,' Dad used to say and I used to reply back that bones can't get tired, but now I know what he meant. Every part of my body and mind aches, and I just want to get to the bench and go home. Except I have no idea how that part is going to actually work. I mean, I can't go to the bench, see the sun and then walk back to our cottage adjoining the doctor's surgery because it's 2016 and someone else lives there, my family are where I left them in London, so I don't actually know what I'm going to do until the magic happens and transports me back. It's too cold to sleep on the bench, and I don't want to hang about the town because I might see someone I know in 2022 and it will all get too confusing. I'll figure it out later; the most important thing is getting off this boat and up the hill before sundown.

I queue up behind the lady with the long brown hair, I still haven't seen her face, and to be honest, I'm hiding mine with my coat collar pulled up, just in case I do know her, which might complicate things. But what's odd is that the man she was joined at the lips with for the whole journey is now at the back of the queue. For two people who barely came up for air the entire sixty-minute journey, it's strange that they're not disembarking together.

I'm now almost running down the gangplank and along the marina wall. I have about fifteen minutes, I'm guessing, before dusk. The lady in front of me hurries too. I follow her up the cobbled main high street, cut through a small lane past the school, up past the butcher's, and The Swan. Everything is shut as it's Sunday afternoon. House windows are illuminated by lamps and flashing TVs projecting bursts of colour. Christmas trees adorn most of them. I run past our house attached to the surgery and see that there's a nativity scene I don't recognise in the window of the living room. It looks nice. We should get one.

The woman is still running in front of me as we turn off the road and along the worn footpath leading to the clifftop. She must know I'm behind her – I'm fitter than I am normally, and five years younger, but I'm still panting with the exertion of rushing this much. It's not until we reach the top, where the bench is, that she turns around accusingly and I gasp.

'Maggie!'

'Do I know you?'

Oh God, I have no idea how to navigate this. In all the dress rehearsals I'd run through in my head, I hadn't considered this. I stammer, 'No sorry, I just – um, sorry, I think we met once before.'

'Did we? Sorry.' She smiles tentatively. 'I can't place you.'

'Don't worry, it's fine, it was very brief. We hardly spoke.' I flash her a polite smile then edge towards the bench.

'You can't sit there,' she says, her voice suddenly sharp.

'Don't mind me,' I say. 'I just want to sit and think a while.'

'But you can't,' she says. 'Not there. Walk a bit further along.'

The panicked urgency in her voice and the speed with which she ran up here tell me that she's about to do it. She obviously has the same thought about me at exactly the same time as her big Bambi eyes widen.

'How do you know about it?' she whispers.

'How many times have you done it?' I ask. Her smooth skin without the wrinkles that line her face now must mean that she's only started doing it recently. It's only been six years, but she looks fifteen years younger, maybe more.

'Only twice,' she says. 'You?'

'A few.' I don't want to give too much away because I have no idea what effect this is going to have on the future. As long as I remain forgettable, Maggie might not remember she's met me when I see her again in 2022.

'You're not planning to win last night's lottery, are you?' Maggie says, her hands on her hips. 'Because they'd never believe that two winners came from the same tiny island on the same night, and I really need the money.'

Of all the nights for me to come back to, it's the night where her life changes.

'Who was the man on the boat?' I ask, keen to fit each piece of the puzzle into the right place. I don't have much time.

Her body stiffens. 'What man?'

'The one you were kissing on the boat.'

A shadow falls over her face. 'A friend.'

'I don't kiss my friends like that,' I say, as lightly as possible. She's not to know that at this point in my life I don't have any.

She scowls. 'Why are you even talking to me? I don't know you.'

'Please don't do the lottery tonight,' I say, suddenly confident in doing what I know I have to. 'It's not because I'm going to, but that amount of money doesn't make things easier. Most millionaires are really unhappy. People asking for handouts all the time, third cousins once removed turning up, cap in hand . . . No one would treat you the same, it would be an incredibly lonely life. It might seem great from the outside, the fancy cars and houses and holidays in the Maldives—'

'How do you know I want to go to the Maldives?'

Tread softly. 'Who doesn't?'

'What, so you're saying don't do it?'

'I'm saying, just have a think about any other options. If you and—' I almost say Tom and then stop myself because she hasn't told me his name. 'If you and this man really love each other, then try to make it work without all the rubbish that comes with being multi-millionaires. Loads of lottery winners end up divorced.' I pull a statistic out of thin air, which she thankfully doesn't question, 'Ninety-two per cent apparently.'

'We're not married.'

'But you could be,' I say earnestly. 'You could get married, you could have children, all on this island. What an amazing childhood for them, running about on the beach every day, riding horses. All this fresh air.'

'But we could still do that, just in a house with under-floor heating.'

'Believe me,' I say, doing a good job of convincing myself into the bargain, 'having money – the type of life-changing money you're talking about – comes with a lot more stress and heartache than you can possibly imagine. Lottery winners are so lonely, so unhappy.'

'You know nothing about me. My house leaks in four different places.'

'So buy some buckets. Or go for five of the numbers, if you have to. Just don't, please don't, win the whole thing. It'll make you so miserable. I can't tell you how I know, but I do. Please.'

Her look of angry suspicion changes to one of dawning understanding. 'Have you seen me in the future?'

I don't know what to reply. If I tell the truth then that will change our friendship in the future for good, but if I don't, then she won't believe me and will sit here and ruin her life.

I nod, deciding to use everything in my arsenal to convince her, consequences be damned. 'Please, Maggie. Don't do this. Don't ever do this again. You have everything you want right now. If you do this, you and Tom will break up, and you'll end up married to someone who bullies you horribly, and you'll be rich but will really regret this. Listen to me: you have a chance to stop that. To live a really good life, doing the job you love, with a man who makes you really happy. Please take it.'

Out of the corner of my eye I spot the sun's base touching the sea. 'I'm sorry, I need to do this, it's really important, but please think about what I said.'

I concentrate on the setting sun, and think about getting the Christmas decorations box out of the loft in our Forth Island house ready to decorate with Mum. I run the scene over and over in my head so there's no room for misinterpretation. This has to work. I need to get back to my family.

As soon as the sun has vanished under the water, I turn back to Maggie but she's gone, running back down the hill with the same urgency she ran up it, her hair streaming behind her.

28

It's beginning to look a lot like Christmas . . .

Thank goodness it's a mild night, despite it being December, and once I'm sure the coast is clear, I let myself in to the storeroom at the back of the surgery, which doesn't have a lock on it – testament once again to the honest nature of the Forthians – and make a bed for myself among the boxes of surgical gloves, swabs and syringes.

If I don't wake up in my own bed in the house next door, I haven't got a clue what I'm going to do. I'm terrified of it not working and being stuck on the island six years before I'm meant to be here. I also have no idea how the me of six years ago is going to explain her absence from home after Westfield closes for the day. I'm assuming I'll blame work, an emergency call-out. Or I may not be missed at all. The thought makes me sad, so I push it away. I've done my best to change things back then – there's nothing more I can do now. I'll just have to wait and see.

I had a sign up above my desk in university halls that said 'Failing to plan is planning to fail', which gives a little indication to my reputation for being fun, fun, fun, but also explains why I'm currently lying awake, sleep completely evading me, running through my options. The obvious thing to do would be to lie low for the day, wait until sunset and try again. If that doesn't work, then I'll have no choice but to go back a day to yesterday morning and wake up again in London. I could find Eileen or Nora, but of course they wouldn't have a clue who I am. Maggie might be the best bet, seeing as we've already met. OK, that's what I'll do. I'll turn up at her door and tell her everything. She already knows that I know her in the future, so I'm sure she'll help me.

I think about calling Dad. It would be the last time I would ever hear his voice, but it's after midnight and it would worry them too much. Why didn't I think about calling him earlier, when they'd still be awake? I can't do it now. I can, I've got to.

His mobile is switched off, as it always is at night – too many reports of those things exploding. By too many, I mean one. And it was a different brand. Their home phone only rings once, and as it's on Dad's side I know he is going to be the one to answer. Phone calls at night are men's business, apparently.

'Dad?'

'Jess, what on earth . . .? What's wrong?'

'Nothing, nothing's wrong. I just wanted to tell you that I love you.'

'But why would you call at – ' There's a pause, and I picture him straining to see the neon flash of the clock radio on the chest of drawers – 'nearly one in the morning?'

'I just wanted to make sure that you knew.'

'Knew what?'

'That I love you. That you're a great dad.'

Another pause. 'Jess, are you sure you're OK?'

I can hear Mum in the background asking what's going on. Where I am. What I want, why I'm calling.

'Tell me,' I whisper into the darkness.

'Tell you what, darling?'

'Tell me that you love me.'

'Of course I do.'

'Say it. Tell me that you do.'

'Are you crying? Do you want to speak to Mum?'

'Dad, please, it's important.'

'Of course I love you, you silly goose.'

I let out a breath and almost cry with happiness.

Suddenly Mum's voice comes on the phone. 'What's this

all about, Jess? Are you alone? Is Fergus with you? Do you need Dad to come and get you from somewhere?'

Memories flash in and out, of them waiting outside different parties, different pubs. At every prize-giving. My graduation. My wedding. A new memory creeps in, hazy at first, it's too far away. I reach further for it. He and Mum are sitting on a bench outside the hospital. His head is in his hands, Mum is bent over him, her arms over his shoulders. They don't see me. I barely register them as I race past, tears blurring my vision, running to nowhere. But they were there. They were there. They've always been there.

'I'm OK, Mum. I just wanted to let you know how much I appreciate all you've ever done for me.'

'You could have told us that at the garden centre on Tuesday, Jessica.'

I smile. Of course I could. And I hope I did.

My eyelids start to feel heavy, and I indulge myself in a loud, deep yawn.

'Love you, Mum. Put Dad back on a second.'

'He's already gone back to sleep, Jess. Snoring like a bear. I'm going to have to sleep in the guest room.'

'You'll miss it when he's gone.'

'Where's he going?'

'I just mean, life's too short not to sleep next to the person you love every night.'

'You're being very strange this evening, Jessica. Have you taken those magical mushrooms? I read about it in the paper, they make you all unhinged and emotional.'

'Night, Mum.'

I don't want to open my eyes.

No one is breathing heavily next to me, so that could mean that I'm still in the store room, or alone in bed in London, or on the island.

I do feel comfortable, which suggests I'm on a mattress, rather than the packing materials I emptied out of one of the boxes last night – Doctor Lewes will probably blame foxes.

It is quiet outside, which does rule out London. So I'm pretty sure I'm still on the island. But in which year?

Do it.

I tentatively open just one eye, because if I only see half the picture then it's not really real. Oh, thank God. My cream curtains. The clothes I was wearing yesterday in 2022 folded on the chair in the corner. The book I'm reading open to the most recent page on my nightstand. Everything is the way it should be. My body sags in relief.

'Come on, lazybones, wake up.' Fergus comes in bearing a steaming cup of peppermint tea and a plate of toast for me. The toast is a new, and welcome, addition to my morning wake-up call. He's got such twinkling eyes . . . was he always this handsome?

'Isn't it a weekend?' I yawn.

'Yes, but the kids have been up for an hour already desperate to go and get the tree. We said we'd be there when it opens.'

'The tree?'

'Yes, we said we'd go first thing. Keith's getting a new shipment in off the first ferry, so we need to be there soon to pick the best one.'

I join the dots quickly, and bound out of bed and straight into the shower. Part of me doesn't want to give in to the thought that by going back and changing that one day, I may have altered how my family view Christmas for ever – that's too hopeful – so I squash it down and wait for the day to unfold itself, my belly fizzing with anticipation.

Liam already has a coil of rope looped over his arm and is standing by the front door in his coat, while Molly is sitting on the doormat pulling on her wellies. Neither of them has needed cajoling or blackmailing to get out of bed on a weekend before eleven, and the sneery looks of distaste are also lacking from the picture. This is very odd.

'Shall we go?' Fergus asks, joining us in the hall wearing a flat cap that I've never seen before.

'Where did you get that?'

He looks back at me in surprise. 'What?'

'The hat.'

'Dad always wears it when it gets cold.' There's a sense of pride in Molly's voice, which baffles me: why would her Dad wearing a hat make her pleased?

Fergus ruffles Molly's hair. 'Best present ever, Molls.'

Since when do the kids buy us presents? And the last time I inadvertently touched Molly's hair last week when I had to reach past her to unhook my coat from the rack, she slapped my arm away so fast it almost flew off.

'Have you got money for the hot chocolates, Jess, or should I take the cash card?'

The question flummoxes me. So much of what's going on is flummoxing me. This wasn't the day that I left. I'd planned to surprise them all by chucking the old plastic tree in the bin and insisting that we get a real tree, but it seems like they're already five steps ahead of me.

'What day is it?' I ask, trying to sound nonchalant as I put my coat on.

Fergus studies me carefully. 'Are you having one of your turns again?'

'No, I'm just a bit sleepy, that's all.'

'Saturday, it's Saturday. Come on, we need to be the first there.'

'Morning, everyone, are you off to get the tree?' Mum floats down the stairs behind us in her dressing gown. Why is she here? Did she sleep here? Why doesn't anyone think that's odd?

'Do me a favour, Joy: turn the oven on at twelve and stick the chicken in at quarter past, will you? It's all prepped and ready.'

He's making a roast dinner?

'No problem. I'm going to have a bath while you're out and listen to Radio Four.'

What is going on?

The kids walk in front of us as we hurry down to Keith's allotment. They appear to be chatting merrily, with no violence involved at all. Fergus is also holding my hand. He threaded his fingers through mine as soon as we shut the front door as though it was the most natural thing in the world. We're leaving the house, we're putting on our shoes and coats, and we're holding hands. It's like I've stepped inside the set of a Hallmark movie as a last-minute stand-in who hasn't had a chance to read the script yet.

'So,' I start, trying to keep my voice from shaking. 'Mum seems pretty settled at ours.' That was good. It was vague but questioning. Now, whatever he replies with I'll be able to figure out what's going on.

'Yep.'

Balls.

'Do you mind, her staying over?'

'Of course not! She's your mum, of course she can live with us. We talked about this.'

I nearly slip on a patch of ice. Live with us? 'I know, we talked about it, back then – ' *When?* ' – but I just wanted to check that you're still OK with it.'

'Yeah, it's fine. I mean, things are hotting up between her and Keith, aren't they, so I'd put a fiver on her moving across the road before too long.'

'Keith?!' It was a question rather than a greeting, but I exclaim it at the exact moment we walk into the allotment and see the man himself. In all his shirt-button-bursting glory.

Keith raises his hand as we approach. 'Jess, Fergus mate, welcome, welcome!'

'Don't you mean Freddie?' I ask in confusion.

Everyone swivels to look at me as though I've stripped naked and am using a fir tree as a dance pole.

'Why would Dad be called Freddie?' Liam says.

Fergus makes a joke of it. 'I'll be whoever you want me to be, Jess,' he says with a wink.

'I thought that's what you liked to be called now?' I say, my voice laced with confusion.

He narrows his eyes at me. 'Since when?'

'Since we moved here.'

'You must have dreamt that. Why would I want to be someone I'm not?' He plants a kiss on my stunned lips.

'I've got a beauty for you, kept it to one side – an eight-footer,' Keith says, dropping his cigarette to the floor, squishing it into the ground and ushering us all towards his shed where about twenty trees are leaning. One stands a good, majestic foot above the rest.

'Eight feet?' I gasp. 'That's massive.'

'We measured it, didn't we, Liam?' Fergus says. 'He stood on a chair with the tape measure. We might need to trim an inch or two off the top, but it'll definitely fit.'

'How are we going to get it home?'

'That's where the sugar injection from the hot chocolate comes in,' Fergus says, grinning. 'Come on, Bays, heave!'

The four of us walk like sentries down the high street, the tree tucked under mine and Molly's right arms, Fergus and Liam's left, Fergus leading at the front, me at the back, the kids in the middle. Everyone we pass comments on the spectacle: 'What a whopper!', 'Aw, isn't that lovely', 'You're going to need a lot of lights for that!'

The tree stands guard outside the cafe in a way it never would have been able to in London, propped up against the outside wall while we're all inside having a hot chocolate, complete with cream and marshmallows.

If you could design a day with your family, today would be it: Christmas music is belting out, the fire is going, a chicken is roasting. We spend the afternoon adorning the tree with all these decorations that are completely unfamiliar to me: peacock-feather baubles, rose gold ribbons, and more lights than I've seen outside of Oxford Street. We dance around each other, reaching up, then down. Fergus catches my eye and winks. At one point, Molly reaches into the bottom of the box and pulls out four baubles that I immediately recognise from the garden centre – they're the ones we bought the day before yesterday, six years ago, with our names on. Molly hangs them prominently on the front of the tree. 'Done,' she announces.

'Not quite,' Fergus says, holding up the battered gold star. 'Whose turn is it this year?'

'Mine,' Liam shouts, grabbing it off him and laughing when Fergus makes a big deal of flexing his muscles before lifting him up at the knees so Liam can reach the top of the tree to put it on the top.

A little while later, the sky is darkening outside the window and I sit in the corner of the living room, surveying them all. Mum's knitting next to the fire, Fergus is lying with his feet on my lap, and thankfully some semblance of normality has been restored because both Liam and Molly are now back on their phones. But they haven't retreated to their rooms as normal. Liam is sprawled on the other sofa, Molly is lying on the rug in front of the fire with Iris. And the fact that Fun-time Freddie doesn't appear to have ever existed is making my head spin. Fergus wanted this move to mark the start of a new him, to become the man he never felt able to be in

London, but obviously he became that person anyway, without changing his identity. But how could that have happened? Could me going back in time, changing one day out of our whole lives together, have made this much of a difference to the way my family functions?

Fergus

It's just gone half ten. The kids have gone to bed, and Joy retreated to her room a couple of hours ago. She's good like that, Fergus thinks. Giving them some space to just be a couple. He'd definitely had his doubts when Jess suggested she move with them to the island, but she couldn't really have stayed in London, not when she'd given up her house to move in with them after Ian died. She'd have had to move to a flat in one of those soulless retirement villages, which she'd have absolutely hated.

He and Jess are one and a half bottles of wine in, a decent three quarters of a bottle sunk each. Enough to feel relaxed and a little tipsy, not enough to see double and to urgently need a kebab. Which is lucky, Fergus thinks, because the island doesn't have a kebab shop. No doubt Liam will probably open one as soon as he spots the gap in the market.

The movie is over, the lovers have met, the obstacle has been overcome, the girl has been kissed, and the credits are rolling. He pretends he hates the romcoms Jess chooses over the world-exploding movies he likes, but actually, they've grown on him. And it's worth it to see her happy. The fire is still flickering and the tree lights are giving the room a lovely glow. Jess would call it romantic. He asks Alexa to play some New Orleans jazz, then he tops up their glasses and they lie on the sofa, end to end. He feels more comfortable than she seems to, for some reason – he doesn't know why, they do this most weekends. His feet nestle next to her shoulder, hers alongside his chest.

Fergus rubs his toe along the side of Jess's jumper. Rhythmically back and forth. She looks up and meets his gaze. She's beautiful. Her toe does the same to his arm, gently grazing his skin. His finger draws a slow circle on her palm. She smiles a lazy smile back at him.

It's quick. It's messy. It's fantastic. Wine spills everywhere.

Jess says that the sofa is absolutely ruined, but then she laughs, a proper head-thrown-back laugh and kisses him again – kisses him as though nothing else in the world matters.

29

Sunday mornings

There are loads of songs about Sunday mornings being brilliant; the Commodores said they're 'Easy' while Etta James sang about wanting a Sunday kind of love, because that's arguably better than a Monday or Tuesday one.

Sunday's always been a day that other people enjoy, while back in London it was always the day that I invariably did three loads of laundry, bleached the bathrooms, whizzed the vacuum round the house and cooked the one meal of the week that didn't come from the freezer. But today couldn't be more different. Waking up on this Sunday, I now know what all the musicians were harping on about.

Fergus has been up a while. He even made me a cup of mint tea and some toast and presented it to me on a tray, stark naked with the plastic stem of a silk flower in his mouth that he'd taken from the vase on the dining table.

'You're so funny.' I pat the duvet next to me. 'Get in, then.'

He jumps in, not needing a further invitation, and burrows underneath it. His whole body covered by duvet moving down the bed until he finds what he's looking for. Considering it's been quite a while since he last saw it, it really doesn't take him long to find it at all, which suggests that in this new reality, he's had lots of practice.

For the rest of the week we act more like teenagers than the two teenagers who we live with. Twice I nip home in between patients for a quick kiss in the kitchen. On Wednesday he draws lewd pictures on the fogged-up bathroom mirror after his shower for me to find, so it's a very good job we have an en suite and don't share the bathroom with my mother and two children. On Thursday he surprises me after work and we walk to the pub together for a drink. We walk Iris together three times – on the beach, of course – and on Friday night, we even cook a meal for everyone from scratch together, music on, wine opened, amiably chopping and laughing and looking less like us and more like we're presenting a cooking segment on a Saturday morning television show.

'You two are so gross,' Molly says, walking into the kitchen and grimacing. Anyone would think she prefers the versions of us that barely spoke. But then I spot her smiling to herself as she turns away in mock-disgust.

'Not gross, my darling Molly-bear, just in love,' Fergus says, trying to twirl Molly around. I laugh along, but a part of me still feels a little wrong-footed. Can it really be this easy? It's as though I'm watching my family from afar, enjoying what I'm seeing, but not really understanding it.

While the weekend was absolutely fabulous, as Monday morning rolls around, it's not going to plan so far. But then I wasn't expecting it to. The 15 December never does.

The book I borrowed from the library a couple of weeks ago isn't next to the toaster, which is the last place I saw it. The toaster is a brand new one, too – gone is my trusty cream SMEG and in its place is a completely transparent one so you can see the bread toasting, just like Liam asked me to try to patent three nights before, six years ago. It's a shame someone else got there first. Is it my fault? Did I forget to call the patent office for him? And where is this damn book? I remember carrying it downstairs, getting distracted by the smell of the toast Liam had just made himself, wanting some myself, putting the book down, and then leaving for work.

Fergus says he hasn't seen it and so do the kids, and I know it's due back today because when Harriet stamped it, 15 December, I remember thinking that Anna would be turning twenty-three today.

Instead of searching for a lost library book I'd be blowing up balloons, sticking up banners, writing a heartfelt message in a card saying how proud I was for the woman she had become. I'd be picking up a suitably extravagant cake and calling round her friends, reminding them about the surprise party we'd be throwing later – not that any of them would forget, it would have been circled then highlighted on their calendars for weeks. She would have had great friends, loyal, genuine friends. I know that she'd have been well-liked amongst her peers, not because she was the prettiest or richest, not that type of superficial popularity, but the kind of girl that everyone just enjoyed being around. I'd have given her the option of having her own party, one with just her friends, of course I would. But she'd have insisted that we were there, too, which was typical Anna: 'You and Dad have to be there, Mum, it wouldn't be the same without you,' she'd have said. Fergus would make a speech, I'd roll my eyes at his jokes, and then he'd raise his glass aloft and say, 'To our darling Anna, happy birthday,' and I'd mouth, 'I love you,' to her and she'd make a heart back at me with her two hands.

I'll have to get a replacement. For the book. That's the thing about living here on the island: even overdue library books become a source of gossip.

The weird thing is, though, when I grovel to Harriet and explain that should it show up again I promise to bring it straight back, she has no record of me even ever borrowing it, and 'my records are impeccable', she boasts.

I shake my head apologetically, say that I must be getting mixed up with a book I borrowed from the ebook library online. She believes me, but I don't. I'm not getting confused. I know I borrowed it.

But that was before I went back.

I have no idea how me changing the events of a day six years ago would influence my choice of fiction now, but it obviously has. This must be what Maggie meant when she said that it's dangerous to play with time.

Maggie.

There are three women who will understand how I'm feeling, and Maggie's the one I feel connected to the most. She'll be able to wind all the threads back together for me. Well, she will after she gets mad at me for doing it again when I'd promised her faithfully I wouldn't. I have no idea what state our friendship is in now, everything seems different. There's even a name for it: the Butterfly Effect, that's what it's called. How a butterfly flapping its wings in an Argentinian rainforest can cause a tsunami in the Indian Ocean. Or how changing a single day in North London six years ago can completely alter a family living in the middle of the English Channel now.

The kids are at school in their final week before the holidays start and Fergus is engrossed in some university prospectuses he sent away for. 'It wouldn't hurt to look to see if I could retrain,' he said when I questioned him. 'People change careers all the time, don't they? You might be married to a world-famous surgeon yet.'

I snatch up my coat and head for the door. The start of Maggie's road looks exactly like the three that run parallel to it, with its rows of 1950s bungalows and fisherman's cottages. On Maggie's road, halfway along it, the waist-height fences and grey brick houses give way to the grand gates and sweeping driveway of Maggie's house, which stands on the site her old bungalow used to.

Or at least it should do.

I walk up and down the road I thought she lived on, but can't find her house. So I go back to the High Street and take the next road along, identical as the one before it. Except her house isn't on that one either. Or the final road.

Her house has completely disappeared.

I tell myself not to be silly, buildings don't just vanish. I must have got it wrong; I've only been there once, and I wasn't really paying too much attention at the time. I'll look up her address tomorrow when I go into the surgery. It's a simple mistake to make, all these roads with white houses and red roofs look the same.

Liam and Fergus are waiting for me outside the school gates for parents' evening when I breathlessly rush up to them. Normally I'd blame traffic for my lateness, but that sort of alibi is redundant on Forth. I give Fergus a look not unlike one that an army major might give a comrade before going into battle. He doesn't return it – he's even whistling as we walk in through the front door of the school.

The hall is really noisy, especially considering there aren't that many students in the school. Each teacher has commandeered a square metre footprint of the space, in which is crammed a small square table with them sitting one side, and three chairs on the other. Historically, this annual event ranks up there with teeth removal and bikini waxes. Supposedly you have to picture people naked to make your nerves disappear. And as I am the only doctor on the island, I have seen the intimate areas of most of the female teachers and a couple of the male ones, which certainly gives me the upper hand for once.

'Liam is very engaged in class, he clearly takes pride in his work.' Liam's English teacher pauses for a second to smile at us, and then at Liam. 'He is a bit chatty in lessons, but for the most part, it's on-task chat, so we don't mind too much about that. On the whole, it's a very encouraging start to the term.'

If Liam wasn't currently sat between us, I'd be showing the teacher a photo of him, pushing it under her nose saying, jabbing it with my finger – 'This is Liam. Liam Bay. You clearly have the wrong child.'

But he is sitting here. Grinning at us. Fergus is looking as though this report is totally to be expected, nothing to see here, just the same old regular praise we always receive, year in year out. Except it's not. Less than six months ago he was suspended for getting most of his year group tipsy on alcoholic ice lollies, and now the most negative feedback we're receiving is that he's 'a bit chatty'?

Maths is much the same, if not a little bit better: 'He clearly has a statistical brain.' Yes, he absolutely knows the probability of getting found out in most situations. Citizenship: 'He is very curious, you must talk a lot at home about world issues.' Absolutely. All the time. Our dinner-table chat yo-yos from what justifies impeachment to how to combat the rising level of the world's oceans. Does it heck. But still Fergus nods and smiles. He even pats Liam on the back at one point, and Liam doesn't squirm away shouting, 'Gerroff!'

Who are these people? Because they are certainly not my family. Molly's parent-teacher conferences are just as extraordinary. Her PE Teacher, Mr Masters, says that she's the top goal scorer they've ever had in a netball team, and has no doubt that if she wants to compete beyond club level, then she'd be accepted in any under-18 team, and in a few years, possibly even at national level. Another teacher says, 'She's very proactive when working alone, and gels very well in group work, sometimes taking the lead, and other times happy to take instruction from her peers.' Her English teacher says that her creative writing is fantastic. I remember her spending the last week or so desperately brainstorming plots and original ideas for her coursework. I tentatively suggested one about time travel and fixing things in your past that has affected your present, but she said she wanted it to be believable. Another teacher says, 'She's very level-headed and mature, making sensible decisions.' So does that mean that French oral-gate didn't happen? What about Cleavage-photo-gate? How many of my memories of the last six years haven't actually happened for the rest of the family? And what memories do they have of the last six years that I haven't got a clue about?

History's next for Liam. We sit down on the hard plastic chairs the other side of the table from his teacher. 'Maggie!' But this isn't the Maggie I know as my friend, it's the Maggie I met up on the cliff two days ago. A much younger, smoother Maggie, who now apparently teaches my son.

She looks back at me, a polite smile on her face, 'Dr Bay, how are you? Mr Bay, nice to meet you.'

Mr Bay? She knows Fergus, they've met many times. Maybe she's just trying to retain a sense of formality as she's Liam's teacher. *She's Liam's teacher.* My heart starts pounding. *You did this,* a voice says in my head. 'I tried to come and see you today, but I couldn't find your house,' I say, hoping no one else can detect the note of frantic desperation in my voice. 'I thought you were on Westbrook Road?'

'I am, number fourteen.'

'That's what I thought, but I couldn't find it.'

'It's right there, between twelve and sixteen.' She smiles, then it wavers. 'Was anything wrong with my results?' She obviously remembers where she is, blushes, and shuffles the papers in front of her. 'Sorry, sorry, it's just the hormones.'

I assume she's referring to the menopause, but then I clock her stroking her stomach.

'You're pregnant!' I gasp.

Her eyes narrow and she tilts her head at me questioningly. *She's pregnant. And I'm her doctor. I'm supposed to know about it. I probably even did the test for her.*

'So, Liam – how's he getting on?' I say brightly, wishing I could run to the bench now and erase the last five minutes from all our brains.

Maggie's still giving me strange looks as she shows us Liam's tick-filled book, and when we rise to leave once our allotted five minutes is up, she holds on tightly to my hand after she shakes Fergus's. 'Is everything OK, Doctor?'

'Yes, absolutely.'

'Why did you want to see me?'

'Oh it was nothing – nothing important, anyway.' I can't talk to her here. Not now.

'So nothing's wrong?'

'Not at all. Take it easy though, get Oscar to run you a nice warm bath when you get in tonight to relax.'

'A bath sounds wonderful,' she says, smiling, 'it has been a long day. But who's Oscar?'

My blood runs cold in my veins.

'Isn't that what your husband is called?' I say.

She laughs. 'Do I look like someone who would be married to an Oscar? I thought you'd met my husband, Tom Masters? He teaches PE.'

30

The past is a foreign country, and I'm the only one with a passport

Maggie's entire life has changed. Because of me.

I – a stranger – said, 'Don't jump off that cliff into that pool filled with the finest champagne,' and she didn't. Now she still lives in her 'sad little bungalow', she probably has never been to the Maldives, and I saw her fingernails, and she has definitely never had a manicure, square- or round-tipped.

But then again, she's having a baby. How is that possible when the Maggie I knew was striding rapidly in the direction of the menopause? She refused the ultrasound I offered, so she still might have been ovulating, it can happen during perimenopause. Maybe she was always going to be pregnant at this time, just with a different man as the father? Would she have even wanted Oscar's baby? He didn't seem like the loving, paternal type.

Maggie seemed happy tonight. I know I'm not imagining it, you can't fake that kind of contentment. And she definitely wasn't before. I'd even go so far as to say that she was miserable. I did the right thing. Definitely. And I didn't actually change anything about her life; I just gave her some well-meaning advice. She didn't need to take it; that was up to her. Totally her choice. Her life. She may have even come to that realisation by herself after weighing everything up. Pros, cons. She may have written a list. Teachers love lists. She seems pretty organised. Logical. I'm probably stressing over nothing.

I'm not stressing over nothing. This is huge. Her entire life has changed, because of me.

'So what do you say, Jess?' Fergus says jovially, as we walk home, one arm draped along Liam's shoulders, the other one resting on mine. Molly's catching us up shortly after seeing her friends. 'A celebratory fish and chips dinner, seeing as we don't have a McD's on the island? It is tradition after a good parents' evening, after all.'

Three things about that sentence make no sense. One, I would never have let the kids have a McDonalds; two, there is no way that would be a tradition of any kind; and three, that was the first good parents' evening I have ever been to that wasn't my own. One day six years ago of both of us being slightly nicer people, being more relaxed with the rules, more engaged with each other and the kids, and we're suddenly the family on the front of holiday brochures splashing each other joyfully in a water park or throwing snowballs at each other on a Christmas TV advert as we wear matching knitted sweaters.

'Fish and chips, definitely,' I say, forcing myself into the role of relaxed mum. 'Maybe even a deep-fried Mars bar.' In for a penny.

'Wow, you've changed!' Fergus laughs. 'Hear that, son? Say yes before she changes her mind and makes you eat a banana.'

OK, so maybe I'm not entirely different, then.

Something else is bothering me about Maggie. We're clearly not friends any more. I know that she's evidently Liam's teacher, and I'm there as his parent, and I'm obviously her doctor, too, but there was this cordial distance between us at the school that went beyond the situation we were in. It was as though we've never actually spoken before, aside from me asking for a urine sample and getting her to stand on the scales. She called me Doctor Bay rather than

Jess, and as she shook my hand, her smile was polite, but professional. We obviously haven't shared any of the chats we had before, we've never been to the pub together, never confided in each other.

She looked different too. Much younger, almost as young as she did on the cliff six years ago. Perhaps a couple of kilos heavier, but none of the lines and wrinkles, or delicate strands of grey peppered through the hair that adorns the Maggie I know. Which means that she doesn't mess around with time at all. But then, why would she, if she's perfectly comfortable as she is? She'd said to me before that the only reason she went back so much was to get everything right, to have a sense of control over her life, when it was spiralling out of her grasp after the lottery win. And if she didn't have the win, then there would be no need for it.

I call Jackie when Fergus goes out to get the fish and chips with the kids.

'I thought you might call today,' she says. 'I remembered the date. How are you feeling?'

'Not great,' I admit.

'Have you spoken to Fergus about it?'

'Not yet.'

'But you will?'

I nod, even though I know she can't see me.

'Jess?'

'Yes, I will.'

'Because it's important to keep letting him in, isn't it?'

'Yes. Jackie, can I ask you something?'

'Of course.'

'If you gave your friend some advice, which they took, and now their life has completely changed, would you feel guilty?'

'Was it good advice? Did it come from a place of love and because you care about them?'

I bite my lip thoughtfully, 'Yes, I think so.'

'Then that's what friends are for, isn't it? To help you see the bigger picture and make the right decisions for yourself. Now, go and talk to Fergus about Anna.'

Fergus

Dinner was delicious. Big fat vinegar-soaked chips and battered fish. Moving to this island has had so many upsides. The kids are now in bed, after yet another stonking parents' evening; the transition from London to here really doesn't seem to have been detrimental to their progress at all. Yes, there aren't any fancy science labs and IT suites, but the teachers seem really good. Fergus noticed that Jess seemed a little out of sorts today, but of course he knows why. He's just as aware as she is of the date. He doesn't know if he should say anything though, it might potentially spoil the mood, but then it would be wrong not to. They'd promised they wouldn't keep secrets again. There's no way that he wants to go back to the arguments and tip-toeing round each other of the past. He still has no idea why or even how things started to get better that Christmas when the kids were smaller; it's as though a switch was flicked and they both became different, closer somehow.

'It's Anna's birthday today,' Jess says, as though she's read his mind.

'Yes,' he replies.

'We'd have probably had a party.'

'Probably.'

'What would she have been like, do you think?'

'Jess—'

'What?'

'It's been a lovely day. Are you sure you want to talk about this? Won't it make you upset?'

'It's her birthday. So if we can't get a bit nostalgic and emotional today, when can we? We said we wouldn't bottle anything up again, didn't we?' She takes a deep breath. 'I think she'd have been very funny. Like you.'

'I do have a good sense of humour,' Fergus says modestly, then smiles. 'I reckon she'd have been driven and ambitious, like you.'

'Is that a bad thing?'

Fergus shakes his head, surprised she'd even think that. 'Of course not. You're incredible. I think she'd have grown up seeing you accomplish all you have done, and feel inspired to do the same.'

'But would I have, though?' Jess says. 'If she'd lived, I mean. Wouldn't I have left the course, and not become a doctor? How would it have worked, with me, twenty-two years old with a baby? I couldn't have done the gruelling placements that I did, working twenty hours straight, eighty-hour weeks. I'd have had to give it up.'

'We'll never know.'

'If you could go back,' she starts, as though all the potential words she could use are lined up on a rack and she's selecting which ones she wants very carefully, 'if you could turn back time, and do it differently, would you?'

'To the day she died?'

Jess nods.

Fergus looks at Jess, assessing whether she can bear his answer. But they've come so far and they promised each other they'd never shut each other out again. 'I think we probably should have given her a proper funeral.' He doesn't meet her eyes. He's never come outright and said it before and he doesn't know if it's too much.

'Would it have changed things though? Really?' she asks. 'You know, if we'd done it ourselves, done a reading, sung a hymn, given her a headstone. How would that have been better?'

'It would have made her real.'

'She was real.'

'Was she?' Fergus says sadly. 'Because we've spent the last twenty-three years pretending that she wasn't. The kids don't know about her, we've hardly mentioned her to each other, there's not a grave we can visit, a photo we can look at. There was one photo of you pregnant with her, but after she died you threw it away. It's as though she never existed.'

From her silence, Fergus knows that Jess knows he's right. She'd kept saying that she didn't want a photo of Anna hooked up to tubes and sick, that they'd wait and take a picture when she was better. She'd even refused the card they'd tried to give her with Anna's tiny footprints on it that they give to parents of babies who didn't make it. 'Why would I want that?' Jess had screamed. 'What am I going to do with it, put it on my fridge? Frame it?'

'I'm sorry,' Jess says quietly as though the blame lies solely at her feet. As though Fergus hadn't smashed his way through the entire contents of their crockery cupboard, screamed into his pillow and felt as though he was going to either sob or be sick every time he saw a young couple with a pram.

'It's not your fault,' he says gently. 'Not yours. Not mine. We didn't know then what we know now. If we had thought then that us giving her to the hospital to cremate, us not even being there at the ceremony, would have caused us so much pain over the next twenty years, then of course we'd have done things differently. But we were kids. We can't blame ourselves for decisions we made then. It's not as though we can change things.'

'But what if we could?' Jess presses on. 'What if I told you that we could go back and make a different choice, would you want to?'

Fergus yawns and stretches, signalling loud and clear that this conversation is over. 'Jess, leave it. It's pointless talking like that, we can't change the past.'

'But if we could?'

Fergus feels a twinge of irritation. Why does she keeps on talking like this? It's futile and achieves nothing. Only more pain.

'If we had said goodbye properly,' Jess continues, 'if we had always had a framed picture of her on the mantelpiece next to Molly and Liam, if we'd made an annual family visit to her grave every year on this day, this day, fifteenth of December, if we'd all gone together and laid flowers, if we'd made her real, would it have made a difference?'

'To what?' he asks.

'To the way we've lived. To the way we've brought the other two up, to our marriage.'

Fergus can tell Jess is getting impatient with his refusal to play her stupid 'What if' game that changes absolutely nothing, except maybe reminding them of their mistakes. It's done. It was done wrong, but they've finally, after twenty-three years, half fixed it.

'I don't think we've done too badly,' he says defensively. 'We've just come back from a parents' evening where the teachers were falling over themselves to give us compliments about the kids. We've just been told Molly could play netball at a national level, we've got a toaster in the kitchen our son invented that people can now buy in John Lewis, for goodness' sake.'

Jess's face jolts in what looks like surprise as though this is the first time she's heard this, when actually she was the one that rang the patent office in the first place and organised the initial meeting with John Lewis's kitchen appliances buyer. And bought every single person she knows one of his toasters for Christmas three years ago.

'We're doing this parenting lark right, Jess. And we're in a good place, you and me, we love each other, and more importantly, we really like each other. Yes we've had difficult times, but who hasn't? You need to let this go.' He remembers the words on a mug he once saw, and repeats them to Jess, feeling grand and eloquent: 'The past is a foreign country and we haven't got a passport.'

He doesn't notice Jess's expression then as he's too busy reaching for a now-cold chip that she'd left on her plate. But if he had, he'd have seen she wasn't listening. She was miles, and years, away.

31

Teenagers in love

The surgery phone rings just as I'm preparing to shut it up for four days. I've laminated a notice that I hang on the front door telling whoever needs to read it that I am still on the island, and can be contacted any time for medical emergencies, but ordinary appointments will commence on 27 December for four half-days, and then we'll resume normal working hours on 3 January.

'Are you sure that's OK?' I ask Eileen, who prompted me to make a sign in the first place.

'If you ask me, you're making yourself a bit too available,' she says, folding her arms across her bosom. 'The old doctor used to shut for three weeks over Christmas.'

'Three weeks! What was he doing for three weeks?'

'He'd normally go to a salsa retreat in the Algarve.'

Wow. 'I was not expecting that.'

'He had quite the pelvis.'

'Wonderful. But no, I already feel really guilty about doing fewer hours – Christmas is a prime time for accidents, burns and cuts etcetera.'

'And should anyone need you, they know where to find you, don't they? Stop fretting, you need a break too. You're like the opposite of Santa.'

I'm afraid to ask. 'How, Eileen, am I the opposite to Santa?'

'Well, you work all year without stopping, then take the one day off when the big man in red is actually getting off his lazy arse to do something.'

'Speaking of Santa, I've actually got a present for you, Eileen,' I say, reaching into my handbag for a very oddly shaped gift, which was an absolute nightmare to wrap.

'Oooh, can I open it now?' she squeals, not waiting for my permission before she pulls off the paper and sees the little china frog with a shower cap on relaxing in a tiny porcelain bath. 'Oh, Jess, I love it! How did you know I collect frogs?' she beams.

Ready for this question, I just shrug, tap my nose and say, 'A little birdie told me.'

Just then the phone rings.

'Forth Island Surgery, Eileen Duggan Mrs speaking. Oh yes, I'll just get her. You just caught her actually, before I switch the answerphone on for the holidays.'

She makes the machine sound like the Oxford Street Christmas lights. I hope it's no one important.

'I think it's someone important,' Eileen says, holding the receiver out to me. 'They're from the local health authority. Says it's urgent.'

I take the phone from her. 'Hello? This is Dr Jess Bay.'

'Your practice in London is desperate for you to return in the new year,' the voice says.

And just like that, the six months that I agreed to for this secondment to Forth are almost up. Somewhere between unpacking the last box and this very moment, I've forgotten that this wasn't permanent. That living here had an expiry date already stamped on it, and our stay on the island is over.

My heart sinks. 'And what about the surgery here?' I ask. 'Is my replacement on their way?'

There's a pause. 'Well, we haven't had as many responses as we were hoping for to the job advert, so we have decided to shut the surgery on the island and the residents can register at one of the many clinics in Guernsey.'

I can't believe I'm hearing this. 'That's not going to help anyone that needs medical assistance when the sea's too rough for the ferry to run, or after six in the evening when the ferry stops, or on public holidays, or when the ferry company strikes, is it? I have two pregnant women on the island at the moment, one hundred and twelve pensioners—'

'How do you know this?' the voice asks, sounding taken aback.

'What do you mean, how do I know this? It's my job to know this. I have a nine year old with a compromised immune system, one adolescent and two middle-aged patients with type one diabetes. The adolescent has had three episodes of severe hypoglycaemia since I've been here, and if I wasn't here, there would almost certainly be a new gravestone in the island cemetery with her name on it. I have a nut allergy, two shellfish allergies, and one man who is rather interestingly allergic to his own sweat, which believe it or not, brought on anaphylaxis during the heatwave in late August. I could go on. Lyme disease? We have a lady with that too. I don't have the exact statistics to hand for the amount of minor injuries I have treated such as cuts needing stitches, infected insect bites needing antibiotics and so on, but I can certainly dig them out for you, if you like? I just—'

'Dr Bay, let me stop you there. I don't know why you're telling me all this.'

'What do you mean, why am I telling you all this? It should be perfectly obvious why: because this island needs a resident doctor on site, and on call, twenty-four hours a day. Anything less would be an absolute travesty.'

I stop and take a breath, surprised about my instinctive protectiveness over my islanders.

'So why don't you do it, then?'

'I'm sorry,' I say, not sure I heard right. 'What did you just say? Can you say it again?'

'I said, if you care so much about the island and its inhabitants, which you so clearly do, I can send a contract over this afternoon.'

When I get home I don't tell anyone about the phone call, or the invitation to make this permanent. It's the day before Christmas Eve, it's too manic. I'll raise it in the new year, when everything has calmed down a little and I've had a chance to think about it all properly.

Fergus is upstairs wrapping my present. As he hasn't left the island for a while and I don't think he's received any deliveries, as I haven't seen any boxes in the bottom of any of the wardrobes, I'm bracing myself for something from the butcher's, grocery store, or a beach inflatable. To be honest, after years where we had agreed to not get each other presents, and instead spend the money on a sofa or a new set of dining chairs, this change in our relationship is very welcome. I'm just glad he mentioned it to me last week, when I still had a chance to do something about it.

Thankfully, I had to go to Guernsey last week to check on an elderly patient who is in hospital there, so a new world of retail possibilities was open to me. I mean, it wasn't Westfield or Oxford Street, but at least I'm not having to give him a windbreaker or a fishing net for crabbing. I saw Nora's ex husband in the food hall of Marks and Spencer's when I was looking for goose fat for the Christmas Day roast potatoes. He didn't see me, or maybe he did but didn't have any idea who I am. We haven't met – I only recognised him from a photo at Nora's when Mum was staying there briefly, in the version of the past that never actually happened. He and his new wife – I heard him call her Kate – were swinging a small child between them, and there was another child, a girl, slightly older, skipping along next to them. Poor Nora.

Liam's out with his friends carol singing for cash. I have to admit I was more than a little relieved when he told me that's what he'd be doing; there was a part of me that missed the old Liam's cheeky entrepreneurialism. Don't get me wrong, I don't miss the weekly calls from his head of year cataloguing all the misdemeanours he'd committed that week, or the subconscious breath-holding when one of the neighbours asked me 'for a word'. Moving into the world of inventing things for the heady world of retail is all well and good. But Del Boy would be more fun round the dinner table than Dyson any day of the week.

Molly's on a date with Nora's son Nico, who has now moved into boyfriend status. After I found out that Maggie and I aren't friends any more, I was so worried that in this new and improved future I'm unwittingly now part of, I don't actually have any friends at all. But the day after the parents' evening Nora popped around to pick up some garlic for a recipe she was following, and while she was definitely looking a fair bit younger than she used to and I couldn't see any sign of a hole in her nose where her piercing usually was, our friendship still seemed to be intact at least. It was she who told me then about Nico and Molly, or more specifically, his intention to ask her out.

'He's never had a girlfriend before,' she confided. 'He's a very sweet boy, I promise.'

'I think it's lovely,' I said to Fergus later, not without a little trepidation; dads can be funny about their daughters dating, mine certainly was. 'She's seventeen soon, so we can't keep pretending she's still a little girl who plays with Barbies.'

After a few moments' deliberation, Fergus nodded approvingly. 'I like Nico, he's on the football team. He's a good lad.'

I straightened Molly's hair for her before she went out tonight. It was a first for me, but apparently I've done it before. She did yank away a few times, shrieking that I was burning her head, but for the most part, the scene was worthy of a #motherdaughter Instagram post, if I was that way inclined. Which I'm not, any more.

Her curfew time comes and goes. It's Friday night, so we'd agreed on eleven, but it's now quarter past. The clock is moving much slower than it normally does, I'm sure of it. If we were still living in Zone 3 in London I'd be more worried, but as we're on the island I just send her a quick text asking if she's OK.

No reply.

Fergus is snoring beside me so I quietly slip out of bed, pull on a fleece and pad back downstairs to make myself a cup of tea and wait for her to get back. I decide that if she's not back by midnight, I'll wake Fergus, call Nora, and set up a search party.

At one-minute-to, I hear her key in the front door, and I nearly faint with relief.

Her eyes are rimmed with red, halting my prepared speech about deals and promises.

'Molly, what's wrong?'

She shakes her head at me. 'I don't want to talk about it.'

'Is it Nico? Did you have a fight?'

She barges past me, and heads for the stairs. 'I don't want to talk about it.'

A minute or so later I hear the shower going. She never has a shower this late.

I sit on her bed and wait for her to come out of the bathroom, not sure how I'm going to ask what I need to ask. When she comes back in she's changed into a pair of flannel pyjamas with little red reindeers printed on them. Her face is scrubbed clean of make-up, her hair pulled back into a tight ponytail. The years have been stripped away from her, making what I need to say so much more difficult.

'Moll,' I start. 'Has Nico hurt you in some way?'

Her face crumples, her chin falls onto her chest and her shoulders start to shake. I gather her into my arms and hold her close, trying to calm my racing pulse. 'You can tell me,' I say, trying to keep the desperation out of my voice. 'I'll help you.'

'He didn't hurt me, Mum,' she says finally between big heaving sobs. 'The opposite.'

I stay silent, my mind racing. That doesn't make any sense, how could the opposite of him hurting her result in her being so upset?

'We did it. I'm so sorry. Please don't be mad.'

'You had sex?'

She nods. 'But it went wrong. He was meant to come out before . . . you know . . . and he didn't, by accident, and now I think I must be pregnant, and I'm sixteen, and I don't want a baby, and oh God, I don't want a baby—' The whole weight of her collapses onto me and I sink down onto the bed with her in my arms, stroking her hair, soothing, saying it's all going to be OK, thinking desperately how I can make it OK.

'When was your last period?'

'What? I don't know.'

'It's important, Molly, try and think. Have you had one in December?'

She screws her face up, thinking, the way she used to when I asked her 'to think really hard and tell Mummy if a camel is a mammal or a reptile', the way she did when I asked which of her feet was her left one. Now I'm sitting here, so many years later, asking her in the same encouraging voice if she might possibly be ovulating.

'About two weeks ago,' she says finally. 'I had it when we had that netball tournament in Southampton.'

Dammit. Damn it.

'OK, this is what we'll do. We'll get a good night's sleep, then in the morning, I'll go to the pharmacy and get some emergency contraception. It'll be fine. We'll sort it out.'

'I don't want a baby.'

'I know.' And I did know, much more than she knew.

What I hadn't remembered when I made this pledge to Molly last night is that today is Christmas Eve. And we live on an island where one pharmacy services nearly seven-hundred people. And due to the average age of the residents, the morning-after pill is not something it usually needs to stock.

'It's for a patient,' I hurriedly say to June the chemist, in response to her raised eyebrow. 'It's urgent,' I add needlessly; I can't imagine a situation where anyone would request emergency contraception not urgently. The clue is in the name for God's sake.

This doesn't stop June telling me that she can order it in for the new year. 'It should come around the third of January,' she says. I make a mental note to research her pharmacist's qualifications.

In my surgery in London, I'd have a ready stock of IUDs, which would do the job too, but here, I prescribe ten times more arthritis medication than birth control.

It's also not as though I can now jump in the car and tour around ten other local pharmacies in the area to find one that does have it. I call the chemists on Guernsey. A couple of them do have it, but being Christmas Eve, there are no ferries running until the twenty-eighth. I'm sure if it wasn't Christmas Eve I could find a fisherman willing to take me over there, for a fee. But that would be impossible this week. I'm running out of options. I need more time.

Molly jumps up from the sofa when I walk back in the door. Liam and Fergus are playing Xbox together sat on the floor, so I motion with my head for her to join me in the kitchen.

'OK, so I'm tracking the pills down. It's all OK, I'm going to sort it.'

Tears well in her eyes. 'But I researched it, Mum. I need to take it as soon as possible.'

'I know, but there's one type you can take up to five days after intercourse.'

She grimaces at my use of the word, but it's a bit late for her to start being prudish now.

'But tomorrow's Christmas, and then everything is shut on Boxing Day,' she wails. 'I'm going to have to leave school! I'm going to be a teenage mother! I want to go to university, I want to play netball, I don't want a baby. Mum, please, you have to help me.'

'I'll make it all OK. I promise.'

As soon as the words leave my mouth, I wish I could take them back. I can't promise something that I don't know I can change. Maggie said that I can't change conception through time travel. If a baby is going to be made, then it will be made. But right now, we have a window. We have a tiny, five-day gap where Molly's pure teenage egg is potentially not yet fertilised, where I can make sure that it doesn't implant, where she can carry on being sixteen and carefree and she doesn't need to imagine a different sort of life.

'Now?' Fergus asks disbelievingly, when I say I'm going out. 'It's Christmas Eve.'

'And Iris still needs to be walked,' I reply.

'Liam and I took her down to the beach this morning, she doesn't need another big walk,' he says.

'Well I just need to pick something up from someone,' I say weakly, glancing out of the window at the rapidly setting sun and darkening sky.

'What from who?' Mum says from the sofa. Why is she always here?

'It's Christmas Eve,' I say brightly. 'You're not supposed to ask questions like that on Christmas Eve, it's a surprise!' I reason that it doesn't matter what I say, because if I get up to the cliff on time, this conversation never happened for any of them, anyway.

Nora's there already after getting my message.

'Did you see Nico when he came in last night?' I ask, sitting down on the bench alongside her.

'He never went out. He and Molly were watching movies in his room until late. I went to bed around ten, and I think she was still there. Why? What's wrong?'

Shall I say it? She seems pretty liberal and understanding. She used to have a nose ring, which must count for something. Teenagers have sex all the time, which is normally fine, except when they're your teenagers.

My silence obviously unsettles her because she says, 'What? What are you not telling me?'

'They slept together last night. For the first time. And they didn't use protection and I think she was probably ovulating, I've been frantically trying to get her some emergency contraception today and I can't, so now I'm going to try to go back to yesterday morning and try to stop them having sex. Somehow. God knows how.'

There's a pause while she processes what I've said.

'There's a way,' she says finally. 'If you just go back then I won't remember any of this, but if we both go back to yesterday, then we can work together to stop them.'

'Is that how it works?' Not for the first time I wish there was a manual next to the bench, with a Do Not Remove stamp on it like the reference books at the library, tied to one of the legs with a piece of string and a knot no one has any hope of undoing.

'I've only done it once before, with Eileen, when I suspected my husband of having an affair and I needed her help to catch him.'

We don't have time to keep talking about it, the sun is already dipping its bottom quarter into the sea behind the clouds. We fall silent, both of us concentrating on thinking about yesterday's breakfast time. I frantically try to recall what I was doing yesterday morning. I am taking the turkey out of the freezer and putting it onto the bottom shelf in the fridge. Fergus is humming along to the radio, Liam is moaning that we've run out of jam, Molly is asking me if it's OK if she sees Nico tonight. She says until midnight, I say ten, we settle on eleven.

And then the sun is gone.

I turn to Nora. 'So what now?'

'Now we make a plan.'

'But I don't see how we can stop them having sex if that's what they want to do.'

'I could say they can't go up to his room?' she offers. 'I should have done that anyway, I don't know what I was thinking. Jesus, we were sixteen once, weren't we? Of course we'd have both done what they did, wouldn't we?'

I don't tell her that my sixteen-year-old self was still collecting novelty erasers and loved nothing more than a good scrapbooking session come the weekend after doing a 1,500-piece jigsaw. But only after any homework was finished. Boys were annoying, and quite often smelly, definitely disruptive, and I had absolutely no inclination to put my hands down the pants of any of them, let alone anything more.

'What, so you set up a movie for them in the living room? Won't they just go out then?' If Molly is determined to do this, I'd much rather her first time was in a warm, safe house rather than round the back of the Co-op. 'Or,' I add, 'we let it happen, but we prepare them more.'

'What, give them a lecture on birth control over tomorrow's cereal?' Nora says with a snort. 'Slip some condoms into their pockets?'

'Why not? If we both do it, me with Molly, you with Nico, tell them that we understand that if this is what they want to do, then they need to make good decisions etcetera etcetera, and we buy them protection, then hopefully that will work.'

'I think we do a mixture of both,' Nora says decisively. 'We'll give them the lecture in the morning, which will mortify all of us, then I'll set up the living room with a movie, popcorn and hopefully they'll stay downstairs and I'll keep popping in and out.'

I smile grimly. 'Let's hope you're the only one doing that.'

32

Here we go again . . .

I take a couple of foil-wrapped squares out of my toilet bag – now that Fergus and I have ignited that side of our lives, I'm apparently the type of person who has a contraceptives' drawer. There's only a few condoms left out of a box of twenty-four; I just wish I could remember the times we've used them.

There's no chance to talk to Molly at breakfast as Liam is lolling in the kitchen armchair, sulking over the lack of jam in the house, gangly limbs spread over the arms, and I have to leave for the surgery soon. The opportunity comes mid-morning, when I pop home between patients to find Liam and Fergus out, and Molly alone in the house.

'Hi, darling,' I start cheerfully, from the door of the living room where she's watching *Polar Express*. By herself. My heart melts as I once again can't reconcile this fresh-faced young girl who loves watching Christmas movies in her reindeer pyjamas while eating a bowl of dry Cheerios like popcorn, with the one who in eight hours' time is going to lose her virginity.

She doesn't raise her eyes from the TV. 'Hey.'

'Um, Molls?' I sit next to her on the sofa. It's less confrontational, more chatty. 'Um, Molls,' I repeat. Mainly because I have literally no clue how to complete the sentence.

'Um, Mum.'

'OK, so here's the thing.'

'What is the thing?'

'The thing is, you're sixteen now.'

'Nearly seventeen.' Her eyes still don't move from the screen, but at least her correction proves that she's listening.

'Yes, absolutely. And there are things that children, I mean people, people your age – any age, my age, your Gran's age even – ' *no need for that,* ' – like to do with one another, that I think we need to talk about.'

Either this is the most interesting film she has ever seen, or more likely, considering the deep red hue her face has now taken on, she can't bear to look at me.

'And I just wanted to tell you that that's absolutely OK, sex is totally natural, but it's also important to make sensible decisions, and as a woman, you need to protect yourself, and not leave it to the boy – man – the man, to pull out, or not, you know, ejaculate, inside you, when he's not wearing a condom.'

I have to ignore her blazing cheeks or I'm never going to get the next sentence out. 'So, I have a couple of packets here, and it's really important that if you and Nico are thinking about progressing to this new level of your relationship, then he has to wear it. Think of it like wearing a raincoat in a storm. It's just sensible, really. Or you'll get pneumonia. From the rain. Not the sex. You'll get pregnant from the sex. Or herpes. Or something else horrible, there's no end of sexually transmitted diseases. Three hundred and seventy-six million new infections each year, in fact.' I thrust the two packets into her hand and then stand up. 'OK then, good to have this chat. Enjoy the rest of the film. Love you, bye.'

Well, that went well.

Nora messages me at eight o'clock. '*They're watching a movie. Fully clothed.*'

I reply with a 'Phew' emoji with a drop of sweat on its brow. An hour later, another ping from my phone where it's perched between Mum and me on the sofa. '*Just checked. All hands where I could see them.*'

OK. Excellent. Everything is going like clockwork.

Fergus

Fergus looks up from the fireplace where he's kneeling down raking the logs in the grate. 'Who's that at this time?'

'Just Nora. Molly's round there, so she's updating me on what her and Nico are doing.'

'Stop fretting,' Fergus says, rolling his eyes fondly. 'She's a good kid.'

'Absolutely. A good sixteen-year-old kid who has a boyfriend.'

'You're not suggesting that they're going to get off with each other?'

'No, I'm not suggesting they're going to get off with each other, I'm suggesting they are probably considering having sex.'

Fergus accidentally pokes a burning log too hard and as it rolls out onto the rug, fiery sparks scatter across the carpet like mini blazing marbles. He lunges for his glass of water and throws it over the smouldering rug. 'That's ridiculous!' He lifts the sizzling log up with tongs and throws it back in the grate while Jess gets down on her hands and knees patting the singed rug with a damp tea towel.

'She's sixteen,' Joy says from the sofa, hating to be left out of any conversation.

'Exactly, she's sixteen!' Fergus echoes.

'How old were you again?' Jess says. 'Fifteen?'

He pulls a face. 'That's different.'

'How? And don't start quoting gender-biased stats at me. Her being a girl makes no difference.'

'No, but her being my daughter does.' He rocks back on his heels. 'Shall I go round and fetch her?'

'It's only nine o'clock, we said eleven.'

'We said eleven when we thought they'd be watching *Love Actually* and the only thing they'd be sharing would be a box of Quality Street! Jesus, Jess, why did you say yes?' Honestly Fergus doesn't understand Jess sometimes. On one hand she can be so over-protective ('wear your coat', 'do up your laces', 'have you taken your well-man vitamin?') but at other times, it's like she's had a personality transplant to a laid-back liberal who apparently thinks nothing of their daughter becoming sexually active.

'I talked to her about it this morning. She knows to be sensible.'

'What? You knew she's having sex tonight and you didn't tell me?' he says, shaking his head in disbelief.

'That was wrong,' Joy helpfully interjects. Fergus spots Jess shoot her mother a glare that says 'shut up', while he cancels hers out by giving Joy one that says, 'Exactly'.

'Well, firstly,' Jess says, in the calm, detached doctor's voice that infuriates him, 'that would be a very strange thing to tell you. And secondly, the way you're reacting right now, even about the abstract idea of it, makes me realise I made the right decision. And thirdly, Mum, this is none of your business – you've hardly had an unblemished sexual past.'

'What on earth do you mean? I have only ever been with your father! And we waited until we were married!' Joy splutters in indignation.

'But . . . but . . .' Jess seems lost for words.

Fergus isn't sure what Jess was alluding to. She knows Joy's still faithful to Ian's memory, moving in with them the week he died and never leaving. It's taken them months to convince her to even have a coffee with Keith, let alone anything else.

'How does she know to be sensible?' Fergus says, trying to move the conversation away from Joy, who is looking hurt and confused. 'She'd never have the nerve to walk into June's chemist and buy some condoms, she'd know June would get right on the phone to us.'

Jess looks a little sheepish.

'What?' he says. 'What are you not saying?'

'Um, I gave her some.'

'Excuse me?'

'Of ours. Just two. He's sixteen, he's not going to need more.'

Fergus springs to his feet. 'Oh my God, Jess, this just gets worse and worse! You basically green-carded her to have a night of unabandoned pleasure.'

'I'm glad you two are getting on. In the bedroom, I mean. It's important to a relationship,' Joy says, her knitting needles going quicker. This time both Jess and Fergus shoot her a 'shut up' glare.

Jess sighs. 'She's losing her virginity, Fergus. Believe me, there's not going to be anything pleasurable about it.'

'So I'm just supposed to sit here, watching rubbish on television while I know that my little girl is being poked and prodded by a spotty oik two hundred metres down the road?'

'Nico has very smooth skin. And you said he was a good lad!'

'Jessica.'

'Fergus.'

'I can't believe that you're OK with this,' he says, shaking his head.

'I don't have any choice, do I? And you don't either. So when she comes in, just say, "Had a nice evening?" and leave it at that. OK?'

He shakes his head grumpily. 'I can't do it. I'm going to bed.'

'Fine. I'll be up later.'

As he reaches the door he hears Joy say over the click clack of her knitting needles, 'The goings-on in this house are better than *Emmerdale*.'

33

I'm raising a teen – what's your superpower?

It's just before midnight when I hear Molly's key in the front door. I wasn't living at home the night that I'd lost my virginity to Fergus, so I didn't have to endure a conversation with my mum, or try to slink through the house unnoticed up to my room where I could lie back and relive every moment in glorious technicolour. So I really don't want to make this awkward for Molly, which is why I'm hiding in the kitchen, and just shout a cheery, 'Hi, Molls, good night?' down the corridor.

I'm expecting a 'Yes thanks', followed by the sound of her skipping up the stairs, but instead she comes into the kitchen, her eyes rimmed with red, and my heart sinks into my slippers. Not again.

'Molly, what's wrong?'

She shakes her head at me, 'I don't want to talk about it.'

'Is it Nico? Did you have a fight?'

'I don't want to talk about it,' she says, giving me mixed messages as she sits down at the table next to me.

I put my hand on top of hers, and she doesn't shrug it away. 'What happened, Moll?'

'You didn't tell me it can come off.'

For a split second I don't follow. Then I do. Oh Christ.

'It doesn't even say it on the packet,' she adds so quietly it comes out as a whisper. 'We didn't know where it went, and then I found it inside me when I went to the toilet, and there was all the ... you know ... sticky stuff.'

I closed my eyes and sat very still. 'It's OK. Molly, it's all OK. Look, it's really late. Try and get some sleep, darling. We'll talk more about this in the morning.'

'Am I pregnant?' Her eyes are wide with horror. 'Mum, I don't want a baby, I'm sixteen, and I don't want a baby, and – oh God, I don't want a baby!' The whole weight of her collapses onto me and I sit with her in my arms, stroking her hair, soothing her, saying it's all going to be OK, thinking desperately what else I can do to make it all right.

In the morning, I text Nora. *Are you awake? We need to talk, it's urgent.*

Yes. Come round.

It's barely even light, none of the shops have opened yet. In fact, there's no sign of life anywhere apart from the early riser who I gave a steroid cream to a month or so ago; she's walking her poodle and gives me a wave as we pass each other.

Nora's waiting for me in the kitchen, a full hot teapot and two mugs ready. Her teapot is shaped like a small cottage, and when she pours it, my tea comes out of the chimney.

'So I take it our plan hasn't worked?' she says. 'Nico told me this morning that it came off.'

'I know.'

'You gave them XL condoms. He's sixteen, Jess!'

I raise my hands defensively. 'They're all I had! Anyway, I thought you were giving them some, too?'

'I made him a natural vegan spermicide out of aloe vera and lemon.'

There's a heavy pause, then I say, 'What?'

'Aloe vera and lemon.'

'I heard you, I just meant, what?'

'It's chemical-free!'

'I'm not worried about the chemicals,' I hiss, 'I'm more concerned about the lack of them. Particularly the lack of sperm-killing ones! We're trying to prevent a pregnancy not cool down sunburn and make a bloody pancake!'

Duly chastened, Nora asks, 'So what now?'

I shrug. 'Go back again, give the right size condoms and a spermicide that might actually work? Or I could go back further than that and get a stash of emergency contraception from Guernsey so that I have it ready?'

In the end I do both.

All bases are covered.

I have now had the sex talk with Molly eleven times. I have given her a variety of different-sized condoms, all of which either come off or break. I went back in time two weeks, gave her the pill, but then she forgot to take it twice and had a bout of food poisoning once, rendering it null and void. She flatly refuses for me or anyone else to insert the coil, saying that it is gross, and I have to stop myself from saying that that is nothing compared to the indignity of childbirth. We've even tried banning them from seeing each other, and that just resulted in both of them climbing out of their first-floor windows and shimmying down the drainpipe, risking an injury that's actually far more serious than an unplanned pregnancy.

Basically, nothing that Nora or I try works and it is exhausting replaying the same day over and over just to get the same results. I even try telling Molly the semi-truth, like I did back in the beginning, with the cleavage picture, saying to her, 'I don't know how I know this, but I have a feeling that if you and Nico are intimate tonight, the contraception won't work, so it's probably best to abstain.' But abstinence and teenagers are not great bedfellows, so when my 'premonition' comes true, she blames me for putting the thought into her head, and says 'the universe must have listened to me'. I'm running out of options.

'There is a chance that she's not actually going to be pregnant, you know,' Nora says to me, on the twelfth day that we've relived. We've met on the bench because unless we come up with a really good reason not to, we're going to try and go back to change yesterday one last time. 'We could be worrying over nothing.'

'But if she is?' I say, voicing the unthinkable. 'What then?'

'Then she is. It is clearly impossible to change it, we've tried everything.'

I give a reluctant nod. I really don't want to admit defeat, but it's looking like I have to. 'Maybe it's like what Maggie said about death, when we were all in the surgery? That death can't be changed. Well, maybe the same applies to conception.'

'Maggie who?'

I realised as I said her name that Maggie said that in the past I erased, not the past that Nora has lived.

'Maggie Masters?' Nora asks. 'The teacher? How would she know?'

I shake my head far more vigorously than I had intended. 'No, no, sorry, it was in a dream, it never happened.'

It's clear Nora doesn't believe me at all. 'I've used that line far too many times to cover up something I've done. What have you changed? What about Maggie?'

I try once again to shake my head. 'Nothing!'

'Jess, how do you know her?'

'She's Liam's teacher.'

'You said we were all in the surgery together?'

I shake my head again, hoping that by doing so I can dislodge my slip of the tongue from her mind.

'Does she know?' Nora presses on, her eyes wide. 'About the bench?'

'Look I—'

'This is really important, Jess, we need to contain this.'

'It is contained. She's fine.'

'But she knows?'

'She's never actually done it. Well, once or twice, but not for years.'

'How do you know?'

There's no way to answer that without telling her everything, and I really don't want to do that. I feel bad enough as it is living with the knowledge that I've completely altered Maggie's life, without Nora adding to my guilt. Although Nora's much more free-spirited and would probably approve of me steering Maggie away from a life of materialism. She did after all make her own vegan spermicide. That's not normal behaviour for someone who secretly covets underfloor heating and a Range Rover with lambs' leather seats. But regardless of that, I can't admit that I ripped the life of a millionaire away from someone, irrespective of how happy they seem about it.

'Jess? Tell me.'

I rub my face with my hands. 'To be absolutely honest, Nora, I'm finding it really hard to know what's actually happened, and what hasn't.'

'That's why you shouldn't do this. I told you that. It gets too confusing and messes everything up.'

Suddenly, I can't be bothered any more. It's not only confusing, it's exhausting, and I'm desperate to actually talk to someone about it, to unburden myself of everything I've done. I've had enough of keeping this massive secret and trying to make sense of everything myself. I take a deep breath and decide to tell her everything. 'When I moved to the island in the summer, you, me, Maggie and Eileen became friends.'

'I was friends with Maggie Masters?'

'Yes, you knew each other really well.'

'I mean, we've lived on the same island for most of our lives, and she teaches my kids, but I wouldn't say that we've ever been friends.'

'Well, you were when I moved here. You had a rota, where one of you would sit on the bench each night, to protect other people from doing it.'

'Actually, that does sound like something Maggie would come up with.'

'I found out about the bench by accident, and you three came to my surgery and warned me not to do it. Then Maggie came again by herself, and told me all the bad things that had come of her winning the lottery and that I shouldn't mess with it at all.'

Nora gapes. 'She'd won the lottery?'

'Yes, and she was really unhappy. But she told me how dangerous it was, and that I should never do it.'

'But you did anyway.'

'I went back six years a couple of weeks ago—'

Nora sucks in her breath through her teeth, making a loud whistle. 'You shouldn't really do that. You can change everything like that.'

'I know. I didn't think I changed very much, but everyone is different now – my husband, my kids, my mum, everyone. But the biggest change was that on the night six years ago when I wanted to come back to the present, Maggie was sat on this bench. It was going to be the night when she would win the lottery, and I persuaded her not to.'

'And . . .?'

'And clearly she didn't do it. She used to live in an amazing house, with a white gravel driveway—'

'Bit over the top for a town with no cars.'

'And she wore beautiful clothes, and had stunning hair—'

'She didn't get it done on this island, then.'

'And her nails were always perfect—'

'She sounds frightful.'

'And she was married to a man called Oscar, who seemed a bit of a bully to be honest. Oh!' I suddenly remember another piece to the puzzle. 'He was the lawyer who defended your husband in your divorce case when you discovered he had another family on Guernsey.'

She stares at me, and her face is deathly pale. After a long pause, she says, 'But I'm not divorced. What other family?'

Shit. Shit. Shit.

34

Mouth open. Foot firmly inside . . .

'But you said . . .' I stutter, grappling desperately to work out what's real, what's imagined. Everything is blurry, nothing is distinct any more, so many times, memories, all melded together like a jigsaw with extra pieces that don't fit anywhere. 'You said the other night that Eileen helped you catch your husband out. That you went back in time together.'

She had definitely said that.

'You definitely said that.'

Nora's voice when she answers is shaky and disarmingly quiet, as though she's concentrating hard on every word. 'I said that Eileen helped me when I suspected him, but we didn't find anything. What do you know?'

I shake my head really fast. 'Nothing really, I don't know – please, just ignore me, Nora. If you're happily married, please don't let anything I've said make you doubt that. I'm sorry, it's just so difficult to remember what's happened when and—'

'What if I'm not happily married?'

'What?'

'What if I have had my doubts about Gareth for years, but have put them to one side for the sake of the kids? What if I've followed him a number of times, trying to catch him with another woman, but I never do?'

'And have you?'

'Please. Just tell me what you know, Jessica.'

'But it might not have happened, it might be a past that you didn't have.'

'I still want to know. Please.'

She looks so earnest, so unsure of herself and her life, so desperate for reassurance and answers that I have to tell her what I know. 'I saw him a couple of weeks ago. With another woman, called Kate, and two children in Marks and Spencer's.'

She looks unimpressed. 'He hates Marks and Spencer's.' Her brow furrows. 'Why didn't you mention this before?'

'I just assumed that you weren't together any more, because you'd told me before that Oscar – that's Maggie's husband that it turns out isn't her husband – was the one who defended your husband when you both went to court to get divorced. Apparently even though he was the one who had another family, Oscar made him look like the victim, as though you'd driven him to it, and he took all your money.'

'What money?'

'Your lottery winnings.'

Nora pales. 'How do you know about that?'

'What do you mean?'

'I haven't told anyone about that. No one knows I've won anything.'

'So where is it? Where's all your money?'

'In trust for Nico and Elodie.'

'Why? Why did you keep that a secret?'

Nora sits back down gently on the bench. 'Because I think I've always known. No one needs to work every other Christmas. Or every other birthday. Or have two different mobile phones, or have long periods where they can't be contacted. "I'm going on a long-haul flight," he'd say. "The time difference in Sydney makes it difficult to call." Or, "I have back-to-back meetings at a conference, don't call me as it'll be really embarrassing if my phone goes off in the middle of it," and like a complete idiot, I always said, "Of course, whatever you think best." Or he'd yo-yo from complete indifference to stifling over-attentiveness.' She barks out a sarcastic laugh that's not a proper one, because there's nothing funny about what she's saying. 'Do you know what first made me think there might be something amiss? He started having his bum waxed. Honestly. After nearly ten years of marriage, he suddenly decides that having a hairy bottom isn't for him. Who does that?'

'Was he particularly hairy?' I ask.

'Like a gibbon.'

'Well then, that's probably for the best.' I smile, and move my elbow a little to try to nudge a smile out of her, too. It works. She lets out a little laugh. Then a louder one. I laugh too. Then we both dissolve in hysterical laughter, tears running down our faces. We're laughing and crying and crying and laughing, the presents, the pasts, the futures, the loves, the money, the losses, the pregnancies, all mixed together, all blended in a complicated multi-colour whirlwind that neither of us has the faintest hope of unravelling.

'So, what are you going to do?' I ask finally, when our laughter has subsided and our tears have been wiped on our sleeves.

'About my husband's other life, or the fact that we might be sharing a grandchild in nine months' time?'

I've almost forgotten why we're there in the first place, sitting on the bench in the middle of the afternoon, on Christmas Eve. 'I'm not sure I can face reliving the day again,' I admit, sighing. 'They're going to have sex, she's either going to be pregnant or she's not. We evidently can't change this. So we have to deal with it.'

Nora nods. 'I agree. We've tried our best, but this is obviously what's meant to happen. Or not happen. I guess we'll see in a couple of weeks' time.'

'I call dibs on Granny,' I say. 'You can have Nana.'

'Nana Nora. It's got a nice ring to it.'

Another memory floats up to the surface, one that I usually pat back down, back inside its box. 'That's if she wants to keep the baby,' I say. 'It's her choice. We can't make her go through with this if it's not what she wants.'

'Of course.' Nora waits a couple of beats before adding, 'You're a good mum, Jess.'

I swivel round to face her. 'Why do you say that?'

'Because I think you need to hear it.'

Molly jumps up from the sofa when I walk back in the door. Liam and Fergus are playing Xbox together sat on the floor, so I motion with my head for her to join me in the kitchen.

'Did you get the pills?' she whispers.

'No. It's impossible. There's none on the island, and by the time the ferries start running, it'll be too late. Sit down for a second.' I pull out two kitchen chairs for us. 'Listen to me, Molls. Sometimes life just throws us down a rabbit hole that we had no idea was even there, and takes us on a journey that we can't plan for. If you are pregnant – ' I rub my hand over hers – 'then we will help you come to a decision that's right for you. But there is absolutely no point worrying about that now, we won't know what we're dealing with for another few weeks, so let's put that beautiful smile on your face, find a carrot and a mince pie to leave out for Santa – ' She grimaces at me – 'and enjoy Christmas. It might be that you're not pregnant and won't even need to make a decision. But if you are, whatever you decide, we will support you, and love you, and be there for you. OK? I love you and it's going to be all right.'

She leans in and gives me a hug, the first one I can remember from her in so long. She's warm, and grown, and beautiful and brave. She's my daughter.

There are two pink lines. Of course there are. I knew there would be. And I'm pretty sure I also didn't misdiagnose the fleeting look of joyous excitement on Molly's face before it was replaced with sheer terror.

'Fucking hell.'

'Language.'

'Fucking hell,' Molly repeats, her eyes not moving from the stick.

'You're right. Fucking hell.'

'I'm having a baby!'

'If you want to.'

'I do. I mean . . . I think I do? I don't know how to change a nappy though.'

'I'll show you.'

'I can't afford a pram.'

'We'll buy one.'

'How will I feed it? How will I know it's hungry?'

I smile at her. 'You'll just know. Much of being a mother is completely instinctive.' As I say it, I'm completely floored by its truth. I've spent the entirety of my children's lives planning, racing, juggling, and never stopping and just being. Because there's noise in silence, and it was always too loud for me to bear before.

'It's OK, darling.' I pull her into a hug, rewriting this moment from my own past. 'We'll figure it all out.'

Molly suddenly stiffens. 'What are you going to tell Dad?'

'Me?'

'Of course you. I can't!'

★ ★ ★

Truth be told, the Fergus I'm currently married to is nothing like the Fergus I left London with, so I have no idea how he's going to take this news. If you'd asked me a year ago, I'd have been able to accurately predict his response, but this version of him? I honestly don't know him well enough yet. My instinct, though, is that this is a conversation that needs to happen in a pub. The proximity to hard liquor coupled with the presence of other people nearby should, in theory, halt any dramatic outbursts in their tracks.

'Well, this is a nice treat,' he says, taking a long sip of the pint of bitter I just put in front of him. 'I thought we were doing dry January?'

'We were. But then something happened today, which makes the need for alcohol slightly pressing.'

He puts down his drink with slightly too much force. 'Is everything all right? Are you ill? Oh no, have you run some tests on yourself and you've—'

'No, no. Nothing like that. Right, well, I'm just going to come right out and say it.'

'OK.'

'I mean, there's no point just beating around the bush and winding myself in knots.'

'No.'

'So . . . the thing is . . . Here's the thing. The thing is . . .'

He takes my hand in his and makes me look at him. 'Jess. What's the thing?'

I take a deep breath. 'Molly's pregnant.' I automatically wince, bracing myself for the gust of breath from his mouth that will accompany a loud lion-like roar.

But none comes.

He takes another sip of his pint and licks his lips. 'Righto.'

'Fergus,' I say, 'did you hear me? Molly's having a baby.'

'Yep.'

This is very curious. Of all the possible responses I'd rehearsed in my head, this was not one of them. Pushing over tables, pummelling Nico's ridiculously smooth-skinned face into a muddy puddle, whipping out a tape measure to get Molly fitted for a nun's habit, or perhaps even a veering into an unexplored territory of emotion and tears, were all possible contenders. But this – this calm, measured, almost mechanical sipping of his pint, is totally off script. He must be in shock. Any minute now he's going to blow.

Fergus

Fergus could never forget the scene in his own parents' house in Dublin when he'd arrived there in a shaking mess the day after Jess had told him she was pregnant with Anna. The words that flew out of his mother's Catholic mouth necessitated an urgent trip to confession to beg forgiveness, both for the colour of her language and the unnatural instincts of her unmarried son. His father just shook his head at him in shamed disappointment. He could imagine the scene in Jess's childhood home wasn't too different. *Well*, Fergus thinks, *not this time.*

'This is our chance to do it differently, isn't it?'

Jess nods. She must know exactly what he means.

'Well, then,' he says. 'That's what we'll do.'

Fergus buys another round. He and Jess are both largely silent as they drink it, but it's a nice silence, one where they're both lost in the same thoughts, with no need to voice them out loud.

'Do you like it here?' Jess says suddenly.

'What do you mean?'

She picks up a beer mat and flips it between her fingers, 'It's been nearly six months, and they need me back in London.'

'What, your old surgery?'

Jess nods.

'So we have to leave?' He tries to keep the disappointment out of his voice.

'Not necessarily. They were planning to close the surgery here down, and make everyone go across to Guernsey because they couldn't find a replacement for me—'

'They can't do that! What about Bernie's asthma?' Bernie's the captain of the skittles team, who has a quick session with a nebuliser in between goes. He definitely needs an island doctor, and perhaps a different hobby.

' – but something changed their minds,' Jess continues, 'and they've offered me a permanent placement here, if I want it.'

'And do you?'

'Do *you*?'

'I asked you first.'

'I asked you second.'

He takes another sip. 'The beer's cheaper here,' he says.

'True.'

'But there's no Chinese takeaway.'

'Also true.'

He fiddles with a beer mat. 'It'd be a nicer place for little'un to grow up.'

'Definitely true.'

'And I am in the skittles team now, I probably can't let them down.'

'Well that's a compelling reason right there.' Jess smiles. 'You didn't even need the other ones.'

'So we're staying put?'

'Looks that way.'

Fergus clinks his pint glass against his wife's wine glass. 'Cheers. Here's to . . .'

'Getting it right,' Jess says.

Fergus knows exactly what she means.

35

Sugar and spice and all things nice

Molly phones at the end of morning surgery in her lunch break at school to ask me to pick up some more ginger tea, which she's been addicted to for the past couple of months now. She likes to drink it in between sticking her head down the toilet. Morning sickness seems to have replaced netball as a sport. The way she's going, she may well make it to the Olympics.

She hasn't started to show yet, despite being twelve weeks along, although every morning she does go through the charade of standing sideways in front of my long wardrobe mirror in her underwear, saying excitedly, 'Look, I'm sure there's a bump.' We've got the scan tomorrow at the hospital in Guernsey. I have got an ultrasound machine in the surgery but it's pretty old, and I'd much rather she visit a special maternity unit for it, although it's taken every ounce of self-restraint not to wheel the ultrasound machine into the house and pounce on her with the probe to listen for the heartbeat while she's sleeping.

It's just going to be the two of us. At first we'd toyed with the idea of hiring a minibus, and Fergus, Nora and Nico coming too to make a day of it, but Molly said she'd prefer it if it was just me and her, and as I'm doing everything differently this time around, I agreed to go along with whatever she feels is right. Fergus thankfully understood without me having to explain it. I could tell Nora was disappointed, as I would have been if it was the other way around, with it being the first grandchild. But anyway, her priority has been Nico recently, who has been a whiter shade of pale for the last three months. He didn't ask for this, any more than Molly did, any more than Fergus or I did when it was us sat there with our whole lives ahead of us.

Fergus took him out for the day fishing soon after the pregnancy was confirmed. I didn't need to ask him to, it was his suggestion, and he told Nico that he understood how he felt, and exactly why that was. I had the same talk with Molly. I told her about Anna and half of me was braced for an angry outburst about her whole life being based on a lie, but instead she just said, 'That must have been so hard,' then started to cry. For me. For the sister she never got to meet. I honestly can't second guess anything about my family any more.

The irony is, time travel has turned them into the family I always wanted, but in doing so, they've become almost strangers who I have to get to know all over again. Fergus doesn't even smell the same – gone is the expensive cologne he bought because of the promised seductive allure from the black and white billboard ads, and in its place is his natural, musky scent that is, in all honesty, far more appealing. Liam's bedroom floor is cluttered with blueprints of his various inventions, meticulous scale drawings propped up on the architect's drafting table we apparently got him for his twelfth birthday. The most incredible addition to the house so far, tiny things that speak the loudest, are the novelty door stoppers that prop open their bedroom doors – a filled hedgehog for Molly and a VW Beetle campervan for Liam. *Come on in*, they silently say, *sit awhile and have a chat*. I can't act surprised when I see these things, items around the house and garden that the others have grown so used to they don't see them, but every new one I notice is a symbol of change, a sign we're different, we're better than before.

'I'll send you the ultrasound picture as soon as we have it,' I promise Nora when I pop round to hers just before the ferry leaves. 'And are you sure you don't want me to take a few of those bags with me and dump them on Gareth's lawn?' I nod towards the four-foot-high wall of bin bags lining her hallway. Nora has spent the last few weeks packing them full of her husband's belongings that he's meant to be picking up.

Far from being an import-export manager for a large multinational with offices in Sydney, Kuala Lumpur and Bangkok, it turns out that Gareth is a self-employed telemarketer for a power-wash company who works from his kitchen table in the three-bed semi he shares with his 'wife' Kate, their two kids and a hamster called Chuckles. We know all this through a series of covert surveillance operations, none of which used time travel, just hours of old-fashioned Internet snooping. Gareth and Kate had a nice week in a caravan in Lyme Regis in Dorset last summer, although the weather was terrible for the whole week (*'Thank goodness for Scrabble! #familytime #triplewordscore'*) and Kate has finally mastered her first soufflé, a rather odd creation of stilton and peach (*#masterchefhereicome #nextstopbakeoff*). Their eldest child just completed her 50-metre swimming badge (*#likeafish*), while the youngest one is a keen horse rider and just did a gymkhana (*#borntoride*). It seems that Kate also sometimes doesn't think through her hashtags.

'How are you feeling?' I ask Nora.

'Excited.'

'About the scan or getting rid of all this?' I gesture towards the bags.

'Both. New starts all round.'

'You're being very brave.'

'I took my time though, didn't I?'

'Better late than never,' I say, smiling.

'Thank you, Jess.'

I bat away her thanks with my hand. 'I've done nothing. Well, apart from blow your entire world to pieces with my big mouth.'

'If you hadn't, I'd still be trapped in a miserable marriage. You've saved me and Maggie.'

'The difference is, she has no idea.'

'From what you've told me, I'm sure Maggie would thank you too, if she knew.'

After the parents' evening back in December, I spent every day that week pacing back and forth, wracked with guilt that I'd robbed Maggie of a life of plenty and consigned her to a life of scrimping and saving, and being – well, ordinary. I'd made up my mind I was going to tell her and went round to her house on Boxing Day, which, now I knew it wasn't a grand mansion with a white gravel driveway, was much easier to find. Tom answered the door dressed in old clothes speckled with flecks of yellow paint.

'Doctor Bay, hello! Do come in,' he said.

'Please, call me Jess.' It's the least I can do, I thought, after ruining your honeymoon by making you go to somewhere in a caravan rather than a suite on stilts in the Indian Ocean.

'I'll just get Maggie. She's currently up a stepladder, even though I've offered a hundred times to do the high bits, but she's pretty stubborn when she makes up her mind about something, as I'm sure you know.'

The Maggie I knew was a people pleaser. A yes-woman, battered into submission by an overbearing husband and a life of being taken advantage of. She was shy, cautious, suspicious, and bore absolutely no resemblance to the beaming, carefree pregnant woman who bounded into the living room, paint roller in hand, greeting me with a massive smile. 'Hello, Dr Bay! What a lovely surprise.'

'Jess, please. I hope you don't mind me just dropping in, but I was passing and I thought I'd pop in and see how you are.'

'That's so sweet of you. Would you like some tea, Jess?'

'Only if you're making some, but I don't want to be any trouble?'

'Not at all. You're more than welcome. I need to pick your brains anyway.'

'Oh?'

'On whether you would be able to give us some antenatal classes? I have no idea what I'm doing, and it would be great if you could teach me – ' Tom cleared his throat in the background – 'sorry, us, everything we need to know about how to keep this baby alive.'

It was a horrible choice of words. But they weren't to know.

'I'm sure I could put something together for you, but maybe there's a midwife on Guernsey or Jersey who would be interested in coming over to do a short course for you? They'd be a bit more up to date with birthing options. I'll put the word out.' It would be a good idea for Molly and Nico to join it, too.

As we drank our tea, my eyes darted around, looking for signs and clues that I made the right choice changing her life, that she was definitely happier now. Tom clearly adored her, and every surface of their home was filled with the happy clutter of married life. A neon LOVE sign hung above the cooker hood; a collection of wedding photos took centre stage on the main wall in the living room, one capturing the two of them embroiled in a cyclone of confetti, both of their heads flung back in sheer sepia joy. I was drinking from a mug with Mr on it, while Tom's said Mrs. Out of the corner of my eye I spotted another photo, of the pair of them with two blonde girls sitting on their laps.

'Who are they?' I asked, feeling a sense of déjà vu that I couldn't place.

'Mia and Talia. They're Tom's nieces, his sister's children.'

Then I remembered. Of course! Maggie told me in the pub that the reason she never erased her life with Oscar and started again was because she'd seen a picture of Tom with these two girls online and assumed they were his. It was an easy leap to make as they looked very similar to him, but if she'd known the truth about them being his nieces not his daughters, she might have wiped out her life post-lottery win herself anyway.

'You seem very happy,' I said to Maggie when Tom went into the kitchen. I just wanted to make doubly sure.

'Of course I am,' she replied. 'Why wouldn't I be? I have everything I could ever want.' She looked as though she was going to say something else, but stopped talking as soon as Tom brought in a plate of biscuits. She'd said enough though to rub balm on my conscience.

I snap back to the present and return Nora's smile. 'You might be right.'

'I know you feel that you took the choice away from Maggie, but you didn't. It was still her decision, you didn't force her not to go through with it.'

'Speaking of choices,' I say, 'you're definitely making the right one getting rid of Gareth and all his rubbish.'

'I know. New starts all round. I know it probably sounds like I'm having a mid-life crisis, but I'm thinking of getting my nose pierced to celebrate my freedom.'

I smile. 'You should. I think it would really suit you.'

36

Saying hello. And goodbye.

'I'm too young.'
  'No you're not.
  'I can't do this.'
  'Yes you can.'
  'I don't know what to do.'
  'You do.'
  'I'm going to let her down.'
  'No you're not.'
  'It hurts.'
  'I know.'
  'It hurts so much.'
  'Hold my hand. I'm right here. I'm not going anywhere.'
She's incredible. She also unnervingly knows far more swear words than I even knew existed. That's all Fergus.

As soon as I can see the baby's head, I take Molly's hands in mine and steer them down so she can guide her own daughter into the world before Nico cuts the cord with trembling hands.

Eloise Bay-Lyons is born at 4.32 a.m. on the morning of 15 September. I stroke Molly's head as she nurses her daughter for the first time, and tell her that she is magnificent, because she is. Then I run out into the hospital corridor and shout to Fergus, Liam, Nora and Mum that she's here, the baby's here. When they're taken back to the ward, we crowd around Molly's bed and a symphony of cooing and adoring aahs fill the room. The nurses, usually so intent on enforcing the two-visitor rule, turn a blind eye. After a while Molly's eyes begin to droop and I usher everyone out, smiling as Nico drops a tender, awkward kiss on Molly's forehead before he leaves, and Fergus plants one on mine that's not awkward at all.

I don't want to leave them, my baby, and her baby. I never want to leave them.

'Mum?' Molly yawns, once it's only us left and a calm silence has blanketed the room. 'You haven't held her yet.'

I reach out for my granddaughter, just an hour old, so small and warm in my arms. She's strong and beautiful, just like her mum.

As Molly sleeps in the bed, I sit in the armchair alongside her, Anna sleeping peacefully in my arms, because somehow Eloise morphed into the auntie she'll never meet sometime around daybreak. Their identical tiny pink rosebud lips and small upturned noses make it easy for me to travel back two decades and have this moment with the baby I never got to hold.

'You're so loved,' I whisper in Anna's little ear as I gently caress her downy head. 'So, so loved.'

I honestly don't know how long I sit like that, with her centimetre-long fingers wrapped around my mine. After a few hours, the baby starts to stir, turning instinctively to my chest to look for milk. 'Darling,' I whisper to Molly, 'someone's a little hungry and wants their mummy.'

And I have somewhere I need to be.

'I was meant to be going to Tenerife for New Year, but I told Mark that they're saying that planes are literally going to fall out of the sky come midnight, so I'm staying put in Enfield, thank you very much.'

'My sister lives near a nuclear power station, and she's terrified it's going to blow up on the dot of midnight.'

'Well, it could do. No one knows.'

'I know. I've stocked up with tins of soup and beans and things and I'm going to fill my bath with water just in case we get cut off.'

'Did you hear President Clinton's speech? Even he seemed worried.'

It worked. It worked, and now I run the risk of ruining absolutely everything just when it's all going right. My legs took me up to the bench on autopilot last night; I didn't even think about it. Holding Eloise just stripped everything else away and all I could think about was Anna, and now I'm here, I'm actually here, and I want to go back to my lovely life, and leave all of this behind. I sit up in the hospital bed and wince with pain, the fresh scar pulling taut across my stomach. I can't be here. Not now. I can't risk losing everything that's come after. My breathing is ragged. I need to leave here as quickly as possible before anything happens. I try to focus on the muted television screen attached to the wall of the ward to calm down, to slow down my pounding heart, to work out what to do. Millennium Bug headlines run along a ticker-tape on the bottom of the screen next to the date and time. Seeing the numbers there: 19.12.99 06.32 jolt me like an electric shock into reality.

I can't leave without doing what I came here to do.

'Excuse me?' I say, holding up my hand to attract the nurses' attention towards my bed that's at the far end of the ward under a window with the blinds not yet drawn for the day.

'Yes, love?' one says, approaching me. I recognise her. She was the nurse that took me down to theatre for the emergency caesarean. She held my hand and told me everything was going to be all right. She wasn't to know.

'I'd like to see my baby please.'

She looks surprised, but then I remember that she would be. Anna was born four days ago, and she was whisked straight off to intensive care, and I stayed where I was. For the first two days the nurses and doctors had constantly cajoled me to go. 'Hold her hand,' they said. 'Sing to her,' another one said, as though trilling Celine Dion songs through the thick glass of an incubator was the most natural thing in the world. I shook my head every time. Eventually they all stopped asking.

'Oh,' the nurse says, 'yes, yes of course. Do you want to have a bit of breakfast first and then we can go?'

I shake my head. 'No, thank you, I want to go now.'

'I'll just get your dressing gown, and take you up there myself.'

She tries to make conversation on the way to the neonatal intensive care ward, but I honestly can't tell you what she says. I'm so hyper aware of not saying or doing anything that might change the future, the future that I actually really like being part of. I just need to see Anna, and then go. In and out, before anyone can see me or speak to me. I can't risk anything about the future we live in changing, not now it's so perfect. I just want to hold my baby, and then go home.

Fergus's head is bowed and leaning against the glass of Anna's incubator. It didn't occur to me that he'd be here. I didn't know that he sat there with her. The night before she died, he came to my ward to say goodnight. He tried to brush the greasy hair out of my eyes, and I angrily moved my head away, telling him to leave me alone. He told me she was very poorly. Those were his words, 'very poorly'. I made a sullen jibe about him being a medical student and that he could do better than that, what was her blood pressure? Heart rate? Respiratory rate? He asked me to come with him, to sit with her, and I said no. I was tired. I then stayed awake all night, trying to make myself brave enough to do it. Brave enough to walk to the end of the corridor, go up one level in the lift and go to her. Three, perhaps four minutes of courage, and I'd be with her. And I couldn't. But Fergus apparently did. He was here for her. She wasn't alone.

Fergus must sense me standing there because he looks up at me, his young face sporting new grey, ugly shadows under his red-rimmed eyes. He lets out a gasp of surprise, and holds his hand out for me to take.

This is the moment that could change everything. But I have to do this. I can't walk away again.

We sit like that for over an hour, our hands entwined, our eyes not moving from Anna's pale face decorated with tubes, the ticking clock on the wall reminding me with every staccato beat that we are one more second closer to losing her.

'Can we hold her?' I ask a doctor who comes to silently, reverently, adjust one of Anna's machines.

The doctor hasn't seen the future like I have, but she knows anyway what it's going to hold. I know that's the reason she says yes, when all hospital protocol would say no. I nod eagerly when she asks if we'd like her to take a picture. Yes, yes, we would. 'Take two,' I say. 'Keep taking them. Take as many as you can.' Anna is so light, weighing barely more than the blanket she's wrapped in. We take turns, Fergus and I, holding, stroking, crying, pointing out her tiny fingers, her button nose, so like the Molly, Liam and Eloise I've met, but who are still strangers to this Fergus.

We have shared so much in this life of ours, all of it yet to be endured and enjoyed, as we sit there, twenty-two years old, half the age of the versions of us I know, holding a child we made by accident, who in exactly nine minutes is going to set every machine she's attached to beeping and wailing.

'You are so loved,' I whisper in her tiny ear, filling every second of the eight and a half minutes we have left with her. 'So, so loved. I know you can't stay with us for long, but we think about you every day. Every single day. You're beautiful, and perfect, and I love you, with every bone in my body, my darling.'

'She's going to be OK,' Fergus says, stroking my shoulder.

No, I think, she's not. But we are.

I wasn't going to, but I stay for Anna's funeral.

So much of my plan has been torn up and shredded. In and out. That's how I pitched it to myself up on the cliff. A quick cuddle, and home to 2023. But I didn't count on seeing Fergus, or sitting with my parents on the bench outside of the hospital an hour after Anna died instead of rushing past them, my tears blinding them from view. Anna was my daughter, my grief, my business, that's how I've spent the last two decades coping with it. But she wasn't. She belonged to all of us.

It's Christmas Eve, we buried Anna yesterday, and twenty-two-year-old Fergus and I are standing looking at the lights on the four-foot-tall Christmas tree that we bought earlier on from a road-side seller and put up on a coffee table in the little one-bedroom flat we used to share at university. We cancelled Christmas the first time it came around in 1999, because I honestly didn't think there was another option. He flew home to Ireland to be with his parents and I stayed shut up in my old bedroom at my parents' house, refusing to join them for lunch, not pulling a single cracker, not letting a morsel of turkey pass my lips. How dare I celebrate the day when Anna couldn't? I didn't even take Fergus's phone call when he rang. That's why I had to stay this time, to do it again, to do it right.

I keep meaning to go home, back to 2023, I do, but then there is another moment that I need to change, another conversation that I need to re-do, to make better. I'm torn between going back and staying here permanently. If I stay here, I have no idea what that means for my body. I know from Maggie, Nora and Eileen that the more time you spend in the past the more your body deteriorates in the present, but what if I just stayed here and never went back? Would I die twenty-four years earlier? Maybe it would be worth it. I could re-do the last two decades and do them right. I wouldn't throw myself into my studies, my work, to heal the gaping wound made by Anna's death. I could be kind when I was harsh, I could be present when I was absent, and I could tell the people I love every single day that I do love them. I wouldn't just assume they know because I feel their forehead for a fever twice a day, or tell them to wear a coat, or buy expensive multivitamins. I couldn't make Anna better, but I was damned if anyone else I loved was going to die on my watch. But I've realised that keeping them healthy and safe is not enough, so this time around, I'd actually say it. Every day. Many times a day. 'I love you.' Because then they'd really know. But what if by staying here, Molly and Liam never happen? What if Eloise is never born? Too much might have changed already, I can't risk anything else being different.

But then, these versions of Fergus, Mum and Dad need me. Every time I think about those other versions of us all, the ones over there in that foreign country that doesn't exist yet, my stomach plummets. I have no idea how me being here has changed them. But I know they can't be the same, not now.

'It's lovely,' Fergus says, looking at the white bauble with the red candy-cane writing spelling out 'Anna' that I picked up from the same garden centre earlier that morning, to match the ones I will buy in many years' time for the rest of the family.

'This way, she'll be part of every Christmas,' I say. 'We'll still be getting this decoration out in twenty-odd years' time.'

'I'll be in my forties.'

'Yes, you will.'

'Bet I'll still be devilishly handsome.'

'You will. But you'll also have grey hair coming out of your nostrils.'

Fergus grimaces. 'I will not.'

'You will. But don't worry, I'll buy you a male grooming kit for your fortieth that's got different scissors for nose and ear hair.'

'You will not! That's a crap present.'

'I bet you a fiver that one day you're going to buy me a hand-held vacuum cleaner for my birthday and I won't talk to you for three days.'

'That will never happen.'

'It will. But I wager that's not going to be the worst present either. I predict that over the next twenty years you'll also give me a handful of women's magazines you've bought from the garage, a gym membership, and a steam iron.'

'You have a very poor perception of future-me.'

'You're not all bad,' I say. 'You're actually pretty fantastic.'

'And you honestly think we'll still be together in twenty years? That we'll have some more children?'

I nod. 'I do.'

'Well in that case, let's make a pact now, that we only ever buy each other highly impractical but brilliant presents. No household appliances, or anything that eliminates body hair from crevices.'

I say, 'Deal,' but can't help wondering what on earth I'm going to buy him from now on. And as much as he thinks he won't, he really will need that grooming kit.

We fall into silence after this back and forth, knowing the banter is merely a distraction from the grief, a way for us not to think about the fact that somehow we need to move on with our own lives, without her. But at least this time I know we can.

And now it's time to go back.

37

My kind of day

I wasn't sure it was going to work. I was a bit late getting back to Forth after stopping at the hospital to thank the intensive care team for their dedication and to tell the nurses on the maternity ward to go to Tenerife, stop worrying about the nuclear power plant and not to waste the bath water on a shortage that's not going to happen come midnight on Y2K.

The sun was already halfway into the sea when I tumbled onto the bench catching my breath. I'd had to duck and dive in and out of doorways as my twenty-two-year-old self tried to avoid younger, but definitely recognisable figures from the island, and I had had a C-section just a couple of weeks earlier, so I wasn't as quick as I'd planned to be.

But from what I can see, all seems to be as I left it as I pad downstairs, definitely in my own house on the island, definitely in September 2023, as the calendar hanging on the kitchen wall testifies. It's the same family planner we had before. That's good. I flick through it, and much of the scribbles on it are familiar (*Start of term, End of term, Iris vet check-up, Liam football*) but some make no sense, which unnerves me. Every Monday, Wednesday and Friday it says *Surgery*, but I open the surgery every weekday, so what can this mean? Did I go down to part-time hours?

Also, even more disconcertingly, I suddenly realise that there are no baby items anywhere. Before I left yesterday, Eloise's new pram was in the hallway next to the new infant car seat, still in its wrapping, ready for us to collect the two of them from the hospital later today. The hallway is completely empty.

My heart skips a beat.

What the hell have I done? I race up the stairs, taking them two at a time and barge into Molly's empty bedroom, it's tidier than usual, school books stacked up on her desk, the same photos of her and her netball team around her mirror, a framed picture of her and Nico on her bedside cabinet, next to a half-full jar of folic acid tablets and pregnancy vitamins. OK, so at least I know she was pregnant. But the baby?

'What are you doing?' Liam asks from behind me, standing in the open doorway brushing his teeth.

'Where's Molly?' I gasp in panic. Please, please tell me she's with the baby. Please tell me I haven't ruined everything.

'She's still at the hospital.'

'With Eloise?' I blurt hopefully.

'Who's Eloise?'

They warned me. All three of them warned me about it being dangerous, of not knowing the consequences of changing the past. The potential tragedy I could unfurl unwittingly. The moan that escapes my body as I sink onto the bed brings Fergus running into Molly's room. He crouches down beside me. 'Liam, go and get your Mum some water. Darling, what's wrong, are you in pain?'

I would have no idea where to start even if I wanted to. I look up at him from between my fingers, which are covering my face. He's wearing a dark suit with a black tie. He doesn't even own a black suit. He must have got it specially for today. Oh God, oh God.

'I need to get going if I'm going to make my first appointment,' he says, 'but I don't want to leave you if you're ill.'

'Appointment?' I say weakly.

'It's Monday.'

'Right. Of course. Monday. So you're . . .' I trail off, hoping he'll fill in the missing blank.

'Going to surgery. Then after you've finished the house calls we can go and pick Molly and Anna up after that as planned.'

My blood runs cold in my veins.

'What did I say? You look like you've seen a ghost?'

'You said Anna. You said we'll pick Molly and Anna up.'

'I know, it's going to take some getting used to.' He leans in closer and picks up my hands, bringing them to his lips. 'She did a nice thing, Jess. I know it's going to be hard for a while, but calling the baby after Anna is really lovely. Like she said, they've grown up with Anna being part of their lives, so it's a lovely way to honour her memory.' He glances at his watch. 'Right, I've already given the car seat and buggy to Keith to put on his cart to take to the afternoon ferry; you can get the same one, then I'll see you at the hospital later. I'd better get going, if you're sure you're OK?'

I nod, even though I'm not sure I am.

'OK, Liam, I'll walk you to school before I get the ferry – we can run through your idea for the solar-powered lawn mower on the way.'

As soon as they're gone, I fly to the laptop and type in my husband's name. Fergus Bay.

M. Fergus Bay, Consultant Plastic and Reconstructive Surgeon MBBS, MSc, FRCS (Plast) at St Mary's Hospital, Guernsey.

He didn't drop out of university after Anna died. He finished his medical training. He's a doctor. I'm still a grandma. We're bringing our babies home today.

I can't help laughing with relief, full, body-wracking laughter that makes me close my eyes and offer up thanks to whoever, whatever, is listening and watching out for us. *Thank you,* thank you, thank you.

Two weeks later, on an unusually warm day at the end of September, Anna smiles the whole way through her christening in the island's charming medieval church. Even when the bells wake her up, even when the vicar is a little over-eager with the amount of water he uses to splash her forehead, her eyes, up her nose, and even when a mosquito lands on her bare arm and Liam thinks it prudent to slap it.

'That baby is clearly more Nora than us,' Fergus whispers to me as we stand watching the scene unfold. 'I've never seen a more zen-like child.'

'She was conceived while Nico was doused in herbal spermicide,' I whisper back. 'I didn't ask which herbs. Maybe I should have done.'

When we had Molly and Liam christened in the church nearest to us in London, they were perhaps one of eight or nine babies lined up on an invisible conveyor belt leading to the font. The vicar had to read from the paper he was holding to see what each baby was called, and as there was no room for godparents to stand up alongside each infant, they just had to shout out their bits from the pews in anonymous unison. Anna's service couldn't be more different. Well-wishers from the island line the path leading up to the church, and those that couldn't squeeze into the twelve pews inside wait patiently outside ready to clap our exit.

So many cards were put through our door this morning, we had to empty the copper basket attached to the letterbox in order to let more through, and as Ruth's shop only has two designs of christening cards, it was easy to create a sense of order with them on the bookshelves: ones with the cross to the left, ones with the pink rabbit to the right. This island has glued our family back together in so many ways. I have no idea why or how we still decided to come here if our family wasn't as broken as it was before; if Fergus hadn't given up his dream career; if we weren't both on the cusp of having affairs; if the kids weren't one more wrong decision away from a very different life. Maybe we just wanted a new adventure away from the frenetic pace of London? Perhaps the lure of island life was too much to pass up? Whatever it was, hallelujah.

As soon as the service is over, we file out to the pretty graveyard for more photos. Maggie comes bounding up, holding Lara, who arrived two months before Anna. We didn't have time to get Maggie to the bigger island for her planned hospital birth, as Lara was in something of a hurry to make her entrance, so I ended up delivering her on a hastily bought new shower curtain on Maggie's living-room floor. It seems fitting that both times I've become proper friends with Maggie I've been peering up her vagina.

'Hello, Granny,' she beams.

'Do you know what?' I say. 'I don't hate that as much as I thought I would.'

'That's good. I made the mistake of calling Joy Great-Granny in the cafe the other day, and she bit my head off.'

'Yes, some of us are taking longer than others getting used to their new names.' I laugh, seeing Mum out of the corner of my eye linking arms with Eileen as they walk down to the pub together. 'Oh, before I forget, are you and Tom still OK to come to ours for dinner on Saturday night? Fergus has got a new pizza oven he's desperate to try out.'

'Absolutely, we're looking forward to it. Right, better go and feed this one. See you later at the pub.'

Most of the congregation have already started the short walk to the pub; Fergus didn't want to be accused of favouritism as he's in the darts team at one, and the skittles team at the other, so we're having the first hour at The Swan and the second at The Fox.

'Oh, by the way,' Maggie says, turning round at the gate, 'I like what you did with the bench.'

I freeze. Maggie's never mentioned the bench to me before, never alluded to the fact that she remembers that I sat on it with her seven years ago. The night I persuaded her not to change her life.

'I just thought it was better this way,' I say finally.

'You're right. It looks nice there. And it stops people making silly choices they haven't really thought through.' She winks at me, alleviating every remnant of guilt I have. 'See you later, Jess.'

Thankfully Nora and Eileen agreed with me the second I suggested it, and even though I'm pretty sure Fergus thought I was completely mad nagging him until he, Liam and Nico carried the bench down from the cliff to the churchyard, it now sits safely under a giant oak tree, happily facing east. Anyone who sits on it, and many people now do, can enjoy a lovely view of the sun rising in the morning through the low branches.

It's been a long, wonderful day, and I take my tea through to the small garden at the back of the house, away from where Liam and Fergus are playing a loud game of beach volleyball on the Xbox in the living room, away from where Mum and Keith are preparing a salad to have with dinner, whilst talking to Molly who is sat on the armchair in the kitchen feeding Anna under a nursing cover that Eileen made for her.

I sit and breathe in the lavender-filled air, hear the gentle buzz of the hovering bees, the sleepy sounds of another day drawing to a close on the island. I tap on my phone to bring it to life. I want to call Jackie, to tell her that finally, everything is OK. We're all doing OK. It's been a few months since we were last in touch, and I think that she'd like to hear that today went well.

But her number's not in my phone. That's strange. I go to my messages and scroll back, I know we were messaging when Molly was almost due – I was feeling anxious about the birth and everything being all right, and she'd given me some relaxation techniques to do. But there's no messages from her in my inbox either. This is very odd.

I google her name, and her website comes up. I tap on the number and it starts to ring.

'Jackie Gerard speaking.'

'Hi, Jackie, it's Jess. I just wanted to let you know that today was Molly's baby's christening. She's called her Anna. Isn't that wonderful? She's beautiful. It was a fantastic day, all the people on the island came, we had a brilliant party. I've never been happier.'

There's a couple of seconds' silence, then Jackie's smooth-as-honey voice comes through again. 'Congratulations, that's lovely! But what did you say your name was again?'

'Jess,' I say, giving a small laugh. 'Jackie, it's me – Jessica Bay?'

'I'm so sorry,' Jackie replies, sounding confused and apologetic. 'I'm normally very good with names . . . Have we met before?'

'I've been your client for years Jackie, it's Jess,' I say weakly, sitting down on a garden chair. 'Jess and Fergus?'

'I'm very sorry, Jess, I really have never heard of you before now. Would you like to make an appointment with me – although it doesn't sound like you need a therapist!'

As I try to take in what Jackie's saying, the back door opens and Molly comes out with baby Anna tied to her front with a fabric sling. Fergus is just behind her holding a wine bottle and four glasses, while Keith lights the patio heater, and pulls out two chairs at the table for Mum and Molly to sit in. Liam is lifting up the lid of the barbecue, saying something to Fergus who puts his arm around his son's shoulders as he listens. Mum fusses over Anna, popping a sun hat on her despite the mildness of the late September evening. Fergus starts pouring the wine and motions to me, asking if I'd like one. I nod.

'I guess I don't,' I reply slowly, looking at my noisy, happy family, realising that what I'm saying is completely true. 'Thank you, though. For everything.'

'I've done absolutely nothing,' Jackie says, laughing. 'It sounds like you've got a lovely life all of your own making.'

The phone lies still in my lap as I sit there in our island garden on a white, wrought-iron bench, allowing the laughter of my family to wash over me. The vivid blue hue of the cornflowers I apparently planted earlier in the summer adds splashes of colour to the borders. Four muddy mountain bikes lean up against the back of the house alongside two well-used surfboards. Lanterns are dotted around the outskirts of the patio, along with burned-down citronella candles stuck in the soil, and Fergus's pizza oven stands next to the upgraded barbecue. It looks like we had a wonderful summer. I feel a sudden pang that I don't have a memory of it, but then I think with a smile that there'll be many more just like it.

And this time, I'm not going to change a thing.

Acknowledgments

It's probably somewhat unconventional to start acknowledgments by thanking a famous person you've never met, but this book may not have been possible without Van Morrison ... I have this ritual when I'm writing of finding a song which matches the story and blasting it out of the speakers every day before I start flexing my fingers over the keyboard – imagine boxers getting ready for a fight – and the song for this book was 'Days Like These'.

Listening to the lyrics: *When everything falls into place like the flick of a switch*, gave me the idea for what it would be like to design the perfect day.

I don't think there's a person alive who hasn't at some point wished they could go back and re-do a moment in their life, whether it's to right a wrong, or just to re-live an enjoyable moment, and this idea kept coming back to me again and again until I had no choice but to make it a book.

There aren't enough words to express my thanks to my agent, Hannah Schofield at LBA, who brainstormed my ideas for this novel with me in the week of her wedding and deftly managed the auction of this book while moving house – proving that she is a superwoman in every sense of the word. Thanks also to Luigi and Alison Bonomi at LBA who saw the potential in me four books ago, and have been such wonderful mentors ever since.

Huge thanks go to the dream team at Hodder & Stoughton. I am so grateful to Thorne Ryan for bringing me to Hodder, and whose passion and enthusiasm for Jess, plus her love of semi-colons, made this book so much shinier. Editor Olivia Barber is an absolute joy to work with, and massive thanks to editorial assistant Amy Batley, Grace McCrum in the Rights team, Oliver Martin in Publicity, Marketing genius Katy Blott, Juliette Winter in Production and the supremely talented designer Natalie Chen for a cover design that makes my heart dance every time I look at it.

My family and friends have been, often unwittingly, the source of much of my inspiration. Special thanks to my treasured tribe of first readers, my very honest friends Anna, Catherine, Claire, Kirsteen, Julia, Rachel and Lisa. A special shout-out to my students, particularly my Year 9 girls who thankfully are nothing like the teenagers in this book, but who did spend a whole library lesson brainstorming titles for me, so thank you!

My family are absolutely splendid and I struck gold being born into this dynasty: Mum, Dad, Hannah and Davinia, thank you for everything. Poulains, Harveys, Poultneys, Haddon-MacMillans, you're quite simply the best family ever. And massive thanks to my in-laws, Edward and Kyaks, whose cheering and popping of corks in France when I got this book deal could be heard in England.

Finally, to my own tribe, Ed, Amelie, Rafe and Theo, you are perfect just the way you are, and if I could sit on a bench at sunset and re-live every day of our time together again, in exactly the same way, then I would.

Nell has always known the date she's going to die.

After a psychic predicted her death date twenty years ago, she has lived life accepting she would never see forty – embracing adventure and travelling the world, choosing fun over commitment and laying down roots.

So, when the fateful day comes, Nell feels ready. She sends five excruciatingly honest confessions to her sister, parents and past loves, knowing she won't be around to face the consequences. Then, with her heart laid bare, all that's left to do is check into a glamorous hotel and wait for the inevitable . . .

But when Nell unexpectedly wakes up the next morning broke, single and very much alive, she must figure out exactly how to seize this second chance at life. And then it also hits her:

What on earth happens now that everyone knows how she really feels?

Morning TV's favourite twin sisters, Alice and Edie, may share the screen, but that's where their similarities end. Their viewpoints are far from identical, and whilst their on-air clashes keep viewers hooked, off-camera, their relationship is far from picture-perfect.

After a heated argument on live television threatens their jobs, the fiery duo make a bet: neither could last a week in the other's shoes. Determined to prove each other wrong, they secretly swap lives – without telling a soul.

What starts as a battle of wills quickly spirals into chaos, as each sister discovers that the other's life is far more complicated than it seems. Between dodging awkward work situations, marital issues, and meddling in each other's families, Alice and Edie's rivalry turns from a competitive bet into an opportunity to help change each other's lives for the better.

But will their relationship survive?

Stella's life hasn't quite gone to plan. She imagined that, at forty, she'd be settled with a supportive husband, two kids and a dog. Instead, she's single and living at home with her mum, Bonnie, and grandmother, Florence. She passes the evenings in her childhood bedroom, obsessively searching for the perfect sperm donor.

Unbeknownst to Stella is that Bonnie and Florence both also had difficult journeys to motherhood. And now that they're writing down their stories for Stella's unborn child, the truth about their family is becoming harder to conceal.

And while you can't choose your family, you can choose what you tell them…